In Honor's
Defense

BOOKS BY KAREN WITEMEYER

HANGER'S HORSEMEN · 3

In Honor's Defense

KAREN WITEMEYER

BETHANYHOUSE
a division of Baker Publishing Group
Minneapolis, Minnesota

© 2022 by Karen M. Witemeyer

Published by Bethany House Publishers
11400 Hampshire Avenue South
Minneapolis, Minnesota 55438
www.bethanyhouse.com

Bethany House Publishers is a division of
Baker Publishing Group, Grand Rapids, Michigan

Printed in the United States of America

Library of Congress Cataloging-in-Publication Data
Names: Witemeyer, Karen, author.
Title: In honor's defense / Karen Witemeyer.
Description: Minneapolis, Minnesota : Bethany House, a division of Baker
    Publishing Group, [2022] | Series: Hanger's horseman ; 3
Identifiers: LCCN 2022002391 | ISBN 9780764232091 (paperback) | ISBN
    9780764240058 (casebound) | ISBN 9781493437207 (ebook)
Subjects: LCGFT: Novels.
Classification: LCC PS3623.I864 I52 2022 | DDC 813/.6—dc23/eng/20220120
LC record available at https://lccn.loc.gov/2022002391

Scripture quotations are from the King James Version of the Bible.

This is a work of fiction. Names, characters, incidents, and dialogues are products of the author's imagination and are not to be construed as real. Any resemblance to actual events or persons, living or dead, is entirely coincidental.

Cover design by Dan Thornberg, Design Source Creative Services

Author is represented by the Books and Such Literary Agency

Baker Publishing Group publications use paper produced from sustainable forestry practices and post-consumer waste whenever possible.

22 23 24 25 26 27 28   7 6 5 4 3 2 1

To my Posse.
I couldn't ask for better brainstormers,
more dedicated readers,
or dearer friends.
Thank you for blessing my
writing journey and my life.

But the salvation of the righteous is of the Lord: he is their strength in the time of trouble. And the Lord shall help them, and deliver them: he shall deliver them from the wicked, and save them, because they trust in him.

—Psalm 37:39–40

Prologue

St. Louis, Missouri
1895

Invisible people rarely received correspondence. A fact Damaris Baxter had accepted long ago. So when the housekeeper entered the parlor and held out an envelope with *her* name occupying the address line instead of her aunt's, it took a moment to process the unprecedented event.

As the youngest of eight children, with no particular radiance of either face or manner to draw attention, Damaris had grown accustomed to being overlooked. In fact, she held the Baxter family record for being left behind on outings most frequently with an impressive total of five. Her brother Joseph had managed the feat twice, being the one most likely to wander off after being counted, but he'd never truly been forgotten, just temporarily misplaced. Their parents had forgotten about Damaris for an entire afternoon on one occasion, not missing her until she failed to appear when called for supper.

Mama had scolded her for being too quiet for her own good, accusing her of hiding away to read books instead of participating in family activities. She'd demanded Damaris pay closer attention in the future so as not to be left behind again. Mama had wept through the entire exchange, of course, then nearly hugged the life out of Damaris at the conclusion of her lecture, assuring Damaris that she was loved if not memorable.

Being invisible had its uses, however. Forgettable girls rarely got called on to recite lessons in front of the class. Or asked to dance when one had a perfectly good book to read. Yet when one reached marriageable age, invisibility became a significant disadvantage. There was always someone prettier, wittier, or more charming to draw the attention of available suitors. Which was how Damaris ended up as a companion to her great-aunt Bertha at the age of twenty-three. Not only was Damaris on the shelf, she was in the back corner behind the knickknacks, collecting dust. At least with Aunt Bertha, she'd found a way to be useful.

Damaris pulled her scattered thoughts together, set aside her needlework, and reached for the letter. "Thank you, Anna." She tried not to sound as astonished as she felt, but her voice carried a touch of breathlessness despite her best efforts.

Anna noticed, of course, and smiled. "It's from Texas, miss."

"Texas?" From Douglas? But the handwriting on the envelope wasn't his. Not that she was an expert on her brother's penmanship. He was fifteen years older and had been absent for more of her life than he'd been present. He'd moved to Texas right after his son was born and had only returned to Missouri once, the Christmas after his wife died.

Seven-year-old Nathaniel had seemed so lost during that visit, so withdrawn. Damaris's heart had ached for the grieving little boy. At sixteen, she knew enough to realize there were no words to take away his pain, so she didn't offer any. She simply made sure he was never alone. She sat on the floor next to him while he played. Brought him cookies from the kitchen. Offered to read him stories. When he finally grew comfortable enough with her to crawl into her lap and help her turn the pages, she'd fallen completely in love. She wrote him letters and sent him small gifts for his birthday and Christmas each year, never really minding that he didn't write her back. Young boys couldn't be expected to correspond with eccentric aunts they probably didn't even remember meeting. She'd been in his life for ten days. A mere drop in the ocean of his young existence. Douglas wrote to their mother a few times a year, so Damaris managed to keep up with Nathaniel through secondhand sources.

"I hope it's not bad news," Anna said when Damaris made no move to open the letter.

Damaris's heart pounded. What else could it be when it came from a stranger? Unless . . . could it be from Nathaniel? He'd be, what, fourteen by now? Perhaps it was *his* handwriting.

Please, Lord. Let it be from Nathaniel, not some stranger with ill tidings.

Damaris placed the envelope in her lap with all the care of a seamstress laying out a piece of expensive Venetian lace. She smoothed her hand over the front before stealing herself to flip it over and discover what lay inside. Her hand trembled slightly as she removed and unfolded the stationery.

Miss Damaris Baxter,
   I write with a heavy heart to inform you of your brother's untimely death. Douglas Baxter was found drowned in Lake Madison on March 7, 1895.

A small cry escaped Damaris. Her brother drowned? It couldn't be. Douglas had been athletic and strong, good at nearly every sport, including swimming. How vividly she recalled the summer after she turned five, when he'd taken it upon himself to teach all of the youngest Baxter siblings to swim. She'd been too young to do much more than cry and cling to him, but by the end of the summer, he'd had them all paddling across the swimming hole unaided—her included. How could he have drowned?

"Are you all right, miss?" Anna turned from where she'd been adjusting the blanket on Aunt Bertha's lap, the older woman snoring softly in her rocker by the window.

"It's my brother Douglas. He's . . . They found him . . ." She couldn't say it. Couldn't make it real.

Anna's eyes softened in sympathy. "I'm so sorry. Should I wake the missus?"

Damaris shook her head. "No. Not yet." She needed time to compose herself, to get a grip on her emotions before she broke the news to her aunt. And what about her mother? Had *she* been informed? Surely a letter of this sort would be sent to the deceased's parents. So why had this one come to her?

Blinking back the mist from her eyes, Damaris refocused on the letter.

> *The cause of death was determined to be accidental. A true tragedy, ending the life of a man in his prime. You have my most sincere condolences.*

Damaris dropped her gaze to the signature—Ronald Mullins, Esquire. A lawyer? She would have expected notification to come from a minister or friend. She'd never heard the name Ronald Mullins, nor did she recall any mention of him in the letters Douglas had written to Mother.

> *Mr. Douglas Baxter named you, Miss Damaris Baxter, guardian of his son, Nathaniel. You have also been named trustee of the boy's estate, including the bank funds and property left behind by Mr. Baxter. I will provide you with a copy of all relevant documents when you come to claim the child.*
>
> *I place myself at your disposal, Miss Baxter. I stand ready to assist you in any way that might prove helpful during your time of mourning.*
>
>

Sincerely,
Ronald P. Mullins,
Esquire

Douglas had chosen *her*? Damaris could barely find the strength to blink through the paralysis of shock. He'd entrusted Nathaniel's care to the baby sister he barely knew. Why not their parents or Bartholomew? Bart was only a year younger than Douglas and had children close in age to Nathaniel. He seemed the logical choice. Yet Douglas had chosen her. Perhaps because she had no attachments to hinder or distract her. Of all their siblings, she was the only one with no family to keep her rooted in St. Louis. She was free to leave at any time, free to devote herself fully to Nathaniel's care.

Or maybe . . . Damaris caught her breath. Maybe the choice had belonged to Nathaniel. The idea kicked her heart into a rapid rhythm. What if Nathaniel had remembered his aunt Maris and requested that she be named his guardian?

To be chosen for herself—it was the secret desire of her heart. To be important to someone. More than a glorified servant who fetched and carried and entertained at her aunt's whim. To be wanted truly for herself. Seen instead of invisible. Valued instead of tolerated.

"I must pack." Damaris jumped up from the sofa with such speed that her forgotten basket of needlework threads toppled to the floor along with her embroidery hoop.

A snuffling sound echoed from the window as Aunt Bertha stirred. "Damaris? Why are you fluttering about, girl? You know I dislike being disturbed during my afternoon respites. Clumsy child," she chided as her gaze landed on the upturned basket and contents spilled across the carpet. "Clean up your mess, then bring me one of my tonics. I can't have my nerves overset."

Anna hurried over to help right the sewing basket. Damaris smiled her thanks but didn't stay to help. She had trunks to fill, railroad schedules to check, and a nephew who needed her.

"Sorry, Aunt Bertha. I don't have time to fetch your tonic. I'm moving to Texas."

ONE

MADISONVILLE, TEXAS
SIX WEEKS LATER

Nathaniel? Is that you?" Damaris looked up from the misshapen loaf of bread she'd just turned out from the pan.

Running footsteps thundered down the hall, but no voice rang in answer to her question. Not that she expected a response. Her nephew preferred pretending she didn't exist to engaging in any form of verbal communication. Sullen looks, exaggerated eye rolls, and stomping frustration were more his style. After she'd arrived in Texas, it had taken less than a day for her beautiful delusions of mothering a sweet, heartbroken boy out of his grief to wither and die in the face of reality.

At fourteen, Nathaniel was more man than boy, at least in stature and stubbornness. He matched her in height and surpassed her in cunning, constantly finding new ways to torture her. She'd been awakened by a chicken pecking at the quilt threads atop her midsection, a snake slithering down the back of her nightgown, and a pair of frogs dropped on her face. It had taken more fortitude than she'd realized she possessed not to run screaming back to Aunt Bertha.

Yet underneath all the pranks, sarcasm, and anger lived the little boy she remembered. A boy who'd lost the linchpin that held his life together—his father. Was it any wonder he was spiraling out of control? He had no one to tether himself to. No one except her, an aunt he barely knew and trusted even less.

After crying herself to sleep for the first week, mourning not only her brother but her starry-eyed dreams of home and belonging, Damaris resolved to meet her nephew's challenge. Self-pity never accomplished anything. If she wanted a real relationship with her nephew, she'd have to fight for it. Stubborn for stubborn. No matter how hard he pushed, she'd prove herself reliable, winning him over with constancy and care. If he lashed out in anger, she'd respond with patience. If he avoided her, she'd seek him out. If he ignored her, she'd persist with one-sided conversations.

"How was school?" she called, lifting her voice to carry down the hall to his bedroom. "Do you have much homework? I can help you with it after dinner if you like."

Miss Tatum had stopped by last week to let Damaris know that Nathaniel's grades had dropped significantly over the last month. He only attended class half the time, and when he did show up, he failed to engage in his lessons. Worst of all, he'd started getting into fights during recess.

He needs you, Lord, but I get the feeling he's pushing you away as much as he's pushing me. Show me how to help him.

Heaven knew she'd need divine intervention to get through to the boy. While she believed in her ability to dose him with a constant flow of affection, she had absolutely no confidence in her ability to discipline him. She'd tried scoldings and reprimands, but they only brought out more rebellion and pranks, so she'd been terribly lax of late. She knew he needed boundaries, but those proved difficult to establish when he didn't recognize her authority.

"We're having sausage gravy on toast tonight." One of the few dishes she made of which he willingly ate a second helping.

Her cooking skills seemed more suited to stove than oven. She could fry, sauté, stew, and boil to some degree of success, but disaster struck whenever she attempted roasting or baking. On the stove, she could move from a too-hot spot to a cooler one or vice versa, but the delicate mathematics of balancing the variables of wood, heat, and dampers never failed to give her the wrong answer when it came to the oven. Hence the lopsided bread in front of her. She flipped the outturned loaf right side up and placed it on a cooling rack. At least it wasn't burnt. Just slightly caved in on one side.

Not everything could be beautiful. A truth Damaris had come to terms with long ago when her own appearance failed to mature into anything other than plain. Yet a thing's outward beauty should not determine its value. Bread's value lay in its ability to fill an empty belly, not in how well it delighted the eye. She wouldn't scorn her misshapen loaf just because it wasn't as pretty as the ones in the baker's window.

"Can we have some of them fried apples you made last week for dessert?"

Damaris squeaked and spun around. "Nathaniel! You startled me."

Her nephew leaned against the doorjamb, his arms crossed defensively over his chest, and his too-long brown hair hanging across his eyes. The prickly pose and droopy mane couldn't hide the satisfaction gleaming in his eyes, however. He was *proud* of making her jump. For someone who had tromped through the house with all the delicacy of a drunken buffalo five minutes earlier, he certainly could move with stealth when he wanted.

"So, can we? Have the apples?"

Damaris smiled, her aggravation melting away as her heart softened. Nathaniel so rarely asked her for anything. "Of course."

There was a half-bushel of tart green apples in the root cellar. Maybe she could even make a brown betty with some bread cubes and extra cinnamon and sugar.

"Thanks, Aunt Maris."

Warning bells rang in the back of Damaris's mind. He never thanked her. Just ate whatever food she placed in front of him and disappeared either outside or into his room.

Nathaniel pushed away from the wall. "I'll be back before suppertime."

Shaking off her cynicism and suspicion before he could sense them, Damaris brightened her smile. "Be careful."

He shrugged as if to dislodge her concern before it could settle on his shoulders, then disappeared down the hall. The front door slammed a moment later.

Damaris sighed. Someday he would accept her affection. Return it, even. After all, love was the strongest force on earth. Because it wasn't *of* earth. It was divine. God's very nature. It would win the day eventually, if she held true to her course. She must focus on the outcome, not on memories of salt in her tea or frogs on her face.

An involuntary recollection surfaced of slimy amphibian bellies against her lips and sticky feet massaging her chin. One frog had even fallen inside her mouth when she woke and gasped in fright. Damaris shuddered. She'd used half a packet of tooth powder that morning, trying to erase the taste and feel of the creature. Thank heaven Nathaniel had yet to repeat the same prank twice. She didn't think she could survive a second amphibious encounter.

Never mind all that, though. She had apples to fetch. She wasn't about to turn down her nephew's first request, not when it was so easily granted.

Leaving her bread to finish cooling, Damaris marched over to the root cellar door built into the kitchen's floorboards. She bent down and hefted it open. Then, sweeping her skirt aside so she could watch where she placed her feet on the ladder rungs, she climbed down into the cool, damp cellar and walked over to the bushel basket of apples in the far corner near the shelves of canned goods. Taking an apple in hand, she squeezed it gently, checking for bruises. She wanted to use the very best. Finding a soft spot on that one, she placed the apple back in the basket and reached for a second. As her fingers closed around the fruit, a shadow fell across the room.

Bang! The cellar door slammed closed. Everything went black.

"Nathaniel!" Damaris dropped the apple and ran toward the ladder.

Surely he wouldn't trap her down here. He was mischievous,

but he wasn't mean. Unless . . . could this be retaliation for his window?

He'd been sneaking out at night despite her urgings that he stop. He gave no heed to her insistence that being out after dark wasn't safe. Arguing him into her way of thinking hadn't worked, yet she couldn't call herself a responsible guardian without doing *something* to stop him. So yesterday she'd nailed his window shut from the outside, hoping that the hindrance would at least make him stop and think before running off into the night. He hadn't said anything about it this morning at breakfast, just rushed off to school like normal. She'd thought he hadn't discovered what she'd done.

Obviously, she'd been wrong.

"All right, Nathaniel. You've made your point," she called as she felt her way through the pitch black, seeking the ladder. "You can let me out now."

Something scraped above her. Something that sounded like table legs on floorboards. Then a thud. Directly above her head.

"I'll make ya a deal, Aunt Maris." Nathaniel's voice echoed through the floor. Tight. Ominous. "You get yourself outta the cellar before suppertime, and I'll stop using my window as a door. But if you're still trapped when I get home for supper, you let me go wherever I want, whenever I want from now on without trying to stop me."

She shook her head. "I can't make that deal. It's my job to protect you."

"No, it ain't. It's my pa's job, but he ain't here no more, so now I take care of myself!"

Footsteps pounded, then faded away.

"Nathaniel!"

A door slammed.

He'd left her here. Trapped. In the dark.

The old, timid Damaris would have sat on the dirt floor and wept. Texas Damaris, however, had more grit. Weeping wouldn't get her out of this cellar. Effort and ingenuity would.

Using the pinpricks of light that outlined the square of the trap door as her guide, Damaris centered herself beneath it and waved her arms until she knocked into the ladder. Grabbing hold of the sides, she fit her foot to the bottom rung and climbed. A few steps up, she reached for the door handle and pushed. It didn't budge. She climbed higher, bending her head forward and hunching her shoulders until her upper back pressed against the door.

Please, Lord, let this work.

Gritting her teeth, she pushed with her legs as hard as she could. The door moved. Not much, but it moved. She tried again, her grunt of effort nearly becoming a scream.

To no avail. The door moved an inch. Maybe less. The table he'd positioned on top was too heavy.

All right, so effort and ingenuity based on brute strength didn't work when one happened to be a woman with muscles accustomed more to needle pushing than table lifting. She'd have to make do with Option Two. Patience.

Her real battle wasn't against wood and hinges. Her opponent was a stubborn, angry, heartbroken boy, and she couldn't afford to lose. Not when Nathaniel's well-being lay in the balance. She might be helpless to get out of this hole, but she could control how her nephew found her when next they met. His aunt Maris would not be weeping and distraught.

Nor would she be defeated and hurt. She wouldn't even be bristling with anger and indignation.

No, Nathaniel would find her calm, smiling, and ready to make him the best fried apples he'd ever tasted.

The strategy of turning the other cheek. The Lord endorsed it, so it must work.

All she had to do was not go crazy in the meantime, imagining the various creepy-crawly things that dwelled in cellars. Things that came out of their holes when the lights went out.

Sitting on the bottom rung, Damaris wrapped her skirt tightly around her legs and hugged her arms across her chest. It would only be for an hour or two. She could manage.

A creak echoed from the corner. Her gaze darted that way, but her vision couldn't penetrate the darkness.

Tiny tapping sounds clicked behind her. She drew her legs closer to her body and began to hum.

She could do this. They were just noises. Magnified by the dark.

Something itched the top of her hair. She shook her head and fluttered a hand over her bun, encountering nothing but hair and pins.

She could do this.

Something tickled her nape. She jumped up from the ladder and wiggled from head to toe.

Perhaps patience wasn't a viable option after all. As she slapped at the itchy spot on the back of her neck, Damaris fervently began praying for an Option Three.

CHAPTER
TWO

Luke Davenport rode up to the ranch house on the Triple G spread, holding Titan to a walk so he could scan his surroundings as he approached. He'd noticed a neighbor to the west, a couple of farms to the north, closer to Madisonville, but nothing developed to the south. The rustlers probably came and went from that direction.

His horse's ears pricked, and Luke leaned forward slightly to pat the big fella's neck. "Yep," he murmured. "I see him."

A man stood in the shadows of the porch, rifle in hand.

Luke signaled Titan to halt. The big sorrel immediately obeyed, seeming to sense his master's desire even before Luke tugged the reins.

Titan was one of the first horses at Gringolet that Luke had broken to saddle after his former captain took over running the respected breeding farm. When Matt Hanger married and declared Hanger's Horsemen officially retired, he'd given all of the Horsemen jobs at the farm, training horses for the army and other local buyers.

Luke liked the work well enough, especially since Matt assigned him the wildest animals to saddle break. The wilder the better, as far as he was concerned. He loved pitting himself against a worthy opponent and giving his own wildness an outlet. Something he'd missed since leaving the cavalry. Riding with the Horsemen had scratched the itch. Chasing bandits, dodging bullets, and infiltrating outlaw gangs kept a man sharp. On top of his game. The military had channeled his recklessness and given it purpose. Then Matt had honed that purpose into a godly mission, protecting the lives and property of decent folk from the wickedness of unscrupulous men. But lately, Luke's sense of purpose had dulled. Like a saber no longer used for battle, his reason for existence was deteriorating. Matt and the others might be content to hang their swords on the wall as a memento of days gone by, but Luke had nothing else. Who was he if not a warrior?

Terrified to contemplate the dark void that yawned wide and empty in answer to that question, Luke had snagged the first available excuse to get back in the action. Wilson Grimes, a trooper who had served under the captain back in their cavalry days, had written to Matt, asking if the Horsemen could look into a rustling problem his brother was facing in Madison County. Luke had volunteered for the job before Matt could even finish reading the letter.

He knew he'd be on his own this time. No Horsemen were available to watch his back, but he'd been on his own before. He'd manage. His friends had more important places to be at the moment. Matt's wife was heavy with their first child, mere weeks from delivering. Jonah had a new bride to keep happy and a ranch to get off the ground. And Wallace wore a deputy's badge now, keeping peace for the good folks of Kingsland. None could just pick up and leave at a moment's notice. None but Luke.

"Hello, at the house," he called. "Name's Luke Davenport. I'm here to see Oliver Grimes. Matthew Hanger sent me."

The man on the front porch stepped out of the shadows, a smile stretching across his face as his rifle barrel dropped to point at the ground. "Mr. Davenport! Welcome." He hurried down the porch steps and strode out to where Luke waited. "I can't tell you how glad I am to have you here. Please, come inside. I'll have one of my men see to your horse." He whistled, and an older fellow emerged from the barn, his bowlegged gait wide enough for a baby buffalo to scamper through. "Quincy, see to Mr. Davenport's horse, would you?"

"Sure thing, Boss." The fellow ambled up as Luke dismounted. "Fine-lookin' horse. What's his name?"

"Titan." Luke patted his gelding's neck, then handed the reins to the old cowhand, whose eyes glowed with admiration.

"Fittin'," Quincy said, his experienced gaze cataloging the animal's features. "He's gotta be, what, seventeen hands?"

Luke grinned. "Seventeen-two." With Luke's own height reaching four inches over six feet, he needed a mount to match.

Quincy whistled softly. "Woo-ee. I'll prob'ly need the step-ladder to unsaddle him."

"Just loosen his girth and give him some water for now," Luke said. "I'll want to ride the property line after your boss fills me in on what's been goin' on around here lately."

Quincy nodded. "Will do." His smile faded into a solemn

expression as he met his boss's eye. He nodded to both men. "Titan will be ready when ya need him."

Luke fingered his hat brim. "Thanks."

"Come on inside." Grimes bounded up the front steps and held the door wide open.

Luke followed, taking his hat off as he crossed the threshold.

"Wilson told me he'd written Captain Hanger for assistance," Grimes said as he closed the door and led Luke through the parlor to a small study at the back, "but I knew the Horsemen were retired. Didn't really expect anythin' to come of it. Yet here you are."

Here he was. So eager to take a job, any job, that he hadn't even wired ahead to notify the client of his plans. Just showed up on his doorstep like a stray dog in search of a bone.

Grimes grinned as he stepped aside and let Luke enter the office ahead of him. As soon as he crossed the threshold, the rancher's demeanor sobered. It was as if the office served as the storage area for all his worry and stress. The heavy atmosphere pressed down on him, and Luke circled his shoulders in an effort to keep it from settling. Grimes waved him into a chair, then took a seat behind the large oak desk that dominated the room.

Grimes propped his forearms on the desktop and blew out a heavy breath. "By yesterday's count, I've lost ten head so far, but this ain't the usual grab-and-run operation. They're bleeding me dry little by little. It's like the rustlers are toying with me."

Luke planted his boots solidly on the floor and pressed a palm against his knee as he leaned forward. "How so?"

"They're taking my beeves one or two at a time. No evidence of horses churning up the soil. No disturbin' the herd. They sneak in at night, find the outliers, and walk one of the beeves away. I've posted a night guard, but I run a small operation. I ain't one of them big outfits with a thousand head of cattle and dozens of men on the payroll. I run about two hundred head and employ three hands, not including old Quincy. Ten missing longhorns means I've lost five percent of my stock. If I can't find a way to stop the rustling, in a month I could be down by twenty-five percent. In three months, I could be out of business."

It seemed risky for the rustlers to return to the scene of their crime over and over. Though maybe it wasn't rustlers—plural—but a single thief.

"Have you found any cut wire?"

Grimes tapped the desktop with the side of his thumb, his mounting frustration adding force and volume to the percussion. "Nope. Been checkin' the fence line every time a steer goes missin'. Ain't found any cut wire or downed sections." He snatched his hand away from the desk and balled his fingers into a fist. "I got no idea how they're getting 'em out."

"Sounds like they might be local if they keep returning. Maybe a poor family lookin' to feed their young'uns?"

Grimes scowled. "I might think so if just one cow was taken. But ten? This ain't about food. It's personal."

Luke straightened. "Someone got an ax to grind with you?" It made more sense that this was an act of spite or revenge. Rustlers were in it for the money, and the only way to make enough money to justify the risk was to grab as much as they could and move on to greener pastures. They'd have to change the brands and find a buyer willing not to look too close. But if the motive *wasn't* money, that opened up new avenues of possibilities.

"That's the problem." Grimes jerked backward and slammed his palm against the chair arm. "I can't think of anyone who'd want to ruin me. I had to let a hand go a couple of years back for havin' a poor work ethic, but last I heard, he'd lit out for Colorado. And I ain't got a beef with any of the folks in town."

"What about your men?" Luke tapped his hat brim against his thigh. "Maybe one of them got liquored up and said or did something to cause offense?"

Grimes shook his head. "Buck and Randall are as steady as they come. They're more into cards than liquor when seeking Saturday night entertainment. And before you ask, no, they don't owe anyone money. Joe's young, so he's still got some stupid in him, but he can also charm the feathers off a goose, so no one stays mad at him longer'n a day."

Luke made a noncommittal sound. A good boss knew his men, but no man knew another completely. Everyone had secrets. It was possible one of the Triple G hands was in on it. Who else would know the land well enough to be able to sneak a longhorn off the property without cutting fence wire?

"What about someone from your past? Any scorned business partners or women who might be seeking revenge?"

"Nah. I bought this land free and clear a decade ago. Earned my starter herd after five years of cattle drives. Left on good terms with my previous outfit." Grimes blew out a breath and ran a hand down his face. "As for women, I ain't been on friendly terms with more than a handful over the years, and none long enough for expectations to develop on either side." He gripped the edge of the desk and met Luke's gaze straight on. "I'm a cow man, Mr. Davenport. My ranch is my life. I ain't got time for politics or courtship or sticking my nose in business that ain't my own. Only man I had a disagreement with lately was Doug Baxter, but he's dead, so it can't be him."

Luke's instincts zinged. "What kind of disagreement did you and Baxter have?"

Grimes shrugged. "The usual." He poked a thumb over his shoulder. "He owned the land next door. A real pretty section with grass for grazin' and a creek that'd be perfect for stock. I wanted to buy. Baxter wouldn't sell. But like I said, the man's dead. Goin' nigh on two months now."

"He leave any family behind who might hold a grudge?" Grief often left folks looking for someone to blame, a place to direct their anger and hurt.

"Just a kid. Nate. You don't think . . ." A thoughtful look crossed the rancher's face before he shook it off. "Nah. The boy's only thirteen or fourteen. He can be a hothead at times, but he's harmless. Although . . . now that ya got me ponderin' on the boy, that might explain . . ." His mouth tightened.

"What?"

"Missin' cattle ain't the only thing I been plagued with lately."

Luke raised a brow, silently prodding Grimes to explain.

"There's been vandalism, too."

"Like what?"

"Half my vegetable garden hacked to bits. Probably lost at least a month of winter's stores. Horses turned out of the corral. One ended up lame. Prob'ly stepped in a prairie dog hole when the vandal spooked 'em. Little things too, like a skunk turned loose in the bunkhouse and manure bombs on the front porch. All takin' place at night, just like the rustlin'. Both started around the same time. I assumed they were related. Some kind of personal attack. None of the other ranchers in the area have lost any beeves, so I'm likely bein' targeted. I just don't know why. But if this is somehow tied to Baxter . . ."

"Let me dig around before you start jumpin' to conclusions." Luke stretched his legs out along the side of the desk. He'd pulled his share of pranks as a boy. Gotten in trouble more times than he could count. It could be the neighbor boy was responsible for those incidents. But rustling? That was a far cry from petty vandalism.

Slapping his palms against his legs, Luke pushed up from his seat.

Grimes rose with him. "That mean you're takin' the job?"

Luke fit his hat to his head and nodded. "Yep."

"Glad to hear it." Grimes slipped a key from his pocket, unlocked one of the desk drawers, then reached inside. "I understand you take half your fee up front. I can write you a bank draft—"

Luke waved his hand and cut off the rancher's words. "We can see to that later this evening. I want to get started while there's still a few hours of daylight left."

Respect lit Grimes's gaze as he straightened away from the desk. "I'll have Quincy ready your horse. You'll want to start with the eastern fence line. The cattle have been grazing in the southeast pasture the last couple of weeks."

Luke appreciated the information, but he wouldn't be riding the fence line today. "I'll check the fence first thing in the morning," he said. "I think I'll pay a call on your neighbor first."

He intended to take Nate Baxter's measure. The boy might be young, but right now he was Luke's only suspect. And if Luke knew anything from his own tarnished youth, it was that angry boys were capable of inflicting man-sized damage when they put their minds to it. And unfortunately, the more they inflicted on others, the more harm they did to themselves in the process. A harm they tended not to recognize until it was too late.

THREE

Luke held Titan to a walk as he turned up the Baxter drive. A small, white clapboard house waited for him at the end of the rutted road, but Luke was in no hurry to get there. He scanned the yard, counting three small outbuildings and a windmill. *Outbuildings* might be a tad generous. There was really just the barn. The other two structures consisted of a chicken coop and an outhouse. Necessary, but not exactly impressive. No evidence of crops or herds, as far as he could see. Baxter obviously hadn't made his living off the land. He must have worked in town. He might have cattle or goats grazing somewhere distant, but with no bunkhouse, smokehouse, or sizeable stock pen in evidence, it wasn't likely.

Unlike at the Triple G, no greeting party came out to meet him. Not even a dog. It could be no one was home. According to Grimes, Nate still lived here. An aunt had come to stay with the boy after his father died. Grimes didn't recall much about the woman beyond the fact that she existed and she refused to sell the Baxter land to him.

Since no uncle had been mentioned, Luke figured she was probably either a widow or a maiden aunt, most likely in her forties, judging by her nephew's age. An image of Miss Prucilla Andicott rose in his mind, bringing on an involuntary shudder. She was a pinched-lipped shrew who had dressed in black from head to toe. She believed her mission in life was to point out the shortcomings of the people around her and report them to those best able to correct the problem. And since Luke had excelled in shortcomings as a boy, he had drawn the wasp's attention on a regular basis. He'd felt the sting of his father's strap after every encounter with the old biddy. If Nate's aunt was anything like Miss Andicott, Luke could understand why the boy might want to lash out with vandalism. Perhaps the Triple G simply had the misfortune of being the nearest available target.

That was *if* the boy was the one responsible for the pranks. Luke wouldn't presume. Once a kid garnered a reputation as a troublemaker, it often didn't matter if he'd done a deed or not. He still bore the blame. By the time Luke had reached Nate's age, he'd long given up on protesting his innocence for offenses he hadn't committed and instead collected blame like badges of honor. If no one was going to believe he hadn't done something, he might as well get what he could out of the situation and pad his reputation.

When his inspection of the house provided no proof of current occupancy, Luke began plotting alternative methods for intelligence gathering. If his conversation with Nate had to be delayed, he'd see that the trip wasn't wasted. A fellow could learn a lot about a man—or a boy—by snooping around in his barn and peering through windows.

He'd best make sure he truly was alone first, though.

Luke dismounted and patted Titan's neck. "Keep watch for me, boy." The animal had keen hearing and a sensitive nature. Luke had learned to trust his horse more than himself when it came to detecting unseen trouble.

He took a few steps toward the house and called out in a loud voice. "Anyone home?" He strolled a few paces to the right so he could see down the east side of the dwelling. "Hello?"

Titan stomped his front hoof. Luke turned at the sound and caught the twitch of the sorrel's ears.

Luke's right hand moved to his holster and hovered in readiness as he approached the house more directly. "Nate? Miss Baxter? Anyone home?"

"Help!"

The cry was muffled. Barely audible. But he heard it.

Luke drew his revolver and climbed the porch steps. The wood creaked beneath his weight. "Do you need assistance?"

Before reaching for the front door, he took a moment to peer through the two windows on either side. Faded curtains hung in each, but enough of a gap existed between the panels to allow him a partial view of what appeared to be a parlor on the right and a bedroom on the left. No evidence of movement in either.

"I'm coming in!"

He fit his hand to the knob and eased the door open, keeping his body behind it as much as possible as he crossed the threshold gun-first.

"In here!" The voice sounded louder but still muffled.

Then something banged deeper inside the house.

"Please. Hurry!"

More banging. Or pounding. Like fists on a wall.

"Where are you?" Luke picked up his pace yet still moved with caution, leaning inside every doorway to scan each room as he passed, making sure no surprises lurked behind sofas or beneath beds.

"Kitchen." The voice was high-pitched. Could be a woman. Or a boy. "Cellar. Please. Let me out!"

Definitely female. Luke jogged the last few steps into the kitchen. As soon as he ascertained no threat waited for him, he holstered his weapon and looked for a root cellar. The banging drew him to a spot near a pinewood hutch, but all he saw was an empty table.

"In here. Please!"

Luke crouched down and peered at the floor. There. A square outline where the floorboards had been cut to make a door. A door that just happened to have the pedestal of a table planted on top of it.

Someone had trapped her in there deliberately.

Grabbing the edge of the oval table, Luke shoved it aside and reached for the door. It nearly caught his chin as it flew open. He dodged backward, almost getting hit again when a woman's head and shoulders popped out of the hole like the clown from a jack-in-the-box. Her appearance startled him nearly as much as the suddenness of her arrival.

This was no prune-faced maiden aunt. The woman in the floor had the unlined skin of youth, her complexion creamy and smooth. Brown doe eyes blinked up at him as she adjusted to the light. She sucked in deep breaths, her chest rising and falling beneath a pleated ivory blouse as she worked to get her bearings. One slender hand moved to rest against her collarbone beneath a jet-black mourning brooch, her fingers trembling. Thick ropes of brownish-black hair sat piled atop her head like a royal coronet, a few haphazard tendrils falling loose around her ears. As she moved, different strands caught the sunlight, blazing for a heartbeat like burnished bronze before submerging again into the backdrop of deceptively ordinary coffee-colored braids. Wide, dark brows slashed across her face with a strength that seemed at odds with the shy way she ducked her chin.

"Here." He wiped his palm on his trouser leg, then extended his hand to her.

Her cheeks reddened. "Thank you. I . . ."

She didn't finish her sentence, but she did fit her hand to his and allow him to help her climb out of the cellar. Although, judging by the speed with which she vaulted up the ladder, his help probably wasn't necessary.

Once she had both feet on the kitchen floor, she did an odd little dance, shaking out her skirt with all the vigor of a dance-hall girl, minus the high kicks. Next, she turned in a circle, brushing at her sleeves, bodice, and backside as if she'd just rolled down a leafy hillside and was trying to dislodge collected debris. Finally, she straightened, running her hands over her face and neck before tentatively meeting his gaze.

"Did I get them all?"

"Yes, ma'am."

Luke had not a clue what she was talking about, but she seemed to need reassurance, so he offered it. With authority.

A relieved sigh slipped past her lips, and he assumed he'd done the right thing. All those years of hangin' out with Wallace must've taught him a thing or two about dealing with women after all. Dealing with, but not understanding. He was still as ignorant as ever in that department. The lady in front of him looked perfectly tidy. Nothing had fallen from her during her odd little jig, so he had no idea what she'd been trying to rid herself of. Hopefully she'd refrain from asking him anything else. He had no desire to look the fool in front of her.

She dipped her chin, aiming the crown of her head at him. "Are there any in my hair?"

Luke swallowed. So much for avoiding further questions. At least there were implied instructions this time. Examine her head. That he could do. Not that he knew what he was searching for, but he'd give it a go.

He didn't even have to bow his back to do so. She was tall for a woman, her forehead level with his chin. Most women failed to reach his shoulders.

As requested, he dutifully scanned her noggin. It looked like a female's head ought. Hair. Pins. Some kind of elaborate braid circle. Nothing that didn't seem to belong.

"All clear." He might not know what he was looking for, but he knew better than to let the troops sense uncertainty. Confidence bred confidence.

"Thank heaven. I swore I could feel them crawling all over me while I was down there."

Bugs. The truth of his mission finally crystalized in Luke's brain. He'd been looking for bugs. Good. His report had been accurate, then. No creepy-crawlies anywhere on her person.

"My imagination probably got the better of me," she admitted as she raised her face, "but it was too dark down there to know for sure." She smiled softly as she lifted her chin, and something tightened inside his chest.

Odd. Usually when he met an attractive woman, the electricity that zinged through him was purely visceral. This was . . . different. Probably because *she* was different. Not exactly pretty. Her brows were too thick. Her nose a tad long and turned up at the end. Her figure tall and willowy. Not many curves or even much meat on her bones. Yet when she looked at him with that small hint of a smile, something about her drew him. Made him feel . . . comfortable. Like he didn't have to try to impress. He could just be himself in her presence. He'd never felt that way around a woman in his life.

Luke cleared his throat. "Are you hurt?" It felt good to be on the shootin' end of the questions.

She shook her head, color rising in her cheeks again. "No. Just embarrassed to be caught trapped in my own root cellar. You must think me the veriest fool."

"Not as big a fool as you must think me if you believe I could hold you responsible for that predicament." Luke crossed his arms and raised a brow. "You might've managed to drop the door on top of yourself on the way down, but unless you can move furniture with your mind, someone else dragged that table over the hatch and trapped you inside."

"Yes, well. I still should have known better."

"Because your nephew pulls stunts like this on a regular basis?"

"No!" Her outrage had more bristles than a washerwoman's scrub brush. "Nathaniel has never done anything like this . . ." She pressed her lips together.

Before.

The word hung unspoken in the air between them. She, not wanting to admit that her nephew had actually perpetrated the deed, and he, hearing the admission anyway.

Luke appreciated a good prank as much as the next fella— had pulled more than his share in his youth—but this crossed a line. Trappin' a woman. Leaving her helpless. Even if the only danger she faced was from imaginary bugs crawling on her, that didn't mean something worse couldn't have happened. Snakebite. A fall from the ladder. Or, God forbid, fire. She would have suffocated in there.

"It weren't right, trappin' you in there."

"No, it wasn't." She crossed the room and positioned herself in front of a worktable with a lumpy brown mass in the center that had to be the ugliest loaf of bread he'd ever seen. "But no harm was done. I'll deal with my nephew as I see fit. He's really none of your concern, Mister . . . ?"

"Davenport. Luke Davenport. And actually, he is my concern." Luke uncrossed his arms and relaxed his stance, making an effort to appear harmless. She didn't look convinced. Luke bit back a sigh. "Is Nate around?"

Any remaining gratitude in her gaze faded behind an increasing wariness. "You know my nephew?"

Luke shook his head. "My new employer, Oliver Grimes, mentioned him. Said he might have some information that could be helpful to my investigation."

"Investigation?" She reached for the table behind her. "Are

you some kind of lawman? Because Nathaniel has done nothing wrong."

Interesting that her mind immediately jumped to wrongdoing.

"No, ma'am. I've been hired by Mr. Grimes to look into some cattle rustling at the Triple G." He smiled at her, hoping to put her at ease. It worked for Wallace, but he must be doing it wrong, 'cause the filly in front of him looked anything but easy. Her gaze kept dodgin' to the window and the back door. Thinking about makin' a run for it? Or worried good ol' Nate might return and have to face up to his misdeeds?

Luke didn't know much about women, but he was pretty sure throwin' accusations around about their young'uns bein' involved in unsavory activities wasn't the best way to secure their cooperation. It'd be best if he downplayed his suspicions.

"Since the two of you are neighbors," Luke said, keeping his voice nonchalant, "Grimes thought Nate might have seen something to give us a clue about who the guilty party might be or how they're getting onto the property unseen. That's what brought me to your door today. I was hoping to ask the boy a few questions."

Her grip on the table let up a bit. "I see. I doubt Nathaniel will be much help, though. He's only a boy."

Luke shrugged. "Boys still got eyes. And something tells me Nate's not the type to sit at home in his room. He's more of an explorer. Am I right?"

She didn't answer, but the truth radiated from her eyes. Nate was a wild one.

"Miss Baxter . . ." Luke frowned. "It *is* Miss Baxter, isn't it?"

"Yes. Damaris Baxter. I'm sorry. I should have introduced myself earlier."

Luke grinned. "When, exactly? During your escape from the cellar or in the middle of defendin' your nephew?"

Her gaze dropped to the floor, but a shy smile winked at him. "I suppose these aren't exactly ordinary circumstances, are they?"

"No, ma'am. But it *is* a pleasure to meet you, Miss Baxter." Luke fingered his hat brim. He probably should've taken it off entirely at some point, but it seemed silly to do it now when their visit was nearing an end.

"Likewise, Mr. Davenport." She pushed away from the table and extended her hand. "And I really do appreciate you coming to my rescue. Thank you."

He clasped her hand, her fingers slender inside his oversized mitt. He lingered an extra heartbeat, enjoying the feel of her hand in his. He couldn't remember the last time he'd touched a wo—

"Let go of my aunt, mister, or I'll blow ya to bits!"

FOUR

Nathaniel!" Damaris couldn't believe her eyes. Where had he gotten a rifle?

When she'd moved into the house, she'd found her brother's shotgun and pistol along with a stash of ammunition in a gun cabinet in the master bedroom, but she had locked that up tight and hidden the key in her jewelry box on her first night. Guns might be normal in Texas, and she supposed they even had their uses when it came to snakes and coyotes and other uninvited creatures, but having them in the house made her uncomfortable. So she'd draped an embroidered dresser runner over the glass front of the cabinet and pretended it was a thin armoire.

She hadn't told her nephew about the key. But then, Nathaniel wasn't holding his father's shotgun. He was holding a rifle. One she didn't recognize.

Mr. Davenport released Damaris's hand and turned slowly to face her nephew, keeping his hands away from his body.

As he turned, he stepped sideways, drawing the aim of the gun away from her.

"Nathaniel," Damaris said in the most soothing voice she could summon, "Mr. Davenport is no threat to me. We were just talking."

Her nephew hid his emotions well, but she knew he must be terrified. Surely he'd never held a gun on another person before. Especially not a person of Mr. Davenport's intimidating size. Why, the man looked like a dime novel hero come to life. His stature and musculature dwarfed the boy.

"Please, Nathaniel. Put the gun down."

Her nephew didn't even glance her way. His full attention centered on the stranger in their kitchen. And while it touched her heart that Nathaniel was trying to protect her, she couldn't escape the feeling that he was the one in need of protection. She took a step toward him, but Mr. Davenport motioned with his hand for her to stay put. Instinct told her to obey. He seemed the type to know what to do in situations involving guns and boys eager to prove their masculinity. Since her knowledge and experience in those areas wouldn't fill a thimble, she opted to follow his lead.

"Your aunt's right, Nate." The words oozed from Mr. Davenport like melted butter. Calm. Smooth. Completely unruffled. "I mean her no harm. You neither."

Nathaniel shifted his feet. His eyes darted from Damaris back to their guest. The gun started to drop as if the weight was taking a toll on his arms, but he jerked it back up in an instant and pointed it straight at Mr. Davenport's chest.

"Don't move!"

Mr. Davenport halted his slow sideways slide. "I'm just

tryin' to make sure your aunt's outta the line of fire. Wouldn't want a stray bullet to find her on accident."

"I hit what I aim at," Nathaniel bragged even as his arms quivered. His gaze darted back toward her for a heartbeat, and in the moment their eyes met, something flickered in his gaze that she'd not seen since she arrived. Regret. And for the briefest of seconds, she swore she saw a little boy's plea for help. He was in over his head and had no idea how to extricate himself.

Give him a way out.

Mr. Davenport couldn't hear her thoughts, of course, but she aimed them at him anyway with as much mental force as she could muster.

"I respect you for protectin' your womenfolk, Nate. But I don't cotton to folks usin' my rifle without permission."

Lord have mercy. Nate had stolen Mr. Davenport's rifle? Damaris bit back a groan.

"Yeah, well, I bet you'd use whatever weapon you could find to protect *your* family, permission or not."

Heavens. Did the boy have to antagonize *everyone?*

"I would, at that," the stranger admitted, surprising an exhale of relief out of Damaris.

Thank you for cool heads, Lord. Now, if you could just soften Nathaniel's stubborn heart . . .

"Tell you what." Mr. Davenport slowly lifted his hands and stretched his arms above his head. His fingers nearly touched the ceiling. "I'm going to turn around and place my palms against the wall. That way you know I won't try to rush you or reach for my revolver. Your aunt can move to your side of the room, out of my reach, and you can set the rifle down on the table. Once I hear you set the gun down, I'll turn, and we can all have a civilized conversation without the use of weapons. Sound good?"

It sounded perfect. At least to Damaris. Nathaniel, however, possessed a more suspicious nature.

"How do I know you won't pull your revolver and shoot me the minute I set the rifle down?"

"You have my word."

Nathaniel scowled. "I don't know you, mister. Your word could be garbage."

The first flicker of impatience tightened Mr. Davenport's face.

Damaris's heart rate doubled. *Please, Lord.*

"Boy, I served with the 7th Cavalry for more than a decade, then rode with Hanger's Horsemen until we hung up our spurs a little over a year ago. If I wanted to shoot you, I would have drawn on you and lodged a bullet in your shoulder before you could figure out how to lever a cartridge into the chamber of that repeater."

Nathaniel paled. "You're a . . . a Horseman?"

"Yep. And I'm gettin' real tired of holdin' my hands in the air. We got a deal or not?"

Damaris had no idea what being a horseman had to do with anything, but a soldier with the 7th Cavalry—*that* she recognized. They'd been responsible for the massacre at Wounded Knee five years ago. Taken the lives of women. Children. Conscienceless atrocities that turned her stomach.

Yet the man standing before her didn't exude the ruthlessness she'd expect from such a vicious warrior. Quite the opposite. He personified patience and calm, like a man going out of his way to avoid bloodshed. If his claim were true about what he could have done to her nephew the instant he'd been threatened—and judging by his size and experience, Damaris found the claim easy to believe—this confrontation would have been over in a matter of seconds. Yet he'd chosen the path of peace and wisdom.

"'A soft answer turneth away wrath,'" she quoted under her breath, half prayer, half observation.

"Proverbs 15:1," Mr. Davenport murmured in equally quiet tones.

Her gaze flew to him. He didn't take his eyes off Nathaniel, but she swore she could feel his awareness of her.

A man of God. Or at least a man familiar with the Bible. The realization assured her as nothing else could. He wouldn't attack Nathaniel.

She turned back to her nephew. Indecision etched his face, and sweat beaded his brow.

"It's all right, Nathaniel," she urged. "I trust him."

She half-expected him to come back with a caustic remark about her being a sheltered spinster with no experience of men, which would have been completely true, but he didn't. He gave a small nod instead, then waved the rifle barrel at Mr. Davenport.

"All right. Turn around. Hands against the wall."

Mr. Davenport complied, turning his back on a scared, inexperienced boy who could shoot him on accident just as easily as on purpose.

"Aunt Maris, collect his gun."

That hadn't been part of the deal. What if Mr. Davenport objected?

Damaris swallowed and took a step. Mr. Davenport turned his face slightly toward her and gave a little nod of consent. Her cresting anxiety ebbed. She took another step.

"Go around, behind the boy," Mr. Davenport said in a low voice. "Don't cross the rifle's path."

Still protecting her. Moisture gathered in her eyes as she changed direction and circled behind Nathaniel. Most of her life she'd felt like a hindrance to her family. One more mouth to feed. The odd daughter who preferred books and embroidery to social interaction. The child with no marital prospects, destined to live off the charity of others. The one more likely to be forgotten than sought after. Yet here she stood between a nephew she barely knew and a stranger whom she knew not at all, both taking extreme measures to protect her. Strange that she should feel more valued and cherished in the middle of an armed standoff than in the middle of her family.

Then again, the Damaris her family knew was a spinster who specialized in fading into the woodwork. The new Texas Damaris was poised to pull a pistol from a giant gunman's holster. A *loaded* pistol. A prospect that churned her stomach. Her mother would never believe her capable of such a feat. But the Texas Damaris had a nephew to raise and a brother to honor. She wouldn't let either of them down with ill-timed squeamishness.

Squaring her shoulders, she approached Mr. Davenport from the right and reached for his weapon.

As if he sensed her nervousness, his low voice rumbled encouragement and instructions in her ear. "It won't go off without being cocked first. Just keep it pointed at the floor, and you'll be fine."

She bit her lip, clasped the handle end with her right hand, and lifted the gun carefully out of the holster. Once she had it out, she pointed the shooting end at the floor, then briefly rested her left hand on Mr. Davenport's back.

"Thank you." For choosing peaceful surrender instead of confrontation. For protecting a young boy's pride and easing a woman's fears. For being the bigger man where it truly counted—in character.

Her touch seeped through Luke like water soaking into scorched earth. It lasted only a heartbeat before she retreated, but even after her hand left his shoulder blade, he could feel the imprint linger. What was it about this woman that affected him so? It had been a simple pat. That was all. A gesture to let him know the sincerity of her gratitude. Nothing more.

So why did it feel like more?

He counted her footsteps as she moved away, then finally heard the sound he'd been waiting for—the soft *thud* of his rifle being set upon the table. A second, lighter *click* followed when his revolver was laid beside it.

"All right, mister. You can turn around."

Luke pivoted slowly, not wanting to spook the kid. He brought his hands down and got his first good look at Nathaniel Baxter without a gun in front of his face. *Luke's* gun. That still rankled. Not to mention the fact that the boy had been responsible for trapping Miss Damaris in the root cellar. Two strikes against him.

On the other hand, when Nate spotted an unknown horse

in front of his house and a strange man inside, he'd taken action to protect his aunt. That evened the score.

The kid stood an inch or two shorter than his aunt and had the gangly, bean-pole limbs typical of a boy struggling to grow into a man. His eyes narrowed as he faced Luke, their steel-blue color radically different from the aunt's soft brown. The boy stood close to the table where the weapons had been stored, his hip cocked against the rounded edge while his fingers pressed into the wood grain mere inches from the revolver. He'd regained a bit of his color and a good deal of his insolence.

Nate flicked his head to get his overlong brown hair out of his eyes. "You really one of Hanger's Horsemen?"

"Yep." Luke relaxed his stance, leaning his left shoulder against the hutch beside him. He kept his right arm free, however, just in case he needed to go for his knife. His gut told him the danger had passed, but his training insisted he always be ready. "Served under Captain Hanger in the 7th, then followed him to Texas. Oliver Grimes hired me to look into some rustling happenin' at his place."

His casual mention of Grimes triggered a reaction. The boy broke eye contact and shifted his stance. Arms crossed over his midsection. Feeling guilty? For the vandalism, or for his involvement in the rustling?

"The other Horsemen here, too?" Nate's voice cracked a little on the question.

"Nope. Just me. Captain Hanger's retired. Runs a horse breeding farm down near San Antonio now. The others settled over in Llano County."

The kid looked far too relieved at that news. Luke couldn't resist an extra little jab.

"They're like brothers, though. One telegram is all it'd take to bring them here in force."

Nate's Adam's apple bobbed up and down.

Luke hid a smile. "But I don't think I'll need them. I'm pretty good at sniffin' out troublemakers on my own."

Another hard bob of the Adam's apple. The boy was definitely nervous.

"In fact," Luke pressed, pushing away from the hutch and closing a few steps of distance between him and his quarry, "I was hoping to ask you a few questions about it. Thought you might have some insight that would—"

"I don't know nothin' about any rustling." The boy's hands dropped to his sides, balling into fists. "And even if I did, I wouldn't do anything to help your boss." His face reddened, and rage visibly vibrated his arms. "Oliver Grimes killed my father!"

CHAPTER

FIVE

Luke steeled his expression to hide his shock. Miss Baxter, on the other hand, hid nothing. Her nephew's angry accusation nearly felled her. She grabbed a nearby chair and collapsed into it.

Luke raised a brow as he regarded Nate. "Those are strong words. You got any proof to back 'em up?"

The kid scowled and sliced his arm through the air as if it were a weapon seeking a target. "Of course I don't have proof. If I did, Oliver Grimes would be behind bars or swingin' from the end of a rope."

A tiny guttural sound that reminded Luke of a kicked puppy echoed from Miss Baxter's location. His attention shifted off the boy and onto the delicate woman who had wrapped an arm around her midsection and was rocking slightly. Her complexion had paled, and her shoulders rounded in on themselves like a shield.

"Why don't you tell me about it outside?" Luke suggested. Talk of hangings and murder wasn't exactly fit for female consumption, especially a female who'd been raised to a more genteel existence. He didn't know much about Damaris Baxter, but her clothes were well-made and more suited to a ladies' drawing room than a cabin in the middle of Texas cattle country.

Nate obviously agreed, for he gave one sharp nod, then strode for the back door. Luke crossed to the table to collect his guns. He'd barely slipped his revolver into its holster before Miss Baxter's chair scraped against the floorboards.

She jerked to her feet. "Stop!"

The word carried all the weight of a command. Luke's hand froze above his rifle, and his gaze sought hers. The pleading in her eyes arrested him, but her attention didn't linger. It shot over to her nephew, who stood with his back turned to her and his hand on the door handle. He'd halted, but he made no move to face her.

"I will not be excluded from this conversation." She gripped the table edge, her knuckles as white as her ashen face. As Luke watched, however, she released the support and straightened to her full height. It was a rather remarkable sight, like a butterfly stretching its wings for the first time after emerging from a cocoon. "I want to hear your reasons for thinking Mr. Grimes is responsible for your father's death, even if you don't have proof." She paused, nibbled on her bottom lip, then worked her way around the side of the table, her gaze rooted to her nephew's back. "I loved your father too, you know. He was my big brother. If his death wasn't the accident I was led to believe, I need to know."

She took a step. Then another. And a third. Halting less than a yard from Nate, she stretched out an arm. Her hand hovered behind the boy's shoulder, poised for contact yet hesitating. A heartbeat passed. Then her elbow folded, and her fingers retracted. "Please, Nathaniel. Let me help."

Nate spun to face her at last, belligerence etched into his features even as moisture glistened in his eyes. "How do you think you can help, Aunt Maris? Read me stories like you did after my ma died? I ain't a kid anymore. Lullabies and fairy tales ain't gonna cut it."

She flinched, yet she didn't back away. She stood fast, caring more about tending her nephew's hurt than her own.

"You can tell me *your* story this time." Her soft voice soothed. Beckoned. Pleaded. "About Mr. Grimes. About your father. About where you go at night."

He'd been softening until she mentioned his nocturnal excursions. His expression turned stony after that, his chin jutting forward in defiance. "Where I go is my business. No one else's. Quit tryin' to mother me, Aunt Maris. It ain't your place."

The boy yanked the back door open and shot out of the kitchen like a jackrabbit chased by a coyote. Grief couldn't be outrun, though. It would catch him eventually, and when it did, he'd need the very thing he swore he didn't want—his aunt.

"Nathaniel, wait!" Miss Baxter charged after him, but the boy ignored her call. She ran as far as the clothesline before stuttering to a stop. She braced a hand against the wooden post. Tears trailed down her cheeks. The sight gut-punched Luke.

"You all right?" He drew up beside her, having grabbed his rifle and raced after them both.

She shook her head. "I pushed him too hard. Asked too many questions."

Luke touched her shoulder, just as she'd touched his earlier, hoping to dispense some measure of comfort. "He didn't run because you asked questions. He ran 'cause he's hidin' something. You didn't do anything wrong. In fact, from what I can see, you're doin' a whole lot right. The kid's lucky to have you."

The woundedness in her brown eyes made his chest ache, but it hurt worse when she tore her gaze away from him to stare forlornly after the ungrateful boy sprinting over the low hill just beyond the barn.

"He doesn't seem to think so."

"Yeah, well, boys his age are stupid." Luke dropped his hand from her shoulder and cocked a grin when she glanced his way. "I should know. I used to be one." He turned and let out a shrill whistle. The quiet thud of hoofbeats followed.

Miss Baxter's eyes widened as she beheld Titan trotting toward him like a giant, faithful hound. Luke hid a smile as he slid his rifle into the saddle boot. "I'll have Nate back to you by supper," he promised as he mounted and took up the reins.

Miss Baxter shaded her eyes with a hand to her brow as she peered up at him. "How? He's gone."

Luke tipped his hat. "I'm a Horseman, ma'am. Hunting down outlaws and bandits is what I do."

"Yes, well, my nephew's not an outlaw. He's a fourteen-year-old boy. Be sure you remember that."

Luke tugged on the brim of his hat. "Yes, ma'am."

Although Nate's age had little bearing on his outlaw status. The boy was knee-deep in trouble of some sort. Of that,

Luke had no doubt. The question was what kind of mud he was slogging around in. The kind that would only muck up his shoes and leave a few stains on his trousers? Or a bottomless bog that would swallow him whole if he stepped wrong?

And how did Oliver Grimes fit into all this? Did he really have something to do with Douglas Baxter's death? Hard to believe when Luke knew Wilson Grimes, Oliver's brother, to be an honorable man, a man of courage and duty. But then, men sharing blood ties didn't necessarily share ties of morality or integrity. And thank God for that, or Luke would have ended up an abusive drunkard like his old man—one who'd rather rail at the world for dealing him a raw hand than actually do anything to make it better.

Shaking off the bad memories, Luke nudged Titan into a slow canter and set off in the direction he'd last seen Nate. He slowed as he crested the hill, but it didn't take long to spot his quarry. The boy made no effort to hide. He just ran. As if exertion and escape could manufacture the freedom he sought. Luke understood the compulsion. There was a reason he'd become one of the most accomplished swordsmen in his unit. Years of stockpiled resentment, rage, and hurt didn't expunge itself. Luke had found an outlet first with his fists, then later with a cavalry saber. The mental concentration required to wield the weapon against a capable opponent quieted the demons, while the physical effort dulled the rage.

After Luke became a proficient swordsman, Matt was the only officer willing to spar with him. The only one willing to take the punishment Luke dealt when the rage simmered too close to the surface. Matt had had his own demons to battle, and while he couldn't match Luke's brawn, his grasp of strategy kept the contest even. And somewhere amid all the sweat and exhaustion, a bond formed between the combatants. A bond that did more to subdue the demons than the sparring ever had. A bond that ultimately led Luke to the One with the ability to subdue the demons permanently. They still raised their nasty heads on occasion, too much a part of him to be fully eradicated until the perfection of heaven arrived, but they'd been chained and stripped of their power.

And the God of peace shall bruise Satan under your feet. One of the many verses he'd memorized over the years ran through Luke's head as he caught up to Nate. God's peace was what the kid needed. But if Nate was anything like Luke had been at that age, getting him to let go of his anger and bitterness would not be easy. It had taken the horrors of war, the bonds of friendship, and a decade's worth of maturing to teach Luke the value of peace. He prayed Nate would catch on quicker than he had.

Luke reined Titan across Nate's path, forcing the boy to halt his flight. Nate scowled, dodged around Titan's head, and tried to take off again, but Luke grabbed him by the back of his shirt and lifted his feet off the ground.

"Let me go!" Nate kicked and squirmed, but Titan was too well-trained to let the flailing limbs rattle him, and Luke was too strong to lose his grip.

"I'll let you go as soon as you start actin' like a man instead of a spoiled child."

Nate stilled, then craned his neck to glare at Luke. "I ain't no child."

Luke raised a brow. "Coulda fooled me. Trappin' your aunt

in the root cellar. Lashing out when she tries to help you. Runnin' away instead of facing your problems. Sounds pretty childish to me. You think your daddy would be proud of such antics? That the kind of man he taught you to be?"

The belligerence fell off Nate's face in a slow slide, starting with a softening around the eyes and working downward until even his chin lost its stubborn tilt.

"Didn't think so." Luke leaned sideways and set the boy on the ground. Then he dismounted, tapped Titan's haunches to let him know he was free to search out some grass, and came around to stand in front of Nate. "Losin' family's hard. You got a right to be angry. Even scared. But you don't got the right to get so absorbed in your pain that you hurt the people around you."

"Yeah, well, you ain't got the right to preach at me."

Luke hid a grin, thinking of the nickname he carried among the Horsemen. "Maybe not, but I know what it's like to get handed a raw deal in life. I wasted a lot of years being driven by anger and resentment. Trust me, it's no way to live. You think the anger makes you strong. But that's a lie. The longer the anger lives in you, the more it erodes your soul and destroys your relationships. If you're not careful, one day it'll hollow you out and leave you with nothing. I'd hate to see that happen to you."

"Why? You don't know me. You think I'm a rustler." Nate crossed his arms over his chest, daring Luke to deny it.

Luke didn't blink. "Are you?"

Nate flicked his head to toss the hair out of his eyes. "I've never laid a finger on a stinkin' Triple G cow."

Which didn't exactly answer the question. He could still

be involved indirectly. Helping the rustlers somehow as a way to retaliate against Grimes.

"All right. What about a vandal? You been causin' mischief at the Grimes spread after dark?" Luke watched for a reaction. "Grimes told me his garden was hacked up. Food stores destroyed. Horses spooked and run out of the corral. Skunks in the bunkhouse. Manure splattered on the front porch. Know anything about those misfortunes?"

Nate looked like he was fighting to hold back a smirk. "Sounds like the critters got a mind of their own over there."

Uh-huh. The kid was definitely involved with the vandalism.

Luke raised a brow. "So those little nighttime excursions your aunt mentioned you taking . . . they don't have anything to do with the trouble at the Triple G?"

Nate shrugged. "I like to walk at night."

Another non-answer. The kid was cagey. Didn't lie outright, but wasn't forthcoming, either. Not much to recommend him as trustworthy.

Time to switch tactics.

"Tell me about Grimes. Why do you think he killed your father?"

Nate's face darkened. "He wants our land. Been tryin' to get us to sell for years, but Pa never would. My ma was the one to pick out the place. Pa said she fell in love with the big black walnut tree growing in the middle of the clearing. Asked him to build the house right beside it so she could enjoy the shade in the summer and harvest nuts in the fall." The boy looked off into the distance, back toward the homestead he'd run from. "Pa planted a second walnut tree at the base of the

hill where we buried her. Said it would shade her year 'round."
He turned back to Luke, his jaw tight. "We weren't about to
let Oliver Grimes's stinky cows trample all over her grave."

Luke nodded, his throat tight. Rough lot for a kid. Growing up without a mother. Luke knew a bit about that. He
didn't voice his sympathy, though. They needed to keep the
conversation focused on the father, not the mother.

"Grimes admitted to me that he's tried to buy your land
on several occasions," Luke said, "but I don't see how that
makes him responsible for your father's death."

Nate's arms swept out in a wide arc. "He was the only one
with anything to gain!" He stomped three steps away, then
growled, "There's no way my pa died in a swimming accident.
He was too good a swimmer. They said he probably hit his
head on something like the edge of a boat, but he never would
have been at the lake in the first place! He always came home
straight after work. To be with me." The boy's voice hitched
on a suppressed sob. "Grimes must've lured him out to the
lake somehow. Held him under, then left him for someone
else to find. He must've thought that if my pa was out of the
way, he could get the land. But I'll never sell it. Ever! Neither
will Aunt Maris. She swore it."

A bothersome seed planted itself in Luke's gut. He could
think of a dozen more plausible explanations for Nate's father's demise than murder. But if someone really did precipi-
tate Douglas Baxter's death in order to get their hands on the
man's land, what would keep them from doing the same to
Nate . . . or Damaris?

CHAPTER

SIX

Damaris welcomed Nathaniel home with a smile when Mr. Davenport dropped him off as promised. She asked a few innocuous questions as he washed up, hoping he'd open up to her on his own accord. All she received from him, however, were a pair of shrugs and one noncommittal grunt. No explanations about his father. No recap of what happened when Mr. Davenport tracked him down. Not even a comment about being hungry for dinner. The angry yet finally vocal Nathaniel had been replaced by a sullen version who seemed determined to avoid interaction altogether. His gaze stayed glued to his plate as he shoveled sausage gravy and toast into his mouth one bite after another, keeping his mouth constantly full and thereby unavailable for conversation.

Patience was a virtue, but sometimes it was an excuse to stay on the easy path of conflict avoidance. Damaris much preferred smooth paths, but if any truth existed in Nathaniel's claim that Douglas had not perished from accidental causes, she couldn't afford continued passivity. Not if she wanted to ensure her nephew's safety.

So when he scooted his plate away from the edge of the table and started chugging down the half-glass of milk he had left, she knew the time for boldness had come. Even though she'd barely eaten half of the dinner on her own plate, Damaris rose from the table, crossed to the stove, and opened the warming oven.

The sweet scent of cinnamon and apples wafted through the kitchen. The milk cup lowered a few inches from Nathaniel's face. He swiveled slightly toward her. His eyes widened a fraction.

"You made fried apples?"

Was that a touch of ruefulness in his eyes? Choosing to believe it was, Damaris smiled and set the plate in front of him.

"Of course. I said I'd make you some." Although she'd kept one eye on the trapdoor opening the entire time she was in the cellar, darting to the apple basket and back to the ladder like a rubber ball on the rebound.

Nathaniel squirmed in his seat, then ran a sleeve over his mouth to remove the thin milk mustache that moistened his upper lip.

"A person of integrity always lives up to his or her word." *Which means no more departures through your bedroom window at night, since I escaped the root cellar before you came home.*

Although, technically, she hadn't actually agreed to his deal, so he might still have a loophole there. But that wasn't her main agenda tonight.

Damaris slid her chair closer to Nathaniel's and lowered herself to the seat. She wanted to cover his hand with hers, to show her love in some tangible way, but boys on the cusp of manhood disliked displays of affection. Or maybe it was just Nathaniel not wanting his aunt to usurp his mother's place.

That comment still stung, even though she'd forgiven him for it almost immediately.

Instead of touching him, she clasped her hands in her lap and sought out his gaze. "Tell me about your father."

He dropped his head and studied the dessert before him as if it were some kind of culinary masterpiece. Which it definitely was not. A couple of the apples bore scorch marks, though she'd made an effort to hide them at the bottom of the pile.

Nathaniel stabbed at a bit of sugared apple with his fork but didn't bring it to his mouth. "Pa woulda whupped me good for lockin' you in the cellar." He lifted his head and made a valiant effort to meet her eyes, though he seemed to get hung up somewhere around her nose. "I shouldn't have done that."

It wasn't an apology, precisely, but it was progress. "No, you shouldn't have. But all is forgiven." One of her hands fled her lap and patted his arm before she realized what she'd done. He frowned slightly yet didn't jerk away. More progress. It nearly made her giddy. The question hanging in her mind kept her sober, though.

Perhaps she could come at it sideways instead of head-on. Make it easier on both of them. "Did you talk to Mr. Davenport about Mr. Grimes?"

"Yeah." A large forkful of apple found its way into his mouth.

He obviously didn't want to talk about it, but she couldn't back down. Not if there was any hope of the two of them building trust and openness between them.

"Do you suspect him because he wants your land?"

Nathaniel slanted a glance at her from the corner of his eye and gave a slow nod.

She'd thought so.

Damaris had met with Ronald Mullins when she first came to town. The lawyer in charge of Douglas's estate had been very kind and had patiently answered all her questions about the trust her brother had set up for his son. As executer, she had the right to sell the land and put the money aside for her nephew. Mr. Mullins even informed her of a standing offer for the property. A generous offer. He'd not mentioned any names, but it made sense that a neighboring rancher looking to expand would be interested in the property. She'd considered accepting. The selling price would secure Nathaniel's future. Pay for his education. Allow him to establish himself in whatever occupation he chose. The land hadn't been farmed or developed in any way except for the house, so it seemed unlikely that her nephew would need the acreage for making his living. Selling seemed a good solution.

Until she mentioned the possibility to Nathaniel.

Children never wanted to be uprooted from their homes, so she'd expected some resistance. Not a full-scale rebellion. She'd told him about the life they could have in Missouri. About the education he'd receive. The advantages he'd enjoy. Gaslights. Baseball. Career opportunities.

The look in his eyes as she spoke, however, sliced her heart to ribbons. Utter betrayal.

He'd been civil to her when she first arrived. Not warm or particularly welcoming, but sufficiently polite. Everything changed after that conversation. Battle lines were drawn, and she'd become the enemy. He'd yelled at her. Called her a traitor. Accused her of selfishness—sacrificing *his* home just so she could return to *hers*. She knew nothing about his father, about their life here. Douglas had loved the land and refused to sell it no matter how many times Mr. Grimes offered or what kind of price tag he attached. This was Baxter land. No one else's. If she wanted to go back to Missouri, go ahead. He was staying.

Then he'd run out the door to the lone tree at the base of the hill behind the house. The tree that sheltered his parents' graves.

She'd followed him. Promised not to sell the land. But the damage had been done. Trust had been broken.

Maybe today she could begin rebuilding.

"When I first heard the news about how Douglas died, I found it hard to believe. He was always such a strong swimmer. In fact, he taught me how to swim when I was just a girl. Did he teach you?"

Nathaniel's vigorous chewing slowed as he nodded, his eyes turning a bit glassy as if he were getting lost in a memory. Hopefully a good one.

Damaris got lost in a few of her own. "I rather idolized him, you know. He was smart. Funny. Good at sports. Nothing scared him. He was so outgoing and easy with people." Even awkward, painfully shy little sisters. She smiled as she recalled him coaxing her out of her hiding place behind the curtains covering the window ledge in her room.

Mother had always sent Douglas to fetch her when company came over, instructing him to toss her over his shoulder like a sack of potatoes if necessary. He'd never had to resort to such tactics, though. He charmed her out of hiding every time with his silly commentary on whichever relative or friend had come to call and his promise to hold her hand all the way down the stairs.

"Everyone loved him," she said. "I missed him terribly when he moved to Texas."

Nathaniel stopped chewing altogether. A sheen encompassed his eyes. "People liked him here, too," he said softly, a slight catch in his voice. "He knew everybody who came into the mill by name and was always the first to volunteer for any work that needed to be done around the church or school. He'd drag me along to those projects, even though I'd grumble about wanting to go fishin' instead. He'd joke that he needed me for protection." He quirked a half grin. "From the ladies set on catchin' his attention. They'd bake cookies and dress up in their Sunday best before they *just happened* to drop by the churchyard or schoolhouse. They put plenty of bait on the hook, but Pa wasn't biting. Not even a nibble. His heart still belonged to Ma and always would."

Nathaniel's smile flattened as he finally lifted his gaze to meet hers. "That's why he refused to sell to Mr. Grimes. This land was *hers*. The house she helped build. The garden where she grew her vegetables. The creek where she slipped and got a drenching, then dragged Pa in after her when he laughed."

The playful memory softened his expression for a moment, but then his jaw tightened. "Grimes wouldn't let it go. He kept after Pa to sell. Especially the last few months.

Pa must've reached his limit, 'cause when Grimes came to the house with another offer, he flew off the handle. I ain't never heard him yell like that. He told Grimes there was no amount of money that would make him sell. Not to him. Not to anyone. Told him to get off our land. Threatened to shoot him for trespassing if he ever set foot on our property again. Grimes called him a stubborn fool. Said Pa would regret rejecting his offer." Nathaniel's nostrils flared as his eyes narrowed. "They found Pa's body floating in the lake four days later."

Four days?

"Did you tell the sheriff about the argument?" Surely there'd been an investigation of some kind. Men didn't just show up floating in lakes for no reason.

Oh, Douglas. What happened to you?

"I tried, but I'm just a kid. Some of Grimes's cowhands vouched for him, said he was riding herd with them all day. The sheriff believed them. Declared it an accident and turned my pa's body over to the undertaker. But there's no way he drowned, Aunt Maris." His eyes pled with her to believe him. "He had no reason to even *be* at the lake. Someone had to have lured him away from the mill and . . . and . . ."

Damaris covered his forearm with her hand and squeezed softly as she blinked away her own grief. He didn't need to say the words. She knew. And it tore her heart to pieces.

It's not fair, God. First his mother and now his father? No child should have to suffer such loss. To be left alone in the world.

He's not alone.

The truth settled in her bones with a depth of certainty

she could not deny. No, Nathaniel wasn't alone. The Lord was with him, a Father to the fatherless, a binder of the brokenhearted. But could Nathaniel sense his nearness? Feel his love, his compassion? Or was he too angry and bitter to let the Lord's comfort soothe the rawness of his grief?

Was that why she was here? Not just to tend to Nathaniel's physical needs but to his spiritual needs as well. To remind him that he wasn't alone.

And perhaps remind herself as well.

"The next time we go to town, I'll ask some questions," Damaris said. "Visit the sheriff, the undertaker, and the mill. See if I can unearth a witness that might be able to explain why Douglas went to the lake that day."

Beneath her fingertips, she felt some of the tension leak out of Nathaniel's arm.

She wasn't sure what she might learn in town that Nathaniel hadn't already been told. Men often dismissed women with the same condescension as they did children. Nevertheless, she resolved not to be put off. She'd persevere, even if the thought of asserting herself among strangers delighted her as much as the prospect of being dragged behind a horse. By her hair. Through a bed of cacti.

She'd do it, though. For Nathaniel. And for Douglas. Her brother deserved justice as much as her nephew deserved closure.

And because for the first time since she'd arrived, she beheld a flicker of something in her nephew's eyes that she'd feared never to see again.

Hope.

— CHAPTER —
SEVEN

An owl hooted somewhere in the distance, drawing Luke's gaze east, around the edges of the rocky outcropping protecting his position. He peered into the shadowy darkness of night but didn't see any movement beyond a tree branch bouncing in the breeze a few yards away. No rustlers. At least not yet.

After two days of scouting Grimes's property line, he'd narrowed the likely entry points down to three options, this one being the top of his list. The rock formed a natural barrier that made wire fencing difficult to implement. Grimes had managed to string wire up over the top of the rock face, but if there were caves or caverns inside, someone who knew the area might be able to lead a cow through an underground passage and out the other side, circumventing the fencing. Luke hadn't found any caverns yet, but his gut told him they were here.

So he'd volunteered for night watch in this section.

Luke hated night watch. Always had. Too much quiet. Too

much dark. Too many chances for a man to get swallowed up by his own thoughts. Especially the ones Luke tried to keep buried beneath a steady flow of hard work and constant activity.

"Stupid kid. Can't do nothin' right, can you?"

"Always knew you was worthless. Even your ma thought so. It's why she took yer sister and left you behind when she ran off. She was ashamed of you. Big ugly lummox. Dumb as a post."

Twenty years might have passed, but Luke still felt the bite of those words every time they bubbled to the surface. His drunkard of an old man loved to run his son down. Had a talent for it. Somehow he always knew the sorest spots to jab, no matter how hard Luke tried to hide them.

After his mother took off when Luke was ten, anger had been his constant companion. It was easier to be angry than to admit he loathed himself, so he embraced the rage. Picked fights at school with boys two to three years older. Broke windows. Started fires. Well, fire. There'd only been the one. He'd thought the stone wall of the livery stable would keep the flames from spreading when he shattered a lit kerosene lantern against the side of it one night. He hadn't expected stray sparks to float up to the haymow and catch the interior on fire. The boarded horses had panicked, the sounds of their distress cutting through his anger to pierce his heart. He'd gone in after them. Set them free in the paddock. Pounded out the fire with a saddle blanket.

Mr. Roper, the livery owner, had given him a job that night, calling him a hero. Luke hadn't had the guts to confess he was the culprit until more than a year later, after mutual respect had sprouted between them. It turned out the old coot had known the truth from the beginning but had taken Luke under his wing anyway. "Shame to let all those muscles go to waste," he'd teased.

Luke had put his muscles to work mucking stalls, forking hay, exercising the horses, and anything else Roper asked of him. He discovered he had a knack with the beasts, and for the first time felt like his being born might not have been a mistake after all. Mr. Roper cultivated that knack until an apoplexy laid him low the summer Luke turned fourteen. Roper lost the use of his left side and then lost his livery. Luke lost his mentor and the only man who had ever cared if he lived or died. When Roper's daughter came to collect him, saying good-bye hurt as badly as the afternoon Luke had found his mama and baby sister gone when he'd come home from school.

Living with his father's abuse became intolerable after that. The constant venom of his belittling. The backhanded cuffs that became full-on swings the larger Luke grew. But when Luke caught his father whipping the hide off one of the livery horses he used to tend, something snapped inside him. Rage erupted to the point of violence. He threw his father to the ground and pummeled his face bloody. If the horse hadn't nudged Luke's back with its head and broken the red haze clouding his vision, he might have killed his old man that day. Instead, he went home, packed his belongings, and left to join the army. He never looked back.

Except on dark, quiet nights, when he was on guard duty.

Luke hefted a sigh and ran his hand over his face, pressing hard enough to stretch the skin down over his jaw. Beard stubble abraded his palm, but it was his mind that itched.

Until something scratched it. Matt's voice in his head. Breaking through the ugliness of his thoughts. *"Got a verse for me, Preach?"*

Captain Hanger had always asked him for a verse before they set out on a mission. Wanting to make a good impression on his commander and friend, Luke had made a point to memorize as many verses about warriors and God's presence in battle as possible. It wasn't until years later that he'd thought to memorize a handful of scriptures for his own personal use.

"'Remember ye not the former things,'" he whispered softly into the night as he adjusted his position, sitting cross-legged with a boulder at his back, "'neither consider the things of old. Behold, I will do a new thing; now it shall spring forth; shall ye not know it? I will even make a way in the wilderness, and rivers in the desert.' Isaiah 43:18–19."

He tipped his face upward and peered at the handful of stars clustered above him. *You must be tired of me askin' for the same favor over and over, but I'm still havin' trouble lettin' go of the past.*

He'd been doing better over the last few years. His work with the Horsemen and his growing relationship with the Lord had muffled the nagging voice of his father and the feelings of worthlessness they stirred. Running across Nate Baxter two days ago had churned up memories, though. All that anger and resentment. The kid reminded him too much of himself at that age.

Ya might wanna give Nate a little help, too. Maybe give him a Roper to set him on the straight and narrow.

Luke contemplated applying for the position himself.

For about three seconds. He likely wouldn't be around long enough to make a difference. And he doubted the kid would want much to do with him if he turned him in on vandalism charges, or worse—rustling. Besides, God had already sent Nate someone: Damaris. True, she was a woman and not really equipped to mentor a half-wild boy into manhood, but she loved him with her whole heart and was more patient and forgiving than the little troublemaker deserved. The kid had no idea how lucky he was. If Luke had a woman in his life who loved him like that, he'd hold tight with every muscle he possessed and never look back.

Behold, I will do a new thing . . . make a way in the wilderness . . . rivers in the desert.

The rest of the verse came back to him in a way that set his heart thumping. Outside of work and his brotherhood with the other Horsemen, Luke had always considered his life a wasteland. Barren and desolate. Barely habitable for himself, let alone anyone else. Asking a woman to share it with him would be selfish at best and downright destructive at worst. But if new rivers were to spring up in that desert—

Four man-sized shadows separated themselves from the rock face in front of him, obliterating thoughts of everything save his mission. Senses heightened, Luke slowly shifted up into a crouch, keeping his head low so as not to draw attention.

Satisfaction rolled through him as the rustlers moved stealthily through the brush. A gang. He'd suspected as much. In all his years of riding with Hanger's Horsemen, he'd never come across a one-man rustling operation. A gang meant he'd need to bring Grimes and his hands in on the capture, though. Tonight, he'd watch. Follow. If he could find their entrance point, he and Grimes could set a trap. Even better, if he could find where they were stashing the rustled beeves, he could recover the stock. They probably had horses waiting on the other side of whatever cavern they'd come through, but if he could mark the exit spot, he might be able to track their trail come morning.

One shadow separated from the rest and pointed to a pair of steers lying in the grass at the base of an oak about twenty yards to Luke's left. The men crept closer. Luke studied them through the dark. Their features were indistinguishable at this distance, but he made note of their gaits. The shape of their hats. Anything that might identify them later. Or now, if one happened to be a smooth-faced fourteen-year-old with an oversized chip on his shoulder. Luke prayed Nate wasn't among them, but he searched for similarities anyway. Better to know what he was dealing with now than find out later when guns were drawn.

A twig snapped somewhere to Luke's right. He fought the urge to turn and instead kept his gaze glued to the rustlers. The leader of the gang signaled with a sharp drop of one arm, and all four men flattened themselves to the ground, disappearing in the prairie grass.

A fifth figure entered Luke's frame of vision. The newcomer moved quickly, with a boldness that paid little heed to the amount of noise he made. A shadowy lump extended from his back. A hat dangling from a stampede string? Or maybe a gunny sack slung over one shoulder?

Luke tensed. Stared hard at the figure's profile, taking in the height. The bare head and hairless chin. The belligerent stride. *Nate.* And he was marching directly toward the rustlers. As if he aimed to join them.

Luke clenched his jaw, wishing he could close his eyes and unsee the truth, but he couldn't. The best he could do now was watch and listen. Determine how involved the kid was and see if there was any way to extricate him before Grimes brought in the law.

Nate neared the rustlers' position but didn't slow. Didn't announce his arrival, either. Just kept walking as if . . . as if he didn't actually know they were there.

Luke's fists clenched. He braced himself against the edge of the rock in front of him. It took all of the restraint he had not to lurch from his hiding place. He tried to think about what Matt would do. The captain always seemed to have a plan at the ready, and it rarely entailed rushing in until all the facts were gathered.

Let it play out. Don't make things worse by jumpin' the gun.

Luke fought to control his breathing. His pulse. There was a chance the rustlers would hold their positions and let the boy walk right by, none the wiser.

Yet even as that hopeful thought started to calm him, reality exploded.

Nate tripped over something in the grass. That something jumped up and grabbed the boy around the middle. Nate yelled. The rustler clamped a hand over his mouth.

Luke drew his revolver. Pushed up from his crouch. Then froze when a low-pitched voice met his ears.

"That one of Grimes's hands?" The rustler from the front of the pack rose from the grass and gestured to Nate.

"Nah. It's just some kid."

74

The leader came to stand in front of Nathaniel. "Out pretty late, aren't you, boy?"

For once, Nate kept his mouth shut. Not that he had much choice in the matter.

"Well, you picked the wrong place for a midnight stroll."

"What should we do with him, Boss?" one of the other rustlers asked.

"He's seen our faces, so we'll have to take him with us. Leave his body somewhere where we can stage an accident. Maybe a broken neck from a fall out of a tree. Boys are always climbin' trees."

"What about the other thing we come for?" The fourth man waded into the conversation.

"We'll get it another night. Gotta take care of this problem first."

Not if Luke had anything to say about it.

Luke crept out from behind the rocks that sheltered his position and stalked toward the gang. Their distraction with Nate allowed him to get within fifteen yards before the first rustler noticed him. His jolt of surprise alerted the rest of the gang. All four spun to face him. The leader snatched Nate from his partner, pulled a knife from his belt, and held the blade to the boy's throat.

Luke aimed his revolver at the leader's head, what little he could see of it behind Nate's wide-eyed face. "Let the kid go."

The leader eyed the revolver and tightened his hold on Nate. A gunshot could bring more of Grimes's men to the scene. *If* they were within range. Grimes was at the house. Joe, Quincy, and Randall in the bunkhouse. Buck was monitoring the west fence line and was probably too far away to hear a shot. But the rustlers didn't know that.

"Can't hit me without hittin' the kid."

Luke shrugged. "Maybe. But I could hit *him*." He shifted the barrel of his revolver to line up with the man standing to the leader's right.

The fellow fumbled for his holster, but the leader hissed at him. "No guns! You wanna bring the whole lot of 'em down on us? He's only one man. We can take him."

"Easy for you to say. His first bullet ain't aimed at your chest."

While the two men at the center bickered, the others started separating themselves from the clump. Either they planned to make a run for it, or they were setting up an attack. Either way, Luke didn't have much time, and with the Horsemen's vow not to use deadly force, he couldn't completely eliminate the four-to-one disadvantage.

He flicked a glance at Nate. The kid looked scared but steady. When their eyes met, Nate shifted his gaze quickly down to the sack hanging from his right hand, then back up to Luke.

Luke gave a tiny dip of his chin, holding back a grin. The kid had grit. A brain too.

"Rush him!" the leader shouted.

Pandemonium erupted. Nate swung his sack upward toward his captor's face. Luke fired at the second man. Numbers three and four charged.

Man Two howled in pain as Luke's bullet winged his arm. Man One grunted, then yelled, "Snake!" as the contents of Nate's bag spilled out on his head.

"Run, kid!" Luke barely got the words out before Men Three and Four plowed into him and knocked him to the ground. He lost his grip on his revolver, but he didn't care. He preferred his fists for close-combat scenarios anyway.

With a roar, Luke grabbed Man Three by the collar and tossed him to the side, making sure to throw him in the direction of the leader. He couldn't afford to let any of the rustlers chase after Nate. He needed to demand all of their attention if the kid was going to have a chance.

"That all you got?" Luke taunted as he threw Man Four off of him and bounced to his feet, fists ready.

Man One grabbed the snake off his head with a growled curse and hurled it into the dark. His gaze locked on the flee- ing boy, but he only managed one step before Luke charged.

Catching the rustlers no longer took precedence. Covering Nate's escape did. And if that meant taking on four men with nothing but his fists and his wits, so be it.

CHAPTER
EIGHT

Luke slammed the leader into the ground, then crashed a fist into his jaw before the other gang members grabbed him from behind. Luke fought like a wild man. When they restrained his arms, he kicked at their knees and used his head as a sledgehammer, cracking the front of one man's skull with the back of his own.

Their grips loosened. Luke started to pull away. Bunched his muscles. Prepared to attack the leader, who was scrambling back to his feet, knife in hand. Luke's focus zeroed in on the weapon, preparing to knock it away with his forearm. But just as he pulled away from his captors, the man he'd winged with a bullet lurched at him from his blind side and drove a blade beneath his ribs.

Luke roared and turned on the injured man. He struck a fierce uppercut to his jaw, and the man fell like a stone, but it was too late. By the time Luke's attention returned to the leader, the man was upon him, his own knife slashing downward. Luke raised his arm to block. The blade sliced into his skin and bounced off bone, but Luke didn't stop.

He punished the leader with his fists. To the midsection, the chin, the side. He took nearly as many punches as he gave. The rustler was a scrappy fighter. Dirty too.

"Hold him!" the leader shouted.

Luke chanced a glance behind him. The others were advancing. Fast. He pivoted and swung, only to have the leader's blade find him again, in the back of the thigh. Luke's leg buckled, taking him down to one knee.

The rustlers pounced. One kicked his face, his pointed boot colliding with Luke's chin and snapping his head back. The second one rammed him from the side. Luke fell.

He tried to rise, but a weight held him down. Boots slammed into his head. Fists pummeled his ribs. He fended them off the best he could, but his injuries sapped his strength. He curled into a ball, arms raised to cover his head, but the blows kept coming. Consciousness began slipping away.

"Enough," the leader called, his voice sounding far away even though Luke knew he was practically on top of him. "Step aside so I can slit his throat and be done with it."

Each man got in one last kick or jab. Two sets of hands pried Luke's arms away from his head. A third set yanked his jaw upward, exposing his throat. Luke peered into the eyes of his killer.

A cavalryman didn't thirst for death, but he knew how to face it with courage. "God . . . will . . . avenge."

The rustler hesitated, knife raised.

All at once, a gun boomed. Hooves pounded the ground.

The leader glanced away as he brought the knife down. The blade glanced off Luke's collarbone, leaving his throat intact.

The rustlers scattered.

A horse whinnied, the sound familiar. Luke strained to see, turning his head a few agonizing degrees to the right.

Titan? But how . . .

A rider slid off his back, Luke's rifle in hand. He crouched in front of Luke's face.

Nate. The kid really needed to quit taking Luke's gun without asking. Nice of him . . . to come back . . . though. . . .

"Mr. Davenport?" The urgency in the boy's tone tugged Luke away from the darkness that beckoned. "Oh no, did they kill ya?" Tears clogged the kid's voice. He grabbed Luke's shoulder and shook him. "Please don't be dead."

Luke managed a moan, praying it was enough to get the kid to stop shaking him.

"You're alive!"

Probably not for long if the kid kept trying to help him. Nate already had Luke's arm wrapped around his neck and was attempting to pull him up. Not that Luke budged, of course. He was far too much dead weight for a boy to move. But the strain of Nate yanking on his arm pulled open the gash in his side and sent excruciating pain surging through his midsection.

"C'mon. You gotta get up."

"No." Luke managed the single word on a croak.

Nate, thank the Lord, stopped tugging on him. "You *gotta* get up. Those men could come back."

"Won't." Oblivion's pull dragged on him. Hard. Luke's eyelids drooped closed. "Get . . . help . . ."

Nate gave a loud sniff, then finally released Luke's arm. "I will, sir."

Luke felt himself slip, but he clawed his way back from the brink. He had to tell Nate. "You're a . . . good kid. Ain't . . . your fault."

"It is." The boy's voice faded into the distance as Luke lost his grip on consciousness. "But I'll make it right. I swear."

"Aunt Maris! Come quick!"

Damaris bolted upright in bed.

Nathaniel.

She threw off the covers and made it halfway to the door before sounds other than his panicked voice registered in her brain. A heavy *thud* from the front room. Footsteps pounding in the hall. A door banging against the wall.

An intruder?

Damaris wrenched open her bedroom door and ran into the hall, ready to battle for her nephew's safety with her bare hands.

But no one was there. Only Nathaniel. One of the parlor lamps sat by his feet, illuminating the hall as he yanked blankets and sheets out of the linen closet and tossed them onto the floor.

"Nathaniel?" She slowed her step, not sure if he'd lost his mind or if she'd lost hers. "What's going on?"

He made a little hiccoughing sound. "I-I need your help."

His voice sounded . . . broken. She gentled hers. "With what, sweetheart?"

Standing behind him, she touched his shoulder. He turned, and her heart stopped. Tears coursed down his cheeks. Snot ran from his nose. He looked utterly lost.

Without waiting for permission, she clutched him to her chest and hugged him tight. "I'm here. Whatever you need. I'm here."

He submitted to her embrace for a few precious seconds before pulling away. "We gotta hurry," he said with a sniff and a wipe of his nose on his sleeve as he bent to pick up the pile of linens. "He'll die if we don't."

"Who, Nathaniel? Who will die?"

"The Horseman."

An image of rugged Mr. Davenport jumped into her mind. So large and strong. And kind to slightly unhinged ladies trapped in root cellars. She'd never encountered a man more competent, more virile. It seemed impossible that such a man should be at death's door.

"He's hurt real bad. He took on all four of 'em by himself." Nathaniel juggled his armful of linens and met Damaris's gaze. "He saved my life, Aunt Maris. Now I gotta save his."

She had a hundred questions—the one topping the list being why Nathaniel had been in a position to need saving in the middle of the night—but this wasn't the time. Her nephew had finally come to her for help, and if Mr. Davenport was really in as dire shape as Nathaniel described, they couldn't afford any delays.

"I'll throw on some shoes and grab my medical basket."

Nathaniel nodded to her, his blue eyes brimming with gratitude. "I'll hitch the wagon and meet you out back."

Damaris didn't take the time to dress. She simply threw a long coat over her cotton nightgown and buttoned it to her throat. Then she shoved her feet into stockings and low-heeled half boots. After retrieving her medical basket from the high shelf in her wardrobe, she headed for the door but stopped, her gaze catching on the gun cabinet in the corner. Should she?

The idea of wielding a gun made her slightly ill, but if the men who had threatened Nathaniel and attacked Mr. Davenport returned, she'd need a way to defend against them.

Determination gripping her, she set her basket on the edge of the bed, then threw open her jewelry box and dug out the key. She moved to the cabinet and flung the lacy camouflage out of the way, then plugged the key into the keyhole and twisted until it clicked. Without letting herself think too much about what she was doing, she snatched her brother's shotgun from the case along with a box of shells. She stored the shells in the basket with her bandages and salves, then grasped the shotgun by the barrel and headed out to meet her nephew.

Nathaniel had the team hitched to the wagon by the time she arrived. His eyebrows arched when he saw the gun in her hand, but the nod of approval he gave her boosted her confidence in her choice.

They both climbed onto the wagon seat, but Nathaniel took the reins. Thankfully, the night was clear. A half-moon shone brightly in the sky, allowing them to see at least a few feet in front of them as they set off. Nathaniel steered the team north, away from the road.

"Where are we going?" Damaris asked as she gripped the bench seat, the uneven ground tossing her about.

"The northeast corner of Grimes's land." Nathaniel's mouth pulled tight. "There's a cavern that joins his land to ours. It's too narrow for the wagon to pass through and too short for the horses, but we can get through with the blankets and supplies. I brought a lantern and the travois my pa used to cart deer carcasses when we went hunting." He tipped his head toward the wagon bed. "Mr. Davenport's a big fella, but with two of us pulling, we should be able to drag him back to the wagon."

Damaris said nothing about the location. The moment his call had awakened her, she'd known Nathaniel had been up to some kind of mischief with their neighbor. Why else would he be running around in the middle of the night?

"Here," she said, holding out the shotgun with one hand and reaching for the reins with the other. "I'll drive. You load." She nodded toward the basket on the bench between them. "The shells are in there."

Heaven knew he would have a better chance of getting the ammunition in the proper chambers than she would. She wasn't sure she could figure out how to load the gun in daylight. At night on a bumpy wagon? Threading her sleeve through one of her embroidery needles would be easier.

Nathaniel took the gun and had it loaded in less than a minute. He handed it back to her and reclaimed the reins, urging the team to a faster pace. Damaris couldn't help but be impressed by his skill with both driving and weaponry. Perhaps locking her brother's guns away was an unnecessary precaution.

Holding the gun across her lap, Damaris peered at her nephew's profile. "What type of injuries has he sustained?" Best to mentally prepare for what waited on the other side of that cavern. She'd need as much time to fortify her nerves as possible.

"It was hard to tell in the dark. I think he was stabbed a couple of times. Maybe more. I did my best to slow the bleeding by stuffing my handkerchief and his in the two holes I found. One in his side and one on the back of his leg."

Damaris closed her eyes against the nausea building in her stomach. This was no time for maidenly sensibilities. A man's life was at stake. A man who'd forfeited his own safety to protect her nephew. She owed him everything, and she'd give everything she had to keep him alive.

Unfortunately, the *everything* she possessed was rather scanty. Her medical experience consisted of mixing tonics and administering smelling salts to her great-aunt. She could make chicken soup and bathe a brow. Dab salve on a burn and wrap a sprained ankle. But tend to a man beaten so badly that he couldn't move? One stabbed at least twice and likely lying in a pool of blood?

Damaris swallowed and begged the Lord for strength.

It seemed to take a lifetime to reach the rocky hill that marked the cavern entrance, but Nathaniel finally drew the team to a halt. Once the brake was set, he jumped down and ran around to the back of the wagon to collect the travois and lantern.

Damaris tied opposite ends of one of the sheets together to form a sling, loaded it with the other linens, and fitted it over her head and one arm so she could keep her hands free. She slid the medical basket into the linen pouch, then swapped her shotgun for Nathaniel's travois, grabbing the two wooden poles and dragging the ladder-like frame behind her as her nephew led the way with the light.

As they moved through the cave, they had to hunch over

in several places as the passage ceiling lowered. When they reached the end of the tunnel, Damaris nearly ran into her nephew's back when he stopped suddenly. He turned down the lantern wick, casting them into near darkness.

"What is it?" Damaris whispered, coming up alongside him.

"Nothin'. Just wanted to make sure none of Grimes's men were about. Davenport got off a shot early in the fight, and I fired a round at the end to scare the rustlers off. It's possible one of the hands on duty heard."

"Wouldn't that be a good thing?"

Nathaniel shrugged. "For Davenport, yeah. For me, not so much."

Because he'd been trespassing. Causing trouble. That was why he'd come to her for help instead of alerting Mr. Grimes. He wouldn't have been able to explain his presence without implicating himself. And if Nathaniel was right about Mr. Grimes killing Douglas, he could have signed his own death warrant by showing up at the man's house in the middle of the night. Damaris shivered. Thank the Lord Nathaniel had chosen to fetch her instead.

"I had to come back," Nathaniel said, his voice small. "I had to know for sure if they'd found him. If no one heard the shots, he'd be alone until morning." He turned, his expression haunted. "I don't think he'll last 'til morning."

Damaris touched his shoulder. "You did the right thing." She offered a reassuring smile, then studied the dark landscape in front of her. "I don't hear any activity out there, but I think I see a horse." She pointed at the large shadow standing a short distance away.

"That's probably Titan. I found him after Davenport told me to run." Nathaniel peered into the dark for one more moment, then turned up the lantern and hurried forward.

Damaris followed, the travois bouncing along behind her.

"I'm back, Mr. Davenport," Nathaniel said as he drew near and set the lantern down next to what she'd thought was a large rock. "I brought Aunt Maris with me. She'll take care of you. Don't worry."

If only she shared his confidence.

The large rock slowly took on the shape of a man as she drew near. Her heart ached at the sight of such a valiant warrior curled on his side like a child, his features almost indecipherable. She blinked back tears as she positioned the travois behind his back. He'd taken on four men to save Nathaniel. His courage deserved to be met in matching mea-sure. Damaris steeled her stomach and stiffened her spine as she moved around to his front and reached inside her linen sling for her basket of medical supplies.

"Hold the light up," she instructed. "I need to see what we're dealing with."

Nathaniel obeyed, and Damaris nearly stumbled at the sight of the battered, bloody body at her feet.

Lord, help us. For only a miracle would save Luke Daven-port's life this night.

— CHAPTER —

NINE

Everything hurt.

That was the first thing that registered in Luke's mind when something jarred him back into awareness. The second was the feeling of falling—or sliding, more accurately. Down some kind of ladder. The rungs bumped against every sore place on his body.

"Catch him!"

Someone sprawled across his front, pressing him hard against the uneven rungs. He moaned.

"Sorry." The feminine voice reached inside the darkness and stirred him. Drew him upward out of oblivion's pit.

The smothering force on top of him shifted. Steadied him. Halted his slide.

"I've got you," she said.

His senses began to register sensations other than pain. Like the delicate scent of lilies. The warm breath against his cheek when she spoke. The closeness of her body pressed atop his. The smothering sensation dissipated, replaced by an odd type of comfort.

"Hold down his top half while I lift his legs."

She slipped away. Leaving him. "No," he protested in a weak murmur.

"I'm here," she soothed, as if knowing exactly what he needed. "Right here."

And he felt her, leaning crosswise over his chest. Holding him secure as his body tipped into a more horizontal position.

"Almost there, Mr. Davenport. As soon as we get you in the wagon, we'll head for home."

Home. He'd never really had one of those. Had always wondered what it would be like. A place with a woman's touch. Curtains at the window. Handmade quilts on the bed. Those white doily things on the dressers. Maybe a sampler or two hanging on the wall. His father had burned his mother's remaining belongings after she left, and the army had no room for anything beyond stark practicality. The bunkhouse at Gringolet wasn't much different. He had a bed, a trunk for his personal belongings, and access to a washstand. Everything a man needed. Yet nothing that made it feel like home.

A loud grunt echoed from somewhere near his feet. That was all the warning he received before the contraption he lay upon was shoved backward. The woman beside him lost her balance and tumbled off him, her soft gasp of surprise awakening his protective instincts. He reached for her, but pain exploded across his side, demanding he retract his arm.

"Don't try to move," she said, quickly righting herself. Her hand gently touched his shoulder, soothing him in a way he couldn't quite comprehend. "We'll get you home, and I'll send for a doctor."

"Madisonville ain't got no doctor." That sounded like the kid. "Just the undertaker."

The hand on his shoulder trembled, but her voice held firm. "Don't worry," she murmured close to his ear as the wagon started to move. "We will *not* be calling the undertaker. We'll figure something out. You are not going to die, Luke Davenport, so just put that idea straight out of your head."

Luke wanted to smile but couldn't manage it. Instead, he focused all his effort on opening his eyes. He wanted to see her. Unfortunately, his eyelids proved obstinate. Heavy and swollen. But he was a cavalryman, and a soldier didn't quit just because something was hard. So he pressed on, and finally his eyes obeyed, cracking open. Night shrouded his vision, and the blows he'd taken to the face and head left his perception blurry, but he could see her. One long braid dangled over her shoulder, making her look young and vulnerable. Her profile glowed in the moonlight as she gazed forward at the horses, worrying her bottom lip with her teeth.

"Damaris."

Her indrawn breath echoed loudly in his ear as she turned her face toward him. "You're awake. Thank the Lord." She smiled at him, but her lips quivered, giving away her anxiety. "Nathaniel will have us home soon. I found three knife wounds. One in your side, one across your forearm, and one in your leg. Are there any I missed?"

He didn't think so, but everything hurt, so it was hard to take stock.

"I'll send to Huntsville for a doctor," she continued when

he took too long to answer. "I came through there on the railroad on my way from Missouri. It struck me as a good-sized town. They're bound to have a physician. He can be here tomorrow, I'm sure. He'll put you to rights, you'll see."

Was she trying to convince him or herself? It didn't matter. No strange fellow from Huntsville was gonna doctor him. Not when he had the best doc in the world on retainer.

Luke gave a small wag of his head. "Wire Dr. Jo Hanger. San Antone. Say Preach is . . . calling in . . . the favor."

"But Huntsville is much closer," she argued. "A doctor from there would get here much faster."

"No. Wire Dr. Jo." He felt himself weakening. Fading. "Promise."

She held his gaze, her brown eyes misting as her judgment warred with his wishes. Finally, she nodded. "I promise."

Confident he could trust her word, Luke surrendered to the darkness once more.

"Hello? I need to send a telegram. It's an emergency!" Damaris pounded on the post office door, praying her voice would carry to the postmaster's personal chambers at the back of the building.

Never in her life had she made such a spectacle of herself, pounding on a door in the middle of the night and hollering like a shrew. No one back in St. Louis would believe her even capable of such a commotion. Invisible people did not carry on in such a way. They were demure, sedate, beneath one's notice.

Well, she couldn't afford to be beneath anyone's notice tonight. Not with a dying man in her bed.

She pounded harder, moving her knuckles from wood to the rectangular glass pane inset at the top of the door. "Open up. Please. A man's life is at stake!"

A few buildings down, a dog started barking. Damaris cringed and glanced around. An upstairs light turned on at the dress shop next door. The curtain twitched, revealing someone at the window watching. Embarrassment heated her cheeks. She hadn't meant to wake the entire block. Just the postmaster. Too bad he was an older gentleman with less-than-acute hearing. But if she had to wake the entire town of Madisonville, she would. Mr. Davenport was depending on her.

Maybe there was a back door. Damaris bent to retrieve the lantern she'd set at her feet but halted when a light appeared somewhere inside. She straightened quickly and renewed her pounding. "Hurry, please!"

"I'm coming," a scratchy voice said from inside. "Quit your banging."

She complied at once, retrieving her lantern as she watched the door for signs of movement.

It finally opened, revealing a gray-haired man dressed in a nightshirt and hastily donned trousers. Suspenders drooped loosely at his hips. A sleeping cap sat atop his head, and a pair of spectacles teetered precariously on the bridge of his nose. She didn't look much better, she knew. After she and Nathaniel had transferred Mr. Davenport to her bed, she'd rushed back to the wagon and driven to town, taking no time to change her clothes or tidy her hair. Fetching the doctor had taken precedence over all else.

"What's so important it couldn't wait 'til morning?"

"I need to wire a doctor." Damaris fought the urge to push the door wide and stride in. Every second she stood still decreased Mr. Davenport's odds of survival. Or at least it felt that way. "Please, sir. A man was attacked near my home, and he's barely clinging to life. A doctor must be summoned at once."

The postmaster frowned up at her. "Clyde Weathers does the doctorin' around here. You should be bangin' on his door."

"Clyde Weathers is an undertaker. Mr. Davenport's injuries are of a critical nature. He requires someone with actual medical training, not someone who will start measuring him for a coffin." Damaris reached out and clasped the man's arm. "Please. I promised him I'd send for Dr. Joe Hanger in San Antonio. I believe that's his personal physician."

The postmaster's bushy brows arched upward. "Hanger, you say? This Davenport fellow . . . his first name don't happen to be Luke, does it?"

"Yes! Luke Davenport. Do you know him?"

"Lady, everybody in Texas knows him. He's one of Hanger's Horsemen. A couple of years ago the papers were full of their exploits. Taking down bandits and outlaws, fighting for justice for the common man. They're heroes." He stepped aside and opened the door wider. "Come on in. If one of the Horsemen needs help, I can sacrifice a few winks of shut-eye."

After sending the telegram, Damaris returned home and immediately took up residence at Mr. Davenport's bedside.

Nathaniel had managed to remove the Horseman's boots and socks along with portions of his clothes. Seeing one long, hairy limb exposed at the edge of the mattress brought a flush to Damaris's cheeks.

"What did you do to his trousers?" she whispered.

Nathaniel stood by the washstand, shifting his weight from one foot to the other. "He told me to cut the leg off. Said it'd be easier to doctor with the material out of the way. I took the scissors to his sleeve too, cuttin' it off at the elbow after we got him out of his coat. He passed out again after that. But before he did, he told me to clean out the wounds with soapy water and pour whiskey on 'em. I couldn't find any liquor in the house, though, so I just wrapped 'em in new bandages." He stopped his fidgeting and met her eyes. "Those wounds are really deep, Aunt Maris. And they're still bleeding. Someone's gonna have to stitch 'em."

Stitch them? Good heavens.

The room swayed, and Damaris reached for the bedpost before her knees completely gave way.

"Aunt Maris?"

"I'm fine," she lied, forcing a tight smile to her lips even as her heart raced at an alarming speed. If she didn't get control of herself soon, Mr. Davenport wasn't going to be the only one lying around insensate. "There's a cookbook on the top shelf in the kitchen," she said, desperate to get Nathaniel out of the room, even if only for a minute, so she could breathe and try to gather her wits. "I think it has a section on home remedies. Perhaps we'll find something in there to help us treat Mr. Davenport."

Nathaniel couldn't seem to leave the room fast enough.

The moment he cleared the threshold, Damaris wilted against the bedpost. She clung to it with both hands, closed her eyes, and pressed her forehead against the wood. A quiet mewl of despair vibrated her throat.

I can't do this, Lord. I lack the experience, the skill, and even the stomach for such a job. Please don't ask it of me.

"The kid's right."

Damaris's eyes popped open at the raspy voice, and she jerked away from the bedpost. "Mr. Davenport. I-I didn't know you were awake."

Had he witnessed her cowardly collapse? This hero of Texas? This legendary Horseman whose feats of bravery were chronicled in newspapers? Never had she wished for invisibility more.

"Dr. Jo won't be here 'til tomorrow afternoon at the earliest. Not sure I'll make it that long if we don't get these holes plugged up."

Releasing her hold on the bedpost, she moved along the edge of the mattress until she was even with his shoulders. Then she lowered herself to her knees on the rug beside him and gently clasped his hand.

His swollen eyes met hers.

She dropped her gaze. "I'm not sure I can do it."

"Damaris." Her name resonated with such strength when he said it. Even in his weakened condition.

She lifted her chin.

"You can."

Not a shred of doubt colored his words, yet an entire mountain of misgiving pressed down on her head.

"I don't know. . . ."

"I do." Again with the penetrating gaze. The certainty. As if he saw something inside of her that she couldn't see. Then his gaze shifted to the wall on the opposite side of the bed. "You did those, didn't you?"

Her samplers? Damaris's brow knit. What did needlework have to do with—

"You got all the skill you need."

She shook her head. "Embroidering linen is one thing. Sewing . . ." She gestured to the bandage around his ribs. "This isn't the same at all."

"Needle. Thread. Knots. It'll get the job done. Well enough to last until Dr. Jo gets here."

Her hand trembled. He squeezed her fingers.

"Damaris."

She met his gaze, her heart thumping, her head spinning.

"I believe in you."

Amazing how such simple words could completely shift her world.

Clasping his hand tight, as if she could draw on his courage and his fortitude, she inhaled a breath and gave a small nod. "All right. I'll do it."

Over the next several hours, Luke's world shrank until it contained only three things—pain, prayer, and Damaris Baxter. She never left his side. Every time he managed to wrest his eyes open, he found her either dozing in a stiff wooden chair next to the bed or hovering above him. Fussing with his covers. Testing the temperature of his brow with a gentle touch of her cool fingers. Lifting his head so he could drink a few sips of water. Even when consciousness waned, he felt her near. Heard her soft voice urging him not to worry. Promising that everything was going to be fine. Help was on the way. He was strong. He could win this fight.

She became his anchor, something solid to cling to within the storm of torment. So much so that when he woke to find her gone, something akin to panic broke loose in his chest.

"Damaris?" Luke craned his neck around, searching each corner of the room for her. Agonizing shards knifed through his head at the movement, but he clenched his teeth and kept looking.

"She ain't here." Nate stepped through the open doorway, worry and guilt softening his normally hostile features.

The kid came in and dropped into the chair Damaris had vacated. It seemed wrong for him to be there, slouching in her chair. Arms crossed defensively over his chest. Eyes not quite meeting Luke's gaze.

Damaris had filled the room with kindness and concern. Her positive spirit made the atmosphere feel lighter as she instilled hope and banished fear. Even the pain seemed less when she was near. Without her, the room felt darker, heavier, despite the morning sunlight streaming between the window curtains.

Nate shifted in his seat, his gaze flicking toward Luke's face before darting up to the wall. "She went to see Grimes. To let him know 'bout you bein' here." His jaw tightened. "I told her not to. Grimes can't be trusted. She shouldn't be goin' there alone."

"You shoulda gone with her."

The kid jerked to his feet. "Someone had to stay here with you."

"Then you shoulda gone in her stead."

Nate's arms unfolded and flopped against his sides. "But I . . ."

Didn't want to explain what he'd been doing on Grimes's property.

Luke skewered Nate with a look. They both knew he'd shirked his duty in order to save his own skin.

Nate ducked his head and kicked at the chair leg. "She should've just waited for Grimes to figure things out for himself and come lookin'," he blustered. "He would've found ya soon enough."

"Your aunt's not the kind of woman to choose what's easy over what's right," Luke said. "If she were, I'd probably be dead by now."

He'd lost consciousness after the first couple of stitches she'd made in his arm, but he remembered the green cast to her features as she'd set needle to flesh. She'd looked on the verge of losing her supper. But she hadn't backed away from what needed doing. She made one stitch after another. And the next time he stirred, he'd felt the tug of her sutures on all three of the gashes the rustlers had inflicted.

She might have a quiet manner, but she wasn't short on grit.

Nor was she short on wits, he discovered a few minutes later, when the front door opened and she called into the house. "Nathaniel? Mr. Grimes has come to check on Mr. Davenport. Are you here?"

The kid jumped from his chair, his eyes wide and desperate.

"He's probably out roaming somewhere," she said with a little laugh, her voice still raised enough to carry through the house. "I usually only see him at mealtimes. It wouldn't surprise me if he slipped out the back door the moment I left the house."

Nate took a step toward the door, then stopped as the sound of the front door shutting echoed down the hall.

"Can I take your coat, Mr. Grimes?"

Luke made a clicking noise with his tongue to gain Nate's attention, then darted his gaze toward the curtain. "Window."

The kid nearly knocked the chair over in his hurry to make

his escape. He slid up the sash, climbed through the opening with the ease of one well used to exiting through unconventional portals, then dropped to the ground and pulled the window closed from the outside.

Nate needed to face up to his deeds one day, but Luke would rather he do so when he was up to the task of watching the kid's back. Right now, Luke could barely manage wiggling his big toe without passing out. He'd be no use to Nate if Grimes *wasn't* the upstanding citizen Luke had been led to believe.

"He's this way."

Strange how Damaris's voice filled him with anticipation even when addressed to someone else. Maybe it was because he sensed her words were intended for him as much as they were for Grimes. Of course, she might have been aiming them solely at her nephew. However, when she walked into the bedroom, her gaze caught his first before making a quick circle about the room. When Luke gave her a tiny dip of his chin to confirm the boy was safe, she understood his silent message and visibly relaxed.

Grimes strode into the room and crossed in front of Damaris, cutting off Luke's view of her. "Good grief, man. You look like my entire herd trampled you."

"I feel like it, too." Luke tried to lift his head to get a better view of Grimes, but a sledgehammer banged on the back of his skull, so he stopped.

Grimes must have noticed the failed action, for he dropped onto the edge of the chair, propped his forearms on his legs, and dangled his hat between his knees as he bent his face closer to Luke's. "I'm right sorry this happened to you, Davenport." He blew out a breath. Fiddled with his hat brim. "Buck found Titan in the northeast pasture this mornin'. Saw evidence of your scuffle. I was rounding up the boys into a search party when Miss Baxter showed up." Grimes glanced over his shoulder at Damaris but made no effort to invite her into the conversation. "Quincy's takin' care of yer mount. Titan's welcome to stay with us as long as you need."

"Thanks." Luke was finding it hard to keep his eyes open. As much as he hated to demonstrate weakness, his energy was completely sapped.

"It was them lousy rustlers, wasn't it?" Grimes batted his knee with his hat, then lurched to his feet and started pacing in front of the bed, the back-and-forth making Luke dizzy. "Dirty thieves." He stopped pacing and made a sharp pivot, leaning over the bed. "Did you recognize any of 'em?" His eyes lit. "This could be the break we need. Now we got a witness. You did see them takin' a steer, didn't you? Maybe we'll finally get them sidewinders in jail."

Luke surrendered the battle with his eyelids and let them fall as Grimes ranted. Too many words. They made his head pound. Especially since he knew he couldn't give Grimes what he wanted. Not completely. Yes, he'd seen their faces. Mostly. Covered in nighttime shadows. No, he didn't recognize any of them, but he'd only been in the area a few days. He'd probably recognize them if he saw them again. Particularly the leader. But he was in no condition to start a manhunt and might not be for weeks. The worst of it was, he hadn't caught them in the act of rustling, so he had no direct proof to convict them.

He could testify against them for attacking him, but that would mean dragging Nate into this mess, and that could create danger for the boy if the perpetrators decided to search out their witnesses. Luke was hoping that if he and Nate lay low for a bit, the gang would decide they weren't threats and leave them alone. Laying low was all Luke was good for at the moment anyway. But he needed to talk to Nate. Damaris too. She needed to know . . .

"Davenport? Can you hear me?"

"We need to let him rest, Mr. Grimes." Damaris. His angel of mercy. Saving him once again.

"But I need him to—"

"Heal," she interrupted. "We need him to heal. There will be plenty of time for him to answer your questions after he's recovered. I'll be sure to send for you when the doctor says he's strong enough for visitors."

Grimes grumbled but complied. The last thing Luke heard before sleep overtook him was the man's boots clomping down the hall.

Damaris herded Mr. Grimes toward the door, anxious to have him gone. The rancher could very well be responsible for her brother's death. Not to mention the threat he posed to her nephew—even if Nathaniel had brought that particular trouble on himself with his midnight forays onto their neighbor's property. There was no telling what kind of mischief the boy had been getting up to over there. Thankfully, Nathaniel had made himself scarce when Mr. Grimes insisted on returning with her. Had she known Grimes intended to interrogate Mr. Davenport about the rustlers, though, she never would have let him come.

Could he not see how much pain Mr. Davenport was in? How weak he'd become? He could barely lift his head an inch off the pillow, for pity's sake.

Damaris opened the front door and did her best to work up a smile for their unwanted guest.

"His doctor should arrive later today," she said as Grimes passed through the doorway. "I'll be sure to let you know when Mr. Davenport feels up to answering your questions."

Mr. Grimes scowled as he slapped on his hat. "I'll come by tomorrow."

Damaris bristled. "You can come if you like, but you will not be allowed inside. Not until the doctor agrees that Mr. Davenport is strong enough for visitors."

"He's bruised and battered, but I've seen fellas look worse after a bar fight."

"Do those bar fight fellows have three gaping stab wounds on their person?" Damaris challenged, her voice raising. "One of those wounds exposed bone, and the other two cut so deep they nearly emptied him of blood!"

Hearing herself shout, she took a moment to breathe and steady her nerves. Her indignation had erupted so forcefully, she now physically trembled from the effort it took to contain it. Heavens, what had come over her? She *never* raised her voice. But then, things didn't usually stir her passions to this extent.

Stepping onto the porch, Damaris pulled the door closed behind her. If her patient did happen to wake, she didn't want him to hear what she was about to say.

"That man nearly died last night." She lifted her chin, refusing to be intimidated by Mr. Grimes's overbearing manner. "He still could, if he takes a fever. You and your cows will just have to wait."

"Those cows are my livelihood, and that man is in my employ. By all rights, he should be in *my* home, being tended by me and my staff." He narrowed his gaze. "Why isn't he?" He took a step toward her. Damaris backed up, her boldness fading as her rear bumped against the closed door. "How did he end up here, Miss Baxter? You never did say."

And she couldn't. Not without implicating Nathaniel. But neither could she meekly roll over and let Oliver Grimes run roughshod over her. Not when she had a nephew to protect and a heroic Horseman to nurse. God had brought her to Texas for a reason, and she wouldn't surrender either of the duties assigned to her just because some man failed to approve of her methods.

Imagining herself as Great-Aunt Bertha delivering one of her infamous reprimands, Damaris stiffened her spine and looked down her nose. "When Mr. Davenport is recovered, he can explain the circumstances to you himself. Until that time, I must ask you to leave."

"It was that nephew of yours, wasn't it?"

Just her luck. Oliver Grimes was impervious to the Aunt Bertha setdown. Or more likely, Damaris had simply done it wrong. Haughty condescension, like most things, probably needed practice to perfect.

"He's working with the rustlers, ain't he?" the rancher pressed.

"Don't be absurd! He's just a boy."

Mr. Grimes advanced another step. Damaris fumbled behind her for the door latch.

"Boy or not, if he's working with the rustlers, he'll pay. Just like the rest of 'em. A crime's a crime. Age don't matter."

"My nephew might be a bit wild around the edges, Mr. Grimes, but he is no thief. And I refuse to stand here and listen to you disparage him in such a manner." Her hand finally found the latch. "Good day to you, sir."

Damaris unlatched the door, slid inside, and closed it directly in her neighbor's face. She turned the lock and waited for the sound of retreating footsteps to tell her he was leaving. Silence was all she heard, though, unnerving her as it stretched from one heartbeat to the next. Finally, heels clicked against the porch floorboards and down the steps. Then the tone changed to the dull thud of boots on dirt.

Thank you, God. He was leaving.

She stayed by the door, listening. Eyes closed. Forehead pressed against the wood and hand still on the lock until the fading footsteps morphed into the hoofbeats of a departing horse.

Only then did she breathe.

CHAPTER

ELEVEN

Damaris's head sagged toward her chest. In a desperate grasp for alertness, she jerked her chin upward and forced her eyes wide. Her book twitched in her hand and nearly fell to the floor. Thankfully she caught it before it could slide off her lap and wake her patient. She glanced at the Horseman. Strain lined his features even in sleep.

Lord, please heal him. After all he did for Nathaniel. Such a brave and selfless man. Don't let evil win this battle.

If Luke Davenport died, Nathaniel might not recover. He was still raw from losing his father. If another man he respected died, and from an attack he blamed himself for, it could break him.

Damaris set aside her copy of *Little Women* and wrapped her arms around her middle, murmuring a whispered petition on behalf of her nephew as well. When she closed her eyes in prayer, however, her lack of sleep from the night before stalked her. Dragged her head back to her chest. Lured her to succumb. Promised just a few minutes of . . .

No!

Damaris shook her head like a freshly bathed dog. She couldn't afford to fall asleep. Not before the doctor arrived. This was her vigil, and she wouldn't shirk her duty.

Rising from her chair, she paced the perimeter of the room before returning to the bed. She studied Mr. Davenport. Luke. Formality seemed out of place in a sickroom. Besides, every time he called out for her, he used her given name. A fact that warmed her insides more than it probably should.

"Who are you, Luke?" she whispered as she circled to the far side of the bed and lightly perched on the edge of the mattress, several inches away from him.

She ran the back of her fingers along the side of his face. The scruff of his whiskers scratched her skin as she traced the line of his square jaw.

He made a sound in his sleep and turned his face toward her. Damaris snatched her hand back.

"Forgive me for taking liberties."

She didn't know why she'd taken to talking to him while he slept. Vowing he'd get through this. Assuring him he wasn't alone. Praying aloud for his healing. Talking filled the quiet, she supposed, but deep down, she acknowledged that it filled another purpose. She needed to hear the encouragement and hope as much as he did. Maybe more. Doubts and insecurities clanged like cymbals in her spirit, enumerating her inadequacies. Of which there were many. After all, she had no experience dealing with giant warriors lying in her bed, bleeding from multiple knife wounds. Wounds that had the power to steal his life if she handled them incorrectly.

"Your doctor friend will be here soon," she said, covering

his left hand with her palm, careful not to bump the bandage on his forearm. She slipped her fingers into the curl of his hand and gave him a tiny, encouraging squeeze. "He'll fix you up in no time. You'll see."

Please let that be the truth, Lord.

"Before you know it, you'll be back to chasing down rustlers and rescuing ladies from root cellars."

Although the idea of him helping other ladies the way he'd helped her didn't sit comfortably on her heart. Which was silly. She was no one special. Luke Davenport likely ran across ladies in need of rescuing all the time in his line of work. She was sure that if he hadn't been attacked and left for dead last night, he would have resolved the rustling issue in less than a week and left Madisonville without giving her a second thought.

But he *had* been attacked. And he was under her care. No ill-timed girlish longings or lifelong womanly doubts were going to keep her from doing whatever she could to aid his recovery.

"You will get through this, Luke Davenport. You will live a full life with all the adventure you want. Surrounded by good friends. Family. Maybe children one day. Grandchildren, even. You have much to live for, so keep fighting, all right?" A touch of unexpected emotion caught in her throat. "Keep fighting."

His fingers tightened around hers. Damaris's pulse jumped, and she quickly stole a glance at his face. His eyes were closed, his breathing deep. He slept. His hand had probably twitched involuntarily. Perhaps he was dreaming of chasing outlaws.

Or maybe . . . just maybe . . . he heard her.

The front door banged open. Pounding feet echoed in the hall. Damaris yanked her hand away from her patient and jumped off the bed as if someone hiding beneath it had jabbed a hatpin through the mattress.

"Aunt Maris! There's a wagon comin' up the drive." Nathaniel ran into the room, his chest heaving as he fought to catch his breath. "Could be the doc. He's got a lady with him, though, so it might just be folks passin' through. But we ain't expectin' any other comp'ny, so it's gotta be the doc. Right?"

Nathaniel had placed himself on watch the minute Mr. Grimes had departed and hadn't left his post at the top of the hill all day. Damaris had taken him a sandwich around noon, but he hadn't returned with her to the house. He'd been adamant about waiting, his gaze glued to the road as if his watching could speed the doctor's arrival. How well she understood his compulsion to do something, anything, to help.

She placed a hand on his shoulder and offered a hopeful smile. "Let's go see who it is."

If it was the doctor, he'd made great time. Better than she'd expected. She'd thought he might arrive by early afternoon if he'd traveled by horseback, but by wagon? He must have found one impressive team.

Impressive was an understatement. The pair of horses trotting into her yard at a fast clip looked like thoroughbreds. Livery horses were never that fine. These were personal stock. Horsemen stock, if she wasn't mistaken.

"This the Baxter place?" the driver called out as he reined in the team of chestnuts.

Damaris ran down to meet him. "Yes. Are you Dr. Hanger?"

The man shook his head as he set the brake. "Nope. But she is." He tipped his head in the direction of the woman beside him. The very pregnant woman.

Good heavens.

The woman rose from her seat, a black bag clutched in her right hand. "Where's Preach?" she asked as her escort jumped down, then turned to assist her.

Damaris blinked, confused that the woman wanted to know the whereabouts of the nearest clergyman, until her sleep-deprived brain caught up and recalled the nickname Luke had her use in the telegram. "Mr. Davenport's inside. I'll show you."

It seemed beyond strange for a woman mere weeks from giving birth to be the doctor Luke would send for, but if he trusted her, so would Damaris.

Nathaniel shot her a questioning look as she led the new-comers into the house, but for once he kept his opinions to himself. No doubt he was as desperate as she was for someone with actual medical training to take over Luke's care. If that someone didn't fit their preconceived notions, their notions would simply have to adjust.

Damaris strode down the short hall and turned into the front bedchamber. As much as she longed to hurry to Luke's side, she left the path clear for the doctor. As heavy with child as she was, Dr. Hanger still moved with a sense of purpose and efficiency, commanding the room like a conductor commanded his orchestra.

She set her black bag on the chair where Damaris had kept vigil, then started unbuttoning her travel jacket. "I'll need hot water, fresh bandages, and a tray for my instruments."

"I'll fetch 'em." Nathaniel darted back into the hall and took off for the kitchen.

Dr. Hanger tossed her jacket over the back of the chair, then moved to the washstand in the corner, rolling her sleeves as she went. Her companion, on the other hand, moved toward the bed and dropped to one knee as he slowly pulled his hat from his head.

"Ah, Preach. This wasn't supposed to happen. Horsemen stand together when danger calls. You should've sent for me." He touched Luke's shoulder, and Damaris swore she could feel the bond between them even from six feet away.

Dr. Hanger's face softened as her gaze turned from the soap and water on her hands to watch the men. "My husband and Preach are very close," she murmured softly. "Out of all the Horsemen, they have been together the longest." The sentiment softening her green eyes sharpened into pointed determination as she resumed scrubbing her hands and arms with vigorous strokes. "Tell me everything," she said. "The wounds. Your treatment. His response. Leave nothing out."

"He was stabbed three times. Once in his right side, once in the back of his right leg, and once across his left forearm." As Damaris ran through the injuries she'd cataloged, Dr. Hanger dried her hands and crossed to the bed to begin her examination.

Her husband stood as she approached and placed a hand at the small of her back. They shared a private look that overflowed with concern for their friend while at the same time establishing a silent promise of partnership. He would do whatever she needed, and she would lean on his strength.

Damaris felt herself slide back into the realm of invisibility as they communicated without words.

Once the charged moment passed, Dr. Hanger glanced back at her. "Continue."

"There was a shallow cut at the base of his throat, but it didn't bleed overmuch, so I didn't stitch it."

The doctor had just bent over her medical bag, but at Damaris's words, she looked up sharply. "You stitched the others?"

Had that been a mistake? Damaris clutched the sides of her skirt, wrinkling the fabric in her effort to hide the shaking in her hands. "Y-yes. He asked me to. He'd lost a lot of blood." Her mouth went dry, and she took a minute to work up some moisture before she continued her confession. "I found a recipe for a poultice of onions, garlic, and honey recommended for treating wounds, so I dabbed it over the stitches before applying the bandages. I hope that wasn't wrong."

The woman with the bright green eyes nodded. "Actually, I'd say you did quite well, Miss Baxter. Onions, garlic, and honey are all known to reduce the risk of infection. They seem to combat inflammation as well, which aids the healing process."

Damaris's grip on her skirt loosened as she let out a breath. "Oh, good." Thank the Lord she hadn't done anything to worsen his condition. "I've been waking him every few hours, checking for fever and urging him to drink some water. He hasn't shown signs of fever yet, but he is very weak. He doesn't stay awake for more than a quarter hour or so at a time. I'm sure he's in a lot of pain. He winces every time he moves his head, and the last time I changed his bandages,

I noticed significant bruising coming to the surface around his middle. There's a good chance there's damage inside."

The idea of hidden damage scared her the most. What might he be suffering from that she hadn't been able to see? Hadn't been able to treat? Thank heavens Dr. Hanger was here. She'd know what to do. Damaris bit her lip as Mr. Hanger pushed to his feet and moved out of his wife's way.

Please let her know what to do.

"Help me take what's left of his shirt off of him."

Mr. Hanger murmured agreement, moved up toward Luke's head, and lifted his shoulders off the bed. The jostling woke the patient.

"Damaris?"

She opened her mouth to answer, but before she could say anything, the doctor responded.

"It's Jo, Preach. Matthew and I are here. We're going to get you patched up."

"Captain?" Luke struggled to open his eyes.

"I've got you, Corporal." Matthew Hanger used his own chest to support Luke's neck as he helped his wife lift the tattered shirt over his head.

Damaris averted her eyes, feeling as if she were intruding on Luke's privacy, even though she had been tending him for the last sixteen hours. She retreated a step. Then another. No one seemed to notice.

Her presence wasn't required any longer. The realization created an ache in her chest, but she ignored the pitiful twinge. The Hangers had things well in hand. She should check on Nathaniel. See if she could help with the hot water and bandages. Dinner would need to be prepared as well.

The Hangers were likely tired and hungry after traveling so long today. Especially Dr. Hanger, carrying a child. She'd need a bed. Nathaniel would have to trade his room for a pallet in the parlor.

Damaris padded toward the bedroom door, doing her best to focus on other work that needed to be done. But she couldn't stop her gaze from seeking out the man on the bed. Nor her heart from wishing she had a reason to remain by his side.

CHAPTER

TWELVE

Luke felt more than saw Damaris slip out of the room. He caught the movement from the corner of his eye as he answered one of Dr. Jo's questions. Damaris's leaving had an odd effect on his chest, creating an ache in the one place the rustlers had managed to miss.

A sudden, searing pain in his midsection tore his thoughts from his hostess as Dr. Jo prodded his torso. When her fingers pressed against one particularly sore spot, he hissed.

"That one's broken," she said, her expression intent as she stared at her hands. "Two other ribs are probably fractured, and we might as well assume the rest are bruised." She raised her head to meet his good eye, one brow arched. "Three deeply penetrating puncture wounds, several broken ribs, contusions to the right eye, a likely concussion, and one laceration far too close to the carotid artery for my peace of mind. Did you take on an entire gang by yourself?"

"Yeah, but it was a small gang. Only four members. I was

holding my own until one of 'em knifed me in the side. Not very sporting of him."

Dr. Jo rolled her eyes. "Imagine that. An outlaw not fighting fair. I'd swat you upside the head if you weren't about to fall apart at the seams. Honestly, Preach, even you know better than to take on four criminals on your own."

"Easy, Josie," Matt said, his voice the same low murmur he used when dealing with a fractious horse. "I'm sure he had a good reason."

"What reason could possibly justify nearly dying? Because that's what would've happened if the Baxters hadn't found him and nursed him as well as they did."

"But they did find him. He's alive, Josie. And we're going to keep him that way. You and me. Together."

Were those tears glimmering in the lady doc's eyes? Luke blinked. He'd never seen her anything but stern and professional when dealing with a patient, no matter how dire the injury. Was it the baby making her emotional, or did she really care about him that much?

Josephine stared at her husband for a long moment, almost as if she'd forgotten Luke was in the room.

Just the babe, then. Made sense. He and the doc got along well enough, liked and respected each other, but they weren't exactly close. He wasn't close to any woman. Although, lately . . .

"All right." Josephine straightened her shoulders and gave a firm nod to Matt before turning back to Luke. "Let's see what's under these bandages, shall we?"

Luke did his best to lie still during the examination, keenly aware of how close his knee was to Josephine's swollen belly.

If he let himself flinch, he might hit her stomach, and he'd rather endure hellfire than cause any harm to Matt's wife and child.

"So, tell me about these outlaws you rousted," Matt said as he slipped out from under Luke to crouch on the rag rug next to the head of the bed. "Rustlers, I'd wager."

The captain was trying to distract him from the pain. He appreciated the effort, but the last thing he wanted to do was involve Matt in this mess. The man had a baby on the way, for Pete's sake. But if Luke refused to answer, Matt would grow suspicious and dig even deeper. Best to give him just enough to convince him this wasn't a Horseman matter.

"Yep." Luke grunted the answer, still focused on keeping his legs as still as possible. "Meant to . . . follow 'em back to . . . the herd, but . . . a kid stumbled across their operation. They took him hostage. Couldn't . . . let that stand."

Matt stroked his mustache. "A kid named Baxter."

Luke didn't bother confirming. After all, it hadn't really been a question.

The captain's eyes narrowed. "You and the boy still in danger?"

"Doubt it." Luke couldn't meet his friend's gaze. Matt always saw more than Luke meant to show. He'd never place Matt in a position where he'd be forced to choose between the Horseman bond and his wife. Right now, Josephine was too near her time for Matt to even contemplate leaving her to chase after some outlaw baggage. Best to downplay the danger. "I 'spect they'll . . . lie low for a while. Prob'ly even head for greener pastures. A cow's a cow. Might as well . . . rustle 'em where no one . . . knows yer face."

The captain made no reply, just got that deep-thinking look he tended to get when he was working out a problem in his mind. And, of course, that was the moment Dr. Jo decided to spray some kind of liquid fire onto Luke's side.

He stiffened and squeezed his eyes shut against the agonizing burn. A moan clawed at his throat, one he was too weak to corral inside.

Then, without warning, the bed dipped behind him, and a warm hand covered his. She didn't say a word, but even without opening his eyes, he knew it was Damaris. He gripped her hand, probably harder than he should—her hand being so delicate and fine inside his rough, callused mitt—but she didn't protest or pull away. She held tight, and somehow her touch made the pain bearable.

Conversation happened around him, but it swirled through the air above him like thick fog. Something about a steaming kettle. Instruments. Torn sheets. Nate tending horses. None of the pieces fit together, but then, he was too weary to figure them out. He picked out Damaris's soft tones among the others and tried to focus on her voice, but then she stopped talking. Dr. Jo had taken over the conversation, talking about catgut and needles. Where was Damaris?

He tried to open his eyes, to look for her, but his lids wouldn't cooperate. He clutched at her hand. Still there. Yet he could barely feel it. Was she slipping away?

"Damaris?"

"I'm here."

Her grip tightened on his hand. He could feel it now. His chest relaxed.

"It's all right to rest, Luke. You're in good hands."

Yes, he was. *Her* hands. He started to drift and this time made no effort to fight the current. Damaris was watching over him.

As he surrendered to unconsciousness, he released all thoughts save one. She'd called him Luke. Not Preach or Corporal or Davenport. But Luke. The man beneath the warrior.

Damaris felt Luke's hand go lax and silently thanked the Lord for sparing him the hurt to come.

"He's passed out, I think," she said, lifting her head as she wiped moisture from her eye with the back of a finger. "You can work freely now. . . ."

Her words died away as she realized that both Hangers were staring at her as if she were a carnival curiosity.

Tugging her hand away from Luke's relaxed grip, she quickly moved from the edge of the bed and stood against the wall. She wrapped her arms around herself, unsure of what she'd done to cause notice. "I'm sorry. I didn't mean to interfere."

For the first time since she'd arrived, Dr. Hanger smiled. "You have nothing to apologize for, Miss Baxter. You're a comfort to him. That's a good thing. The calmer he stays, the less likely he is to pull stitches or worsen his injuries. I'm glad you're here."

Damaris smiled shyly in return, some of the tension leaving her shoulders. "What can I do to help?"

"Why don't you unwrap that bandage on his forearm?" Dr. Hanger nodded toward the arm folded across Luke's chest, the one attached to the hand she'd been holding. "I'll disinfect and suture that area next."

A blush warmed Damaris's face, but she nodded and followed instructions.

She worked with the Hangers for the next hour as the doctor inspected every wound, bruise, and bump. The only difficulty arose when it came time to tend the injury he'd sustained to the back of his right thigh. Male limbs were not precisely proper viewing material for unmarried ladies, even ones who'd previously dressed wounds on said limbs. Thankfully, Dr. Hanger put Damaris in charge of protecting the patient's wounded forearm while Mr. Hanger rolled Luke onto his belly.

Careful to keep Luke's arm away from his body so it wouldn't be pinned beneath him, Damaris raised it above his head and guarded it while he rolled. And when the doctor took up a pair of scissors and started cutting his trousers clean away, Damaris tied her gaze to that forearm bandage with such a tight string that there was no available slack for looking anywhere else.

Luke wore a pair of short drawers beneath his denims—a fact she'd discovered most gratefully after Nate cut away the leg of his trousers—but he still deserved his privacy. Keeping herself at his head while the others worked on his injured leg, Damaris talked to him in low murmurs. Telling him what a magnificent job Dr. Hanger was doing. Assuring him that he would feel much better the next time he woke. Promising to bring him a cold compress for his poor, swollen eye. Anything to distract her and encourage him. By the time the Hangers were ready to roll Luke back over, she'd resorted to quoting some of her favorite Bible verses, having run out of other things to say.

"That's how he got his nickname, you know." Matthew Hanger came around to the side of the bed where she knelt by Luke's head and offered her a hand up. "Quotin' verses."

She was thankful to find a sheet covering Luke's form. Dr. Hanger stood at the washstand, cleaning her instruments with the last of the hot water from the kettle. She must have finished her treatments. *Thank you, God.* Damaris had done her best to remain outwardly positive and encouraging, but the longer the doctor worked, the more the worry had built up between Damaris's shoulder blades and through her neck. Perhaps now that the examinations, cleaning, and suturing were complete, she and Luke could both rest.

Releasing her hold on the mattress, Damaris allowed Mr. Hanger to pull her to her feet.

"Luke has a memory like a steel trap." Mr. Hanger grinned slightly, his gaze drifting over to his friend on the bed. "He knows more scripture by heart than most parsons I've met. That's why the boys in the 7th took to calling him Preach. He got a kick out of it. Said he was about as unsaintly as they came. Wild to the bone and born for trouble. But it wasn't true." He turned the force of his gaze on Damaris, and it cut straight through to the barren parts of her heart. "Preach might have a wild past, but no man on earth is more loyal or dependable. Or fiercer when it comes to protecting his own. If I had to choose only one man to go into battle with, I'd choose Preach every time."

Damaris had no response. Polite niceties would only cheapen the moment. These two men shared a powerful bond. A bond the likes of which she'd never shared with anyone. A bond she envied. What would it be like to have someone in her life who could be counted on always to be there, always to take her side? One who saw her even when she was at her most invisible?

"Thank you for being there for him." A touch of emotion clogged Matthew Hanger's voice. "For nursing his wounds. For bringing us here." His focus returned to the man on the bed. "Preach is as tough as they come, but if it hadn't been for you, he might be quotin' verses from inside heaven's throne room right about now."

"My husband's right," Dr. Hanger said, slipping up beside him and sliding her hand through the bend in his elbow. "You saved his life, Miss Baxter, and we are in your debt."

Damaris searched the doctor's face. "So you expect him to recover, then?"

Please, Lord!

Dr. Hanger nodded. "As long as nothing turns septic and we manage to keep any fever at bay, yes. He's weak from blood loss, but with a restorative diet and plenty of rest, I expect he'll be back to his ornery, stubborn self soon enough." She made the last comment with the kind of fond smile that spoke of true affection.

Damaris smiled in return as relief nearly floated her feet off the ground. "Just let me know what needs to be done, and I'll do it."

The doctor straightened and patted her husband's arm as if communicating something to him without words, then faced Damaris. "Right now, what he needs is rest. As do you." She laid a hand on Damaris's arm. "Let me fix you a cup of tea."

"Just don't let her fix you anything else," Mr. Hanger said with a chuckle.

His wife slapped at his arm. "That's enough out of you, Matthew Hanger. I'd never repay Miss Baxter's kindness to Preach by subjecting her to my cooking, and well you know it." She linked arms with Damaris and leaned close. "Don't worry, tea is my one specialty. Though we might need the kettle."

She led Damaris to the door by way of the washstand, picking up the empty kettle as she went. Her playful diversion as they wove through the room on a ridiculously circuitous path lightened Damaris's spirit.

"I'm afraid I'm not much of a cook, either," she confided in a whisper. "My specialty is sausage gravy on toast. I don't do too badly with pots and skillets, but I can't seem to master the oven."

Dr. Hanger's face lit up in a broad grin. "Oh, Miss Baxter. We are going to be *great* friends."

"Then you must call me Damaris."

"And you must call me Josephine." She leaned close as they meandered past her husband and approached the door. "And you must tell me absolutely everything about how you and Preach met."

Damaris's cheeks warmed, but so did her heart. Shared confidences with a woman near her own age? No judgment over her lack of culinary expertise in the kitchen? Compliments instead of criticism? She hadn't enjoyed many friendships as a child and even fewer as an adult. Her shyness and the shadow of Great-Aunt Bertha prevented most such doors from opening. But nothing barred her way today.

Damaris leaned her head close to Josephine's. "It all started when I found myself locked in the root cellar. . . ."

— CHAPTER —
THIRTEEN

The Hangers stayed four days, and Damaris could not remember enjoying a visit more. A rather odd happenstance, since a man nearly had to die to bring the captain and his wife to her door. Thankfully, Luke no longer perched precariously outside heaven's gate. Except for a slight fever that plagued him the first two days, he'd been improving steadily. He stayed awake hours at a time now instead of mere minutes, though he still napped a couple of times a day. His appetite was improving, and Josephine had allowed him to start incorporating solid foods into the broth-heavy invalid diet she'd insisted upon initially.

Mr. Hanger had gotten Luke out of bed the last two days for short walks around the house. This morning, Luke had managed the feat more or less on his own after Nathaniel found him a V-shaped branch to use as a crutch so he could take some of the weight off his injured leg.

A noticeable change had come over her nephew since the incident with Luke and the rustlers. Nathaniel seemed more subdued, more helpful around the house, and significantly less angry. Remorse surely played a role, but Damaris believed other factors were at play as well. Two factors in particular: Luke Davenport and Matthew Hanger. Nathaniel lapped up the male attention like desert sand absorbed water. He hounded Mr. Hanger's heels whenever the head Horseman traipsed to the barn to tend the stock. Josephine's husband had fetched Titan from Mr. Grimes's ranch the first morning of his visit, determined to see to Luke's horse himself. He allowed Nathaniel to tag along and watch him work, and even enlisted his help from time to time.

Not only that, but the two of them rode for an hour every afternoon after school, apparently at Luke's suggestion. The men claimed Titan needed the exercise, but Damaris was pretty sure it was bribery, pure and simple, for Nathaniel wasn't allowed to ride unless he'd completed all his chores and schoolwork the previous day. The boy had actually opened a book at the kitchen table the last two nights after supper. Damaris had nearly dropped the dish she'd been washing the first time it happened. Never again would she question whether or not miracles happened in the modern age.

While her nephew bonded with the Horsemen, Damaris enjoyed a growing sense of sisterhood with Josephine. Damaris usually found herself uneasy around guests, but Josephine had a no-nonsense way about her that removed all societal expectations and pressures. They shared many a cup of tea, discussing Luke's progress and all the things Damaris should watch for after the Hangers left. Doctoring did not dominate their conversations, however. They shared stories of kitchen disasters, secret worries about raising children—both infants and teenage boys—and Damaris's favorite topic: Luke.

"Preach must have known he'd need my services one day," Josephine reminisced as Damaris helped her pack her traveling bag. "When I tried to hire the Horsemen to rescue my brother, all I had to offer was one of my father's mounts and my medical services. Matthew was quick to point out that one horse couldn't be split between four men, but Preach liked the idea of having a doctor at his beck and call. Especially since I'd proven capable of keeping a man alive after a rustler's bullet nearly did in one of their own. I'd hoped, for their sakes, that after Matthew retired the Horsemen there'd be less need for my skills, but I love those men like brothers, and I'll come running whenever any of them call."

Even when she was nine months pregnant. And experiencing pre-birthing pains, if the creases that had just appeared across her forehead were any indication.

"Come. Let's wait for your husband in the parlor." Damaris took charge of Josephine's carpetbag and steered her new friend into the front room, urging her onto the sofa.

Josephine didn't protest the assistance, which was unusual for the take-charge doctor. She lowered herself somewhat awkwardly onto the cushion, then rubbed her belly in a circular motion, her mouth tight. After a moment, her face relaxed, and she let out a sigh.

"Are you sure it's safe to travel?" Damaris dropped her voice in case Mr. Hanger appeared sooner than expected. Josephine had declared earlier that he worried far too much as it was, and she didn't like to upset him with conversation best left to women. "What if the baby comes early?"

Josephine waved away Damaris's concern with a smile, but she couldn't quite mask the uncertainty in her eyes. "These are just preparation contractions, the ones Dr. John Braxton Hicks described in 1871 in his article in the *Transactions of the Obstetrical Society of London*." Her hand rested lightly on her protruding stomach. "Believe me," she said with a wry grin, "I made a very thorough study of the literature after I started experiencing the sensations early in my third trimester. They tend to worsen when I'm particularly active, so it's not surprising they've been more frequent of late, but now that Preach is out of danger, Matthew is anxious to get me home. He probably wants to wrap me in cotton wool and keep me from engaging in anything more exerting than turning pages in my medical journals."

"Well, after rushing all this way and expending so much energy looking after Mr. Davenport, you're due a rest." Damaris would be sad to see her new friend leave, yet she wanted Josephine safely home in case those preparation contractions turned into the real thing. "Besides," she said, taking out the small tablet she'd stashed in her skirt pocket, "I've taken notes on all of your instructions. I promise to take exceptional care of your patient."

Josephine smiled and touched Damaris's arm. "That's the only reason I let Matthew talk me into leaving before Preach was stronger. He told me that Oliver Grimes offered to put Preach up at his ranch, but I don't know anyone in that household and don't feel comfortable trusting strangers with his care. You, on the other hand, I trust completely."

Heat rushed to Damaris's face. She couldn't recall ever

receiving a finer compliment. She prayed she wouldn't prove a disappointment.

"You care for him." Josephine made the statement without the smallest tinge of doubt in her voice.

Damaris's head shot up. "He saved Nathaniel's life. I owe him a great debt."

Her friend's green eyes twinkled. "It's more than gratitude that keeps you by his bedside."

"I-I don't know what you mean."

Josephine's brows arched. "Don't you?"

All right. Yes. She knew precisely what Josephine meant, but any fondness she felt for Luke was immaterial. He would only be here long enough to recover from his injuries. Then he'd be out of her life. She wouldn't be so foolish as to expect anything else.

"Of course," Josephine continued, "I wasn't the only one who vetoed the option of Preach convalescing at the Grimes ranch."

Damaris lifted her face.

"Preach refused the offer before I could raise any concerns." The twinkle in Josephine's eyes brightened. "And I'm pretty sure it's not just your nursing skills that have him wanting to remain here."

"Thanks for buildin' this bunk for me, Cap." Luke sat on the edge of the wooden box Matt had nailed together in the front stall of the Baxter barn. It was taller than most bunkhouse beds, so Luke could lower his oversized frame onto the straw tick Damaris had sewn for him with minimum bending.

"Make sure you can lie down and get up again on your own," Matt said, fussin' over him like an old woman. "I don't want to strand you out here with only a boy and a woman to lug your heavy carcass around if you get stuck. You'd prob'ly flatten them."

Luke obediently went through the motions of lying back and rolling his legs onto the mattress until he was sufficiently horizontal, doing his best to hold back the grimace and groans that begged for release. "They're stronger than they look," he said as he lay flat, catching his breath before attempting to rise. Who knew lying down would take so much out of him? "They managed to haul my carcass off the ground, into a wagon, and then into a bed that first night. If I fall on my face, they'll find a way to straighten me out."

Not that he planned to give them a chance to prove their mettle. A man stood on his own two feet. His feet might be a bit wobbly these days, and his step might be slow and lopsided, but he'd manage.

Gathering himself, Luke rolled onto his left side and braced his right arm against the wooden frame. Sweat beaded his brow as he slowly levered himself into a sitting position. Gritting his teeth, he pivoted until his legs dangled over the side. He made sure to place all his weight on his left hip so his right thigh wouldn't press against the wood. Dr. Jo would tan his hide if he popped any of her stitches. Not to mention the fact that any time he bumped the back of his right leg against something, it hurt like the dickens.

He felt absurdly proud of himself when his feet hit the barn floor and his legs once again supported his weight.

Matt looked less than impressed. Probably because Luke's

muscles were quivering like a newborn foal and he couldn't hide the raggedness of his breathing. But he'd passed the test. Proven his mobility. Even if he did feel like he'd have to sleep the entire afternoon to recover from the effort. The captain didn't need to know that, though. Matt would never leave one of his men behind if he wasn't convinced that man could take care of himself.

But Matt also had a wife to consider, a woman he loved more than any other human on the planet. And a baby that could arrive at any moment. Matt had been watching Josephine like a hawk, frowning every time her face registered a twinge. He needed to get her home to Gringolet. Today. Luke intended to make sure that happened.

"I'll be fine, Cap. The Baxters are good folks. They'll take care of me until I'm back in fightin' shape again."

"Speaking of fightin' shape . . ." Matt's expression morphed from that of an overprotective big brother to a hardened professional in a blink. "I had a lengthy conversation with Oliver Grimes this morning. He wasn't too pleased with you leaving his employ, but he understood that you're in no shape to continue your investigation and wouldn't be for some time."

"Did he try to recruit another Horseman for the job?" Luke wrapped an arm around his aching side and leaned his rear against the edge of the bunk to take the weight off his leg.

"Yep." Matt stroked his handlebar mustache. "I told him none were currently available. I did give him your descriptions of the rustlers, though, so he can pass those along to the local law. It placated him somewhat."

Luke hadn't expected Grimes to be happy about losing the Horsemen's help, but he also didn't want the rancher pestering Damaris and accusing Nate of being part of the gang. It rubbed against the grain, asking Matt to play messenger, but Luke couldn't intimidate a flea in his current state. "You make it clear the kid wasn't involved?"

Matt nodded. "I did. Grimes didn't look convinced, though. He believes the boy's a troublemaker with some kind of vendetta against him."

An accurate assessment. Still . . . "Nate's pulled a few pranks, but nothing overly serious." Luke had given Matt an accounting of what transpired that night, including Nate's appearance. "The kid risked his life to come back for me. If it weren't for him, I wouldn't be standing here."

The captain scowled. "If it weren't for him, you wouldn't have been injured in the first place."

Luke just shrugged.

Matt blew out a breath. They both knew that even good intentions could have unforeseen dark consequences. Wounded Knee was supposed to be a peaceful weapon confiscation, and look how that had turned out. Luke still had nightmares about the carnage left in the wake of the Hotchkiss guns his company had fired on the Lakota. The regret ate at his soul. Were it not for God's grace . . .

As he'd trained it to do, his mind immediately turned to the words of Paul to tame the ravenous beast of guilt when it raised its ugly head.

This is a faithful saying, and worthy of all acceptation, that Christ Jesus came into the world to save sinners; of whom I am chief. Howbeit for this cause I obtained mercy, that in me first Jesus Christ might shew forth all longsuffering, for a pattern to them which should hereafter believe on him to life everlasting.

He'd been shown mercy so that he might be an example of Christ's grace to others. And right now, Nate Baxter needed the same mercy Luke had received.

Matt broke the silence. "Look, I know there are things you aren't telling me about this situation."

"Cap," Luke began, but Matt waved him off.

"You don't need to explain. I understand what you're doing, and part of me even appreciates it."

"Your place is with your wife now," Luke said softly, "not with your men."

Matt's sharp gaze speared him. "You're my family, Preach. You and Wallace and Brooks. That doesn't go away just because I married Josie."

"I know that, Cap. We all do." Though the small, raw place inside Luke's heart that had never quite healed from his mother's abandonment or his father's abuse lapped up the reassurance like an affection-starved pup. "Brothers to the end. That will never change."

"You better believe it."

"But your commitment to your wife comes first." Luke scratched at an itchy spot on his jaw where a half-grown beard stubbled his face. "Had I been thinking more clearly, I never would've asked Damaris to send for her. I should've just used the doc from Huntsville."

Matt set a firm yet gentle hand on Luke's shoulder. "No, you did right. You know how possessive Josie is about you boys." He cocked a grin. "She never would've let me hear the end of it if some other doctor tended you."

Luke chuckled.

"Seriously, though, Preach." Matt tightened his grip on

Luke's shoulder and waited for Luke to meet his gaze. "If trouble comes calling, pack up the Baxters and head to Gringolet. You're not in this alone. Remember that. Horsemen stand together."

Luke held his captain's gaze, knowing the words were not idle. Matthew Hanger and the others had his back no matter what.

He gave a jerky nod, acknowledging the kinship that ran deeper than blood. "Horsemen stand together."

Later that afternoon, Luke hobbled back to the barn after spending an hour showing Nate the best way to build a small game snare. Nate's daddy had taught him the fundamentals of shooting, but Douglas Baxter had grown up in town, just like his sister, and relied on butchers and store owners to keep him in meat. Luke wasn't sure how Damaris planned to provide for her nephew without a regular income, so he figured passing on what he knew about foraging and hunting might make at least small inroads to paying her back for nursing and feeding him for the duration of his recovery.

Nate had seemed interested and engaged in the lessons. Eager to try out a new skill. After Luke showed him how to form a wire noose and explained the proper technique for crafting a trigger, he'd sent Nate off to scout game trails and burrows so he could set up a few practice traps. If the boy actually managed to catch something, Luke would teach him how to skin and dress whatever he caught—rabbit, squirrel, opossum.

He couldn't wait to see Damaris's reaction. He could picture her horrified but desperately trying to hide her disgust in the face of her nephew's pride in his prowess. Maybe he should warn her of what might be coming. Give her time to prepare and scour that recipe book of hers. Surely if it contained recipes for onion poultices for stab wounds, it would have something for a squirrel stew or braised rabbit. Shoot, maybe Luke would just teach Nate how to roast his catch on a spit over a campfire. The kid would probably enjoy that more anyhow.

Nate craved the outdoors like a fish craved water. It was his natural habitat. Unlike his aunt, who preferred a cozy nest indoors. The two couldn't be more opposite, yet when push came to shove, their differences melted away, leaving the bond of family to stand firm.

Damaris had earned Nate's respect the night the two of them rescued Luke. He saw it in the way the boy looked at her, heard it in his tone of voice. He was still an ornery little cuss with a mischievous streak a mile wide, but Luke would bet a month's salary there'd be no repeat of the cellar incident. Nearly getting himself killed when he'd stumbled into those rustlers had given the boy a shift in perspective. Maybe Luke could help him get a little farther down the path to manhood before he left.

Having reached the barn, Luke braced his hand against the corner post to catch his breath, surprised at the ache that had developed in his chest—not from the short walk across the yard, but from the idea of leaving. He turned his gaze toward the house and pictured Damaris sitting near the window in the parlor, working on a piece of embroidery. She tended to stitch in the afternoons.

Strange how he'd learned her routines even though he'd been unconscious more often than not the last few days. Yet almost every time he woke, he found her by his bedside, occupied with something. A book or some needlework. Usually with a cup of tea at hand. She'd always been ready with a smile, a helping hand, and distracting conversation.

He was going to miss waking up to find her near now that he'd moved to the barn. Propriety had to be respected, though. And really, separation was in his own best interest as well.

He had no business imagining a life that included a woman. Especially one as refined and proper as Damaris Baxter. All Luke knew of family life was brokenness. A mother who ran away from her problems. A father who solved his with fists and a bottle of whiskey. Not exactly a promising pedigree. Better for everyone if he kept his focus on horses and outlaws. That way any mistakes he made wouldn't damage the people he cared about.

Because as much as he hated to admit it, he was coming to care for the Baxters. A lot.

Having rested a moment, Luke pushed away from the corner of the barn and crutched the rest of the way inside. It took a moment for his eyes to adjust to the dimmer interior, but the smells were immediately familiar. Horses. Cows. Manure. Leather. Straw.

Yep. This was where he belonged. Barns, bunkhouses, maybe a small one-room cabin someday when he got tired of wanderin' from job to job. That was what he was made for. A simple, masculine existence. No furbelows or feminine trappings. Just plain old practical living. That was the life for—

His thoughts broke off when he turned the corner into the first stall. Every muscle in his body seemed to have forgotten how to move. Except the ones in charge of his eyelids. He blinked once. Then again, trying to clear away the hallucination, but the stubborn vision refused to be banished. His throat tightened. An odd pressure pushed against his chest. What had she done?

Leaning a hip against the jamb, Luke slowly reached up and removed his hat. It seemed the right thing to do when entering a home. For that was what she'd created—a home. An honest-to-goodness home. In a horse stall. For him.

A blue-and-red quilt topped the straw tick mattress on his bunk, the edges hanging over the side to hide the unfinished lumber. The rag rug from the room where he'd convalesced—*her* room—now adorned his floor. A set of nails protruded from the wall to his right, one of which held his overcoat. Luke hung his hat on the peg closest to him, his hand trembling slightly. He took one step past the threshold, propping his crutch in the corner by his hat, and used the edge of the bed to work deeper into the room.

A pillow lay at the head of his bed. Beneath the bunk sat a bootjack and a chamber pot. His face warmed at the thought of her considering that particular need even as he appreciated the independence it would allow him.

A pair of crates stacked one atop the other formed a washstand in the corner behind his bunk. A basin sat on top of the stack, with a small bar of soap on a saucer in the right corner. A shaving mug and brush that must have belonged to her brother sat in the left corner. An ewer filled with water perched on the shelf made by the open, sideways crate. A folded towel had been tucked onto the shelf next to the ewer, and a small shaving mirror hung from a nail centered over the basin. He touched the towel, not surprised to find it soft. Luke was used to coarse, worn-out scraps, but no such thing existed in this magical place.

Having saved the best for last, Luke braced himself by flattening his palm against the back wall as he pivoted to face his sitting room. What else could he call it? There was a chair, one of the wooden ones from the kitchen, though it sported a bright red cushion he didn't recognize. Beside it stood a small table, one he thought he recalled seeing across from the hearth in the parlor. And on top of the table stood an oil lamp. Not a sensible lantern like one would expect in a barn, but a glass parlor lamp, one that transformed an ugly barn stall into a place of beauty and light.

Not only was there a lamp, but she'd left him a pair of books.

He picked them up and examined the spines. *Twenty Thousand Leagues Under the Sea* by Jules Verne and James Fenimore Cooper's *The Last of the Mohicans*. Inside the front cover of each, a name was written in a small, tidy hand— Damaris Baxter. Books from her private collection. Ones she'd obviously selected with care. Books that would appeal to a wild, adventuring soul. The corners showed wear, and the spines sported creases. These were not titles collected to look good on a shelf. She'd read them. Multiple times, he'd guess. Perhaps the prim and proper Damaris Baxter had a bit of a wild, adventuring soul herself.

The thought made him smile as he stepped away from the table to admire the last piece of her handiwork.

In the middle of the wall across from his bunk, in the space between his sitting area and the pegs for his clothes, hung the most remarkable item of all. A framed needlework sampler, signed with the initials DB and the date of 1894. A little house made of x-shaped stitches sat near the bottom of the picture with a road leading out to the edge of the frame. Trees and bushes dotted the linen landscape, while embroidered flowers formed a border around the perimeter.

In the center, she'd stitched a verse, one that made his chest squeeze.

> Choose you this day
> whom ye will serve.
> But as for me and my house,
> we will serve the Lord.
>
> —Joshua 24:15

Me and my house. Everyday words, yet they carried such profound meaning. A household. A family. People under his protection. People for whom he was responsible. People he loved and who loved him in return.

Since the day he'd left home, he'd only ever been responsible for himself. Yes, he'd looked out for his fellow cavalry troopers while in the army and later his Horsemen brothers, but they were grown men, in charge of their own lives.

He had no use for any other family. They'd just steal his freedom and tie him down. And what if he ended up like his old man? Unable to control his temper. Cruel. Abusive. Or what if he grew weary of the fetters and just up and left one day like his ma had?

But if any provide not for his own, and specially for those of his own house, he hath denied the faith, and is worse than an infidel.

The verse rose up in warning, the last word ringing in his ears like a prophetic accusation.

Luke shook his head. Nope. It didn't matter how attractive she made it look with her homey touches and thoughtful gestures. The family life was not for him.

She deserved better than his sorry hide, anyway.

"Oh, I'm sorry. I didn't realize you were here."

Luke's head swiveled toward the stall opening so fast, his brain felt like it bounced off the inside of his skull. His head started to throb.

Damaris stood in the doorway, dressed in a work apron over the same dark blue skirt and white blouse she'd had on this morning. Yet for some reason, he felt as if he were seeing her for the first time. Everything about her seemed new.

When he stared at her without saying anything, her gaze dipped down to the floor, and her hands twisted inside the blanket she held.

Man, but she was somethin'. He couldn't figure out what it was about her that called to him, but there was no denying that she did. She wasn't petite and curvy like the women most men considered beauties. Nor was she bold and brimming with a confidence that would draw a man's attention and appreciation. She was simply . . . Damaris. Quiet, kind, and exceedingly generous. And despite his resolve to ignore all thoughts of households and settling down, when he looked at her, he found it difficult to think of anything else.

Finally, she looked back up at him, the slash of her brows

arching in confusion. "Are you all right?" She laid the blanket on the bed and took a step closer to him. "Are your injuries paining you? I could brew some willow bark tea or—"

"I'm fine." Luke tried to smile but couldn't seem to manage it with so many emotions churning inside him. "It's just . . . this." He gestured to the miracle she'd created in the middle of a barn. "No one's ever . . ." What? Made him a home? He couldn't say that. Even if it were true. He settled for, "Thank you."

A pretty pink color flushed her cheeks as her warm brown eyes lit with pleasure. "You're welcome. And you're *welcome* . . . here." She ducked her face away from him to fiddle with the blanket on the edge of the bed. "This stall just seemed so inhospitable and cold. I didn't want you to feel like you were being banished. You're a hero to us, you know." Her gaze darted his direction, almost meeting his eyes before it skittered back to the blanket. "A few little items to brighten the space and add to your comfort while you recover seemed the least I could do."

"I've been in hotel rooms that weren't half this fine."

Her smile widened at his praise. "I'm glad you like it."

"Like it?" he scoffed. "You've gone and ruined me for all future bunkhouse life."

Something shifted in her eyes. She peered at him as if plumbing his depths. "Is that how you see your future? A series of bunkhouses?"

He shrugged off the question, as if it didn't challenge everything he believed about himself. "It's what I know. First the cavalry, then the Horsemen. Even my quarters at Gringolet are more bunkhouse than cabin."

"And you've never longed for more?"

Of course he had. What man didn't dream of having a woman to share his bed at night, to cook his meals and darn his socks? A woman to believe in him when he didn't believe in himself. To stand by his side in good times and bad. To love him even though he knew he didn't deserve it.

"Ain't nothin' wrong with bunkhouse livin'. It comes with a roof over your head, food to eat, and enough wages to keep clothes on your back and a saddle on your horse. I'm content with that."

Mostly.

"Yes, well, I was content playing companion to my great-aunt Bertha, too. Until I learned of Nathaniel's need. Contentment isn't chained to a certain set of circumstances, Luke. It's portable. You can take it with you wherever you go."

"Not everywhere." The bitter words slipped from his mouth before he could call them back. His feet suddenly itched to escape, to walk out of the stall before the ugliness inside him seeped out and stained her pretty white apron. "Some places are so harsh that hanging on to survival is all a person can handle. Lofty ideals like contentment and peace wither on the vine."

"Is that what it was like on the battlefield?" Her voice gently touched his ear, evidence of a soul too innocent even to imagine the truth.

"Nope." He threw the word down like a gauntlet. "That's what it was like at home."

Then, before she could offer a kindhearted platitude—or worse, ask him to explain—he grabbed his crutch and hobbled out of the barn.

Damaris reached for the bed frame behind her, too shaken by what Luke had revealed to stand unaided. What kind of home life had he endured that he considered it more devastating than the horrors he'd encountered on the battlefield?

Her eyes misted at the thought of a little boy hiding from danger in his own home. Alone. Frightened. Maybe even bloodied and bruised. Home was supposed to be a place of safety. Security. Love. Who had stolen those things from him?

Growing up, she'd often felt overlooked and undervalued, but she'd never feared for her survival. How insensitive she must have sounded to him, advising him to carry contentment with him from place to place, as if it could be stored in a saddlebag or a pocket. She knew nothing about what it meant to walk in his shoes or live in his skin. How foolish to expect the wisdom she'd gleaned from her own experience to translate automatically to his. Especially when her motivation for mentioning it had stemmed from pure selfishness.

She'd wanted him to see more than a bachelor existence in his future. Not because she didn't think he could be content living bunkhouse to bunkhouse, but because she wanted him to envision family life as a viable option. The same way *she'd* started to envision it. A future with Luke Davenport. His gaze seeking her out instead of looking through her. His hand covering hers. That teasing spark in his hazel eyes. His mentoring Nathaniel. Teaching him the things she couldn't.

She'd allowed those daydreams to take root over the last few days, convincing herself she had something to offer a man like Luke. As if a warrior had need of a quiet mouse who felt more at home in fictional worlds than in the real one.

Perhaps he *had* needed her a little. At least as a nurse. He had nearly died, after all. But now she'd gone and run him out of his only sanctuary with her careless words. He'd no doubt come to the barn seeking respite, and here she was, lollygagging around in his private space, keeping him from the rest he needed. Josephine would be disappointed in her.

"Come on, Damaris," she murmured under her breath as she pushed away from the bunk. "Do what you came to do, then get back where you belong." Up at the house. Out of Luke's hair.

Reaching into her apron pocket, she retrieved the length of heavy cording she'd brought and tied one end to the nail she'd hammered earlier into the left edge of the stall opening. She had to stretch up on tiptoe since the nail was a full arm's length above her head. Luke Davenport was a tall man, and she didn't want to knock the hat off his head every time he walked through the doorway. Pulling the cord as taut as possible, she stretched it across the top of the opening and tied it off on the nail on the opposite side. The line wasn't perfectly level, but it would do.

Next, she grabbed the extra blanket she'd brought from the house and attached it to the line with clothespins. Finally, she took the curtain tie pilfered from the front parlor, looped it around the blanket, and hooked it over the last nail.

There. Now he had a door. Privacy and protection from nosy nurses who had no business inserting themselves into his life. She just had to find him to let him know it was safe to return.

It didn't take long. He was too injured and sore to hobble more than a few dozen yards away. She found him leaning against the paddock fence, nose to nose with his horse.

Damaris approached the fence but left plenty of space between her and Luke. "I'm finished," she said softly, not wanting to disturb him more than she already had. She kept her gaze on the horse, too embarrassed to look at his owner. "I'll send Nathaniel to fetch you when dinner's ready."

She backed away.

"Damaris, wait."

She halted. Turned to face him. But she couldn't find the courage to look him in the eyes.

He heaved a sigh and ran thick fingers over his short-cropped hair. He'd been so eager to escape her that he hadn't even paused to collect his hat.

"I'm sorry." They both blurted the words at the same time.

Luke frowned. "What on earth do *you* have to be sorry for?" Now he sounded angry.

Damaris shook her head, her shame keeping her face pointed toward the ground. "I spoke out of turn. It was presumptuous of me to lecture you on contentment as if I were an expert. Which I'm most certainly *not*." Her need for him to believe her sincerity overcame her embarrassment and dragged her gaze up to meet his. "I never meant to minimize your personal experiences and hardships, Luke. I'm very sorry."

"And I'm a horse's backside."

"What?"

He grunted quietly as he shifted to lean his weight against the fence slats and hooked one arm around the post, probably for extra support.

"You need to rest." She frowned in concern and took a step toward him. "We can talk later."

He scowled at her. "We can talk now. I ain't gonna topple over in the next five minutes."

Wonderful. Now she'd insulted his manhood. Only *she* could manage to make things worse with an apology.

Afraid to dig herself any deeper into the Pit of Good Intentions Gone Wrong, she buttoned her lips and let him take the lead.

"First off," he said in a near growl, "you had every right to say what you did. Speak the truth in love. That's what the Bible teaches, and that's what you did. Ain't nothin' wrong with that. The wrong came in when I let old hurts get the better of me and walked out on you after you worked so hard to turn that stall into something special. You deserved better."

She did her best to smile but feared the attempt was too wobbly to be effective. "It's all right."

"No, it ain't. I'm a rough man who's lived a rough life, but even I know better than to walk out on a woman who's been nothing but kind to me."

Hearing him denigrate himself sparked her ire. He had saved Nathaniel's life, and she wouldn't allow him to speak poorly of himself in her hearing. "You might be a little rough around the edges, Luke Davenport," she said, stepping close enough to lay her palm lightly on his chest, "but in here beats a noble heart. I don't know what harsh circumstances you endured as a child or on the battlefield, but I do know that the man standing before me today is a man to admire. One who places the well-being of others before himself. One who loves God's Word and inspires loyalty in his friends. One who forgives the faults in others faster than he forgives his own. You're a good man, Luke, and I thank God for bringing you into our lives."

For however long you decide to stay.

Damaris dropped her hand back to her side and retreated, her pulse zigzagging in crazy patterns through her midsection as she realized just how boldly she'd acted. What must he think of her?

He didn't say a word. Or move. Or even breathe, as far as she could tell. To be honest, she was having difficulty breathing herself. Touching him, feeling his heart pound beneath her fingertips, wasn't exactly the best way to keep from growing too attached.

Yet she didn't regret it. She'd spoken the truth in love.

What kind of love was a question better left unexplored. For now.

Luke watched Damaris leave, too dumbstruck to do anything but stare. It was a good thing his elbow was looped over the paddock post, or he might have proven himself a liar and toppled right over onto his face.

Her touch had been featherlight, yet he could feel the imprint of her fingers as if they'd branded themselves on his skin.

Never in all his born days had a woman touched him like that. Sure, a saloon gal or two had made friendly with his person on the occasions he'd found himself seeking a meal or a game of cards in such a place. But they hadn't *touched* him. Not in a way that left a lasting impression. Luke was pretty sure he could live to be a hundred and not forget Damaris's gentle hand pressed against his chest and her earnest words pressed against his soul.

He rubbed the spot on his shirt where her hand had lain, trying to preserve the feeling. How had she reached inside him like that? Grabbing hold of his heart as if it were a book on her shelf. Cracking it open and peeking inside before he could snap it closed again. The crazy thing was, part of him actually wanted to let her see those hidden places. To share those dark memories with someone so awash in light. Thank goodness the sane part of him knew better.

But that sanity had its limits, apparently, for he couldn't stop himself from caring about her. Her well-being, her feelings, even her interests. And when had a cavalryman ever cared about needlework and novel reading? Lord, have mercy. He was losing his mind.

A man to admire. Her words echoed in his head, warming his blood and kicking his pulse into a bouncy trot. It was probably a good thing he could barely walk to the barn at the moment. Otherwise, he'd be sorely tempted to follow her into the house and let her know exactly how much he admired *her*.

Titan nudged him from behind, snorting into the back of his neck.

"I know," Luke muttered as he turned slowly and patted Titan's neck. "She's too good for me. But I don't have to court her to protect her. She needs a man with my kind of skills around, with those rustlers out there. Maybe with Grimes too, if there's any truth to Nate's accusations. I ain't leaving 'til I know she's safe."

And when she was?

Luke swallowed. Walking away from Damaris Baxter wouldn't be easy. But he'd do it. Even if it meant leaving a piece of himself behind.

CHAPTER

SIXTEEN

"Y ou goin' to town today?" Nathaniel peered at Damaris from across the breakfast table, oddly uninterested in the flapjacks on his plate.

Something was bothering him. She searched his face for clues but found none, only the shuttered expression he wore when he expected her to disappoint him, an expression she hadn't seen since Luke came to stay with them.

It had been two days since the Hangers left and Luke moved into the barn. Luke was steadily growing stronger, recovering enough that she didn't worry about leaving him for a few hours. And since today was Saturday, Nathaniel would be around to check on their patient occasionally. He and Luke got along well. At least, they seemed to. Nathaniel continued to exercise Titan every day and kept up with his chores with few complaints. Things had been progressing so well, Damaris had started to believe that the sullenness and anger were a thing of the past.

Until this morning. The chip had returned to her nephew's shoulder, and Damaris couldn't escape the feeling that she was forgetting something—something that would explain the change in his demeanor. But for the life of her, she couldn't figure it out.

She hesitated over her answer, sensing a trap. "Yes." She set the coffeepot on the back of the stove to stay warm. She'd take Luke's breakfast out to him after Nathaniel finished. "I need to pick up some supplies at the general store."

Nathaniel cut off a slab of pancake far too big for his mouth and shoved it in. His eyes glowed with rebellion. "That all?" The flapjack distorted his words, but she made them out.

"I think so?"

Wrong answer. His eyes narrowed, then dismissed her. He dropped his gaze to his plate and stabbed at his food with a force that would penetrate armor.

What had she forgotten?

"Do you need me to get something for you while I'm there?"

He shrugged. No eye contact. No words. Just a defiant lift of his shoulders that made it clear she'd failed to measure up to some invisible standard. Again.

Why wouldn't he talk to her? She couldn't rectify her error if she didn't know what she'd done wrong.

Damaris blinked as an idea flickered to life. Maybe *she* should talk to *him*. He couldn't guess her needs any more than she could guess his.

Butterflies took flight in her stomach, but she did her best to ignore them as she pulled out a chair and sat next to Nathaniel. Needing to busy her hands, she reached for the platter of flapjacks and forked one onto her plate, then reached for the blackberry jam.

By the time she found the courage to look up at her nephew,

he'd finished over half his stack. He was shoveling in food as fast as he could chew. If she didn't find her courage soon, she'd lose her chance.

She set down her fork, then reached across the table and touched his arm. He jerked away. Not an auspicious start.

Curling her fingers inward, she withdrew her hand a few inches, leaving it to rest on the table between them. "I can tell I've upset you, but I don't know what I've done. Whatever it is, I want to make it right. Talk to me, Nathaniel. Please. What have I forgotten?"

"My pa! You forgot my pa." He shoved his chair backward and lurched to his feet. "You're so busy fussin' over Mr. Davenport that you've forgotten your own kin. I shoulda known better than to expect you to actually follow through on your promise."

"Nathaniel, wait!"

But he didn't. He stormed out the back door, nearly running over Luke in the process.

"Whoa there, partner." Luke shuffled sideways and grabbed the door before it slammed closed.

"I ain't your partner." Nathaniel's voice echoed from a distance, piercing Damaris's heart.

Luke made his way inside, taking care to close the back door gently.

Damaris swiveled in her chair, turning her back to him as she quickly ran a knuckle beneath each eye to dry the evidence of her dismay. After a quick sniff, she jumped to her feet and crossed to the stove to fetch his coffee.

"You didn't have to walk all this way," she said, desperate to fill the silence. "I would have brought breakfast to you."

"You already do too much for me. 'Sides, I ain't gonna get my strength back if I just laze around all day. I plan to be back on Titan by this time next week."

His words barely registered. Nathaniel's accusations overshadowed them. Without thinking, she reached into the warming oven to grab Luke's plate and burned her fingers.

She cried out softly as she snatched her hand back and curled it against her chest. The plate of flapjacks flung from her grip and clattered to the ground, breaking the dish and tossing pancakes onto the floor. Part of her wanted to collapse on the floor with them and let the tears fall, but she'd already let one person down this morning. She wouldn't compound her error by ruining a second one's breakfast.

"I'm sorry," she mumbled without turning. "There are some leftover flapjacks on the table. They're not as warm, but at least they're not wearing the floor."

Her poor attempt at humor failed, just like everything else this morning.

Then all at once, he was there. Surrounding her. His tall, broad body so close she could feel his warmth. It stole her breath.

He reached for her hand. "Let me see."

Embarrassed at her own ineptitude, she tried to wave him off. "It's fine." In truth, it stung mightily, but she could tell it wasn't serious.

"Damaris." The authority and concern in his tone snatched her attention and stilled her fluttering about the stove. "Give me your hand."

Slowly, she unfurled her arm. His fingers, thick and

callused, gently cupped the back of her hand as he bent over to examine the red marks on her fingertips.

"Let's get some water on this."

He didn't release her hand, just led her to the sink pump and worked the handle until water flowed. He held her fingers under the cool stream, his hand still cupping hers as he pumped the handle with the other to keep the water coming.

How could something so practical feel so . . . intimate? Was it his nearness? The tenderness of his touch? The way their heads bent together over the sink?

Invisible fairies danced over her arms, sending shivers directly into her belly.

It doesn't mean anything. He's just being kind. Taking his turn playing nurse.

Damaris tried to react with practical stoicism. Tried not to infer things he likely didn't mean. But her heart was raw from Nathaniel's ire and the knowledge that he'd been justified in his anger. And no matter how much rose tint she scrubbed from her proverbial glasses, she couldn't imagine Luke taking this kind of care with one of his Horsemen friends or even Nathaniel. It made her feel special. Almost . . . desirable.

So much better than feeling like a failure.

And so much more dangerous.

She tugged her hand away from his and blotted it dry on a towel hanging by the sink. "Thank you." Her voice came out in an embarrassingly breathy whisper. She stiffened her spine along with her resolve. "I'll dab some salve on it after I clean up the breakfast dishes."

"Doesn't look like you ate much yet. Why don't you join

me at the table?" He pulled out her chair and leaned a bit on the ladder back.

Where was his crutch? Had he walked all the way from the barn without it? Damaris pressed her lips together, concern welling in her breast. He was pushing himself too hard.

She lowered herself onto the seat, then surveyed his movement as he rounded the table to sit across from her. He moved gingerly, his limp pronounced. But he didn't look unsteady. On the contrary, he looked quite capable as he grabbed the coffeepot on his way past the stove and hooked a finger through the ear of the mug she'd set on the tray she'd planned to bring to the barn. He snagged the fork and knife from the tray as well, storing them in the front pocket of his shirt, then rounded the table edge and reached his place. Once seated, he poured his coffee, then scooted the entire platter of remaining flapjacks from the center of the table to the spot in front of him. He retrieved the utensils from his pocket, but instead of tucking into the quickly cooling food, he bent his head and closed his eyes.

Catching the action, Damaris quickly did the same.

"Thank you, Lord, for this food, for the hands that prepared it, and for the chance to be alive another day to eat it. I'm mighty grateful for all three. Amen."

Damaris opened her eyes to find his peering directly into hers.

"Now," he said as he reached for the honey and started drizzling it over his massive stack of flapjacks, "why don't you tell me what's got you rattled?" He pointed his fork in her direction. "I'm guessing it has something to do with Nate, since he nearly ran me down on my way in."

Her shoulders slumped. "I'm afraid so."

"Did you have to scold him for something?" Luke jabbed a three-layer bite and stuffed it into his mouth. Apparently oversized bites were a point of masculine pride in Texas.

Damaris cut her own tiny bite, but she didn't lift it to her lips. Her appetite had left with Nathaniel. "No. He scolded me. And I deserved it."

Luke raised a brow. "I find that hard to believe."

She briefly considered eating the bite poised on her fork, if for no other reason than to give herself an excuse to avoid the unpleasant admission of being in the wrong. But she'd never admired characters displaying cowardice or dishonesty in the books she read, and she'd promised herself when she left Missouri that she'd become an admirable heroine like Jane Eyre, Elinor Dashwood, or Jo March while adventuring in Texas. A woman who didn't shrink from challenges but met them with grace and determination. And with honesty.

Her fork returned to her plate untouched.

"I made a promise, then allowed it to slip my mind as if it were nothing of importance. But it *is* important. Very important. Especially to Nathaniel."

Luke didn't seem shocked or horrified, just interested. He fed himself another bite and looked at her with questions in his eyes, waiting for her to explain.

She took a sip of lukewarm tea to fortify herself, then held his gaze and continued. "Do you recall Nathaniel's accusation against Oliver Grimes?"

He gave a short nod as he swallowed. "Hard to forget."

Apparently it wasn't. At least not for her.

"Well, after you brought him home that day, Nathaniel

finally opened up and told me all the reasons he thought Mr. Grimes was responsible for Douglas's death. I promised that the next time I went to town, I'd visit the undertaker, the sheriff, and employees at the mill where Douglas worked to see if I could learn anything about how he died or why he left work early to go to the lake. I owe it to my nephew *and* my brother to discover what answers I can, or at least to make a worthy attempt."

The interest on Luke's face darkened to something resembling displeasure. "You should wait until I can go with you. If someone *did* have a hand in your brother's death, stirring the pot with a bunch of questions is a good way to make yourself a target."

"No one will think it the least bit strange for me to ask questions about Douglas. It's only natural for a sister to wonder about the details of the accident that cost her brother his life. Besides, I excel at being unremarkable." She smiled as she lifted her teacup to her lips. "Most likely, by this time next week, the people I speak to won't even remember our conversation."

He didn't smile at her quip. In fact, he frowned. Glowered, really. As if angry on her behalf. Sweet man. Yet as much as his protectiveness warmed her heart, she wouldn't let it derail her.

Damaris set down her teacup. "I appreciate your concern, Luke. Truly. But I promised Nathaniel I'd look into it, and I intend to keep my word." She dipped her chin. "Now that I've been reminded." She sighed. "I can't believe I forgot."

Luke quirked a half-grin. "Well, you've been a mite busy the last week, tendin' to the fella who had the bad manners to bleed all over your bed."

"I still should have remembered. Nathaniel did. You should have seen his face when he asked what I would be doing in town. It was like he had hope on a tight leash, expecting me to disappoint him. And I did. I have to follow through. For both our sakes."

Luke reached across the table and took hold of her fingers. "I know it ain't my place to interfere, but please promise you'll be careful. If someone is less than forthcoming, don't push too hard for answers. Just gather what information comes easily and bring it back. I can help you sift through it. Nate too. This isn't all on your shoulders."

Damaris blinked back the thin sheen of moisture that crept across her eyes. How long had it been since someone offered to ease her load without trying to dictate how she carried it? She couldn't recall.

Rubbing the edge of his palm with her thumb, she nodded. "I'll be careful. I promise."

Careful in town. *That* she could promise.

Careful with her heart? She'd slid past *careful* the moment he took her hand. Now she was careening toward reckless. Hopefully, she wouldn't find sharp rocks at the bottom of this particular hill, for at her current pace, a crash would leave her shattered.

SEVENTEEN

I t's a right tragedy, what happened to your brother, miss. I was the one who fished him out, you know." Sheriff Conley shook his head. "Nearly fell in myself tryin' to get him into the boat. Good thing Clyde was there to steady us. I mighta ended up swimmin' with the fishes, too." He chuckled, then caught Damaris's eye and stifled his amusement. "Sorry," he mumbled.

Damaris pressed her lips together. Hearing the details of Douglas's death was more difficult than she had expected. She'd thought she'd come to terms with his loss, that enough time had passed to allow her to be objective in this fact-finding mission. Yet listening to the sheriff chronicle his retrieval made her stomach clench and her heart ache.

Focus on the facts. Glean details. Douglas is with Jesus, not in that horrid lake water.

"You said you used a boat to fetch him. How far was he from shore?"

The sheriff gave her a strange look, then scratched his

bearded jaw. He looked to be around fifty. His skin had the tan, creased look of worn leather common in those who worked outdoors, but his potbelly hinted at a tendency for leisure. "Not sure, exactly. Close enough to be spotted by folks walking by, but too far to wade in to get him. Why do you ask?"

Luke's warning about not pushing too hard for information echoed in her mind. She gave the sheriff one of her more insipid smiles, the kind she used to placate Great-Aunt Bertha while paying only half-attention to one of her aunt's long diatribes on the deterioration of society. Some of the sharpness in the sheriff's expression dulled in response.

"I suppose I'm just trying to understand how this accident happened," she said. "I'm sure you can imagine how hard it is to lose a loved one in such a sudden manner. It's taken me months to recover enough from the shock to even consider asking questions. I suppose I'm seeking closure, Sheriff, some way to make sense of things so I can move on."

The lawman leaned forward in his chair, his hands folding across his belly as his expression turned dutifully somber. "Sometimes there ain't no good reason, miss. Just bad luck. Best we can tell, he hit his head on somethin' and fell into the water. Prob'ly out there fishin'."

"Was there a boat near where you found him?"

"Nope. But it was hard to tell how long he'd been there. The wind was blowing pretty good that day, if I recollect properly. Coulda blown the boat to shore somewhere else. After Clyde cleaned Doug up, he noticed some bruises around his face. Woulda been consistent with a fall."

A fall forward. If a man fell out of a boat, wouldn't he fall backward? Unless he was hit from behind. Either way, the damage should have been to the back of his head, not his face.

Damaris wanted to press for more answers, but the sheriff's gaze was beginning to sharpen again. She might be better off dividing her questions between him and the undertaker so neither one would pay too much attention.

She sighed and let her shoulders droop. "I'm sure you're right. It's just so hard to accept that Douglas is gone. But I must, mustn't I?" She gave a little sniff, not at all feigned. Tears were closer to the surface than she wished.

She rose from her chair. Sheriff Conley stood as well and steered her toward the jailhouse door.

"Thank you for your time, Sheriff. And your patience with my questions."

"Not at all, miss." He stopped beside the door and hooked his thumbs into his gun belt. "I'm glad I could help put your mind to rest."

Her mind was far from being at rest, but she didn't let on. Just offered him another insipid smile and wished him a good day as she stepped into the sunshine.

She followed Sheriff Conley's directions to the local carpentry shop two streets over where Clyde Weathers displayed rough-hewn tables and chairs alongside the pine boxes he kept on hand for his undertaking business. The careless mixture of items for the living and the dead made the separation of the two states seem dangerously fragile, as if one could pass from chair to coffin at any moment.

She supposed one could. Douglas had.

The thought sobered her even as it hardened her resolve.

If Douglas had been pushed into death, she needed to know who was responsible. Not just to provide justice for her brother, but to provide protection for Nathaniel. If the culprit was after the land, a new Baxter stood in his way now. One equally disinclined to sell.

Damaris pushed open the door and entered the shop, a prayer on her heart. *Show me the truth, Lord.*

An overhead bell clanged as she closed the door behind her. She wandered to the side of the room dedicated to furniture, carefully turning her back on the coffins leaning against the opposite wall. The dining set she came to first appeared sturdy and functional, but it lacked style. No spindled legs or carved designs. No craftsmanship. Of course, she was accustomed to the offerings found in a large city. Perhaps tastes ran simpler in Texas.

"Can I help you?" A thin man with dark hair and pale skin stepped through a curtained doorway, flakes of sawdust stuck to his clothing.

Damaris turned and offered a smile. "Mr. Weathers?"

"Last I checked." He offered no smile in return.

Not exactly a salesman, was he? Utilitarian with no frills. Like his furniture. Perhaps instead of being a carpenter who took on the duties of an undertaker when the need arose, he was actually an undertaker who made furniture to make ends meet.

Crossing the floor to meet the gruff fellow halfway, Damaris dropped her smile in favor of a more solemn expression. "My name is Damaris Baxter. Douglas Baxter was my brother. I understand you were the one who tended him."

"That's right." He brushed a bit of sawdust from his sleeve. "Helped the sheriff pull him out of the lake, too."

"I appreciate the care you took preparing him for burial."

She had no idea if Douglas had been laid out properly or not. By the time she'd learned of his passing, the burial had already taken place. Yet at her compliment, a bit of warmth finally seeped into the undertaker's eyes.

"Not many folks think about the work entailed with undertakin'. Buildin' the coffin, diggin' the grave, makin' sure the deceased is presentable for meetin' his Maker. It's God's work, you know. Givin' the departed a bit of dignity in death."

"I'm sure it is." Though talking about it was making her queasy. She pressed a hand against her midsection, hoping the pressure would stop the churning within. "I was wondering if I might prevail upon your expertise and ask you a few questions."

He glanced toward the window, as if gauging the likelihood of another customer walking through the door. "I s'pose I can spare a minute or two." He gestured toward the dining set she'd been inspecting earlier and then, as if just remembering his manners, hurried ahead of her and pulled out one of the chairs. "Have a seat."

"Thank you."

He lowered himself into a second chair, then crossed his arms over his chest and leaned backward as if bracing for an inquisition. "Shoot."

"I spoke with the sheriff a few minutes ago, and he mentioned that my brother's face was bruised. Do you think he might have been in some kind of altercation before he drowned?"

"Ya mean, like a fight?"

"Yes."

A thoughtful look crossed Mr. Weathers's face. "It's possible. I noticed some other bruises and scrapes on his chest when I changed him into his burial clothes."

Damaris's heart pounded, and a knot formed in her belly.

The undertaker shrugged. "Although, them scratches coulda come from him tryin' to pull himself back into the boat after he fell out."

"But if he were conscious and able to grab for a boat, he wouldn't have drowned. My brother was an excellent swimmer."

"Maybe, but I doubt he was used to swimmin' with his boots on. Them things fill with water and weigh a man down. And if he were weak from a knock on the head, well . . ."

Her throbbing pulse slowed. His explanation made sense. But there was still the matter of the missing boat. Surely if Douglas had been fishing, as the sheriff surmised, they would have found a boat somewhere in his vicinity.

Damaris eyed the man across from her. He might not be the most polished fellow around, but he seemed to know his trade. "Besides the scratches, did you notice anything else odd after pulling Douglas from the lake? Any lumps on his head? There must be a reason he fell out of the boat. Some injury that incapacitated him to such an extent that he was unable to recover."

Mr. Weathers uncrossed his arms and leaned forward. "You think there was someone else in the boat, don't ya? Someone who fought yer brother, then tossed him over the side and left him to drown."

"I-I don't know. . . ." Damaris stammered, but the undertaker didn't seem to notice. His gaze turned introspective, as if he were too taken with the puzzle to worry about his company.

"It'd explain the missin' boat," he mumbled as he rubbed his chin. After a moment, however, his expression soured back into a frown. "But there weren't no lumps on his skull. No dents, neither." He slapped his palms against his knees and looked her in the eye. "I can't tell ya how yer brother ended up in the lake, miss, but I can tell ya what *didn't* happen. No one bashed his head in. His noggin was fully intact when we dragged him out."

"Well, I suppose that's some small comfort."

So why didn't she feel comforted in the slightest? She should be glad her brother hadn't suffered the pain of a horrible injury prior to his death. Yet he was still gone. And she had no explanation as to why. If he hadn't fought with someone, how had he ended up in the lake? And where was the boat? And why did he leave work early? She might not have known her brother well, but she knew he believed in hard work and providing for his family. The only reason he might have left early to fish would be if he had planned a special afternoon for Nathaniel. Yet Nathaniel knew nothing about a fishing trip. It just didn't make any sense.

Damaris rose to her feet and offered the undertaker a small smile. "Thank you for your time, Mr. Weathers. And thank you, again, for tending to my brother."

He nodded as he pushed to his feet, but his face already exhibited distraction. A common reaction to her departure, as people turned their thoughts to more interesting pursuits. Like sawdust.

As Damaris reached the door, however, Mr. Weathers surprised her by calling after her.

"Miss Baxter?"

She turned her head. "Yes?"

"There was one more thing I noticed that seemed a bit odd about your brother."

She dropped her hand from the door handle and pivoted more fully. "Oh? What was that?"

"I found a piece of straw in his mouth." He shrugged as he said it. "Prob'ly don't mean nothin', but I remember thinkin' it strange."

"That *is* strange." A man might chew on a piece of straw if it were at hand while he worked in a barn or a haymow. But in the middle of a lake? "Thank you for telling me."

The undertaker nodded, and Damaris turned to go.

"Miss Baxter?"

She glanced back, surprised to see a touch of softness in the gruff man's eyes.

"I'm sorry fer yer loss."

She'd heard that sentiment dozens of times since coming to Madisonville from churchgoers, merchants, and anyone else she had reason to introduce herself to. All well-meaning and kind, but none of those polite sympathies rang as true as the one coming from this man in this moment.

Clyde Weathers dealt with death all the time. She'd thought it had hardened him, but looking at him now, she wondered if perhaps that crusty shell was just an armor he wore to protect himself.

Her eyes growing damp, Damaris blinked quickly to dry them. "Thank you," she murmured softly as she ducked her head and reached again for the door.

He made no effort to halt her this time, and she soon found herself outside, breathing fresh air and staring at a world awash in sunshine. A group of boys ran across the street. A small dog gave chase. A pair of ladies stood outside the milliner's window two doors down, exclaiming over a new design. A farmer's wagon rolled past, supplies piled up in the bed behind the driver.

Everything was blessedly normal. And somehow, the ordinariness of it all gave her the stability she needed to square her shoulders and continue her mission.

Until she pivoted to her right and came face-to-face with the man she least wanted to see—Oliver Grimes.

EIGHTEEN

Mr. Grimes's eyebrows shot up to hide behind his hat brim when he spotted Damaris. His gaze darted from her to the door she'd just exited.

"Miss Baxter. You're not here on . . . official business, are you? Surely Davenport hasn't passed. Hanger led me to believe he was expected to recover."

"Oh. No. Mr. Davenport is still with us," she assured him, relief spearing through her belly at the realization that he hadn't divined her true purpose in visiting the undertaker. "He's actually out of bed and hobbling around. Gaining strength every day."

She might be painting Luke's health in slightly overgenerous terms, but it seemed unwise for Grimes to believe she and Nathaniel were unprotected. Just in case her neighbor had any nefarious schemes in mind. Besides, she had a feeling that if Luke could stand, he would fight, and fight hard.

Grimes let out a breath. "I'm glad to hear it. My brother

would never forgive me if my troubles caused the death of one of his beloved Horsemen."

"Your brother knows the Horsemen?"

Grimes nodded. "Served under Captain Hanger in the 7th Cavalry. It took a good deal of wheedlin' on my part to convince Wilson to write to his captain on my behalf. They're supposed to be retired from this kind of work, but I was losin' cattle right and left and too desperate to be deterred. I thought God had answered my prayers when Davenport showed up. Then the big fella went and got stabbed all to pieces, and I'm back where I started."

Any sympathy she might have felt for her neighbor's predicament vanished the instant he made it clear he cared more for his cows than for the man he'd hired to protect them.

"Have you lost more cattle, Mr. Grimes?"

"Not yet, but those criminals are still on the loose. They could come back at any time."

She tapped her toe against the boardwalk, her agitation too high to contain. "I'd still say you are in a much better position now than you were prior to Mr. Davenport's arrival. Not only do you know how many rustlers you are dealing with, but you have a physical description of the guilty parties. Information you'd be missing were it not for the Horseman you hired. It's likely the rustlers have abandoned the area completely thanks to their encounter with Mr. Davenport, so you are most decidedly *not* back where you started."

He looked stunned that she dared contradict him. She was rather stunned herself. Avoiding confrontation had always been her preferred path. She'd swallowed her pride so many times, all the edges had been worn smooth. Had his discontent been aimed at her, she would have dipped her chin and meekly accepted whatever criticism he dealt, letting it roll off her back as usual. But when he spoke of Luke with callous disregard, something stirred inside her. Something righteous and indignant that could not be ignored.

Mr. Grimes didn't seem particularly impressed with her show of spirit, however. His shock quickly gave way to displeasure. "I might have more information now, but I still don't have my beeves, do I? Davenport wasn't just supposed to catch the rustlers, Miss Baxter. He was supposed to retrieve my cattle. And thanks to your brat of a nephew, he failed on both counts."

Red-hot anger roared through Damaris like a forest fire as she fought the unladylike urge to kick Grimes in the shin with the pointed toe of her shoe. "I'll thank you not to slur my nephew, sir." She squeezed the words out through the crevices of her clenched teeth. "Now, if you'll excuse me, I have supplies to gather at the mercantile."

Leaving him on the boardwalk, she swept down the steps into the street and strode away as fast as she could without actually running. However, it wasn't merely anger that drove her. Fear propelled her as well.

Had Grimes shared his suspicions about Nathaniel with the sheriff? The lawman hadn't spoken of it when she'd visited the jailhouse earlier. Was that because he didn't deem the charge worthy of merit or because he didn't want her cognizant of a secret investigation? And what about Grimes himself? Had he killed Douglas? Would he target Nathaniel next? Grimes certainly held no fondness for her nephew. Was that due to his certainty that Nathaniel was responsible for the recent rash of pranks on his property, or was a deeper animosity at work?

Her thoughts distracted her so thoroughly that she completed her shopping, had the wagon loaded, and sat perched on the bench with reins in hand before she recalled that she still needed to visit the mill. Unfortunately, she hadn't yet learned her way around town well enough to know precisely where to find it. She recognized the businesses that made up the courthouse square, and she could find her way to the church on Price Street without Nathaniel's direction now, but she hadn't explored much beyond those two landmarks.

To be honest, she wasn't even sure what a grist mill looked like. She'd always pictured something idyllic by a stream with a waterwheel, but she'd seen nothing like that in Madisonville. Nathaniel had mentioned that a steam engine powered the mill, not a waterwheel. For all she knew, she could have driven past it a dozen times without realizing it.

Letting out a sigh, she reset the wagon's brake and climbed down from the driver's seat. Too embarrassed to go back inside the mercantile to ask for directions, she chose instead to cross the street to the Feed & Seed that stood next door to the livery. Vanity, not practicality, dictated her choice. She hated giving people reason to doubt her intelligence. She could tolerate a poor opinion of her looks, her deportment, her cooking, even her singing voice, but she took pride in being a woman of learning. If taking a few extra steps allowed her to preserve a piece of that pride, she'd gladly stretch her legs.

"Miss Baxter!"

A jolt passed through Damaris at the sound of her name, so unaccustomed was she to being hailed. Her step slowed as she raised her head and turned, searching for the source of the call.

"Miss Baxter!"

A man in a light gray suit waved as he jogged toward her. She squinted until his face came into focus. Mr. Mullins? Why would her brother's lawyer be flagging her down in such an urgent manner? She'd thought their business completed weeks ago with the creation of Nathaniel's trust and the legal arrangement of her guardianship of her brother's property and accounts. Had he found another paper for her to sign? She slowed in front of the Feed & Seed and awaited his arrival.

The lawyer was younger than she'd expected. She still recalled the surprise of finding him free of the gray hair and paunchy middle she'd always associated with men of his trade. Silly, really. Old lawyers had to have been young lawyers once upon a time, didn't they? And where better to get one's start than in a place offering little to no competition for legal services?

Mr. Mullins's office had sported fine furnishings and a set of lovely matching walnut book cabinets that she'd instantly envied. Even knowing they were filled with uninteresting law tomes couldn't dim her appreciation. He spoke with a cultured voice, wore tailored suits, and his blond mustache and beard boasted the craftsmanship of a skilled barber. Abundant proof that a young man of ambition could nurture a successful law practice even in a small Texas town.

He slowed his approach as he neared, then tipped his hat with a grin. "So glad I caught you, ma'am. It will save me from having to make a trip out to your place." A sheepish look softened his features. "I should have paid a call before now to see how you were settling in. I worry about you living out there on your own so far from town. A delicate woman such as yourself must be unused to the wilds of Texas. Forgive my neglect."

His intentions might be kindly meant, but his assumption that she wouldn't be able to handle herself rankled. Nevertheless, Damaris pasted on a smile. "There's nothing to forgive, Mr. Mullins. I'm managing quite well. And I'm not on my own. I have Nathaniel. He might be young, but he knows his way around the property."

"Of course, he does." The curled ends of the lawyer's waxed mustache twitched slightly as his countenance brightened. "Do you have a few minutes, Miss Baxter? There is a matter of business I need to discuss with you. It won't take long. I promise."

Damaris hesitated. She'd been away from home long enough as it was and still had the mill to visit. Yet she didn't particularly care for the idea of him dropping by unannounced to check on her. Especially not while Luke was there. Unflattering rumors often started with less. Mr. Mullins might not be one to jump to conclusions or to gossip about suppositions, but she didn't know him well enough to be sure. It might be best to get whatever business he wished to discuss over and done with while she was in town. Besides, he could provide directions to the mill as easily as anyone else. And in a more private setting.

"I suppose I can spare a few minutes."

"Excellent!" He sketched a shallow bow. "Let's repair to my office, shall we?"

Turning back the way he had come, he led her down Trinity

Street, then crossed the square to the redbrick courthouse that was still under construction. The building would be a beauty when finished. Most of it had been completed already in a lovely Romanesque Revival style that reminded her of some of the churches back in St. Louis. It was a grand sight, standing three stories tall, covered in stately brick with a plethora of arched windows. A clock tower stretched toward the sky from the center of the building and, when finished, was sure to be as grand as any church spire.

Mr. Mullins held the door open for her as they stepped inside, and then they climbed the stairs to the second story and his office located on the southeast corner. As Damaris followed him inside, light filtered through the many windows lining the exterior walls. The sunlight should have warmed her, but she found herself rubbing her arms.

This was the first place she'd come after arriving in Madisonville. The place where she'd learned the details about Douglas's death and obtained directions for finding Nathaniel. The place she'd made a legal commitment to care for her nephew, putting on paper what she'd already vowed to do in her heart.

Instead of watching Mr. Mullins take his seat behind the desk and riffle through his papers, Damaris studied the walnut cabinets behind him, focusing on the rows and rows of books on display as if they were old friends waiting to comfort her. A silly bit of nonsense, to be sure, but it helped dispel the chill left by unpleasant memories.

"Ah, here it is." Mr. Mullins looked up from his papers and smiled at her. "I've received a new offer for your land. Fifty percent more than the figure you turned down last month.

I know you said you weren't interested in selling, but this particular buyer is quite determined. To be honest, the price they are offering is more than the property is worth. If you and your nephew are set on remaining in Madison County, you could buy other land in the area and still have a handsome sum left over."

She started shaking her head, fully intending to keep her promise to Nathaniel not to sell, but Mr. Mullins raised a hand to forestall her refusal.

He leaned across the desk and lowered his voice. "I hate to be indelicate, Miss Baxter, but with no source of income, how long do you think you can provide for your nephew? You've yet to experience a Texas winter. Not even the most fruitful garden will produce enough canned goods to see you through." He leaned back in his chair and let out a sigh. "I was hoping that enough time had passed for the shock of Douglas's death to have worn off and for reality to have set in. One must be practical, after all, when one is in charge of another's well-being." His brown eyes softened with regret. "I'm afraid sentiment won't keep Nathaniel's belly full."

"I have a little money of my own put aside, Mr. Mullins," Damaris said as she shifted in her seat. The chair that had been perfectly comfortable a moment ago seemed to have sprouted stinging nettles from its upholstery. "We won't starve this winter."

Though she really couldn't say what future winters would hold. Douglas had put aside a small nest egg, but without his regular income, there was no telling how long that would last. She'd been so focused on tending to Nathaniel's immediate needs and helping him through his grief that she hadn't given much thought to their future. Perhaps Nathaniel could find work in town. Something he could do after school. Or maybe she could sell some of her embroidery or take in mending. She should speak to the local dressmaker, see if—

"What of next winter?" Mr. Mullins broke into her thoughts. "And the winter after that? I don't mean to be cruel, Miss Baxter, but I wouldn't consider myself a Christian if I didn't warn you of the dangers that lie ahead. Dangers that can be avoided with a little wisdom and forward thinking." He slid a paper across the desktop to face her. It contained a number that made her breath catch. "An offer like this doesn't come around very often, ma'am. If you turn it down this time, I can all but guarantee there'll be no third chance."

Her fingers trembled as she touched the bottom corner of the page. Was she being foolish, letting sentiment overrule practicality? Was she so concerned about Nathaniel liking her that pleasing him in the short term took precedence over feeding him for the long term?

She withdrew her hand from the paper. No. She'd made a promise, and she aimed to keep it. They could always return to St. Louis for a year or two if they became destitute. Then, when Nathaniel was grown, he could return to his land and do with it whatever he wished.

"I'm sorry, Mr. Mullins. Your advice is sound, but I've promised my nephew that I won't sell his land to Oliver Grimes. No matter how large the offer, I must decline."

"But, Miss Baxter," he said, leaning again across the table as he slid the paper a few inches closer to her, "this offer is *not* from Oliver Grimes."

Her gaze dropped back to the page. This time instead of

focusing on the number in the center of the page, she studied the printed heading at the top. A company's name stood out in bold font—*Harbinger Land Development Company.* Out of Austin, Texas.

Not Oliver Grimes.

Her head swam as implications and possibilities flew at her from every angle. Heaven help her. There were *two* people trying to buy Nathaniel's land.

— CHAPTER —
NINETEEN

W here's Aunt Maris?"

Luke looked away from the stove, where he was warming a pot of beans, to peer at the boy who'd finally decided to put in an appearance. A frown wrinkled Nate's brow as he slouched against the kitchen doorjamb. Luke had figured the kid would show up in time to eat the noon meal. If a growing boy could be counted on for anything, it was eating. Which was why he'd let himself into the house and thrown together a quick luncheon when he realized Damaris would be delayed in town.

Besides, it was past time he and Nate had a conversation about the boy's behavior toward his aunt.

Luke held Nate's gaze as he answered. "She's still in town."

Nate straightened away from the wall, his eyes widening slightly. "She should be home by now. Don't take more'n a couple of hours to fetch supplies."

"You know she's doin' more than just fetchin' supplies." Luke raised a brow. "After that temper tantrum you threw this mornin', did you really think she wasn't gonna do everything in her power to make things right by you?"

Nate said nothing, but his glare returned.

Luke did his best to bank his own temper, but it had been on a low simmer ever since Damaris left that morning. His worry over her didn't help matters. So many things could go wrong during an investigation. Suspicions could be raised. Guilty parties could sniff out trouble and decide to eliminate it before it could bite them. The longer she was gone, the tighter the knot pulled in his gut.

He jammed his spoon back into the beans and stirred, muttering under his breath, "You got no idea how lucky you are, kid."

"Lucky?" Nate's voice rose in disbelief. "To have my pa killed by some greedy land-grabber? To barely even remember my ma?"

Wood scraped harshly against wood as Nate yanked a chair away from the table and launched it toward the wall. One of the legs broke free of the seat, leaving the chair listing drunkenly. Only the smallest hint of remorse touched the kid's face before the belligerence took over.

Luke pointed his bean spoon at the damaged chair. "After we eat, you're gonna fix that."

Nate's frown darkened.

Luke's voice brooked no argument. "I'll help, but you're fixin' it, hopefully before your aunt gets home."

"Why do you care?"

Luke turned away from the stove to face Nate straight on. "Why do you *not*?"

Nate blinked a few times, then dropped his chin to stare at the floor.

"Life has dealt you some serious blows, Nate. I ain't dismissin' your wounds. They're as real as the gashes those rustlers stabbed into my hide. They hurt and will take time to heal. But you can't let that pain blind you to your blessings."

"Right." The sarcasm dripping from that word was so thick, Luke wouldn't have been surprised to see a puddle forming at the kid's feet.

Making a grab for the patience that was quickly slipping through his fingers, Luke took a second to breathe, then came at the issue from a different angle.

"All right," he challenged, "let's look at the night of my stabbing."

The kid's face hardened, but he met Luke's gaze.

Deciding to take that as permission to continue, Luke dove in. "Was I lucky to be cut up by a gang of rustlers and left for dead? No. But I *was* lucky that the kid I rescued had enough honor to go for help. Lucky that the boy's aunt was willing to leave her bed in the middle of the night to fetch me and tend my wounds. Lucky to have a Horseman brother with a doc for a wife who traveled over two hundred miles to ensure I'd recover. Even in the middle of the worst pain I ever experienced, God was raining blessings down all around me. But I woulda missed 'em if I'd been too consumed with my own hurt to look around."

Speaking of hurt, Luke's leg had started throbbing. Standing still seemed to hurt more than moving, for some reason. He shifted his weight to find some level of relief but held his position. Nate needed to hear him. He'd stand here all day if he had to.

"I know what it's like to have anger running so hot through

your veins that you can't see anything else. It poisons you. Hardens your heart until you stop caring about anyone or anything. It would've destroyed me if God hadn't intervened. He stuck me in the army. Put me in Matt's unit. Broke me down little by little until the blinders finally fell off my eyes, letting me see God's goodness again. A goodness that had been there all along.

"Kinda like your Aunt Maris. You could've been shipped off to Missouri after your pa died, but instead, your Aunt Maris left her home to come here. She cooks for you, washes your clothes, helps you with your schoolin'. She puts up with your crabby attitude, forgives your mischief, and is always ready with a kind word. She loves you, Nate. Not everybody has that. I didn't when I was your age. So, yes, in my book, you're a very lucky kid."

Nate said nothing, but Luke didn't mind. The boy had a lot to chew on, and he wouldn't be able to swallow truth in the big chunk Luke had just handed out. He'd have to break it down into bite-sized pieces and digest it over time.

Luke gave the kid some space and turned back to the stove to collect the bean pot he'd nearly forgotten. Hoping nothing had burned at the bottom, he hobbled two steps to the table, plunked the pot down on the cast-iron trivet in the center, then gestured toward one of the still-standing chairs on the opposite side.

"Take a seat. I'll dish it up."

Nate hesitated, and for a moment Luke thought he might refuse, but the boy's stomach overrode his obstinance.

Luke unstacked a pair of shallow soup bowls, then broke off a hunk of Damaris's leftover skillet corn bread and dropped half of it into each bowl. The bread was dry as all get-out, but if he crumbled it and poured the beans over the top, it'd be tolerable.

"Rib-stickin' food," Luke said as he placed a bowl in front of Nate and handed him a spoon. "That's what our old mess cook would call this. He claimed that fancy vittles would never keep a soldier's belly full through a day of drills. A cavalryman needed food that stuck to his ribs."

Nate frowned down at the bowl but dug his spoon in anyway. "I ain't in the cavalry," he mumbled before shoving in a bite.

"Maybe not," Luke conceded, "but now that I can get around without my crutch, I was hoping you might be willing to spar with me. Help me build my strength with some sword and combat drills."

Nate's chin came up. His eyes widened in his face, and for once they were free of insolence. "You'd teach me to fight?"

Luke hid a smile, remembering his own eagerness to jump into manhood at that age. He schooled his features into a stern line. "I'll teach you to *spar*. There's a difference."

Fighting might seem glorious to a boy who felt powerless to control his own life, but Luke had learned the hard way that fighting, even for a just cause, extracted a price. But if Luke could focus Nate's aggression and frustration in a positive direction, maybe the kid would quit funneling them into revenge plots and pranks against his aunt.

Luke caught a hint of a smile playing at the boy's lips before Nate covered up the evidence by shoving another bite of beans into his mouth.

Propping his elbows on the table and lacing his fingers

together over his bowl, Luke gave Nate a meaningful glance. "Forget something?"

Nate's chewing slowed, and he set down his spoon.

Luke nodded in approval, then closed his eyes. "Lord, we thank thee for food to eat and a friend to share it with. Amen."

Nate scooped up another spoonful, but he cast a cautious glance at Luke. "Friend, huh? Is that what we are now?"

Luke shrugged. "Don't see why not. I saved your life. You saved mine. That kind of thing bonds cavalrymen. Figured it might as well bond us, too." He took a bite of bean mush, his heart thumping in his chest as he tried to gauge Nate's receptiveness. He took a couple of chews. "If your dance card ain't full up, that is."

Nate fiddled with his spoon, then gave his own shrug. "I might have some room."

"Good. Then it's settled." Luke extended his hand across the table.

Nate looked at it, then slowly straightened in his chair before reaching his arm out to clasp Luke's hand.

Something wrapped around Luke's chest as they shook. Something that felt an awful lot like purpose. As if everything he'd gone through in his life had prepared him for this moment.

The realization terrified as much as it energized.

He met Nate's gaze and dipped his chin in an unspoken promise to have the boy's back, come what may.

Nate nodded in return. The pact was made.

No other words seemed necessary as they each finished off their beans and corn bread. Nate finished first. He carried his bowl to the dry sink, then stopped to eye the chair he'd broken.

"I'll fetch my pa's toolbox."

Luke nodded as Nate pushed open the back door. "I'll be here when you get back."

The door swung closed, and Luke's thoughts turned heavenward.

I don't know how much time you're plannin' on givin' me with these folks, God, but whatever time I got, help me make a difference in that boy's life.

For that boy had already made a difference in his.

TWENTY

Damaris ran so many mental circles on the drive home from town that she was exhausted by the time she rolled into the yard. She set the brake and just sat for a moment on the wagon bench, eyes closed, praying for the Lord to grant her enough energy to climb down without toppling face-first into the dirt. Hopefully, once her feet planted themselves on solid ground, she'd find the strength to unhitch the horses and tote the supplies into the house.

"Glad to see you made it back."

Surprisingly, the low, husky voice didn't startle her. It melted into her instead, like butter into toast. Soothing the charred, dry crevices inside and softening muscles that had hardened from hours of chasing elusive answers and battling growing suspicions.

Odd how the simple reminder that she wasn't alone eased the weight of her burden.

She dipped her head, slightly embarrassed to be caught sitting in a wagon with her eyes closed. Yet opening them to find Luke Davenport gazing up at her with genuine solicitude in his more-green-than-blue hazel eyes diluted the chagrin.

"I'd offer to help you down, but I'm probably more liability than asset at the moment." True regret tinged his voice as his attention drifted down to her waist and lingered.

Good heavens. Was he actually imagining where his hands would fit? Damaris warmed at the thought, and her pulse thrummed at a slightly higher velocity.

Men had helped her from wagons before. It was an act of practicality and chivalry, an innocent maneuver designed to speed a lady's descent. If a gentleman offered assistance, she accepted. Otherwise, she scrambled down on her own. Nothing to contemplate or ponder. Yet here she sat doing both. Pondering the possibility that a man like Luke Davenport might actually find something about her attractive enough that he would seek an excuse to touch her. And contemplating the keen sense of disappointment spearing through her at the realization that she wouldn't be feeling his hands close around her waist. Nor would she have an excuse to place her own palms atop his exceptionally broad shoulders. Or hover above the earth for a wisp of a moment with nothing touching her but him.

"Damaris?" Luke stepped closer to the wagon and braced his hand on the footboard near her shoe. "Are you all right?"

She blinked in an effort to focus on reality. "I'm fine." Or she would be as soon as she emptied her brain of the romantic twaddle swimming around her cerebellum like pickling liquid. A dangerous concoction that demanded immediate remedy. One couldn't *un*pickle a cucumber, after all. Once the damage was done, there was no going back to one's original, sensible state.

Don't lose your head over a man who's going to leave.

Damaris pushed to her feet and plastered a quick smile on her face. "Things took longer than I anticipated in town, and I fear I'm a little tired."

Not to mention that she hadn't eaten more than a few bites today. After her confrontation with Nathaniel, she'd had no appetite and no desire to delay further when she could be setting matters right. Was it any wonder she was falling prey to fanciful notions? After a hot cup of tea and some sustenance, she'd be back to her old self.

Unless Luke kept looking at her as he was now. Concern etched his features as he peered up at her, his gaze searching her face as if she were a painting and he a collector determined to examine every brushstroke for insight and meaning.

Rather unsettling to a lady used to drawing no more notice than a passing glance from gentlemen. Completely ill-equipped to handle such attention, much less make an accurate assessment of what it might mean, Damaris took refuge in practicality. Turning her back on the man threatening her equilibrium, she concentrated on handholds and foot placement as she climbed down. It didn't help her already throbbing pulse when Luke made no effort to back away and allow her a comfortable cushion of space in which to descend. He stayed right where he was, mere inches from the wagon seat. And when he placed his hand lightly upon her back as she dismounted, her shoe nearly slipped from the wheel spoke.

Thankfully, she made it to the ground without incident, though she found it amazingly difficult to face him again. Not because of any particular shyness on her part, but because it would mean removing her back from the touch of his hand.

With a stern mental reminder to act her age and leave the schoolgirl swooning to those still young enough to be in school, Damaris turned to face him. Before she could think of anything halfway intelligent to say, however, he relieved her of the need.

"I'll see to the horses," he said as his hand fell back to his side. "Go rest for a spell. I'll get Nate to unload the supplies."

"Nathaniel's home?" She twisted her neck to search the yard for evidence of her nephew. Usually he didn't show up until mealtime.

Lunch!

Oh dear. Luke and Nathaniel must be starving.

"I'm sorry I'm so late getting back. I'll get something on for lunch right away." Lunch at three in the afternoon? "Or maybe I'll just make a big early supper."

"No need," Luke said as he patted the horse nearest him and reached for a harness buckle. "The boy and I ate at noon."

"You did?"

Luke chuckled softly. "Don't sound so surprised. I never would have made it to the ripe old age of thirty-three if I hadn't figured out how to feed myself when there weren't a woman handy to do it for me." He leaned close and lowered his voice to a rumbly rasp. "Don't tell anyone, but entire battalions of soldiers have been known to stay fed and watered for months without a woman within a hundred miles." His eyes danced with humor. "We fellas like to keep the truth hushed up 'cause we much prefer eatin' cookin' that ain't our own, but we're not completely helpless in the kitchen."

Damaris grinned, the last vestiges of her guilt swept away

by his teasing. "I'll not tell a soul," she vowed in a dramatic murmur, barely able to suppress the giggle tickling her throat.

"Whatcha whisperin' about, Aunt Maris?"

Her nephew's question sounded more like an accusation, pointed and barbed. Well, at least she knew where he was now.

Damaris flushed slightly as she pivoted, her lighthearted mood dampening at his scowl.

"You found out somethin' about Pa, didn't ya?" Nathaniel marched forward, his face a mixture of hurt and anger. "Whatever it is, I deserve to know." He shot a heated glance at Luke before returning his focus to her. "No secrets."

Damaris immediately stepped away from Luke and laid a hand on her nephew's shoulder. "I'd never keep something like that from you, Nathaniel. We weren't talking about your father, I promise. Luke was just assuring me that the two of you hadn't starved while I was away. I thought I might have to whip up some eggs to keep your stomach from collapsing in on itself, but it seems there's no danger of immediate implosion."

She smiled, hoping Luke's example of teasing good humor into a person worked as well on suspicious boys as it did on spinster aunts.

Nathaniel's posture relaxed slightly, and a wry quirk of his lips gave her hope that trust had been restored. "He fed me army food. It didn't taste like much," he said with a gibing glance at Luke, "but he was right about it sticking to my ribs." He wrapped an arm around his midsection. "I've been guzzlin' water all afternoon, and I still ain't managed to wash it down."

"I told him marching was the only cure." Luke looked up

from the harness strap he was folding out of the way and winked. "An hour of drilling around the paddock perimeter woulda cleared him right up, but he wasn't interested. Can't imagine why not."

Nathaniel rolled his eyes and groaned, but a smile lit his expression.

Luke was good for him. Understood him in a way Damaris couldn't. A tiny part of her felt excluded from that connection and wished she could find a way to join. But a larger part of her rejoiced that God was bringing blessing to a boy who desperately needed it. If connecting with Luke drew Nathaniel away from the dangerous precipice he'd been flirting with of late, the pain of watching her Horseman ride away one day would be worth it.

Her Horseman? Oh, heavens. That didn't bode well. She readily admitted to admiring Luke and feeling a greater-than-usual attraction to him. It was only natural to feel a kinship with the man she'd nursed back from the brink of death. But to think of him as hers? *Not wise, Damaris. Not wise at all.*

Unfortunately, banishing her feelings for him was not an option. They were sprouting far too fast to cut down. And if she were honest with herself, she'd have to admit that she didn't want to cut them down. They made her feel alive in a way she'd not experienced before. As long as she kept reminding herself that his being in her life was temporary, she'd be able to handle the loss when it came.

"Aunt Maris?"

At the sound of her name, she shook free of her thoughts and quickly tried to piece together the bits of conversation that had floated around her while she'd been woolgathering.

"Sorry, yes. You can leave the crates on the table. I'll put the supplies away."

Nathaniel nodded and moved around to the back of the wagon to grab the first box.

"Oh, and Nathaniel?"

He paused and looked up at her.

"I did learn several things about your father today."

His eyes darkened, and a muscle in his jaw clenched.

Damaris held his gaze, silently vowing to be his ally no matter what the future held. "After dinner, I'll tell you everything. And maybe between the three of us," she said as she tossed a quick glance in Luke's direction, "we can start to make sense of what really happened that day. All right?"

Nathaniel gripped the crate in front of him, his fingers flexing and unflexing. All at once, his grip and face hardened. He dipped his chin in a sharp nod, then dragged the box out of the wagon and marched it toward the house.

Luke listened to Damaris recount the details of her investigation while sipping his after-dinner coffee, impressed by her instincts and intelligence. He'd known she was educated, but he'd thought her bookish and naïve. Not the sort to question an undertaker about injuries on a body or a sheriff about missing boats. But there was nothing naïve about her logic nor her ability to ferret out information from a variety of sources. She could work for the Pinkertons if she wasn't so dedicated to raising her nephew.

"Just because my pa didn't have any dents or cracks in his head don't mean there weren't someone else there," Nate insisted after Damaris related the undertaker's response to her fight theory. He banged the flat of his hand against the tabletop and raised a few inches off his seat. "Someone coulda pushed him out of the boat, then held his head underwater when he tried to get back in."

Damaris fiddled with her teacup, twisting it back and forth within the divot of her saucer, her expression more thoughtful than provoked by her nephew's outburst. "I hadn't considered that scenario. That's a solid possibility. It wouldn't explain the straw, though."

Luke sat forward. "Straw? What straw?"

She blinked twice, as if she'd forgotten he was in the room. Not terribly flattering to his ego, but she did tend to lose awareness of her surroundings when she was in the middle of a good ponder. It had happened earlier today too, by the wagon. He'd wanted to see if he could draw some of those ponderings out after Nate traipsed into the house, but she hadn't given him the chance. She'd followed on Nate's heels, pausing only long enough to thank him for seeing to the horses.

"The undertaker mentioned finding a piece of straw in Douglas's mouth," Damaris said, her eyes once again clear and bright. "It struck me as odd." She turned back to Nate. "I don't recall Douglas being one who liked to chew on straw. Was that a habit he picked up in Texas?"

Nate shook his head. "Nope. I never saw him chew on nothin' besides food. What do ya think it means?"

Damaris sighed and leaned back in her chair. "I have no idea. I suppose it must mean there was straw around when he died. Maybe it was floating in the lake? Or lying in the bottom of his boat?"

Luke tapped the side of his thumb against the rim of his coffee mug. "Or on the killer."

Damaris and Nate both turned to look at him.

"Things get messy in a struggle," he said with a shrug. "Blood, dirt, sweat. After a fight, you got as much of the other fella's mess on you as you do your own."

"So you admit my pa was murdered?" Nate's tone was weighed down with defensiveness, but his eyes pleaded for affirmation.

"I admit there's a whole lot that don't add up about the way your pa died. From what you and your aunt have told me, he doesn't sound like the kind of man to shirk work for a fishin' trip. Which means something else was afoot. Something that likely entailed foul play. Whether that interference was on purpose or accidental, we don't yet know."

"Actually," Damaris said, her voice low and intent, "I think we do."

— CHAPTER —
TWENTY-ONE

Luke's gut tightened the way it did before a battle. Damaris had learned something. Something big. And when she met his gaze, he could sense the weight of it pulling on her soul.

"I spoke with one of Douglas's coworkers at the grist mill. A Mr. Green." Damaris turned her attention to Nate. "He remembers someone delivering a note to your father that day. The contents must have been urgent, for Douglas dropped everything and ran from the mill the minute he read it. He offered no explanation beyond saying he had to get home."

Luke shoved his coffee cup aside. "Home? Not to the lake?"

She nodded, the look in her brown eyes making his chest ache. "Mr. Green assumed the note had something to do with Nathaniel. That maybe the teacher had sent word that he'd become ill or been injured somehow. He couldn't imagine Douglas leaving so abruptly for any other reason."

"But I was fine," Nate interjected, his brows knitting together. "I was at school. All day."

Damaris reached across the table and covered Nate's hand with her own. "I know. Someone lied to get your father to leave the mill. Maybe they waylaid him on his way home."

Nate jerked his hand away from hers. "It was Grimes. I know it!"

"Easy there, sport." Luke held up a hand, hoping to calm the boy. "Gettin' riled won't help you think clearly."

Nate shot to his feet and braced his palms on the tabletop. "What's there to think clearly about? Grimes is the only one who had a reason for wanting my pa out of the way. It had to be him!"

Damaris flinched slightly at the kid's angry tone, but the compassion never dimmed from her eyes. "That's just the thing," she said softly, her gaze darting over to Luke before refocusing on her nephew. "Oliver Grimes might *not* be the only one."

Nate plopped back down into his seat, confusion visibly cracking through his wall of belligerence. "What?"

"Mr. Mullins chased me down in town today and insisted we talk."

Luke frowned, not liking the idea of this Mullins fellow ambushing Damaris.

"The lawyer?" Nate asked.

She nodded. "There's been another offer for the property. A significantly larger offer."

"I don't care how big the offer is. I ain't selling."

"I know. I tried to tell Mr. Mullins that, but he refused to take no for an answer. He insisted I take some time to think about it. But that's not the important part of the conversation."

Luke leaned forward in his chair. "The new offer wasn't from Grimes, was it?"

Damaris shook her head. "No. It was from a company down in Austin. The Harbinger Land Development Company."

A land development company? Luke sat back. This added a whole new level of complexity. Land development companies didn't just buy up land willy-nilly. There was always a strategy. One calculated to earn profits. And if they were offering Damaris above market value for her property, there had to be something here they wanted.

"That still don't mean it weren't Grimes." Nate huffed as he crossed his arms over his chest in a pouting motion.

"No," Luke agreed, "but it does mean that we have more than one suspect. And we aren't likely to find the truth if we don't consider the whole picture. So we gotta get rid of any preconceived notions that are blockin' our view. Think you can set yours aside long enough to look at things from a more objective angle?"

Nate glowered and shrugged.

Well, at least the kid was honest.

"Once I can sit a horse, I'll pay the land office a visit. See if this Harbinger Company is buying up any other land in the area. That might give us a clue about why they're so interested in this piece."

"I still don't see how that makes any difference," Nate protested. "The company's in Austin. Grimes is here. He might not be the only one who wanted Pa's land, but he's the only one around who coulda hurt him."

"That we know about." The kid had a point about opportunity. But if Matt had taught Luke anything in their years of bringing criminals to justice, it was to verify the facts you had and never assume there weren't more out there to gather. "These companies have got to have people scouting out the land they want to buy, don't they? Could be one of them tangled with yer pa."

Nate just sat there, hunched and scowling. Then all at once, he jumped to his feet and strode to the back door, mumbling about having chores to do.

"Nathaniel?" Damaris started to rise, but Luke stopped her with a hand on her arm.

"Let him go. He's been hangin' on to that grudge too long to give it up easily. He needs time to sort his thoughts."

Her shoulders dipped as a quiet sigh escaped. "I thought I'd sorted mine on the ride back from town, but I feel like I came home with more questions than answers."

Since she hadn't pulled away from his touch and his hand was still sitting on top of her arm, it seemed only natural to use the connection to try to offer a measure of comfort. Luke rubbed his thumb back and forth along the edge of her arm, then dipped down to her wrist where her skin emerged from her sleeve. So soft and delicate. Just like Damaris herself. A vivid contrast to his callused hands and rough ways.

She peered up at him, and he expected her to pull away. A coarse cowboy had no business pettin' a fine lady's wrist, after all. But when her eyes met his, he didn't find unease or a lack of welcome in their depths. Nope. What he saw was longing. The kind one lonely soul recognized in another. His chest tightened.

"You're not in this alone, Damaris. I'm here. I'll stay as long as you need me."

A touch of pink colored her cheeks a heartbeat before she dropped her chin.

As long as you need me? He'd meant that he'd stay until they found her brother's killer. And the rustlers. And ensured she and Nate were safe. But that wasn't what he'd said. He'd vowed to stay as long as she needed him. And now he couldn't stop himself from the ridiculous hope that she might need him for more than her current troubles.

"You're a good man, Luke Davenport."

He shook his head. "You wouldn't say that if you knew who I really was."

Her head lifted, and something fiery sparked in her eyes. "Then tell me. Who are you? Really?"

His blood pumped hard at her challenge. She'd thrown down a gauntlet, and he'd never been able to resist a dare. Yet unlike the time he'd stripped down to his skivvies and run through the mayor's garden howlin' like a banshee to win two bits off Bobby Langren, taking up this gauntlet would mean stripping his soul bare in front of a woman whose opinion mattered. A woman who might take one look at the ugliness inside him and decide she and Nate were better off without him. Yet Luke was no coward. If she wanted to know the real him, he'd show her every gory inch.

Drawing his hand away from her wrist, he leaned back in his chair and crossed his arms over his chest.

"I'm a troublemaker who spent more time in school swingin' his fists than opening books, an arsonist who nearly set an entire town on fire, and a bully who almost beat his own father to death."

She didn't flinch. Didn't even blink.

Had he shocked her senseless? Maybe she needed another shock to snap out of it. He had plenty in his arsenal. He pulled out one he figured would do the trick.

"'Course, then I joined the army, where I took countless lives on the battlefield." He swallowed hard, the last piece of truth dragging its feet.

Confess your faults one to another . . .

"I served at Wounded Knee." He forced the words out. "My unit slaughtered women and children." He'd followed Matt and done his best to protect the innocent, but those Hotchkiss guns had rained fire on the Lakota without discriminating between armed combatant and unarmed civilian. So much chaos. So much death. So much guilt left to taint his soul.

If we confess our sins, he is faithful and just to forgive us our sins, and to cleanse us from all unrighteousness.

He'd been cleansed. He knew that. Believed God's promise. Yet whenever he recalled that day, he couldn't help but feel soiled. Stained. Like he needed to be cleansed again. And again. And again.

The sounds of chair legs lightly rasping against floorboards focused his attention outward in time to catch Damaris getting up from the table. Her shock must've finally receded enough to allow her to move away from him. She was too polite to criticize him. She'd probably busy herself with rinsing out the coffeepot. Change the subject to the weather until he took the hint and made himself scarce. He might as well save them both the awkwardness and just—

Damaris picked up her chair, rounded the table, and placed it directly beside his. Then, before he could figure out what to do, she covered his oversized paw with her slender, delicate hand and squeezed with surprising strength.

"I didn't ask you to tell me who you were, Luke. I asked you to tell me who you *are*."

He stared. He couldn't help it. She'd stunned him. Utterly and completely. Define himself without referencing his past? Was that even possible? The man he was today had been built on a lifetime of experiences. Good. Bad. Worse. He *was* his past.

Wasn't he?

Her thumb moved against the back of his hand, imitating his attempted comfort from a moment ago. "'Therefore if any man be in Christ, he is a new creature: old things are passed away; behold, all things are become new.'"

"Second Corinthians 5:17." He knew the verse well. Meditated on it often. Yet in his experience, people were far more interested in the old creature than the new.

So why wasn't Damaris asking him about what he'd revealed? The violence. The fighting. The killing. Was she truly not curious? No, there were hundreds of questions brimming in her eyes. He wagged his head, her reaction making no sense.

A soft smile touched her lips. "You're a warrior, Luke Davenport. And warriors aren't formed by ease and tranquility. They are forged in battle. Battles it sounds like you've been waging since childhood. I want to know your story, Luke, because I want to know you. Where you came from, what shaped you, who shaped you. But I will not judge you on the man you were. Only on the man you are. A man of courage. Sacrifice. Honor. A man with flaws and imperfections, but one who strives to be better. To protect those in his care and bring evil men to justice. A man who knows the Word and strives to emulate the God who gave it."

Luke chuckled softly, embarrassed by her praise even as it poured over his dry, cracked heart like anointing oil. "Most of them verses I learned as a kid. My teacher made me memorize and recite scripture every time he caught me misbehaving." He grinned. "I misbehaved a lot."

"And now that you're a man grown? I saw the Bible you carry in your saddlebag. It's well worn. I doubt it got that way because your old schoolmaster is still demanding recitations."

Luke looked away from her sweet, far-too-trusting eyes and focused on the grain of the wooden table. "I'm no saint, Damaris. I got a knack for memorizin' things, but I'm still workin' on the livin'-it-out part. I'm a rough man who's lived a rough life. I've got something wild inside me that pushes me into danger 'cause I know I'm expendable. I tried livin' like a normal fella, surrounded by friends, with work I enjoy. But even then I couldn't settle. Couldn't find peace. So I took the job with Grimes. On my own. With no Horsemen to back me up. Because livin' on the edge made more sense than livin' in a peace that didn't belong to me."

He forced himself to look at her. "That's the man I am, Damaris. Discontent, dangerous, and a tiny bit deranged."

"Hmm. I think I prefer driven, devoted, and dependable."

He started to argue, but she wouldn't let him.

"If there's something wild inside you that drove you to leave a comfortable position with the Hangers, then I thank God for that wildness. Without it, Nathaniel would be dead, and I never would have met you." She shifted in her seat and leaned close. "We need you, Luke. And not just because you're a Horseman. Nathaniel connects with you in a way he never will with me. He respects you. Listens to you. Admires you. And I . . ."

His gut clenched. And she . . . ?

"I'd be lost without you. I try to believe that I'm strong. That I can handle life in Texas. But I don't know the first thing about how to protect Nathaniel from real danger. I know nothing about guns or how to recognize a killer. For all I know, I've stood face-to-face with the man who killed my brother on numerous occasions. I want to be courageous and smart and capable, but inside I'm terrified that I'm not enough. Having you here makes me feel stronger. Safer. Braver."

Luke twisted to face her. His heart pounded so hard, not even his injuries could compete with the ache rising in his chest. Unable to resist the way she called to the core of him, he cupped her cheek in his palm and gave her his pledge.

"I'll keep you and the boy safe, Damaris. I swear it."

She leaned into his hand, her eyes closing for a heartbeat before her lashes lifted. "I know you will."

He didn't deserve her unwavering faith, yet he'd do everything in his power to be worthy of it. Of her.

Slowly, he drew her face closer. Memorized the shape of her lips. Watched them part ever so slightly.

"I'd walk through fire for you." His murmured vow rumbled deep in his throat an instant before he sealed his promise with a kiss.

— CHAPTER —
TWENTY-TWO

An entire garden filled with enchanted fairies sprang to life in Damaris's belly the moment Luke's lips touched hers. Desires and delights unfurled, blossomed, and climbed to extraordinary heights.

For a self-proclaimed *rough man*, Luke's kiss was amazingly gentle. His lips smooth. His touch tender and tentative. There was nothing rough about it.

Damaris stretched forward and did her best to kiss him back, though she had no idea if she was doing it correctly. Her only experience in the realm of kissing entailed bussing family members on the cheek, and this was as different from that as a thunderstorm was from a light sprinkle.

Perhaps cooperation counted more than skill, however, for once she leaned into him, Luke's intensity shifted. Some of the gentleness retreated, exposing a hunger that shocked her. Not because of his boldness, but because she—invisible, shy, plain-faced Damaris Baxter—had inspired such intensity.

Feeling emboldened herself, she touched his face, wanting him to know he wasn't alone. She felt it, too. Something more than mere attraction. Something deeper. Something that could grow into love.

His arm wrapped around her waist and clutched her to him with such strength, she felt herself lift from her chair.

But then he stopped. Relaxed his hold. Ended the kiss.

"I'm sorry. I shouldn't have—" A groan cut off his words, reminding Damaris of his injuries.

"Did we aggravate your wounds?" As much as she enjoyed his kiss, she didn't want to cause him pain. She ran a hand down his side and tested for any dampness that might indicate bleeding through damaged stitches.

His hand covered hers and gently, almost reluctantly, pulled her palm away from his waist. "My wounds aren't the problem." A self-conscious chuckle echoed between them. "My lack of control is. I got carried away, I'm afraid. A gentleman would have done a better job curbing his ardor."

Heat rose to Damaris's face, but she refused to let him believe he'd offended her in some way. "I rather liked your uncurbed ardor."

His eyes turned the deep blue-green of a fathomless sea, stirring a longing within her to plunge back in, but she wouldn't abandon all propriety. Unchaperoned, unmarried ladies did not linger in the company of bachelor cowboys for precisely this reason. When a legend of a man like Luke Davenport looked at a woman with heat in his eyes and said things that led that lady to believe she actually inspired ardency, morals that had been easy to adhere to all her life suddenly grew slippery.

Recognizing the danger, Damaris got to her feet and walked

on trembling legs to the dry sink. Behind her, she heard Luke's chair scrape backward, heard his boots scuff the floorboards, and imagined she even heard his breathing, so fully had he consumed her senses. She turned and smiled, but she kept her hands behind her, gripping the edge of the sink as if it were the anchor that would keep her from being swept away.

"Can I offer you more coffee?" It seemed an inane question after what they'd shared, but perhaps they needed a little inanity to reestablish the necessary boundaries.

Luke limped toward the doorway and reached for his hat. "Better not." He fiddled with the hat's brim, but when his attention returned to her face, there was nothing sheepish about his gaze. It pierced her, warmed her, and left her slightly breathless. "As much as I'd like to stay, I'm gonna bid you good evening, Miss Baxter. I think I'll do some reading. I feel a hankerin' for Second Timothy. I'll likely start with chapter two, verse twenty-two, and see where the Good Lord leads from there."

Damaris couldn't recall the scripture he referenced from memory, but with the heat building between them, she could guess its contents. Something about avoiding temptation and holding fast to purity, no doubt. "I think I might do some reading myself." And she knew precisely where to start—Second Timothy. It might be unwise to share his company any further tonight, but she could share a bit of his spirit. "Good night, Luke."

He dipped his chin. "Night, Damaris."

Fitting his hat to his head, he strode out of her kitchen, but the memory of what had transpired between them lingered behind, swirling through her mind and tingling upon her lips.

She released her hold on the dry sink and lifted her fingers to press against her mouth to hold the memory captive. Luke Davenport had kissed her. *Her.* And all evidence indicated it hadn't been a mistake.

A grin, wide and no doubt excessively bemused, stretched beneath her fingertips.

For the next three days, Luke pushed his physical limitations harder and further than he had since his early army days. He and Nate sparred with their fists and with wooden "swords" made from sturdy branches, though they focused more on defensive instruction than offensive action. At least when the kid was around. When alone, Luke turned himself loose on a feed bag filled with sawdust and sand.

He tired quickly the first day, but he kept at it. Punch the bag. Rest. Spar with Nate. Rest. Muck stalls. Rest. Then repeat. When he couldn't lift his arms, he'd walk. Lead Titan around the paddock. Stroll down to the creek. When his legs gave out, he'd sit in the chair Damaris had placed in his barn room and oil harness leather. Anything to gain strength and occupy his mind.

He still replayed that kiss about a hundred times a day, but at least when he collapsed into bed each night, he was too exhausted to dwell on it for long before sleep claimed him.

Seeing Damaris around the property was a kind of sweet torture. He'd made a point to avoid the house when it wasn't mealtime, but she still managed to cross his path several times a day. Hanging laundry. Feeding chickens. Sometimes even just carrying a book out to the pretty little spot beneath the hickory tree on the far side of the paddock. She liked to spread a blanket beneath the branches and lean against a fence post while she read.

So pretty and serene. He had the hardest time tearing his gaze away from her and found excuses to linger in the paddock. It was a miracle Titan didn't get dizzy from all the circles Luke led him in when Damaris was around.

Today was different, though. Today he was going to attempt to mount. His wounds still ached like an old woman's rheumatism, but they were healing. Enough that he figured it was time to pay the doc in Huntsville a visit to get the stitches removed. Dr. Jo had instructed him to wait ten to fourteen days. Today marked day ten. That meant he should be able to sit a horse without fear of popping a stitch. 'Course, he'd have to build up his stamina before attempting a full day in the saddle.

Damaris kept fretting over him, telling him he was pushing himself too hard. But he couldn't escape the feeling that he needed to be ready for battle. Whether it was his military training, the Holy Spirit, or just his gut talking to him, he'd learned the value of listening. That inner voice had saved his life more than once through the years. How much more vital to listen to it now that Damaris and Nate were depending on him. If pushing himself harder than was comfortable meant he was ready to defend them when the time came, he'd gladly accept the aches and exhaustion.

Besides, he needed to get away from Damaris before he did something stupid. Like kiss her again. He'd made a point not to be alone with her in the house or even the barn after that night at the table, but like a pair of stray calves, the two of them kept gravitating toward each other. He might make a point to keep the paddock fence between them while she read beneath the tree, but the moment she closed her book and stood, his arm was draped over the fence slat nearest her with him having no recollection of crossing the paddock to get there.

They chatted every day. She regaled him with tales of her vast collection of siblings and the fearsome Great-Aunt Bertha. He told stories about the Horsemen's adventures. About the time they were stripped of weapons, boots, and horses and left to die on the prairie. And the time they had to dig the youngest Horseman out of a collapsed mine. The widow they'd saved from a scheming foreman, and the prodigal brother they'd rescued twice from the same band of outlaws.

They'd spoken of deeper matters, too. He shared pieces from his childhood. Told her about his mother leaving and his father's drinking. About working in Mr. Roper's livery and battling his demons with Matt. She admitted to feeling like a misfit and a burden to her family. Her failure to fit the Baxter mold. She shared her longing to create a family with Nate and the discouragement she did her best to hide when she hit one obstacle after another.

Luke had kept his hands to himself, but the intimacy between him and Damaris just kept growing, like plant shoots undeterred by cobblestones, winding through tiny crevices to sprout green in the midst of a stone street. She was becoming important to him. As important as his Horsemen brethren. Maybe more so. The thought scared him. And tempted him. Tempted him to believe that his future might hold something other than dodging bullets and chasing outlaws. Something that would make growing old a pleasure instead of a liability.

Titan stamped a hoof in impatience, eager to leave the barnyard and stretch his legs.

"I know, buddy. I'm dallyin' worse than a slug on crutches." He patted the big sorrel's neck in apology. "Got a lot on my mind, it seems." And a serious ache in his body. His side still throbbed from lifting the saddle onto Titan's back a few minutes ago.

All right. Time to quit pussyfootin' around and get to business.

Checking his grip on the reins, Luke inhaled a breath, grabbed the horn, and raised his left boot toward the stirrup. Thankful that the rustlers had done him the courtesy of stabbing him in his non-mounting leg, he fit his toe into the stirrup and swung up and over. His side protested the stretching, but it was his right thigh that most concerned him. The constant rubbing that would come with a ride over uneven terrain would test the seams in his hide.

He'd start small. A ride into town and back. He could break up saddle time with a visit to the land office. Ever since Damaris had revealed the existence of a second buyer, he'd wanted to check their records for other properties owned by Harbinger. Maybe he'd find a pattern. Or a clue to what they planned to develop in the area. Either way, he hoped it would provide him with a motive for Douglas Baxter's murder.

"You're riding today?"

Damaris's voice snagged Luke's attention, jerking his gaze from between his horse's ears to the woman who had just appeared around the corner of the barn.

She looked lovely. Her simple green calico dress wasn't anything fancy. In fact, it was probably the simplest dress she owned. Yet of all the dresses he'd seen her wear, he liked this one best. It didn't carry any drawing room formality or big city airs. It made her seem more approachable. More . . . attainable.

Luke cleared his throat, hoping his hat brim hid his thoughts. "Yep. I've been itchin' to get back in the saddle. Figured I'd ride to town and back. Test out the leg."

He could read the worry in her eyes, but she didn't try to talk him out of going. Just walked up to Titan and patted the horse's shoulder.

"Be gentle with him," she murmured as she stroked Titan's dark mane. "And make sure he gets home."

Home. Luke swallowed. This wasn't home. It was just a temporary stopover. A place to recover from his injuries and do a bit of good looking out for Nate and Damaris. It was their home, not his.

Yet for the first time in his life, he found himself hankering to have a place where he could hang that word.

Home had been the small clapboard house with the peeling white paint and rotted front steps he'd grown up in. The place where the walls smelled of pipe tobacco, the carpet smelled of spilled whiskey, and the curtains shut out the light and muffled the cries of a young boy who wasn't always fast enough to dodge his father's blows.

He'd wanted nothing to do with that home. Or any other. Until now.

As Damaris tipped her chin up to look at him, Luke recognized the truth staring him in the face. Home wasn't a place. It was a person. *This* person. Madisonville, Texas. St. Louis, Missouri. The moon. Location didn't matter. If Damaris waited for him, it would be home.

But what if he broke that home like his father had? Drove the people he loved away? Maybe not with drink and abuse, but Luke had plenty of other faults to choose from.

A slight pressure against his ankle pulled him from his spiraling cogitations. He looked down to find Damaris's hand resting against his boot.

"Take care, Luke." She smiled up at him, cutting through the darkness of his thoughts like a sunbeam through a storm cloud. "Josephine will scold me good if you open one of those wounds again. If you won't think of yourself while you're riding, think of me."

He grinned and tugged his hat brim in salute. "Oh, I'll be doin' plenty of thinkin' about you, ma'am. Don't you worry."

Fire flamed in her cheeks. "That's not what I . . . Get out of here, you." She swatted his leg.

Luke laughed and nudged Titan into a walk. He waved, enjoying the pink lingering in Damaris's cheeks before he turned his mount toward the road. At the end of the yard, he clicked his tongue and set Titan into an easy canter, feeling so good that he barely felt his injured thigh at all.

TWENTY-THREE

The haze of infatuation had worn off by the time he reached the courthouse. Luke bit back a wince as he dismounted and looped Titan's reins over the hitching post. The leg still held his weight. He'd count that as a win and try to ignore the itchy throbbing of the healing flesh as he entered the large brick building and hunted down the land office.

When the clerk pulled the county records and set them in front of him, Luke immediately regretted not bringing Damaris with him. He could stare down an entire gang of bandits without blinking, but a pile of papers left him craving escape.

After an hour, Luke's head throbbed worse than his thigh. Sitting at a table in the corner of the small lobby, he pored over documentation for survey reports, mineral rights, grazing fees, and leasing agreements, all carrying more legal mumbo jumbo than he could wade through in a year. He'd found several bills of sale with the Harbinger name attached, but he didn't understand the survey reports and therefore couldn't figure out where they were located on the map.

He was about to sound the retreat in order to fight another day when the door opened and a familiar pair of boots strode inside.

"Jonesy? Ya here? I got that bill of sale you been pesterin' me about. Signed it over at the lawyer's office. Ink's probably still damp."

Harland Jones, the clerk, got up from his desk behind the counter and held out his hand to collect the paper. "Thank you, Mr. Grimes. I'll get it recorded this afternoon."

Luke straightened his hunched-over posture and lifted a hand in greeting as Oliver Grimes turned. His former employer's eyes widened in surprise a moment before a smile split his tanned face.

"Davenport! Glad to see ya still in town." He moseyed over to the table and extended a hand. Luke shook it. "I don't guess you're feeling up to chasing rustlers again, are ya? My beeves are still missin'."

Luke shook his head. "Sorry. This is my first day back in the saddle, and I 'bout wore myself out just gettin' to town. I won't be in rustler-chasing shape for at least another week. Maybe more." He shifted in his chair, trying to find a comfortable position. An impossible proposition, he'd learned over the last hour, but one he couldn't seem to stop himself from attempting every few minutes. "Sheriff Conley hasn't uncovered any new leads?"

Grimes rolled his eyes. "Conley wouldn't be able to find his badge if it weren't pinned to his vest. Why d'ya think I was so desperate to hire the Horsemen?" He blew out a breath and apparently his temper with it. "Conley handles town matters well enough, I s'pose. Keeps the peace and kisses enough babies to get himself reelected. He just don't do much for those of us outside the city limits."

Luke understood Grimes's frustration, but he also understood the challenge of one man overseeing an entire county. The sheriff couldn't be everywhere at once, though Luke had hoped the descriptions he'd provided of the rustlers would have garnered more fruit.

"Any new cows go missing since the night I was attacked?"

"Nah." Grimes massaged the back of his neck. "I guess I should be thankful you scared 'em off. I hate to think of the money I'll lose from those ten beeves, though. It sours my stomach."

Luke nodded in sympathy. Ten prime cattle at market could mean the difference between a lean year and a prosperous one.

Grimes glanced at the papers strewn over the table in front of Luke, and his gaze sharpened. "What's all this?"

"Lookin' into a land development company called Harbinger. Trying to determine how much land they've bought up in the area and where it's located."

Grimes scowled. "They make that Baxter woman an offer? She ain't sellin' to them, is she? Dad-burn it. It ain't fair. That land should've been mine."

"Cool your kettle, Grimes." Luke shot a glance at the peeping office clerk, who quickly ducked his head and resumed his work. Pushing to his feet, Luke stepped close to the hotheaded rancher and lowered his voice to a murmur. "She ain't sellin' to anyone. You need to let it go. Heed the tenth commandment."

"I *did* let it go. Today, as a matter of fact. That's what got me so worked up. I thought fate had tricked me, giving that land to the very company I just sold to."

Luke's chest tightened. "You sold your ranch to Harbinger?"

"Just a small strip along the eastern property line. When Doug's sister refused my offer, I resigned myself to not being able to expand my holdings in that direction. Harbinger has been after me to sell for the past few months. I turned 'em down. Until they came back with a counteroffer last week. They offered to swap acreage with me, giving me two hundred and forty acres bordering my property on the west in exchange for a strip of eighty acres on the east. The land to the west ain't as well-watered, but there's patches of prairie grass that would allow for expandin' my herd. And with three times as many acres, it didn't make sense to refuse."

The Baxter land lay directly east of Grimes's property. If Harbinger had bought the east section from Grimes, then they wouldn't give up easily in obtaining Nate's land.

Grimes bent over the table and started riffling through the papers Luke had sorted. "Hmm. Looks like Harbinger is buying up land between here and Navasota."

Luke peered at the papers again, but he still couldn't make out any patterns. "How can you tell?"

"Here's a bill of sale from Carson Howser. I used to ride by his place on my way home before he decided to move to town." He tapped a second paper with his pointer finger. "And this is Old Zeb's place. He ran a small outfit south of here. His daughter married a farrier from Midway and moved there about five years back. Zeb's wife's been wantin' to move closer to them ever since. I guess Harbinger managed to sweeten the pot enough to bribe old Zeb into givin' the wife what she wanted."

Grimes chuckled, but Luke didn't see anything funny.

What he finally saw was a pattern. A line stretching from Navasota to Madisonville. A line that probably meant a future railroad. And if Damaris and Nate were the only holdouts, things could get ugly real fast.

"Aunt Maris!"

Damaris brushed the dirt from her garden gloves and pushed to her feet, letting the weed she'd been battling claim a temporary victory. Shading her eyes with a hand to her forehead, she searched the road for her nephew. She spotted him on the drive, waving something over his head.

"Aunt Maris! We got a telegram!"

Catching his excitement, Damaris abandoned her weeding tools and hurried down the row between the carrots and summer squash. She'd just closed the garden gate when Nathaniel reached her. His cheeks had reddened from his run, and his breath came in labored huffs, but his eyes danced with anticipation.

They'd received a letter from her mother a few weeks after Damaris arrived, and one rather ill-humored note from Great-Aunt Bertha full of complaints about being abandoned, but not much else. Certainly not a telegram. Her belly fluttered even as her mind spun, trying to imagine who could have sent it.

Nathaniel held out the small yellow envelope. "The lady

from the post office said it was for Mr. Davenport, too. Should I fetch him?"

"He's not here." Damaris took the envelope, her flutters increasing at the sight of her name next to Luke's on the front.

"Where'd he go?" Nathaniel's eyes shuttered a bit as uncertainty overrode excitement. "He didn't say nothin' about leaving when I headed out for school this mornin'."

"He'll be back. Soon, I hope." How well she understood Nathaniel's wariness. With all the time he and Luke had been spending together the last few days, she wouldn't be surprised if he dreaded Luke's departure as much as she did. She turned her mouth up in a reassuring grin, hoping it looked more convincing than it felt. "He took Titan into town. Said he wanted to see how his injuries held up in the saddle."

The furrows in Nathaniel's brow smoothed, and enthusiasm reignited in his gaze. "We don't have to wait on him, do we? It's got your name on it. That means we can open it. Right?"

"Why not?" The boy had had enough disappointments in his life of late. She didn't have the heart to deny him such a small request. Not to mention the fact that she'd never been very good at subduing her own curiosity.

Sharing a conspiratorial wink with her nephew, Damaris flipped the small envelope over and tore open the flap. Her breath caught as she pulled the message out and read the first words.

Baby arrived. Eleanor Louise.
All well. Matt

"The Hangers had their baby!" Joy for her new friend swelled through Damaris's chest, and her soul reached out to the Lord in silent gratitude. "A little girl." She handed the telegram to Nathaniel so he could read it for himself.

"Eleanor Louise? That's an awful big name for a tiny baby."

"I'm sure they'll shorten . . ."

The dull sound of approaching hoofbeats distracted her, leaving her sentence to taper away into nothing as she turned her attention to the road. Her heart leapt at the sight of Titan cantering toward them, Luke upright in the saddle.

Nathaniel dashed off to meet him, waving the telegram in the air. Damaris's feet followed at a respectable pace even as her heart galloped like a racehorse at the derby.

Luke slowed his mount as he entered the yard, his eyes finding hers before his gaze shifted to Nathaniel. Her pulse stuttered, and a flood of warmth unleashed within her midsection at his small display of preference.

"Dr. Jo had her baby!" Nathaniel announced as he came abreast of Titan. "A girl!"

The worry and discomfort lining Luke's features disappeared in an instant. A broad grin split his face. "Boy, howdy. You don't say. Cap's got himself a daughter?" A deep chuckle rolled out of him. "I feel sorry for the boys who hope to court her someday. Riding through a battlefield might be easier on a fella than getting past Matt to his daughter. 'Course, if the girl's as independent-minded as her mama, she'll have her own say in the matter."

"Well, it's a good thing they have sixteen or seventeen years to prepare," Damaris said, her smile widening when Luke turned the full effect of his grin in her direction.

Nathaniel chattered about the baby's name and what nick-names he'd suggest while Luke brought Titan to a halt outside the barn and dismounted. Damaris didn't miss the stiffness of Luke's movements nor the tightness around his mouth as he made his way to the ground. He was hurting.

She wanted to help but wasn't sure how to do so in a way that wouldn't dent his pride. So she simply positioned herself at his side, ready to offer assistance in any way possible.

"You know," Luke said, his face growing thoughtful as he took the telegram from Nathaniel without really looking at it, "maybe we ought to go for a visit. See the new baby. What do you think?"

Nathaniel gazed up at him, cautious hope in his eyes. "Me and Aunt Maris, too?"

Luke ruffled his hair. "Yep. You and your aunt, too." He peered over the boy's head to meet Damaris's eyes.

A knot formed in her belly. Something was wrong. The way he looked at her, it was like he was trying to communicate a warning she didn't understand.

Nathaniel ducked away from Luke's hand, moved to her side, and clasped her elbow. "Can we, Aunt Maris? Miss Tatum can give me school assignments early. She did that for Johnny Reed last month when his ma took sick and his pa sent him and his sister to stay with their grandparents in Huntsville."

"I don't know," she murmured, unable to look away from Luke's face as she tried to read him. Finally, she gave up and turned to her nephew. "Why don't you take care of Titan while Mr. Davenport and I discuss it?"

"All right." Nathaniel took charge of the reins and started leading Titan away. "But I vote we go."

"Duly noted." Damaris made a point to keep her voice light, but the moment Nathaniel disappeared into the barn, she dropped the façade. "What's going on?"

Luke clasped her hand, his large palm engulfing hers in a way that should have brought comfort and security but, in this instance, only promised the revelation of bad news.

"The people who want your land aren't going to stop." His low tone sent a shiver down her spine. "In fact, I'm pretty sure they're about to intensify their efforts. I need to get you and Nate out of here before that happens. Get you someplace safe. Someplace where you have more than me watching out for you."

Damaris's stomach dropped to her knees.

Lord help them.

CHAPTER
TWENTY-FOUR

Luke squeezed Damaris's hand, wishing he could have done more to cushion the blow. She did her best to hide her distress, but he felt it in the trembling of her fingers and saw it in the way her gaze automatically moved to the barn doorway where Nate had disappeared. It made Luke want to pummel something.

But he couldn't pummel a company. Especially one based in a city located over a hundred miles away. Plus, he didn't have any actual proof of wrongdoing. If Harbinger was anything like the unscrupulous land speculation companies he'd heard tales about, that proof would be hard to come by. They'd take measures to keep their hands clean. Hire others to do their dirty work. Cause *accidents* that couldn't be traced back to them. Accidents like a strong swimmer drowning in a lake he had no reason to visit.

"Do you really think we're in danger?" Damaris peered up at him, her gentle brown eyes larger than usual in her delicate face.

"Not immediate danger, perhaps, but in situations like this, it's hard to know when things will start getting ugly."

"And just what situation are we in?" She turned to face him, her backbone stiffening and her shoulders rolling backward.

She might be an elegant lady with hands more suited to needlework than war, but she wouldn't shy from this fight. Already he sensed the change in her. Her voice had lost its wobble. She'd shoved the fear aside in favor of plotting a course that would allow her to protect her nephew.

"I stopped by the county land office in town to see if the Harbinger Land Development Company had been buying up other properties in the area. They have. In a pattern that seems to stretch between here and Navasota. My best guess is that they're expecting the railroad to come through in the next few years, and they plan to turn a profit on the land."

"But surely they wouldn't actually harm someone just to increase their profits. What's one piece of land when they have so many?"

Luke wished he could relieve her mind, assure her that everything would be fine, but sugarcoating danger only left a person ill-equipped to respond when it came calling.

"It isn't just one piece of land, sweetheart. If you won't sell, that jeopardizes the entire enterprise. The railroad won't build if they don't have a clear path between cities. If they choose a different route, all the land Harbinger bought to this point will be worthless. They'll lose thousands of dollars."

"You think that's what happened to Douglas, don't you? That someone tried to force him to sell and ended up killing him."

Her chin dropped, and her hand slid from his. Heedless of sore muscles and irritated wounds, Luke wrapped his arm around her waist and steered her over to the back porch, limping only slightly. If he had his druthers, he would've just swept her into his arms and cradled her close to his chest. Sheltered her from the pain knocking at her heart. But she had enough surprises crashing over her at the moment. He wouldn't add to them. So he settled for sitting next to her on the steps and tugging her into his side. He worried for a moment that he was being too presumptuous, but then she laid her head against his chest, and everything settled into place.

She needed him, and nothing was going to keep him from being there for her.

"Harbinger likely hired someone to force your brother's hand," he said.

Damaris tipped her face up to look him in the eye. "You're sure it wasn't Oliver Grimes?"

"I am now."

Her brows arched.

He rubbed his hand up and down her arm. "I ran into Grimes at the land office and learned he just sold a strip of land to Harbinger. The section that runs along your property line. Harbinger offered him three times as many acres to the west of his ranch in exchange. Now that his land no longer borders yours, there's no motive for him to try to buy your place."

"But there's an even stronger motive for Harbinger." Her voice flattened, and her cheek came to rest against his chest once more.

Luke laid his chin atop her hair and hugged her close. "'Fraid so."

"What am I supposed to do?" She straightened and pulled a few inches away from him. "I can't risk Nathaniel's safety, but I don't want to sell his birthright, either. This isn't right. Can't the sheriff do anything?"

"Not unless there's proof that a crime's been committed." Luke ran a hand down his face and rubbed at the stubble under his jaw.

She's right, God. It ain't fair for greed and power to rule the day. Where is your justice? Where is your provision?

Lowering his hand, he gripped the edge of the step with enough strength that the wood bit into his hand. He was a Horseman, for pity's sake. It was his *job* to fight injustice. To protect people like Damaris and Nate. But he didn't know how to fight an invisible opponent. He needed his team.

"Maybe I should take Nathaniel home to St. Louis."

The soft words struck him so hard he flinched. St. Louis? She might as well retreat to Boston or New York.

"As much as I would love to visit the Hangers," she continued, "we can't stay there permanently. We'd have to return here after a few days or perhaps a week, and the danger would have likely intensified while we were away. Nathaniel's safety takes priority. I can protect him better in Missouri."

"And I can protect the both of you better at Gringolet."

He sounded desperate, and he knew it, but his gut was screaming at him not to let her leave. It might be pure self-ishness, him grasping at any available straw in order to keep her in his life. But it might also be instinct, the kind that kept him alive on the battlefield. The kind that kept those around him alive.

"Give me a few days," he pleaded.

He scrambled to come up with a reason to justify her staying, something tangible. But Matt was the one who came up with the plans. Luke just carried them out. So what would Matt do? Who would he—? *That's it!*

"We've got a newspaper contact in Austin who can look into Harbinger for us. Matt trusts him completely. He used to funnel jobs to us before the Horsemen retired. His name is Francis Kendall. If anyone can dig up dirt on Harbinger, it's Kendall. Give me time to write to him, ask him to investigate. In the meantime, maybe we can stave off the wolves if you pretend you're considering selling. Didn't you say that lawyer fella didn't want to take no for an answer? What if you told him that you want to accept the offer, but you need time to convince Nate to go along with it? Maybe even ask him to look into the possibility of moving your brother and sister-in-law's graves. I know it's morbid, but it would make the story believable and give him something to take to Harbinger that sounds like progress."

Damaris nibbled on her bottom lip, looking as torn as he felt. "Wouldn't that be dishonest?"

He had to work to keep a growl of frustration from rumbling out of his throat. Not that he was angry with her. She was right. What he proposed *did* veer toward dishonesty. But Abraham lied about Sarah being his sister to protect his household. David pretended to be crazy in order to escape from Saul and take refuge among the Philistines. Rahab lied to protect the spies hiding in her house. All were heroes commended for their faith. God must've understood.

But had the Lord actually approved?

Doubtful.

One of the verses his old schoolmaster had assigned him to memorize and write on the blackboard rose in his mind to jab at his conscience.

Lying lips are abomination to the Lord: but they that deal truly are his delight. Proverbs 12:22.

That didn't leave much room for justifications about the greater good.

"Perhaps I could simply ask Mr. Mullins for more information about the buyer."

Luke snapped his attention back to Damaris.

"The more we learn about Harbinger, the better, right?"

Luke nodded, his heart pounding. She was considering his plan. Considering staying.

"I could mention that I heard about Mr. Grimes selling a parcel of his land and ask if the company would be interested in buying only our unused acreage, leaving the section with the house, barn, and family grave site in the Baxter name. I truly *would* be interested in his answer. If there is a way to remove the danger by giving them a portion of land while preserving the heart of the homestead for Nathaniel, I'd consider it."

"That's brilliant!" Luke slapped his knee in excitement. Not as satisfying as planting a kiss on her lips like his first instinct had demanded, but it would have to do.

A smile blossomed across her face, nearly stealing the breath from his lungs. How in the world could any man think this woman plain? She was the most remarkable creature the Good Lord had ever formed.

"I, ah, better get started on supper," she said, ducking her face away from him as she pushed to her feet.

Luke grabbed the railing and heaved himself upward as well. "And I have a letter to write."

There was little chance Harbinger would consider Damaris's counteroffer. The section of land she wanted to keep stretched east-west, perpendicular to the north-south path a railroad would need to travel. Nevertheless, the offer would do exactly what he needed it to do—buy time. Time for Kendall to investigate and time for Luke to get back into full fighting shape so he could protect the people he cared about.

One of whom was jogging this way across the yard.

"So what did y'all decide?" Nate asked. "We goin' to see the Hangers?"

Luke turned to Damaris, letting her take the lead with how much she wanted to tell the boy. Her eyes sought his, and he nodded in a show of support. He'd have her back, whatever she decided to share.

"Not just yet," she said. "A new baby creates lots of changes in a household. I think we should give them some time before showing up on their doorstep."

Nate's smile flattened, and suspicion entered his eyes. "There's something you're not telling me, isn't there?"

Damaris's hands found her hips. "Yes, there is." Her cheeks flamed red.

Nate jutted his chin forward. "You gonna tell me?"

"No, I'm not. Not everything that happens in your vicinity is your concern, Nathaniel Baxter. I'm allowed a few secrets, and I intend to keep them. Now, if you'll excuse me, I have supper to get on."

Her dress belled out as she spun in retreat, and the door closing behind her put an exclamation mark on her words.

Luke watched her go, downright impressed. Not only had she stood up to her nephew instead of bending over backward to please him like she usually did, but she somehow managed to be completely honest while cleverly redirecting his attention.

Nate's jaw hung loose.

"Close your mouth before you let flies in." Luke chuckled, slapping the boy's shoulder as he moved past him toward the barn.

Nate shook off his stupor and gave chase. He circled around in front of Luke and blocked his path. "Is she sayin' what I think she's sayin'? Are you and Aunt Maris . . ."

Luke's humor vanished. He wouldn't let anyone, even her nephew, imply anything improper about Damaris. "I think she said it was none of your concern." He crossed his arms. "Your aunt is one of the finest women I've ever met, and I intend to respect her wishes on this matter. I expect you to do the same."

Nate quailed a bit under the force of Luke's glare, but he held his own, just like he had the first day they'd met. "All right. I won't ask her. I'll ask you. What are your intentions toward her?"

Luke intended to make sure that what happened to her brother didn't happen to her. Or to Nate. But he couldn't say that without stirring up more hornets than he'd be putting to rest. That left him with only one viable source of honesty. The one that most men, him included, preferred to pretend didn't exist.

"I'm fond of your aunt," Luke finally managed to admit aloud. "Real fond. But all this"—he waved his hand through the air as if his emotions were suspended around him like a fog—"is too new for me to have formed any official intentions. I can promise you, however, that I'll never do anything to hurt or dishonor her. You have my word."

Nate held his gaze for a long moment, then slowly extended his hand. Luke fit his palm to Nate's and gave it a firm, solemn shake. Nate nodded in approval, then strode away to tend to his chores.

That approval buried itself deep in Luke's chest and magnified his determination not to let either Baxter down.

Ignoring the lingering aches and stiffness from his ride to town, he marched to his barn room and sought out pen and paper. He had letters to write.

CHAPTER
TWENTY-FIVE

The following day, Damaris drove to town and parked her wagon in the empty lot across from the courthouse. She didn't climb down right away. She couldn't. Not with the mini cyclones spinning her insides into tangled knots.

Pressing her hand to her midsection, she closed her eyes and willed her nerves to steady. Initiating business calls always had this effect on her. Paying calls with an appointment was hard enough, but showing up uninvited, without an invitation? She felt a bit like Esther going in to see King Xerxes.

Don't be ridiculous. It's just a conversation. One Mr. Mullins will probably welcome. You might very well be bringing him business, after all.

The logic failed to settle her stomach, but it did give her the gumption she needed to disembark the wagon and stride across the street. Only when she stood outside the lawyer's door did she falter. Her hand trembled as she reached for the door handle. Yanking her hand back, she balled it into a fist.

You can do this, Damaris. For Nathaniel.

Luke wouldn't let a door stand in his way. He'd march in and take charge of the room in an instant. Strong. Brave. Certain of his purpose. She could do the same. She *would* do the same.

Unfurling her fingers, she straightened her spine and lifted her chin. Imagining herself to be a powerful Horseman intimidated by nothing, she clasped the handle and let herself into the office. She strode across the small reception area and rapped on the glass pane of the inner office door directly below the etched insignia that read, *Ronald Mullins, Esq.*

At the knock, Mr. Mullins glanced up from the four open tomes spread across his desktop. Recognition lit his eyes. He smiled, jumped to his feet, and hurried around his desk to the door, pulling it all the way open.

"Miss Baxter! How lovely to see you. Please come in."

Her knotted nerves loosened just a tad at his gracious reception. He showed her to a chair, then stacked his books to the side so he could face her over a clean section of desk. "What can I do for you today?"

Perched on the edge of the upholstered chair, Damaris fiddled with the metal clasp on her handbag. Forcing her fingers to still, she balanced the purse on her knees and met the lawyer's gaze. "It's about the offer on my nephew's property."

"Wonderful! I knew you'd reconsider after you had time to think things through." His eyes glittered with satisfaction. "A generous offer like that doesn't come along very often. It would be foolish to turn it down when such a sum would allow you to provide for young Nathaniel in fine fashion. I will be happy to draw up a bill of sale for you." He opened a drawer and reached inside for a pre-printed document page that only lacked pertinent property details, signatures, and dates.

He was moving so fast that her head began to swim. "Wait."

Pen in hand, he paused before inking the nib, his brows arching.

Damaris tightened her grip on her bag. "I'm not ready to accept the offer yet. I have a few questions first."

His face lost a bit of animation, but he hid his disappointment behind a mask of professionalism. "Of course. What questions do you have?"

"I'd like to know more about the Harbinger company. Who are they, and why are they interested in our property?"

Mr. Mullins smiled. "Let me assure you that the Harbinger Land Development Company has a stellar reputation. I've had the honor of brokering a handful of sales for them here in Madison County over the last year, and I've found them to be excellent to work with. They pay their fees promptly and allow plenty of time for the previous owners to find new living situations before asking them to vacate.

"I can't speak to any particulars regarding their interest in your specific property, but development companies tend to do precisely as their name implies. They develop. They anticipate future needs and purchase land accordingly. It might entail speculating on a mining venture, expanding a town site, bringing in a rail line, or any of a dozen other enterprises."

He certainly had no qualms about singing the company's praises. His enthusiasm gave her pause. Could she and Luke be mistaken in their conclusions about Harbinger? Could there be another explanation for her brother's death?

"Do you know if Harbinger has any agents working in

this area? Scouting properties and whatnot? I would feel better if I could speak directly to someone employed with the company."

Mr. Mullins grew thoughtful. "Hmm. I don't know of anyone. All of my communication with the company has been through letters and telegrams. I have visited their offices in Austin a few times as well."

Damaris's hopes deflated. She'd wanted to uncover a name. Someone she could investigate. If she could place the agent in town at the time of Douglas's accident, it might be enough to get the sheriff's attention.

Unfortunately, it seemed that was not to be.

"That's disappointing." But she had a mission to accomplish, and while she didn't remotely resemble Matthew Hanger or any of his mighty Horsemen in physical prowess, temperament, or skill, she intended to mimic their gritty determination in seeing this mission through to its completion.

She straightened her posture and moved on to Phase Two.

"As I've mentioned before," she began, "my nephew has no desire to leave the only home he's ever known. However, I believe I might have come across a compromise that could satisfy both parties."

Mr. Mullins leaned back in his chair and opened his arms expansively. "I'm all ears."

Damaris scooted to the edge of her chair and lifted her chin. "I recently learned that a neighbor of ours, Mr. Oliver Grimes, sold a small section of land to the Harbinger company while the majority of his holdings remained in his possession. I'd like to propose a similar agreement."

Mr. Mullins began to shake his head, but Damaris dove into her proposition before he could interrupt.

"I'd be willing to sell all of our undeveloped land, keeping only the five or so acres surrounding the house, barn, and garden. That would allow us water from the creek and the well along with access to the road. It would also preserve the grave sites of my brother and sister-in-law."

The deepening frown on the other side of the desk did little to inspire optimism, yet Damaris soldiered on.

"I realize, of course, that this arrangement would greatly reduce the property's value. I expect the gentlemen at Harbinger to rescind their original offer and return with a figure substantially lower. However, as you made clear to me at our last meeting, a woman with a child to support must consider her finances. Therefore, I am willing to entertain any reasonable offer within my stated parameters."

Mr. Mullins leaned forward, a frown tugging his mouth downward. "I'm sorry, Miss Baxter. Your situation is different than that of Mr. Grimes. When Harbinger approved that renegotiation, they made it clear it was a one-time compromise. The other properties they sought would not serve their purposes unless they obtained the full acreage. So I'm afraid my hands are tied. I cannot present your new offer to them."

A response that fit with Luke's railroad theory. Still, she'd had to try. For Nathaniel.

"I understand." Damaris pushed to her feet, grateful that her legs held her up despite their shaking. "Still, I would like you to communicate my offer to them. Perhaps they can see a way to put the land to use in a way that you cannot."

Mullins stood as good manners demanded, but his frown did not abate. "I sincerely doubt—"

Damaris raised her hand to cut off his protest, shocked at her own boldness. Perhaps Luke's courage had rubbed off on her more than she'd realized. "Please, Mr. Mullins. Pass along the offer. If you are correct and they refuse, I'll know where we stand. As will Nathaniel." She let her mask of strength slip for just a moment, allowing the lawyer to glimpse her true concern. "I need my nephew to see me as an ally, not an enemy in this, Mr. Mullins. To do that, I must make every effort to preserve what he holds dear. Surely you can understand."

"What I understand is that you are far more accommodating of a child's feelings than most adults would be in your shoes." He dipped his head in deference, but a touch of censure rang in his tone.

Damaris raised her chin. "Nathaniel has lost both his mother and his father. It would be a shame for him to lose his home as well."

Mr. Mullins crossed his arms and peered at her as she imagined he would peer at a judge he was trying to sway in court. "What would truly be a shame is if he lost his chance for a solid future because his guardian was more concerned with preserving his immediate happiness than securing for him the advantages of education, opportunity, and financial prosperity."

Blowing out a breath, he uncrossed his arms and relaxed his posture. Even the scowl he'd worn softened into a look more in the category of brotherly concern than condescending disapproval.

"I'm not a parent, Miss Baxter, so I cannot begin to understand all the nuances involved in making a decision such as the one before you. Yet I feel compelled to offer some unsolicited advice."

She nodded. Not because she particularly cared to hear his advice, but because she sensed he was going to share it regardless, and the less resistance he felt from her, the more quickly she'd be able to make her escape.

"Don't let your desire to earn Nathaniel's approval supersede your job of doing what is ultimately in his best interest."

He could not have aimed a better shot. The arrow cracked open her armor and sank into the vulnerable flesh beneath.

"I suppose it all comes down to determining what is truly in the child's best interest," she said as she grabbed the back of the chair she'd just vacated, seeking support.

He nodded. "I suppose it does."

The lawyer's words lingered in Damaris's mind long after she left his office. She prayed most of the way home, asking the Lord for discernment to recognize what was best and for courage to see it done no matter the personal cost.

When her wagon rolled into the yard and she spotted Luke and Nathaniel laughing together by the water pump, dirt and sweat coating them from head to toe, the scene soothed her worries. *This* was what was best for Nathaniel. A godly man to mentor him. A mother figure to love and nurture him. Memories of his parents surrounding him with encouragement and purpose. If only she could capture this moment and make it last.

Luke caught sight of her first. He lifted a hand in greeting, then gave the pump handle a few good thrusts before washing away the grime from his face, neck, and hands. Nathaniel, on the other hand, bolted away from the pump, perfectly content in his mud-encrusted state, and ran up to the wagon.

"Can Luke and me go shooting before supper? He said I needed to ask your permission, so can we?"

She pulled the wagon to a halt and looked over at Luke, who stood at a distance, rubbing a towel over his short-cropped hair. His eyes met hers, but she sensed no direction from him. He'd abide by whatever she decided.

Damaris returned her attention to her nephew. Her first instinct was to please him, to make him happy and perhaps in the process make him like her a little better. Yet equally strong was the desire to keep him safe. He was still a child, after all. A child on the cusp of manhood. How did mothers stand back and allow their sons to become men when the journey was fraught with so many dangers?

"Don't you already know how to shoot?" she asked, trying to find a way to squirm out of making an actual decision.

Nathaniel rolled his eyes at her. "There's a difference between knowing how to shoot and being good enough to hit your target nine times out of ten. It takes practice, Aunt Maris." He stepped closer and lowered his voice to a husky whisper. "And who better to practice with than one of Hanger's Horsemen? Please, Aunt Maris? Luke's gonna be gone all day tomorrow. This is our best chance."

Her head snapped up, and her eyes immediately sought out Luke. "You're going to be gone tomorrow?"

He strode toward the wagon. "Yep. Gonna ride to Huntsville. Get these stitches out. I'll be back before nightfall."

He was leaving?

Just for a day. Not permanently. Still, the panic that hit her chest at the news would have knocked her flat if she hadn't still been sitting on the wagon bench.

"All right." She hid her churning emotions behind a stern façade as she lowered her gaze to Nathaniel. "But you listen to Luke and do everything exactly as he says. Understand?"

"Woohoo!" He jumped and pumped a fist into the air. "I'll get Pa's gun."

"Not until you clean up at the pump," Luke said, one eyebrow raised.

"Yes, sir!" Nathaniel dashed off to do just that.

Luke closed the remaining distance to the wagon and held a hand out to her. "I'll keep a close eye on him."

Was he going to help her down this time? Had he healed enough? His gaze held no uncertainty. Only a heat that melted her insides and set her head to spinning like a weather vane in a windstorm.

"I trust you," she murmured, her meaning seeming to broaden from shooting lessons to something much more personal as she rose to her feet and turned to face him.

He said nothing more, just fit his hands to her waist and slowly lowered her to the ground. The trip seemed to last forever, yet it ended far too quickly. Their eyes never wavered from each other. Her hands settled on his wide shoulders, and his fingers twitched against her stays. Her feet gradually came to rest on the earth, but neither of them cared. His hands retained their position. Hers did the same.

"*I'll stay as long as you need me.*" The promise he'd made days ago reflected again in his eyes.

Her heart thumped out the question she didn't yet have the courage to ask aloud. *What if I need you forever?*

TWENTY-SIX

S trange how a house that had never felt lonely when she'd been alone in it before could suddenly feel soulless and empty despite the fact that nothing had physically changed. The clock on the parlor mantel still chimed every hour. The same creaky floorboards in the hall greeted her each time she passed. Yet the silence felt magnified.

Breakfast had been a bustling affair. Nathaniel had chattered nonstop about the target shooting yesterday afternoon while Luke praised his improved marksmanship and made suggestions about what they might try next. Damaris couldn't imagine a more perfect way to start the day. So many smiles had circled their table that she'd almost grown dizzy from watching them make the rounds. Not a single belligerent scowl or sarcastic comment emerged to take the shine off the morning. Add to that the warm glances she'd collected from Luke along with his quiet thanks and sincere compliments, and she found herself wishing she could somehow capture the moment with needle and thread in one of her samplers so she could treasure it forever.

Then they'd left. Nathaniel to school, Luke to Huntsville. Hours later, she could still see her Horseman turn in his saddle to tip his hat to her before riding away.

He'd ridden away before. To go to town or to exercise Titan. Yet this time felt different. It felt like a practice run for when he would leave for good. And it left a hole in her heart that ached with loneliness.

Damaris closed her copy of *Little Women* and folded it against her chest as she leaned her head back against the trunk of her reading tree. Maybe she should rename it her wishing tree. Not much actual reading had transpired today. Her eyes had dutifully scanned the pages, but she'd absorbed nothing. Her mind was too filled with Luke. Recalling how he would work Titan in the paddock, then come stand at the fence. Smile at her. Ask about her book. Share an anecdote about some scrape he'd gotten into at school as a boy in order to *avoid* reading.

No story bound in paper could compare to the one she longed to live in the real world. The one where Luke Davenport never left.

As if her newly dubbed wishing tree had heard her heart and granted her desire, the sound of an approaching rider met her ears.

Damaris scrambled to her feet, heart pounding. She brushed the dust from her skirt, then lifted a hand to check her hair. She hadn't expected him back until closer to suppertime, but maybe he'd felt well enough to push his pace. She hurried along the fence line to the edge of the barn and waved a greeting.

Her hand slowed mid-wave, however, when she realized

that the rider looked significantly smaller than Luke. Shorter in the saddle. Narrower across the shoulders. Wrong color of hat.

Moving her hand to shade her eyes, Damaris studied the rider for distinguishing features. The afternoon sun glinted off something on the man's vest. A badge, perhaps?

Before she could confirm, a second rider appeared on her drive. This one she recognized. She'd seen him ride in before. The day after Luke had been attacked by rustlers.

Oliver Grimes.

Dread settled into her belly as the two men drew closer. They tipped their hats to her, but neither moved to dismount.

"Afternoon, Miss Baxter." The leather of Sheriff Conley's saddle creaked as he shifted his seat and offered her a weak smile. "Your nephew home from school yet?"

What did they want with Nathaniel? Her gaze darted from one man to the other. Had Mr. Grimes filed a complaint? She didn't know precisely what type of trouble Nathaniel had stirred up during the nighttime visits he'd paid to the ranch next door, but surely they were mere pranks. Nothing criminal.

Choosing her words with care, Damaris focused on the sheriff, preferring his tepid smile to the scowl on Grimes's face. "Nathaniel's not home yet, but I expect him soon. Can I ask what this is about?"

"It concerns the boy, ma'am. I'd just as soon wait fer him before we start discussin' things. I've never been fond of repeatin' myself."

And she'd never been fond of arrogant men who enjoyed

sitting on their high horses and looking down on people. In this case literally as well as figuratively.

"Can I at least offer you some coffee while we wait?" Anything to get them down off their horses and level the playing field a little. "I don't know how long Nathaniel will be. He doesn't always come straight home."

"He will today, ma'am." The sheriff sounded awfully sure of himself. Too sure. "I left a deputy outside the school to watch for him. Cal will let him know to come straight home."

No doubt this Cal person was also under orders to make sure Nathaniel cooperated. Which could ensure exactly the opposite result, knowing her nephew.

Mr. Grimes, who had been content to wait in the background, nudged his horse and moved up alongside the sheriff. "I ain't got all day to wait around, Conley. I say we just head up to the canyon. See if your report is accurate. Cal can bring the boy along later."

Sheriff Conley shook his head. "I said we were gonna wait on the boy, and that's what we're gonna do." He turned back to Damaris. "As the boy's guardian, you'd be within your rights to go up to the canyon with us, ma'am." He scanned her from head to toe, then raised a skeptical brow. "If you ride, that is."

Damaris bristled. "Of course I ride. And if you think you're taking my nephew anywhere without me, you are severely mistaken, sir. I'll fetch the horses."

She had little actual experience in saddling mounts. Her father or a liveryman had always taken care of the task for her in the past. She could hitch a team to a wagon, but saddling was a different story. No matter. She'd ride bareback if she had to. These men would not be leaving her behind.

She marched into the tack room and took down a pair of bridles, then exited into the paddock and approached the first of her brother's geldings. Leaving the extra tack draped over the fence, she clicked her tongue and held out her hand. The black nuzzled her palm, then stood still while she removed his halter and slipped the bit of the bridle into his mouth. Speaking softly to him, she fastened all the straps, then turned to lead him into the barn.

She stopped short when she spotted Oliver Grimes standing at the barn door, a blanket tossed over his shoulder and a saddle across his arms.

"I'll saddle this'un while you round up the other." His expression had lost none of its displeasure, and his grumbled offer sounded far from solicitous. Yet there he stood, ready to help, while the sheriff remained mounted in the yard. Perhaps Oliver Grimes wasn't as heartless as he seemed.

"Thank you."

He had the first horse saddled by the time she retrieved and bridled the second. Minutes later, the mounts were ready, and she and Mr. Grimes both led one down the barn aisle. They paused at the tack area to allow Damaris to hang up the halters.

"Where's Davenport?" Grimes murmured in a low voice.

Damaris debated how much to reveal. The sheriff's timing for this little visit had not escaped her notice. It was almost as if he had waited for Luke to leave town in order to catch her and Nathaniel alone. On the other hand, Mr. Grimes seemed genuinely surprised by Luke's absence. Did that mean he wasn't party to the ambush? Or just not privy to all the details?

"He had some business to tend to out of town, but I expect him home soon." No harm in letting him believe Luke could show up any minute. With God, all things were possible, after all. "Do you know why the sheriff is here?" The lawman hadn't been eager to share, but maybe Grimes would be more forthcoming.

"All I know is he sent a message out to the ranch to meet him here at three o'clock. Somethin' about my missing beeves." He met her eyes for a heartbeat, an odd mix of pity and indignation radiating from his gaze.

They believed Nathaniel knew where the cows were! But he didn't. He had nothing to do with the rustling or the criminals who'd left Luke to die in the dark on that horrible night.

"Aunt Maris?" Nathaniel's voice jabbed at her from outside the barn. "Where are you?" He sounded angry. And afraid.

"I'm here!" she called, pivoting away from Mr. Grimes and his disturbing gaze and hurrying out into the yard, her horse following in her wake.

She tossed the reins over the horse's neck, then dashed over to her nephew. A man she assumed to be Cal was being waved on his way by the sheriff, but Damaris barely spared him a glance. All her energy belonged to Nathaniel. Reaching out, she clasped his hand and gave it a squeeze.

"What's going on?" he whispered, turning his face toward hers.

"I don't know. Something about the rustled cattle, I think."

Mr. Grimes exited the barn, leading the second horse, and Nathaniel instantly stiffened.

"What's *he* doing here?" There wasn't much whisper in that question.

Damaris had no time to explain or to calm Nathaniel because in that moment the sheriff decided to take charge of the conversation.

"Mount up, boy. We're going to ride up to the canyon at the north end of your property." Conley crossed his wrists over his saddle horn and eyed Nathaniel. "I assume you know the one I mean."

"We only got one canyon, so yeah, I know the one you mean. But there ain't nothin' out there 'cept dirt and a few scraggly trees."

Sheriff Conley seemed unimpressed by Nathaniel's assurances. "I got me a witness that says different. He claims he saw near a dozen longhorns holed up there. All wearin' the Triple G brand."

Nathaniel pulled away from her, his face reddening as he strode two steps toward the lawman. "That's a lie! I never touched those cows."

Damaris ran after him, quickly inserting herself between her nephew and the frowning sheriff.

"That's what we're here to find out." Sheriff Conley's right hand moved to the butt of his revolver, but he didn't draw the weapon. Thank the Lord. "Now, get on yer horse, and let's take a ride. See who's right."

"Please, Nathaniel." Damaris kept her voice low as she gently pushed him toward the horses waiting outside the barn. "We need to keep cool heads. I know you didn't have anything to do with rustling that cattle. Soon the sheriff will, too."

Only the truth they knew failed to agree with the truth they found in the canyon.

Ten steers wandered around a small enclosure that had been roped off to keep the cattle from escaping.

As soon as the animals came into view, Oliver Grimes kicked his mount into a canter to get a closer look.

"Well?" Sheriff Conley called after Grimes had dismounted and inspected the stock. "Them your beeves, Grimes?"

The owner of the Triple G glared up at Nathaniel. "Yep. They're mine, all right."

The sheriff moved close to Nathaniel's horse and caught the reins. "Nathaniel Baxter, you're under arrest for cattle rustlin'."

"But I didn't do nothin'!" Nathaniel swung a panicked gaze toward Damaris, and she nearly crumpled from the force of his fear. "I didn't do it, Aunt Maris. I swear."

"I know you didn't." Damaris turned a scowl on Conley. "This is ridiculous, Sheriff. Luke Davenport already gave you a description of the rustlers. Four grown men who left him for dead after attacking him with knives. My nephew has nothing in common with those men. I don't know how these cows came to be here, but Nathaniel had nothing to do with it."

"The other rustlers coulda hired him to show them how to sneak onto my property," Grimes said as he rejoined the group. "Makes him just as guilty as them."

"But they didn't," Nathaniel insisted. "I never saw them before that night."

"So you *were* there." Grimes jabbed an accusing finger toward Nathaniel's chest. "I *knew* it. This scamp has been sneaking onto my property for weeks. Destroying my food stores. Cripplin' my horses. Scatterin' my hens. He's a menace and deserves to be locked up."

"Well, you're a murderer who deserves to swing at the end of a rope!"

Damaris gasped.

Grimes, however, just wrinkled his brow. "What in tarnation are you talkin' about, boy?"

"You killed my father." Tears formed in Nathaniel's eyes as he spat the angry words at the man he'd hated for months. "You wanted his land, and he wouldn't sell it to you, so you killed him."

"Is that what you think?" Grimes wagged his head. "I did no such thing. Yes, I wanted your land, but not so bad that I would *kill* someone over it." Some of the anger drained from Grimes's features. "Look, son, I might not've liked your daddy all that much, but I respected him. He stuck to his guns and didn't let me or anyone else push him around. It's a right shame what happened to him, but I had no hand in it."

Nathaniel's shoulders hunched. He looked so lost and adrift. Yet Sheriff Conley remained unmoved. If anything, his grip on Nathaniel's reins tightened.

"My nephew will admit to the vandalism," Damaris said. She had to do something to stop this farce from continuing. "And he will make whatever restitution the law requires. But he is *not* involved in the rustling. You have Mr. Davenport's testimony. I demand you release Nathaniel at once."

"Ain't gonna happen, ma'am." The sheriff took the reins

completely out of Nathaniel's hands and began edging the horses back toward town. "Facts are facts. The boy admits to trespassin' on Triple G land, being in the vicinity of the rustlers on the night Mr. Davenport was attacked, and the stolen cattle were found on his property and therefore in his possession." Conley's eyes turned granite-hard. "The arrest stands. I'm takin' him in."

— CHAPTER —
TWENTY-SEVEN

Damaris had never felt more helpless in her entire life than on that horrible ride to town. The anger she'd come to expect from Nathaniel had vanished, leaving a desolate hopelessness in its wake that broke her heart. He wouldn't look at her. Wouldn't talk to her. Just stared straight ahead as Sheriff Conley led him to the jailhouse.

When the lawman escorted him to a cell and closed the barred door behind him, the metallic click of the lock echoed like a gunshot in the quiet room. One that sent a bullet straight through Damaris's heart.

A tear threatened to roll down her cheek, but she blinked it away. This was no time for hand-wringing and despair. This was a time for bold faith. For unshakable hope.

She marched up to the cell and wrapped her hands around the bars. "We'll figure this out, Nathaniel." Not a shred of doubt colored her tone. "The truth will set you free. You'll see."

She reached through the bars and clasped his hand. He

clung to her for a moment. His eyes met hers, his gaze brimming with fear and regret. Then he pulled away. His shoulders folded inward, and he turned his back, shuffled over to the cot on the far wall, and sat down. He stared at the floor, practically willing her to leave.

But she wouldn't. She'd stay here all night if she had to. He would not be left to face this alone.

A pair of hands gently fit themselves to her upper arms and urged her away from the cell. "This ain't no place for you, ma'am," the sheriff said. "Come away now."

She tightened her grip on the bars. "I will not," she gritted out softly between clenched teeth. "My nephew needs me, and I will stay here until this tragic miscarriage of justice is made right. Nathaniel is no rustler. He's just a boy."

"It ain't my job to determine guilt, Miss Baxter. The circuit judge'll take care of that. All I do is collect evidence and arrest folks who possess motive, means, and opportunity to commit a crime. Your nephew has all three."

She turned to glare at the unfeeling man. "But there is evidence against others as well. Evidence you are conveniently ignoring. Four other men trespassed on Triple G land. Mr. Davenport caught these same men in the very act of rustling. They attacked Mr. Davenport and left him for dead. Those are the men guilty of this crime, not Nathaniel."

"So you've said. Repeatedly." The sheriff blew out a breath and worked his jaw as if he was physically trying to keep his temper in check. "You'll have a chance to explain your side to the judge, but I've made my call, and your yakkin' ain't gonna change my mind." He took hold of her arm and put a little more strength behind his tug, dragging her a few steps away from the cell. "Now, if you want to help your boy, I suggest you find him a lawyer."

A lawyer. Of course! Why hadn't she thought of that before?

"Nathaniel?" She leveraged herself back toward the cell. "I'm going to hire Mr. Mullins. I'll be back as soon as I can."

Sheriff Conley must have realized she would soon be out of his hair, for he released his hold on her and gave her a modicum of privacy with her nephew, retreating toward his desk.

Her nephew, on the other hand, just sat on the cot, head in his hands, making no effort to connect with her at all.

"Nathaniel, please," she murmured. "Look at me."

She waited. And waited.

Finally, his head lifted. Tears glistened in his reddened eyes, and moisture immediately pooled in her own as her chest clenched. Punching down the pity swelling inside her, Damaris hardened her heart. Luke had been teaching Nathaniel to fight and defend himself. It was time to apply those lessons to a new arena.

"Hold your head up," she challenged, lifting her own chin in example. "You are no criminal. You're the son of Douglas Baxter. And Baxters don't retreat when things get hard. Neither do Horsemen, and you have two of us on your side. I'm going to fight for you, Nathaniel. Luke will, too. And God, the mightiest warrior of all, will fight for you. You are not alone in this. Do you hear me? You are not alone."

He gave a tiny nod. It wasn't much, but it was a start.

"Good. I don't know how long I'll be gone, but I *will* be back." Hopefully with Luke.

Heavens, how she wished he were here right now. He dealt with criminals and lawmen all the time. He'd know exactly how to handle this situation. But he wasn't here. Which meant Nathaniel's well-being rested solely on her shoulders.

As she released the bars and turned to leave, she kept her chin up, doing her best to practice what she'd just preached. She wasn't alone. God was with her. Fighting for her.

"'Ye shall not fear them,'" she quoted softly beneath her breath, "'for the Lord your God he shall fight for you.'"

"What's that you're sayin'?" Sheriff Conley looked up from where he'd just retrieved a coffeepot from atop a potbelly stove.

Damaris smiled at the lawman, and oddly enough, the gesture felt authentic, unlike the pieced-together patch of false politeness she usually manufactured in situations like this.

"Just recalling a verse that a friend of mine likes to quote." *And doing my best to emulate his confident, warrior mentality.* "It seemed appropriate."

"You talkin' about that Horseman fella?" Sheriff Conley scowled. "Be careful around him, ma'am. Vigilantes like that care more about collecting bounties and reward money than who might get caught in their crossfire. Now that Oliver Grimes has his stock back, Davenport's got no reason to stick around. And that's fine by me. We don't need his kind around here."

Damaris burned with the urge to give the pompous nitwit the setdown of his life, but angering the sheriff would do her nephew no favors. So she tamped down her outrage and pulled out one of those manufactured smiles she kept handy, even though it had to stretch a little too tightly over her indignation and likely wouldn't fool anyone.

"I can't say I agree," she said, adding a heaping tablespoon of sugar to her tone, "but I won't argue with your conclusions. Now, if you'll excuse me, I think I will heed your advice and seek legal counsel for my nephew."

He saluted her with his newly filled coffee cup and waved her toward the door, no doubt as eager to see her gone as she was to be rid of him.

Hurrying up Elm Street to the courthouse square, Damaris prayed that she'd find Mr. Mullins in his office. When she found the door to his office unlocked, she nearly wilted in relief. After letting herself in, she dashed through the reception area and burst straight into the inner office, where she found Mr. Mullins standing by a coatrack, reaching for his hat.

"Miss Baxter. Are you all right?" He abandoned the coatrack and made his way to her side. "You look quite distressed."

"I need to hire you," she blurted. "To defend my nephew. He's been arrested."

"Arrested?" He drew back in shock. "But he's just a boy."

"Precisely! The very idea of him being a cattle rustler is ludicrous. But Sheriff Conley will not be swayed. Nathaniel is locked in jail at this very moment."

Mr. Mullins lightly touched her arm and steered her toward a chair. Then, instead of seating himself behind his desk as he usually did, he sat in the empty chair next to her. "I assume the sheriff has evidence of some sort that precipitated the arrest?"

Damaris nodded and told him about the stolen cattle being found on Baxter property, about Nathaniel's past forays onto

Triple G land, and about his grudge against Oliver Grimes. "We are ready to make restitution for the vandalism," she rushed to assure her lawyer, "but Nathaniel is no cattle thief."

Mr. Mullins grew thoughtful. "I believe you, Miss Baxter, but I'm not sure a judge will. Having those steers found on your property is compelling evidence. And given the boy's history with Grimes, he appears to have motive."

"But Luke Davenport can testify that Nathaniel was not part of the rustler's gang that attacked him. He saw four men and could likely recognize them if he saw them again. My nephew knows nothing of these men. He'd never seen them before that night and has not seen them since."

Mr. Mullins let out a sigh. "I'm afraid that Mr. Davenport's testimony might not be as convincing as you hope."

"What do you mean? He's one of Hanger's Horsemen, for pity's sake. No one has more experience when it comes to identifying and capturing rustlers. His credibility is unmatched."

"That would be the case in most situations, but in this instance, that credibility has been compromised."

Damaris didn't believe him. She couldn't afford to. Luke's testimony was the only viable weapon she had at her disposal. "How?" she challenged, preparing arguments to rebuff whatever he might say.

"Well, if I were the opposing attorney, I would point out to the judge that Mr. Davenport is only alive today because of the nursing he received from you, Miss Baxter. The entire town has heard about the attack that left him near death. The very fact that he is still among the living is due solely to your care."

"That's not entirely true. Josephine Hanger handled most of the doctoring," Damaris corrected. "She and her husband, Matthew, were here for four days. If anyone should be credited with saving Mr. Davenport's life, it's Dr. Hanger."

Mullins nodded. "That's good to know. I can argue that in rebuttal, but I don't think it will make much difference. Not when my opponent is sure to bring to light the fact that Mr. Davenport has been living at your place during his recuperation. Growing close to you and your nephew. Nathaniel talks about him at school, you know. And children spread tales faster than adults. Why, just this morning on my way to the café for breakfast, I overheard a pair of young lads talking about how exciting it must have been for Nathaniel to have one of *the* Horsemen take him shooting. They were quite envious."

Damaris crossed her ankles and tucked them beneath her chair. "I fail to see what that has to do with anything."

"My dear Miss Baxter. It would take very little effort for a lawyer to argue that a man like Luke Davenport, one who is known far and wide as a protector of the innocent, would do whatever was necessary to protect a young lad with whom he had struck up a friendship. Not only is Mr. Davenport indebted to you, the boy's aunt, but he is genuinely fond of the boy himself. A protector protects. It's his nature. Therefore, someone could argue that Mr. Davenport's description of the rustler attack deliberately omitted Nathaniel's involvement in order to protect the boy from blame."

"Luke would never lie."

"Of course not." Mr. Mullins patted her hand, but the gesture failed to impart any reassurance. "Unfortunately, the law isn't always about what is true. It's about what you can get a judge and jury to *believe* is true. And I'm afraid that far too many people would find it easy to believe that Mr. Davenport has a soft spot for you and the boy."

All of her arguments turned to dust in her mouth. She had truth on her side, but what if truth wasn't enough?

Ye shall not fear them, for the Lord your God he shall fight for you.

She heard the verse from Deuteronomy in Luke's voice as he'd taught it to Nathaniel after one of their sparring sessions. She tried to cling to the promise, but doubts assailed her, filling her mind with the sounds of a guilty verdict being handed down and images of Nathaniel being carted off to prison.

"Cattle theft is a felony offense." She barely heard Mr. Mullins over the rushing in her ears. "It carries a penalty of up to five years in prison."

Damaris whimpered. Shook her head. This couldn't be happening.

You're supposed to be fighting for us, her soul cried. *Where are you?*

"I have an idea." Mr. Mullins patted her hand again to get her attention. A light filled his eyes that buoyed her hopes just enough to keep her head above the floodwaters. "I'm friends with the man who clerks for the circuit judge. He has an office just down the hall. Let me go to him and see if we can propose some kind of plea that won't require prison time."

Damaris straightened. "Do you think it possible?"

Mullins shrugged. "It doesn't hurt to try." He pushed up from his chair and started pacing the office. "Judge Kilmore is tough, but this is Nathaniel's first offense. And with his youth, I might be able to convince the judge that prison is not the right place for him. I can use his father's recent passing as exigent circumstances."

He suddenly stopped and banged the flat of his hand against the corner of his desk. Spinning to face Damaris, he reached into his vest pocket and pulled out a watch.

"I've got to run if I'm going to catch him. Wait here, Miss Baxter."

She barely managed a nod before he ran out of the office.

Time ticked by so slowly. She prayed and paced, then paced and prayed. She stared out the window, hoping for a sign of Luke returning, but he failed to materialize.

Nearly an hour passed before the creak of the outer office door finally broke the silence. Damaris turned from the window and met Mr. Mullins as he strode toward her. The beaming smile on his face set her heart pounding in expectation.

"We wired the judge," Mr. Mullins declared, "and after some negotiating, he's agreed to dismiss the charges when they are brought to him if you and Nathaniel agree to a few unconventional terms."

To have the charges *dismissed*? She'd agree to almost anything. "Of course. What are the terms?"

"Judge Kilmore agrees that prison should be the last resort for a boy of such tender years. Thankfully, he is on the side of those who believe prison is for reformation more than punishment. And since Nathaniel's grudge seems focused solely on Oliver Grimes and not the community at large, the judge is willing to consider removing the boy from the target of his aggression as a possible solution. I told him of your family in St. Louis, that you would be able to take him there and provide a good home for him. But that wasn't enough for Judge Kilmore. He insisted on removing all of Nathaniel's ties to the Madisonville community to ensure he doesn't return. I happened to mention there was an offer on your property. That you could sell the land and remove the boy to St. Louis within a week's time."

Damaris took an involuntary step back. Sell the land? She'd vowed not to. It was Nathaniel's birthright. All he had left of his father.

"I . . . I can't sell."

"You have to." Mr. Mullins took hold of her shoulders and squeezed gently until she looked him in the eyes. "If you don't, your nephew's going to prison."

CHAPTER

TWENTY-EIGHT

Luke hit the outskirts of Madisonville about an hour be-fore sunset. Weariness dragged at his bones, causing his spine to bend and his shoulders to slouch. He was a poor excuse for a cavalryman, worn to a nubbin by a single day in the saddle. But he'd made it to Huntsville and back. Almost by suppertime, too. For a fellow who'd nearly been dead a couple of weeks ago, the effort wasn't completely pitiful.

To his left, a man in a suit was locking up the hardware store. Catching sight of Luke, he offered a wave. Luke nod-ded in return as Titan clopped down the street. Diagonally across the square, a handful of ladies sat on the boarding-house porch, chattering like a flock of magpies. And down the boardwalk to his right, a couple walked arm-in-arm toward a restaurant. It made him long for Damaris's company even more than he already did. Which was fairly significant, since he'd been thinking about her all day.

As he neared the northeast corner of the courthouse, a movement at the edge of his periphery drew his gaze back toward the boardwalk where he'd seen the couple a moment ago. A woman exited the restaurant, struggling with the weight of the door while she attempted to maneuver a basket through the opening. Her shape seemed familiar, and a distinctive braid of dark brown hair formed a crown atop her head. Damaris? What was she doing in town this late?

Tightening his knees, Luke urged Titan into a trot and reined him onto a path to intercept. Once she cleared the door, Damaris moved faster than he anticipated, jostling the basket with her hurried stride.

Not wanting to draw undue attention, he waited to call out until he was nearly abreast of her.

"Damaris?"

She visibly jumped, then almost turned her ankle as she pivoted sharply toward him.

A mule kicking him in the gut would've shocked him less than the sight he beheld when she faced him. Red, puffy eyes. Strands of windblown hair falling haphazardly around her ears. Clothing wadded and wrinkled. And dirty. He couldn't recall ever seeing her dirty.

"Luke?" Her voice broke as recognition lit her eyes. She took a step toward him, and her desperation, her heartbreak, her *need* slammed into his chest.

He was off his horse in an instant and leapt onto the boardwalk to wrap an arm around her. "I'm here."

"Thank God," she whimpered right before she buried her face in his chest and wept.

Luke cupped the back of her head and held her against him, not caring one iota about who might see them or what they might think. Damaris needed him, and not even a Texas twister would pull him away.

A handful of minutes passed before she lifted her head from his shirt and inhaled a long, shuddering breath. He reached into his trouser pocket, pulled out a handkerchief, and pressed it into her hand. She wiped her eyes and blew her nose, her movements rushed and impatient.

After tucking his handkerchief into her skirt pocket, she grabbed his hand and started marching as if a bugle had just sounded the advance. She descended the stairs to the street at the end of the boardwalk, then turned right on Trinity. Luke shot a look at Titan over his shoulder and clicked his tongue. The horse obediently followed.

"They've arrested Nathaniel for rustling."

The words punched him like a hidden jab right as they rounded the corner.

"On what grounds?" He lengthened his stride to move in front of her, then reached for the basket she carried in her far hand, taking the burden from her. He wished he could do more.

"They found the missing cows in a canyon on the northern section of our land. I reminded Sheriff Conley of your testimony about the rustlers and your certainty that Nathaniel was not among them, but he wouldn't be swayed. He insisted that since Nathaniel bore a grudge against Oliver Grimes and had been seen in the company of the rustlers that night, he was a viable suspect. Finding the stolen cattle on our land sealed the deal and provided the evidence he needed to make the arrest."

Luke frowned. Those longhorns showing up out of the blue on the day he left town seemed suspiciously convenient. He'd ridden Titan around the north end of the property a few times while building up his stamina, and he'd never seen so much as a single steer.

"Someone must've driven the rustled cattle onto Baxter land during the last day or two," he said. "I've been to that canyon as recently as three days ago. I can testify there were no beeves there then. Someone is trying to make Nate look guilty."

But why? To shift blame off of themselves? Or for some bigger reason?

"I don't think your testimony will help."

"Why not?"

Damaris made a left at the boardinghouse, still holding his hand. A fact that did not go unnoticed by the ladies on the porch.

Unable to tip his hat to the busybodies with one hand captive and the other fit around a basket handle, Luke settled for a smile and a nod. He'd seen Wallace deploy that technique with great success, distracting women with a flash of charm. But the porch ladies didn't appear charmed. Or distracted. If anything, their interest seemed to heighten. One even rose from her chair to shadow him and Damaris around the porch corner until she finally hit a railing that halted her progress.

Despite his companion's unwavering focus on the road in front of her, Damaris must have been aware of the ladies and their straining ears, for she didn't answer his question until she was a good half dozen yards past the boardinghouse.

"I spoke to a lawyer. He thinks your testimony will not be viewed as reliable due to your . . . closeness with Nathaniel and myself." As if just realizing she still held his hand, she released him and ducked her chin. "He told me that a judge might be swayed to believe that you would lie to protect us. I told him you were too honorable to do such a thing, but he didn't think it mattered."

Luke wasn't quite as certain of his honorable nature as she seemed to be, but it didn't matter in this case because no bending of the truth would be required.

Damaris slowed as they neared the jail, then turned to face him and halted. "Mr. Mullins wired the circuit judge and preemptively worked out a deal. The judge agreed to dismiss any charges brought against Nathaniel if we remove him from the area. I would have to take him home to St. Louis. Then, to ensure he didn't return to threaten Mr. Grimes again, we would have to sell the land as well."

Luke frowned. "That's a strange proposition."

And mighty convenient for the company wanting to buy the Baxter land. A company who just happened to broker its sales through the same lawyer giving Damaris advice.

"I don't know what to do." She looked up at him as if he had the answers. He didn't. But he had plenty of questions poking holes in his brain. "I'll talk things over with Nathaniel, of course. I intended to do so over supper." She nodded toward the basket Luke had confiscated. "But ultimately, I have to make the decision." She shook her head. "I can't let him go to jail, Luke. Not when it's in my power to prevent it."

"We don't have to make any decisions tonight." He took her hand and pressed a quick kiss to her knuckles. "If I've learned anything from Captain Hanger, it's that there are always more options than you see at first glance. You just might have to get a little creative in where you look for them."

"But Mr. Mullins said—"

"I'm not so sure you should be listenin' to Mr. Mullins."

Lines appeared in Damaris's forehead. "Why not? Douglas trusted him."

"With drawing up his will, yes, but I'm not so sure he'd trust him with his son's defense."

She tugged her hand free of his hold and wrapped her arms around her midsection as if she felt attacked by his lack of faith in her judgment. But it wasn't her judgment he didn't trust. It was the slickness of this lawyer who seemed to have his thumbs in too many pies.

"He can keep Nathaniel out of prison," she insisted, desperately holding on to the only thing that mattered to her—protecting her nephew.

"But don't you think it odd that his method of doing so also gets him what *he* wants?"

"The land?"

"Exactly."

Plodding hooves and creaking wood signaled the approach of a wagon. Luke glanced behind him, then placed a hand on Damaris's back and steered her to the edge of the road, taking care to keep himself between her and the vehicle. The farm wagon passed without incident, but Luke made no effort to reinsert distance between himself and Damaris. He wanted her close. Wanted her fingers on his arm. Even if she didn't particularly care to hear what he had to say.

"You're not his only client, Damaris. He works for Harbinger, too. He probably gets a percentage of every sale he brokers on their behalf. Who's to say he didn't suggest the land sale to the judge in the first place? He might've even sweetened the pot with a bribe. Promising the judge a share of his cut in exchange for making the land sale a condition of the boy's plea."

"Surely a judge wouldn't agree to something so . . . unethical."

Luke loved her innocence. The way she believed in people. In their capacity for good. Especially when it came to her belief in him. But one couldn't effectively fight the darkness if he didn't know where it lurked.

"In my line of work, I've seen a lot of corruption. The more power a person holds, the easier it is to succumb, since few, if any, will challenge them. Judges, politicians, cattle barons— I've seen plenty of those types choose greed over morality."

She shook her head slightly, wanting to deny his claim. She looked so lost, as if she were drifting on the open sea, only to have him start dismantling her boat, board by board.

Needing to shore her up somehow, he cupped her cheek and stilled her wagging head. Her gaze lifted. Met his. Pleaded for something solid to hold on to. Never had his towering frame felt quite so flimsy.

"I don't know anything about this particular judge. He might be a straight arrow. I hope he is. But the more I hear about this Ronald Mullins fellow, the more he strikes me as a slippery sort. I'm not suggesting you turn down his offer to work a plea for Nate." Not yet, anyway. "But I am asking you to give me some time to look for another way out of this mess. One that doesn't entail selling Nate's land." He stroked her cheek with the pad of his thumb. "Can you do that?"

She held his gaze for a moment, then pressed her lips together and nodded.

"Thank you." He tugged her against his chest and hugged her close. "We'll get through this, Damaris," he murmured against her hair. "All of us. Together."

She pressed her palm against his shirt, directly over his heart. Then she leaned into him, giving him not only her agreement, but her trust. The most precious thing he'd ever owned.

Now he just had to find a way to prove himself worthy of the gift.

Luke held the jailhouse door open for Damaris to pass through, then followed her inside.

"Davenport. You're back." The sheriff didn't look terribly pleased by that development. Probably figured Luke wouldn't be as easy to push around as an inexperienced woman who knew little about the law.

He'd be right.

Luke tipped his hat, acknowledging the lawman's authority even as he pinned him with a glare that made his opinion of the situation clear.

Conley pushed up from his chair and met Luke's stare with one of his own, making his claim to the righteousness of the arrest clear in his bowed-out chest and jutting chin. He stood a good six inches shorter than Luke, but he held his ground well.

The sheriff lifted a hand to stave him off, even though Luke hadn't said a word since entering. "I don't need you to remind me about the night you were attacked, Horseman.

Your woman done wore my ear off already repeatin' the tale multiple times. I got cause to hold the boy, and I ain't changin' my mind."

His woman? Luke's collar heated at the implication even as his chest expanded. Man, but he liked the idea of Damaris belonging to him. He'd been careful thus far not to let himself think of her in those terms. Not consciously, anyway. He admired her, respected her, and would gladly sacrifice himself to protect her, but he'd turned the key against considering anything further. Hearing the claim shoot off the sheriff's tongue as if it were a done deal busted through that locked door like a shotgun blast, sending splinters every which way and leaving Luke off balance.

Forcing his mind back to the lawman in front of him instead of the pretty lady at his side, Luke thanked the Lord for the military training that kept his thoughts from showing on his face.

"I'm not here to argue with you, Sheriff. Miss Baxter filled me in on today's events, and I agree that the arrest was justified based on the evidence available to you at the time." He dropped the food basket onto the lawman's desk with a *thump*. "You want to look through this before letting Miss Baxter into the cell to share the meal with her nephew?"

The touch of relaxation that had slid into the sheriff's posture when Luke supported the arrest tightened at the insinuation that Conley wasn't in possession of all the evidence. It didn't slacken any when Luke made the presumption that Damaris would be allowed into the cell, either. Allowing family visitors in the cells was a common practice, but each lawman had the power to decide what would or wouldn't take place in his jail.

Luke had calculated the risk entailed in asserting himself and decided it was worth it to let Damaris know she had options as Nate's next of kin. And if the sheriff decided to deny her meal privileges with her fourteen-year-old nephew, Luke wanted *Conley* to know that word would get out about his callous treatment of his boy prisoner.

After glaring for a good, long minute at Luke, Conley snatched the basket handle and rifled through the contents. "You can have twenty minutes with the kid," he groused as he shoved the basket toward Damaris. "No more."

She collected the food and dipped her head. "Thank you."

Conley grabbed the ring of keys on his belt and marched down the hall toward the pair of cells that stood at the back of the building. Damaris followed but paused to look back at Luke when he didn't join her.

"You go ahead," he urged softly. "I want to chat with the sheriff. I'll check in on Nate when you're done, then see you home."

She nodded, her eyes locking with his. The connection he felt in that moment nearly knocked the wind from his lungs. Her brown eyes tugged so hard at his heart, he felt compelled to rub a hand over his breastbone to make sure it stayed in his chest.

How could a woman look so utterly vulnerable and so courageously strong at the same time?

"I'm glad you're here, Luke."

"Me too."

She blinked and sighed out a breath, effectively cooling

some of the heat radiating around him. Tucking a stray piece of hair behind her ear, she straightened her shoulders and smoothed the front of her dress. Then, arming herself with a somewhat believable smile, she pivoted and followed the sheriff, leaving Luke to stare after her like a lovesick calf.

Until Conley clomped back into the office area, muttering and scowling. "I guess you plan on waitin' for her." It was less of a question and more of an aggrieved resignation.

"I do."

The lawman waved at a chair pushed against the wall to Luke's right. "Might as well take a load off, then. Don't need you towerin' over me like some disapprovin' tree."

Luke chuckled. "You picked up on that, did you?"

Conley's mouth twitched as if fighting a smile. "You ain't exactly subtle."

Luke grabbed the ladder-back chair with one hand, spun it around, and took a seat.

"Coffee?" Conley lifted a dented pot from the small stove behind his desk and held it up in question.

Luke's stomach growled loudly in answer.

"I'll take that as a yes." Conley smirked as he pulled a second cup off a shelf. He blew out a smattering of dust, then filled it with dark brew.

He plopped the cup on the desk in front of Luke before taking his own seat. A groan escaped him as he folded himself into the chair.

"You might find this hard to believe," he said, "but I generally tend to avoid arresting half-grown boys." He shook his head. "Grimes has been breathin' down my neck for a month about his missing beeves, though, and when a witness reported seein' cattle holed up on Baxter's land, I couldn't just let it go. This is cattle country. Rustlin' can't be ignored. Even when the rustler's a kid."

"I agree." Luke lifted his coffee to his lips. "When the kid actually *is* a rustler."

The sheriff shrugged. "Guess that's up to Judge Kilmore to decide."

Luke took a swig of coffee and grimaced at the strong, bitter taste. It wasn't any worse than what he'd drunk in the army, but he'd gotten used to the way Damaris fixed it, sneaking in a tiny bit of sugar to soften the flavor's rough edges.

She probably thought he hadn't noticed. And for a while he hadn't. Until he poured his own cupful the day she'd gone to town and it hadn't tasted the same. Apparently the fighter who'd spent the majority of his life proving himself the toughest man in the unit had a secret craving for the sweeter things in life. Damaris had recognized it. How, he had no idea. No one else ever had. Not even him. She might be quiet on the surface, but her observations ran deep.

Luke stretched his legs out in front of him and shifted his weight in the chair to avoid the tender place on his thigh where the doc in Huntsville had removed his stitches. "So, who was the witness who spotted the stolen stock?"

Conley raised a brow. "You know I ain't gonna answer that. I can't have a certain Horseman harassin' him about his testimony, now can I? Don't change nothin' anyways. The cattle were found right where he said they'd be."

Luke swallowed his disappointment along with another dose of corrosive coffee. He'd hoped the sheriff would be more forthcoming. Conley might be lazy when it came to investigating crimes, but he wasn't void of intelligence.

"Mighty convenient, don't ya think?" Luke asked. "Especially since the stock weren't there a couple of days ago when I rode the Baxter property line."

A spark of curiosity lit the lawman's eyes for a moment before he hid it behind his coffee cup.

"I know the kid ain't doin' it alone," Conley admitted after setting down his cup. "He seemed as surprised as his aunt did to find them cows in their canyon. But that could just mean he didn't expect his partners to sell him out."

"His partners." Luke scoffed. "You mean the four full-grown men who tried to kill him when he accidentally stumbled across their evening activities?" Maybe he'd been too quick to credit Conley with a working brain. "I saw that whole encounter, Sheriff. Nate had no idea the rustlers were there, and the only thing those men cared about was ridding themselves of a witness. There's no partnership."

"Tell it to the judge."

"I will." Luke glanced away, giving Conley the satisfaction of winning their little staring contest. Antagonizing the lawman wouldn't aid his cause. Besides, Luke had nothing to prove.

Except for Nate's innocence.

"I guess Grimes has already pressed charges." Luke abandoned his coffee and leaned back in his chair. His stomach might be empty, but half a cup of sludge was his limit.

Conley, on the other hand, gulped down the dregs from his mug and wiped the back of his sleeve across his mouth in satisfaction. "Not yet, but he will. I expect him first thing in the morning. He was more concerned with roundin' up his beeves than ridin' back to town with us this afternoon. Only natural."

Luke nodded, his expression carefully solemn. It wouldn't do to jump out of his seat and throw his hat in the air with a mighty whoop.

If Grimes hadn't pressed charges yet, Luke still had time to talk to him. Try to convince him to let Nate go. It'd be a long shot. Oliver Grimes had been obsessing over his missing stock too long to turn a blind eye. But maybe with the right argument—

"Visitin' time's almost over," Conley groused. Apparently he told time by how long his cup of coffee lasted. "If you want to see the boy, best do it now. Leave yer guns out here, though."

Luke unbuckled his gun belt, lowered it onto the sheriff's desk, then strode toward the back of the small building. He found Damaris in the first cell, sitting on one end of a thin cot. Nate sat on the other end with the food basket between them. Damaris glanced up, a small smile touching her lips. Sadness lingered in her gaze, though, making his chest ache.

Luke circled his hands around the bars and turned his attention to the boy staring at his shoes as if afraid they'd run off without him if he looked away. "Holdin' up all right, Nate?"

The kid just shrugged and didn't look up, acted as if shame and self-pity were tied to his chin like twin anchors, mooring him to the floor. Luke had made enough poor choices in his younger years to be familiar with the posture.

Luke's fingers tightened on the bars. His biceps tensed. How he longed to bend these bars wide. To step into that cell and ruffle Nate's hair. Squeeze his shoulder. Shoot, grab him up in a bear hug and hold on until those anchors weighing him down disintegrated.

"Hey." Luke sharpened his tone.

Nate finally lifted his face.

"You forget the first lesson I taught you about fighting?" Luke never thought he'd miss this kid's sass, but right now he'd give a day's wages to see some spirit in Nate's gaze.

"Believe you can win." The mumbled recitation barely carried across the few feet separating them.

"That's right. It don't matter how dark things look or how big your opponent is. If you believe you can win, you're already halfway to victory. Now, I happen to believe we can win this battle. In fact, after chattin' with the sheriff, I even have a plan."

"You do?" Nate set down the fried chicken leg he'd been gnawing on and sat a little straighter.

Luke felt Damaris's curiosity roll over him as well, but he kept his focus on Nate. "Yep. Gonna have me a chat with Oliver Grimes tonight. See if I can work out a deal to get him not to press charges against you. If it works, it will get you out of jail, but it will mean lettin' go of your resentment and makin' restitution for the pranks you pulled. You man enough to do that?"

Nate's Adam's apple made a slow rebound as he swallowed. "Aunt Maris told me about Harbinger. You sure Grimes isn't the one who killed my pa?"

Luke nodded. "As sure as I can be without proof. But I plan to watch your back anyway. If Grimes agrees to let you make restitution, I'll be part of the deal. I won't send you over there alone." The sound of clanging keys urged Luke to hurry. Their privacy was about to end. "You willin' to do the work if Grimes agrees?"

Nate rose from the cot like a soldier coming to attention. "Yes, sir."

"Good." Luke released the bars and dipped his chin at the boy. "I'm proud of you, Nate."

The kid blinked, then gave a wobbly nod.

Conley arrived, keys dangling from his hand. "Move over, Davenport." He peered in at Damaris. "Time to go, ma'am."

While Damaris packed up the food basket, leaving a napkin with Nate's unfinished chicken on the cot along with a pair of butter cookies, the sheriff unlocked the door and swung it open with a squeak. Placing himself in the opening, his hand on the butt of his pistol, he waved Damaris out.

Luke stepped to the side to let Damaris pass, but after Conley closed and locked the door, he stepped back up to the bars. "If I'm going to have your back," he said to Nate, "I need you to have mine."

The boy's forehead scrunched. "What can I do from in here?"

"Pray, son. You can pray."

← CHAPTER ←
THIRTY

Titan stood next to the two Baxter horses at the hitching post outside the jail. Luke moved toward his mount, thinking to grab a piece of jerky from his saddlebag to eat as they rode, but Damaris stopped him with a light touch on his back.

"Here." She reached inside the food basket and pulled out a napkin-wrapped bundle. "You must be starving after riding all day." Instead of handing the bundle to him, she backtracked a few steps to the wooden bench against the wall of the jail. "I saved you some food."

She laid out the napkin like a picnic blanket and revealed two chicken thighs, corn on the cob, a biscuit, and two more of those butter cookies.

Saved him some food? Saved him *all* of her food was more likely.

He frowned. "I can't take your supper."

"I'll eat when I get home." She circled behind him and gave him a nudge toward the bench. "You've been on the road all day, and I don't intend to send you off to battle Oliver

Grimes without proper nourishment. I don't have much of an appetite anyway."

He let her push him to the edge of the bench, then turned to face her. "Damaris, I—"

"You can spare five minutes to eat a few bites while I take this basket back to the restaurant." She met his gaze, and suddenly he understood.

She needed him to eat. Needed to feel like she was contributing something to the fight. Needed to feel like there was one thing in this flood of swirling circumstances that she could actually control.

"All right." He cupped his hands around her arms and rubbed her sleeves with his thumbs.

Her eyes grew shiny, but she blinked away the excess moisture. More than anything, he wanted to pull her into an embrace. To shelter her from the emotional storm pelting on every side. But they both knew they didn't have time for comfort. The sun would set soon, and with it would go his chance to bargain with Grimes.

Turning slowly, Damaris broke free of his hold and headed back to the restaurant on the square. Luke dropped onto the bench and gobbled down the food she'd left him. He barely tasted it, with the speed of his consumption and his level of distraction as he plotted out the best approach to use with Grimes. But it filled the empty hole in his belly, and for that, he was grateful.

By the time Damaris returned, he had her horse unhitched and Nate's horse standing ready, its lead line looped around Titan's saddle horn. When she circled to the left side of her mount, Luke laced his fingers and offered her a leg up.

Riding astride caused her skirt to bunch and exposed a few inches of her stockinged leg. Luke told himself not to look but did a poor job of obeying the order. Thankfully, his mission kept him on task and boosted him into his own saddle before he could embarrass himself by gawking. That flash of trim ankle and shapely calf might have set his blood to pumping, but it was the memory of a dejected Nate sitting slumped on a jailhouse cot that set his course.

He didn't linger at the Baxter homestead, just tossed the spare horse's lead line to Damaris and rode for the Triple G. The deep orange of the western sky warned that time was short.

He found Grimes in a rocker on his front porch.

"I thought you might be payin' me a visit tonight," the rancher said before lifting a half-smoked cigar to his mouth and taking a long draw. The end glowed red for a second before paling to an ashy gray. Grimes lifted his chin and blew out a cloud of smoke, then dropped the cigar butt and ground it into the porch floor with his boot.

Not sure what to make of the rancher's somber mood, Luke dismounted and approached the porch with caution. "I heard you got your cattle back." He might as well start by focusing on the good news. "I'm glad they turned up."

Grimes pinned him with a sideways look. "Probably wish they'd turned up on someone else's land, though, huh?"

Luke nodded, easing his way up the porch steps. "Yep. Woulda made proving Nate's innocence a mite easier."

Grimes stopped rocking and planted his boots flat on the floor. "You sure he ain't involved?"

Luke met his gaze without hesitation. "I am."

Grimes exhaled a groaning breath, then slapped palms to knees and pushed himself up from the chair. "He thinks I killed his pa."

Whatever Luke had been expecting him to say, it wasn't that.

Grimes wandered to the railing and gazed out over his land. "I know I ain't exactly the friendly sort. Don't have time to play nice with the neighbors when there's work to be done, and there's *always* work to be done. But for the boy to actually believe I killed Douglas . . ." He ran a hand over his face. "It shook me to hear him shout those words at me, Davenport. Shook me hard. I can't get it outta my head." He turned to face Luke. "Did you know?"

Luke nodded. "Nate shouted the accusation at me the first time we met, after I told him I was workin' for you."

"Did you think that I . . . ?" Grimes swallowed the rest of the sentence, shadows lurking in his eyes.

Luke leaned against the wall of the house and idly brushed at the travel dust coating his trousers. "I considered it."

Grimes lurched away from the railing. "How could you think me guilty of such a thing?"

Luke held up a hand. "I didn't say I thought you were guilty, just that I considered the possibility. I didn't want to believe Wilson's brother capable of such an act, but I didn't really know you. And the more I learned about the way Douglas Baxter died, the more suspicious the circumstances appeared. You seemed to be the only one with motive. Until we uncovered another party who had something to gain from Baxter's death. One who's probably responsible for framing Nate for rustling your cattle, too."

Grimes's indignation cooled a bit, and a new spark of curiosity flared. "This got somethin' to do with them maps you were lookin' at in the land office?"

"It might."

His mental wheels churning, Grimes turned to ponder the horizon. "You know, it *is* rather curious that my missing beeves showed up less than forty-eight hours after Harbinger got their hands on my acreage."

"Especially when I rode the perimeter of Baxter's property a few days before, and there wasn't so much as a hoofprint in that canyon."

Grimes pivoted to face Luke once again. "You think Harbinger tried to encourage me and Baxter to sell our land by stirrin' up trouble?"

Luke shrugged. "It's possible."

"And when trouble failed, they moved on to bribery. Which I fell for hook, line, and sinker." The rancher kicked the rocking chair, skidding it sideways a few feet. "I ain't nothin' but a pawn in their game. Moving me around the board like I don't have a will of my own. And Baxter . . ." He stopped his fuming and swallowed long and slow. "You really think they killed him?"

Luke hesitated. He had no evidence. Only theories. But having Grimes as an ally could be an asset moving forward. "I can't prove anything. Yet. But if they *are* responsible for bringing in those rustlers, then they're not above hiring killers to do their dirty work." He rubbed his side where the doctor had just pulled seven stitches from a wound that nearly ended his life. "That crew had no compunction about stabbing me and leaving me for dead."

"If that's the case, that woman of yours ain't safe as long as she refuses to sell."

That was the second time today someone spoke of Damaris as if she already belonged to Luke. Were folks jumping to conclusions because he'd been staying at her place, or was the Lord trying to tell him something?

Either way, Grimes was right. Damaris wasn't safe. Neither was Nate.

"I think that's why your stock suddenly showed up on Baxter land."

"They're still tryin' to play chess with the lives of real people." A sour look crossed Grimes's features. He leaned over the railing and spat. "It sticks in my craw. Lettin' some rich bigwig dictate the destiny of the workin' man."

"Damaris talked to a lawyer. Ronald Mullins. He was quick to work out a preemptive deal with the judge. The judge agreed to drop all charges against Nate if he leaves the area, sells the land, and never returns. Mullins said it was to guarantee *your* safety," Luke said with a nod toward Grimes, "but I'm pretty sure it's just a manipulation to force a sale."

"Mullins has got to be in Harbinger's pocket." Grimes spat again. "He's the one who persuaded me into givin' up them eighty acres to the east in exchange for his two hundred and forty to the west. He prob'ly bribed the judge, too."

"Which is why I'm hoping to play a little chess of my own."

The rancher's brows lifted. "Oh? Whatcha got in mind?"

"They think they've got Damaris cornered. Either sell the land or watch her nephew be carted off to prison on a felony rustling charge. With as vocal as you've been about catching the rustlers and making them pay, no one expects any mercy from your quarter."

Grimes scowled. "You're askin' me not to press charges, aren't you?"

"I don't expect you to let Nate off without paying for the wrongs he did you. I'll bring him over every day after school, and you can put him to work until you decide he's made restitution for his vandalism."

The rancher's scowl didn't lift as he stared out into the growing shadows.

"I'll continue looking into the rustling." It wouldn't hurt to add some extra incentive to the pot. "I've got a score to settle with them too, after all. And I'll supervise any work you ask Nate to do. I'll see that it's done right. You have my word."

Grimes tilted his head toward Luke, revealing a half smirk. "That kid's gotten under your skin, hasn't he?"

"He reminds me of myself at that age. Angry with a wild streak in need of guidance."

"Had me one of them streaks myself." Grimes looked back out across the yard. "The barn *could* use a new coat of paint. And I got half a garden that needs to be replanted."

Luke's stomach clenched. "That mean we have a deal?"

Grimes pushed away from the railing and held out his hand. "Yes, Horseman. We have a deal."

— CHAPTER —
THIRTY-ONE

The moment Nathaniel stepped out of the jail cell the following morning, Damaris enveloped him in a smothering hug designed to pour love and gratitude directly from her heart into his. For once, worries about how he might react offered no hindrance. Nor did she give a single thought to the three rugged men bearing witness to the display. When Nathaniel embraced her in return, pressing his cheek against hers and leaning into her instead of pulling away, tears squeezed between her closed lashes.

Thank you, Lord. You made a path where there was none and gave me back the child of my heart.

"Let's go home," she said when Nathaniel began to pull away.

He didn't say anything, but the way his eyes shimmered as he nodded his agreement spoke volumes. A night spent alone with the very real fear of losing either his home or his freedom had changed him. Matured him. Given him perspective.

In fact, once he untangled himself from Damaris's embrace,

he straightened his shoulders and walked past Luke to stand before Oliver Grimes. "I'm sorry for the pranks I pulled and any damage I caused, Mr. Grimes. I promise to work hard for you to make it right."

Damaris caught Luke's eye and found the same pride in his gaze that flooded her chest.

"Thank you for not pressing charges, sir." Nathaniel's voice quavered, but he cleared his throat and continued. "I know it looks bad, but I swear I didn't take your cows."

Mr. Grimes dipped his chin slightly. "And I swear I didn't kill your father."

Nathaniel nodded. "I know that now."

"Good. Then I'll expect you at the Triple G straight after school on Monday. You got a barn to paint." Grimes held out his hand.

Nathaniel stared at it a moment, then clasped the rancher's palm with a firm grip. "I'll be there."

And he was. Every day after school the following week, Nathaniel and Luke headed to the Triple G and worked until suppertime.

Damaris knelt beside her brother's grave and laid a small bouquet of wildflowers near the headstone. "You'd be proud of him, Douglas. He's grown up so much in the past few days. It's as if when he stepped out of that jail cell, the anger and resentment he'd been carrying fell away like shedding skin. He's raw and confused and still misses you terribly, but I think he's finally starting to heal. Luke is helping. Picking up where you left off in showing him what it means to be an honorable and godly man."

A small chuckle erupted as she recalled last night's impromptu recitation. "It turns out Luke has been helping Nathaniel memorize scripture while they work on the barn. Your son quoted all of Psalm 15 to me yesterday before sitting down to supper. He squirmed a bit at the part about a righteous man doing no evil to his neighbor, but there was something about the way he held himself as he recited the verses. As if the psalm had become a creed of sorts for his life, not just an assignment he'd been forced to complete as a punishment. God is at work in him, Douglas, and it's a remarkable sight to behold."

Damaris took a handkerchief from her pocket and spread it upon the sundried ground behind her brother's grave. Lowering herself to sit on the cotton square, she let out a sigh and leaned against the tombstone as if she were resting against her big brother's back. "I think I'm falling in love with him, Douglas. Luke sees me. And instead of merely tolerating my presence like most people, he actually appreciates what I have to offer. If a bluestocking old maid could actually offer anything worthwhile to a Texas legend. He's a Horseman. Did I tell you that? A former cavalry officer who makes his living training horses and rounding up criminals. As opposite from my quiet bookish existence as one can be. Yet he actively seeks my opinion. Not only seeks it but honors it. Honors me. He looks at me as if I were a rare treasure he'd never thought he'd find, and when I look at him . . . Oh, Douglas. It's as if all my odd, misshaped edges finally fit somewhere."

As if God himself had handpicked Luke just for her.

Is that the case? her spirit asked as she looked over the landscape with unseeing eyes. *Did you send Luke to us for more than just Nathaniel's protection? Did you send him for me, too?*

Oh, how she wanted that to be true. To have the assurance that he wouldn't leave after the job with the rustlers and Harbinger was done. That he'd have a reason to stay. Two reasons. Both carrying the Baxter name.

"I wish you could've met him," she murmured as the wind started to pick up and blow against her face. "I think you would have liked—"

An acrid odor crinkled her nose, cutting her off mid-thought.

Damaris frowned as she pushed to her feet. It smelled like . . .

Smoke! A line of charcoal clouds marred the horizon to the north.

Lifting the hem of her skirt, she ran to the top of the rise and scanned the countryside. There. The dark clouds met the ground in the distance. A flash of orange caught her eye. Then another. Her heart clenched.

Prairie fire!

And with the south wind, it would head straight for the house.

God, help us!

Damaris spun and raced down the hill toward the barn. Nathaniel had taken one of the horses to the Triple G, and Luke had Titan. That left one horse for her to ride and a cow to turn out just in case the fire couldn't be stopped.

Saddling the horse would take too long, so after fitting a bridle over the gelding's head, she positioned him near the paddock fence and used the bottom rail as a mounting block.

With an inelegant lurch, Damaris threw herself over the back of her brother's second-best steed. Praying she wouldn't fall off, she grabbed a generous handful of mane along with the reins and urged the horse into a canter.

She had to get to Luke before the fire grew too large to fight.

Luke stood at the base of the ladder, trying not to get dripped on while Nate painted the trim along the top of the barn door. They'd finished the second coat of red paint on the siding yesterday and started on the dark brown trim today. They should complete the job by the end of the week if all went well.

Nate was proving to be a good worker, now that he'd set his mind to the task. He heeded direction, focused on the job, put forth quality effort, and didn't complain. Luke was downright proud of the boy. If he kept this up, he'd soon be a man who garnered respect from all who crossed his path.

"Luke?"

He craned his neck back to find Nate turned sideways on the ladder and squinting at something in the distance.

Nate raised an arm and pointed. "I think that might be Aunt Maris. Why would she be riding over here this late in the day? We're nearly done."

Shifting one hand to a rung to ensure the ladder stayed steady, Luke pivoted in the direction Nate pointed. This was no neighborly visit. Her posture was too hunched, her pace too fast. Luke stiffened. Something was wrong.

He spun back around and grasped the ladder with two hands. "Hurry down, Nate."

The boy grabbed his brush and paint can in one hand and scrambled down the rungs faster than he probably should. "You don't think the sheriff's comin' after me again, do ya?"

"Not a chance." Luke might be impatient to get to Damaris, but he couldn't ignore the raw fear in the kid's voice. He gripped Nate's shoulder and looked him in the eye. "Whatever it is, we'll face it together. All right?"

Nate swallowed and gave a shaky nod.

"Good. Now, let's go see what's going on." After thumping his charge on the back, Luke set off down the road at a jog. In a heartbeat, Nate caught up and matched his pace.

As they closed the distance, Luke noted the missing saddle. Then he saw Damaris start to list dangerously to one side. He picked up his pace.

"Take charge of the horse," he called to Nate as he zigged to the right just in time to catch Damaris as she slid off the horse's back.

Her awkward spill had her head knocking into his chin and her elbow jostling his rib cage, but even so, having her in his arms was a tiny slice of heaven.

Until she dropped a bucket of brimstone on his head.

"Fire." She twisted to face him, her beautiful eyes wide with trepidation. Her chest heaved against his as she fought to control her breathing and finish her explanation. "Prairie fire. Behind the house."

Prairie fire? Usually those started with a lightning strike or a campfire jumping its ring. But the sky had been clear all day, and no one but Nate ever ran around on that extra acreage.

Her small hands closed over his forearms. "What do we do?"

Luke turned to Nate. "Run up to the house and ring the dinner bell as long and as loud as you can. That'll bring the hands in. Explain what's happening and ask them to load up a wagon with shovels, blankets, and as many tubs of water as they can manage. I'll take Titan and get started on digging a firebreak. Maybe we can turn the fire away from the house."

"I'll help!" Nate insisted.

"No." Luke's heart kicked at the thought of what could happen to the kid. Fires were unpredictable and fierce. He didn't want Nate anywhere near the flames. "You need to stay here with your aunt."

"But—"

"I don't got time to argue, Nate. Follow orders and ring that bell."

A flare of the old belligerence tightened the boy's features, but he ran off to obey.

Luke turned to the woman still in his arms. Man, but he wished he had time to enjoy the feel of her against him. "I've got to go, darlin'. But you'll be safe here."

Her fingers clutched at his arms. "I don't care about safe. I care about *you*. You can't fight a prairie fire by yourself, Luke. Let me help. I might be close to useless with a shovel, but I can beat out flames while you dig. Take me with you."

His arms tightened around her and pulled her close. She cared about him. His heart thumped hard against his ribs to hear her admit such a thing out loud. He cared for her, too. More than his own life. Which was why he couldn't let her put herself in harm's way.

"I won't be alone for long. The Triple G hands will pitch in." He pressed his cheek to the side of her head. "I need to know you're out of harm's way, Damaris. I can't be worryin' about a spooked horse tramplin' you in the smoke or a stray spark catchin' your skirts on fire." The dangers were too numerous to count, and even imagining them iced his blood.

"What about you?" She pulled back and pressed her palms into his chest. "You're just as susceptible to stray sparks and choking smoke." Her soft brown eyes pleaded for guarantees he couldn't give. "You escaped one near-death encounter. What are the chances you'll escape another? You're not allowed to die on me, Luke Davenport. The land, the house, the Baxter legacy—none of it is worth your life."

Her passion ignited a gunpowder fuse that exploded through Luke with shocking force. He captured her lips in a fierce, frantic kiss that left little room for gentleness. Her fingers found their way around his neck as she lifted up her heels to return his embrace with equal fervor.

The discordant clanging of the dinner bell broke them apart and brought reality crashing down over his head. He reached up and cupped her face, her skin soft under his callused hands. "I've got to go."

"I know."

Forcing himself to release her, he stepped away. He'd gone no more than three or four yards when her call stopped him.

"Luke?"

He glanced over his shoulder. Her eyes looked slightly frantic, and one of her arms lingered in mid-air as if she'd stopped herself from reaching for him.

"I love you."

His throat closed up, and his body turned to stone. Three words. So small. Yet so powerful. No one but his mother had ever said them to him, and after she left, he convinced himself that she'd never really meant them. The bond he had with the Horsemen was a form of love, but men didn't talk about such things. And while the Good Lord had written love words in his holy book for him to receive, hearing them aloud was . . . different. Hearing them from *her* was different. The words changed him. Cracked his insides open even as they healed old scars and made him throb with new life.

A life he would lay down in a heartbeat to preserve hers.

With the dinner bell clanging in the distance and his throat too choked to speak, he held her gaze for a single, charged minute as he battled a flood of raw emotion. Then, with a tip of his hat that was a woefully inadequate response, he took off running for the paddock where Titan waited. Perhaps he could prove in deeds the truth he couldn't yet say.

He loved her, too.

CHAPTER

THIRTY-TWO

By the time Damaris made it up to the house, Luke had collected Titan and was galloping down the drive. Never had a man looked so confident and strong in the saddle. A mighty Horseman capable of feats beyond those of ordinary men. Even so, her chest ached as she watched him ride past.

Watch over him, she prayed, for she knew Luke well enough to know that his safety would not be high on his list of concerns. He wasn't reckless, but he cared more for those under his protection than himself, and she feared he'd take unnecessary risks to save Nathaniel's inheritance.

"What in tarnation is goin' on?" Grimes rode into the yard with two of his men behind him.

Upon seeing him, Nathaniel finally stopped circling the striking rod inside the triangular cast-iron dinner bell and vaulted over the porch railing. "There's a grass fire at my place. North of the house. Mr. Davenport's headed there now to start digging a firebreak. He needs a wagon loaded with water tubs, shovels, and as many blankets as you can spare."

"Buck, grab the blankets from the bunkhouse," Grimes ordered from the back of his horse. "Randall, round up every washtub and hip bath Mrs. Olson can find and load 'em up. We'll fill 'em on site."

Nathaniel darted over to the trough at the edge of the paddock. "Aunt Maris and I can fill some of them here while Quincy is fetchin' the wagon. Save the men some time when they get to our place."

Mr. Grimes nodded. "Good idea. I'll head out and give Davenport a hand. Tell Quincy that I left Joe with the stock. Ask him to ride out to the west pasture and tell the kid what's happening so he can be on the lookout for any spread onto Triple G land."

Nate ran off to do as Mr. Grimes bid, and Damaris quickly stepped up to the pump and worked the handle, filling the trough to the brim. As the rancher turned his horse toward the road, Damaris called out her thanks.

Grimes acknowledged her for the first time, tipping his hat, his hard eyes oddly sympathetic. "Ma'am."

The next twenty minutes were a chaotic blur. Mrs. Olson, the Triple G cook, brought out tubs and pots and milking pails while the men filled them. Once the wagon was loaded, they set out, leaving an eerie stillness in their wake.

"It ain't right, Aunt Maris," Nathaniel complained as he stepped away from the pump, his trousers as wet as her skirt due to water sloshing from trough to pail to tub in their hurry to fill what vessels they could. "That's *my* land. My job to protect it. I'm not a helpless kid. I can dig."

"I know you can, but fires are dangerous. They can change direction in an instant if the wind shifts." Even so, she longed to be out there, too. Doing something to help. It felt cowardly sitting here where it was safe just because she was a woman.

Nathaniel kicked one of the paddock fence posts. "Waiting here is a waste of time. I'm going after them."

He headed to the barn, but Damaris scurried into his path. "Not without me." She was not letting him out of her sight.

Nathaniel's brows arched. "You're coming, too?"

She nodded. "I think we should head home and load our own wagon with water and blankets. Double the resources. We'll stay back from the worst of the fire to keep the men from worrying about us, but we can take over the water runs so they can keep working."

"Good plan." Nathaniel gave her a nod, then dodged to her left to continue to the barn. "Let's go."

Damaris didn't hesitate. She'd seen the fire. Four men would have a hard time curtailing the spread. Two sets of extra hands would increase the odds of success, not only of stopping the fire, but of keeping those who fought it safe. And that was what mattered most.

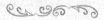

The enemy shall not prevail. Luke repeated the vow as he worked, one hour after another. When he'd first arrived, it became clear that digging a firebreak on his own would take far too long. Instead, he'd set to work beating back the fire with a gunny sack he'd snatched out of the barn when he paused long enough to ensure the stock had been turned out. Thankful for the creek that ran along the east edge of the property, he ran back and forth time and time again, extinguishing flames and kicking dirt over smoldering sparks. But for every foot of progress he made, the fire gained three more on another front, closing the distance to the house standing less than half a mile away.

When Grimes arrived, the two of them worked in tandem, but still the fire gained ground. Thankfully, when Randall showed up with the wagon, he brought wisdom born of experience with him.

"Quincy says we gotta plow a break." Randall set the wagon brake, then hopped down and lowered the tailgate. Buck dismounted to assist in unloading an ancient-looking plow from the back of the wagon. "It's more efficient than digging. If it's wide enough, it'll keep the fire from jumping. Then we can set a backfire to steal its fuel."

They unhitched one of the wagon horses and hooked him to the plow. There wasn't time to plow a complete perimeter around all the buildings, so Randall turned earth from the creek westward until a long line stood between the house and the fire. The rest of them spread out across the two hundred yards of burning prairie a quarter mile out from the plow line and focused their attention on keeping the blaze contained until they could risk setting the backfire.

Heat blistered Luke's skin. Smoke stung his eyes and choked his lungs. His arms felt like dead weight hanging from his shoulders, but he kept shoveling. For Damaris. For Nate. For justice.

Because only one cause for this fire made any sense.

Arson.

When framing Nate failed to force the Baxters to sell, Harbinger must've decided to take away their reason for staying. A house fire would have been too suspicious, but a grass fire could be attributed to natural causes, stalling any investigation. They'd set it when Luke and Nate had been away, probably hoping it would rage out of control before anyone noticed. But they hadn't counted on Damaris catching it early and riding for help. Her quick thinking had given them a chance. Now it was up to him to right the wrong.

He dug his shovel into the ground and threw another scoop of dirt onto the sputtering flames in front of him. How many shovelfuls had he spread? Two hundred? Three? Even through his work gloves, he could feel blisters forming on his palms. He glanced up from where he worked and spotted a new area of flames to his left. Too big for the shovel. He'd need a blanket. One heavy with water. His shoulders ached at the thought of swinging the weighted fabric, but he ignored the pain and stomped over to where the Triple G wagon waited.

"You need a break, Davenport." Grimes, his face a sooty mess, met Luke partway and handed him a canteen.

Thankful for the moisture, Luke drank deep, the warm liquid soothing his scorched throat. He longed to dump the contents over his head, but water was too precious. They couldn't afford to waste a drop.

He handed the canteen back to Grimes and kept moving toward the wagon. "I'll rest when the fire's out."

"As to that—Randall finished plowing the break. We're ready to set the backfire. He and Buck are using the last of the collected water to wet down the grass south of the plow line. As soon as they're done, we'll retreat behind the line and set the second fire. With any luck, that'll slow this beast down, and we'll finally be able to kill it."

We need more than luck, Lord. We need you.

Luke reached over the side of the wagon and grabbed a blanket from the top of a pile, his brain so tired that it took him a moment to recognize the blanket he'd been sleeping under for the past couple of weeks. One of the hands must've gone through the Baxter barn and retrieved anything that could be of use.

"There's a new flare-up on the west. I'm gonna beat that down." He moved to the tailgate and dunked the blanket into a washtub that still held a few inches of water. "Once everyone has retreated behind the line, come fetch me. I'll work until then."

Grimes scowled at him. "Pace yourself, Horseman. We still got a long ways to go."

"I know my limits." And he knew his God—the source of all strength. He'd keep going until the Lord stopped him.

Ignoring Grimes, Luke tossed the wet blanket over his shoulder and marched back into battle.

Half an hour later, Buck came to fetch him. "We're ready to light the backfire."

Luke slapped the flames in front of him two more times before straightening. He rubbed the sweat from his brow with a grimy sleeve, knowing he was only spreading the soot around, but he had to protect his eyes. The smoke wreaked enough havoc without his own perspiration blinding him.

It grated against his spirit to walk away from an enemy not yet defeated, but this wasn't a war he could win with blankets and shovels and his own waning strength. He needed to fight fire with fire. Which meant he needed to step away from the front line and temporarily retreat.

"Here," Buck said as Luke came abreast of him. He held out a thick carrot. The top was still on and a bit of dirt clung to the skin, but it made Luke's mouth water. "It ain't much, but it'll help keep yer strength up."

"Thanks." Luke took it and bit off a large hunk.

"Miss Baxter has a whole basketful of food back at her wagon. Carrots, peaches, blackberries, some strange-lookin' bread. I think she grabbed any portable food she could find during her last water run."

Luke stopped chewing and grabbed Buck's arm. "Damaris is here?" In the path of the fire? His gut knotted in an instant.

His weariness forgotten, he took off running.

"She's been behind the break the whole time," Buck called after him. "She's not in any danger."

Maybe not at this moment. But what if the wind shifted? Grass fires jumped over breaks all the time. Even creek beds and streams. There was no guarantee she'd be safe.

The hissing sound of dying fire mixed with the crackling of living flames drove Luke to run faster. An urgency he couldn't explain spurred him on. Blackened earth gave way to grass not yet consumed. And still he ran. Nearing the plowed firebreak, he spotted Randall wrangling Titan and the other horses. Grimes stood north of the break, matches in hand.

"What's yer hurry?" the rancher called as Luke sped by.

Luke didn't stop to answer. He spied the Baxter wagon to the right and veered in that direction. His heart pumped faster when he caught a glimpse of a second fire to the west. It must've started from a stray spark carried on the wind, for it had sprung to life well inside the break. Where no one was looking as they prepped for setting the backfire. The flames were contained to a small area, but they flickered unnaturally high and only a few yards from Damaris's wagon. A wagon with no driver.

Where was she? Why hadn't she driven away? Did she think she could fight the rogue fire on her own?

Terror like he'd never felt surged through his chest. *Please, God. Wherever she is, get me to her in time.*

THIRTY-THREE

Where was she? Damaris groaned and reached a hand to the back of her head where a sharp pain jabbed at her skull. All at once, memories flooded her consciousness. The flash of a new fire. Calling Nathaniel to get in the wagon. Him running toward her, shouting for her to look out. Something striking her from behind.

No. Not some*thing*. Some*one*.

Damaris shoved up from the ground and pushed to her feet. "Nathaniel?"

A wall of fire formed a semicircle around her, cutting her off from the wagon and the water and blankets it carried. Heat from the flames scorched her face. Dark smoke clouded her vision, stirring panic in her breast.

"Nathaniel!" A cough choked her as she tried to inhale and call again.

Oh, Lord. Help me find him!

Something moved to her left. Crooking her elbow around her mouth to reduce the amount of smoke she inhaled, she stumbled in that direction. Her eyes watered and burned, but she peered through the haze and spotted a shadowy form. Two forms. Struggling. A man held her nephew from behind, an arm wrapped around his throat. Nathaniel kicked and tugged on the man's arm, but the villain gave no quarter.

"Get away from him!" Damaris charged.

She rammed the man holding Nathaniel at full speed. Hitting him felt like hitting a fence post, but her momentum caused him to lose his balance and stagger backward, releasing his hold on her nephew. Nathaniel crumpled to the ground, fighting to get air into his lungs.

"You shoulda left well enough alone, lady," the man sneered. His thick mustache twitched as he spoke, and his dark eyes scanned her with derision. "I was gonna give you a chance, but now you'll just have to die with the boy." He drew a wicked-looking hunting knife from his belt and brandished it.

She dropped to her nephew's side and cupped an arm around his back, helping him sit up.

The man, tanned from years of outdoor living, backtracked a few steps to where a horse stood waiting. "It's a right shame that prairie fires are so hazardous."

He reached for a canteen slung over his saddle horn and unscrewed the lid. Instead of taking a drink, however, he poured the liquid over the grass in a long line. It took a moment for her to register the pungent, oily smell over the smoke already hanging thick in the air.

Kerosene!

"You never know when a stray spark will set a new section ablaze and kill the very people fighting it." He pulled a match from his pocket and struck it with his thumbnail.

"No!" Damaris jumped to her feet, but it was too late.

With a raspy laugh, he dropped the lit match onto the kerosene-soaked grass in front of him. A new wall of flame roared to life. It spread right and left, joining up with the existing fire and completely circling them. Cutting them off from any escape.

Snatching her skirt back from the flames, Damaris rushed to Nathaniel's side. She grabbed his arm and tried to hoist him to his feet.

"Get up. We have to find a way out."

He leaned on her and levered himself to his feet, but his coughs kept him doubled over. He trembled against her, still weak from his near-strangulation, and almost fell to the ground again when he tried to walk. Damaris forced his arm around her neck and held on to that hand while she supported his back with her other.

The fire ate up the grass and crept closer, shrinking the circle. She searched for an opening, any opening, but found nothing. Her only hope was for one of the men to notice the new fire behind the break and investigate, but they were so focused on the main fire that the chances of rescue were slim.

She stumbled in the direction of her wagon anyway, her spirit crying to the Lord for help.

"Don't worry, Nathaniel. I'll get you out." Somehow.

Maybe she could take off her skirt and wrap it around his head and shoulders. If it caught, she could fling it off of him as soon as they cleared the ring.

And if her own clothing caught? Damaris clamped her jaw tight. Such thoughts accomplished nothing. Her job was to save her nephew. She'd focus on that and leave the rest in God's hands.

Luke reached the Baxter wagon and confirmed that Damaris and Nate weren't there. He checked the bed and even peered underneath to be sure, but found nothing beyond a bunch of empty pails and washtubs.

"Damaris!" His gaze turned toward the fire even as his heart prayed he wouldn't find what he most feared. "Nate! Where are you?"

Flames danced as high as his waist, taunting him. Thick smoke obscured his vision and stung his eyes. He set his jaw. Either Damaris was safely away, or she was in that fire. Either way, the fire had to die before it spread. Otherwise all their efforts on the main front would be for naught.

He backtracked to the wagon bed and grabbed a blanket. Two pails still held water. He dumped one into a larger washtub and dunked the blanket into it. He rolled it around until it absorbed all the water, then squeezed out what little extra remained.

With forced stoicism, he marched toward the flames, blanket over his shoulder. As he closed in on the wall of fire, a movement on the other side drew his attention. Was that a . . . person?

"Damaris!" All stoicism gone, he ran to the edge of the flames and peered through them. The heat burned his face, but he didn't back away. "Damaris!"

"Luke!"

He caught his name over the crackle of the fire, and his heart soared. She was alive! For now. "I'm coming! Hang on!"

He sprinted back to the wagon and grabbed the last pail

of water. His heart demanded he race back, but he needed every drop of that water, so he forced himself to keep to a smooth canter instead of an all-out gallop.

"'Fear not: for I have redeemed thee, I have called thee by thy name; thou art mine.'" Luke quoted the promise made to Israel, his soul praying that the words might also apply to him and those he loved this day. "'When thou passest through the waters, I will be with thee.'" His eyes locked on the ground before him, watching each step to ensure he didn't misplace a foot and lose the water he carried. "'. . . and through the rivers, they shall not overflow thee.'"

Reaching the edge of the flames, he set the pail down on a flat section of ground. Then tugged the wet blanket off his shoulder and opened it wide. He draped it over his head, using his hat brim as a shield to preserve a small field of vision. The fabric fell heavy over his back and wrapped around his arms like a giant shawl. He picked up the bucket, then tucked both arms as close to his torso as he could without jostling his cargo.

He tipped back his head. Heat scorched his face. He searched for the best entry point and set his jaw.

"'When thou walkest through the fire, thou shalt not be burned,'" he quoted, his voice ringing loud in defiance of the wall in front of him. "'Neither shall the flame kindle upon thee.'"

Raising one blanketed arm to shelter his face, he ducked his head and ran forward, shouting, "For I am the Lord thy God, the Holy one of Israel, thy Saviour.'"

"Luke!"

As soon as he cleared the inferno, someone wrapped his

back in a hug. He pulled away immediately, not wanting Damaris to try to extinguish any flames with her hands or clothing. His woman had grit in spades, though, and refused to relinquish her hold. The blanket peeled from his body, taking his hat from his head. He had to move fast to free it from his arms before her enthusiasm sent the water cascading from the bucket he held.

After setting the pail down an arm's length away from him, he spun to face Damaris, ready to pull her away from any flame that could leap onto her clothes or sear her skin. But the sight of her so startled him that he couldn't move.

The prim and proper Miss Damaris Baxter was stomping out the last few smoldering spots on his blanket, wearing only her drawers. Well, not *only* her drawers. Her shirtwaist was still in place and buttoned to her chin per usual, though it took him a couple of heartbeats to get past the outline of her legs to notice. Other oddities jumped out at him as well. Like the fact that her skirt was wrapped around her hands like a protective bandage and a giant white kerchief was tied around her neck like a cowboy's bandana. A piece of her petticoat?

She looked up and caught him staring, then immediately unwound the skirt fabric and held it in front of her.

"I was planning to run Nathaniel through the flames right before you got here." She ducked her face away from him. "I thought less fabric volume might give me a slightly better chance of getting through unscathed."

Without water to deter the flames? Lord, have mercy. She never would have made it.

Back in charge of his senses, Luke strode forward and grabbed her arms. "You're a brave woman."

He did a quick visual sweep of the area. The flames were closing in around them quickly. Odd that they had formed a circle and not moved forward from a single point of origin. Had there been multiple sparks and separate fires that joined into one?

His gaze snagged on Nate, and the puzzle of the fire's formation vanished from his mind. The kid looked shaky, hunched over and hacking into the remainder of his aunt's wadded-up petticoat. He couldn't take much more of this smoke.

"I'm going to get Nate. Take your skirt and dampen it in the water, but save as much as you can."

Damaris nodded. "Got it."

Luke hurried to Nate's side and grabbed him by the shoulder. "Climb on my front and wrap your legs tight around my waist."

Nate's eyes looked glazed over, but he nodded. Luke grabbed him beneath the arms like he would a toddler and hugged him close. It would be easier to carry the kid on his back, but Luke wasn't about to risk the blanket catching fire with Nate underneath.

Back protesting the weight, he tromped over to Damaris. "Your skirt wet?"

Her eyes met his as she straightened from bending over the bucket. Fear and trust mingled in her gaze. "Yes."

"Good. Get my blanket and turn it scorched side in, then drape it over my back. Make sure Nate's legs are covered."

She did as instructed, quickly fitting his hat to his head, then adding the blanket curtain and wrapping it around Luke's arms.

"If there's any water left," he said, "drizzle it over your hair and down the front of your legs. Then use the skirt as a shield. We're going to run through together. You'll guard him from the front, and I'll cover the back."

Her gaze settled on her nephew, then hardened with determination. She used every last drop of the water, then took her place in front of him.

Luke clasped the blanket in one hand and fixed his other above Damaris's hip. He leaned close to her ear. "Ready?"

She hoisted the skirt in front of her face and nodded. "Ready."

His fingers tightened around her as he leaned forward. "Go!"

Damaris took off. Luke matched her stride for stride. She screamed as she leapt through the flames. His heart clutched at the sound an instant before the heat of Hades swept over his body.

— CHAPTER —
THIRTY-FOUR

Damaris's feet left the ground as a powerful hand launched her into the air from behind. The heat of a thousand ovens engulfed her, tearing a scream from her throat. When she landed on the other side, she tumbled and rolled. Without her petticoats to tangle her legs, she jumped up, tossed her skirt shield away from her, and did a quick patting inventory to make sure she wasn't on fire. Not feeling any searing pain, she turned to look for Nathaniel and Luke.

Like a dragon unfurling its wings, Luke opened his arms wide and shrugged off the blanket. Nathaniel unhooked his legs from Luke's waist and slid down to stand on his own.

Damaris rushed to her nephew's side. "Are you all right?"

He coughed but nodded.

She craned her neck left and right, checking every inch of him just to be sure, but he looked unscathed.

Luke, on the other hand, had steam rising from his back and was yanking shirttails from his trousers with desperate hands. She didn't see any actual flames, but something was burning him. Perhaps the blanket had still been smoldering when she draped it over him.

She ran to the wagon. The washtub barely had a quarter inch of water in the bottom, but when tilted, it made a decent-sized pool.

Grabbing the tub, she ran back to Luke and shouted for him to get on his knees. He dropped. She poured. Then she tossed the tub aside and slid her hands up under his shirt, tenting it away from his skin.

He sighed, then relaxed. Then slowly rose, his height pulling his shirt back into place and leaving her fingers to trail slowly down the muscular ridges of his back.

When he turned, the look in his eyes seared her heart more fully than the fire around them seared the earth. "Damaris?" His voice rasped as he cupped her face. "You're all right?"

Tears misted her eyes at the awe in his tone. She nodded, her lips pressed together to keep them from trembling as the shock began to set in.

With one tug, he clutched her to his chest. His other hand reached for Nathaniel and pulled him into the embrace as well. "Thank you, God," he murmured as his arms tightened around them. "Thank you. Thank you. Thank you."

A flood of emotions swelled within Damaris's breast as she held on to the two people most important to her in all the world. Not only had God spared their lives, but he'd brought them together and formed a family. For nothing had ever felt so right as the three of them clinging to one another, everything stripped away except what truly mattered—love and gratitude. For each other, and for their Savior.

Nathaniel pulled away first. He turned to face Damaris, a protective fierceness about him that reminded her of Luke. "How's your head?"

Bringing it to her attention made it start throbbing. She reached a hand to the back of her head and probed gently at the knot that had formed. "It's sore, but I'll be fine."

Luke drew her in front of him so he could examine the wound. "Did you fall?"

Nathaniel scowled. "Only after the rustler knocked her on the skull with his pistol butt."

"What?" Luke's roar nearly deafened her.

"I saw him, Luke. The rustler who attacked us that night. He set the fire by our wagon."

A wracking cough interrupted Nathaniel's explanation. Damaris hurried to his side and rubbed his back. Once he had his breathing back under control he stepped away from her cosseting and moved closer to Luke.

"I think he set the main fire, too. After he conked Aunt Maris, he came after me. Tried to strangle me." His hand moved to his throat, and Damaris bit her lip, recalling how close she'd come to losing him. "The snake kept goin' on about how tragic it would be for the last Baxter male to be found burned to a crisp in an unfortunate prairie fire. How no one would ever know my demise had been helped along. If Aunt Maris hadn't flattened him . . ."

Nathaniel swallowed, then pivoted to look at her. Admiration and unqualified acceptance radiated from him. Her heart nearly burst.

"That settles it," Luke said, his voice hard. "The two of you are sticking to my side until we get this fire out. And the minute we do, I'm wiring Matt and putting you on a train bound for Gringolet."

"Then I suppose I ought to put my skirt back on." Damaris winked at Nathaniel, and he let out a burst of surprised laughter.

Luke joined in, his deep rumble helping to cover her embarrassment as Nathaniel fetched the scorched wad of clothing and tossed it to her. Both men turned their backs as she dressed.

"There," she announced, letting them know she was finished. "Perfectly presentable, wouldn't you say?" She fanned out the skirt to show off the new holes riddling her attire. "I hear charcoal lace is all the rage these days."

Nathaniel snickered, and Luke grinned. But when he came up alongside her, wrapped his arm around her waist, and growled in her ear that she'd look good no matter what she wore, a warmth spread through her that had nothing to do with the grass burning behind them.

It took well into the night to ensure the fires were completely extinguished. After the backfire proved effective and Grimes and Buck helped beat out the second fire, the threat waned. As the sun set, the Triple G crew headed back to their ranch, bedraggled yet victorious. Whatever rift had existed between the Baxters and Grimes had been obliterated by the partnership forged in fire this day.

Luke escorted Nate and Damaris back to the house, where they all grabbed a quick bite of cold chicken and day-old biscuits. Then, after checking the lock on every door and window,

Luke left them to clean up and recover while he walked the charred ground with a shovel, searching for embers glowing in the dark. He turned over sections of earth until he could barely lift his arms. When his bleary eyes could pick out no more suspicious red or orange specks against the dark landscape, he finally dragged himself back to the house and the coffee Damaris had promised to leave for him on the stove.

Letting himself in the back door with the key she'd loaned him, he locked the door behind him and headed to the stove. The coffeepot sat right where he expected, but two other kettles also stood ready. He glanced around the room for an explanation and found a screen set up near the pantry. The screen hid a large bathing tub filled with water. All it needed was the hot water from the stove to provide the perfect soak. He'd intended to dunk himself in the horse trough and scrape off the worst of the grime before heading to bed in the barn. To have a bath—a *real* bath—after the last six hours was a luxury. And the fact that Damaris and Nate had gone to the trouble to provide it for him made him feel like a true member of the Baxter family.

A family he vowed to keep safe.

Safe from fire-setting, child-strangling rustlers and the money-grubbing, coldhearted investors who paid their salaries.

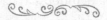

Luke awoke the next morning to the lowing of a cow near his ear. He opened one eye to find Bessie's muzzle an inch from his face. Drawing back slowly so as not to spook the old girl, Luke reached out and patted her neck.

"Glad you found your way home, girl. Give me a minute to get dressed, and I'll get that milking taken care of for you."

Feeling oddly shy about undressing in front of a cow, Luke shooed her out of his stall and closed the curtain. He dressed quickly, sparing only a brief minute to stretch out sore muscles. Finding a milk pail proved tricky, but he pulled one out of the wagon bed and rinsed it off at the pump. The lingering odor of smoke in the air firmed his resolve as he worked. He would defend this land. These people. *His* people.

Twenty minutes later, he stood on the back porch, full milk pail in hand, as he fumbled in his pocket for the key. He needn't have bothered, though, for the door opened wide, revealing Damaris in a dark blue traveling dress with an apron tied around her waist. Her welcoming smile kicked him in the chest and set his blood to humming.

"Good morning."

He pulled his hat from his head. "Mornin'."

She stepped aside and showed him where to set the milk pail. "Nathaniel is packing a bag upstairs. We'll be ready to go as soon as breakfast is done."

"Good." Luke hung his hat on a peg as Damaris returned to the stove and stirred a pot of oatmeal. "I hate sending you away, but you and Nate aren't safe here. Now that I'm on my feet again, I plan to hunt down the scoundrel who's causin' all our trouble. It should only take a day or two, now that I know he's in the area. With any luck, he'll turn on Harbinger, and we can put them all away."

She pivoted to face him as he leaned against the worktable behind her. "I wish you'd call in the others to help you."

He'd thought about it, but he didn't want to pull Matt

away from his new baby. Besides, he needed the captain to watch over Damaris and Nate. He might wire Mark or Jonah if he ran into trouble, but he'd wait to see how things progressed. Sheriff Conley might be lazy, but he was capable when properly motivated. The two of them should be able to dig out the rat and trace him back to his nest.

He crossed his arms. "I'll call in the cavalry if I run into any trouble I can't handle."

Damaris removed the oatmeal from the stove and set it on a wooden trivet on the counter next to a stack of bowls. Instead of serving up the hot cereal, though, she walked over to him. He uncrossed his arms and stood a little straighter at her approach. When she reached a hand up to fiddle with the lapel on his coat, his pulse started a chaotic ricochet that made it hard to concentrate on anything other than her nearness.

She didn't meet his eyes, just stared at his chest while she smoothed the lapel flap. "Promise me you'll be careful, Luke. I've grown rather . . . attached to you." The fiddling stopped, but her hand lingered on his chest. His heart pounded against his ribs as if trying to escape its cage and reach the comfort of her fingers. "And not just because you've managed to save my nephew's life twice, mine once, and spared our house from going up in flames."

Slowly, her head tilted back, and her soft brown eyes met his. "When I wake each morning, the anticipation of seeing you makes me eager to start the day. When I read a passage of scripture, I find myself wanting to discuss it with you. Every time I hear a horse come up the path, my heart races in the hope that the rider is you." Her gaze dropped again, her hand moving across his chest to fiddle with one of his buttons. "I know we haven't spoken about what might happen after all this is over, and I'm not expecting you to do so now. But before you put us on that train, I need you to know something."

She forced her chin up. A pink blush colored her cheeks. "We want you to stay, Luke." Her lashes lowered, stealing her beautiful eyes from him. "I realize it might not be what you want, and I'm not trying to take you away from the Horsemen or your calling to help others, but if you ever find yourself longing for a place to call home, you could have one here. With us. With . . . me."

How was a man supposed to react when a woman offered him everything he'd ever wanted but never had the courage to dream was actually possible?

Obviously *not* with stunned stupor, for her hand fell from his chest at his silence, and she stepped backward.

Not about to let her get away, Luke snatched her straight off her feet and held her flush against him. She gasped and grabbed him around the neck as if there were a chance she might fall. Which was impossible. After a speech like that, he was never letting her go. Ever.

"Damaris Baxter, I can't think of anything I want more than to make a home with you. To make a *life* with you. And Nate. The two of you mean more to me . . . than . . ." Emotion clogged his throat. He coughed to clear it, and when he finally found his voice again, it was a raspy mess. "You mean more to me than anything. I think I've been falling in love with you since the day you climbed out of that cellar."

An extra loud sniff echoed from the doorway. Luke glanced

up to find Nate leaning against the wall, a mischievous grin stretched across his face. "Guess I did you both a favor with that stunt, then, huh? You're welcome."

Luke chuckled as he loosened his grip on Damaris and returned her feet to the floor. "All that proves, you rascal, is that the Almighty can bring good out of any trial."

A fact that had been proven true several times during the past few weeks.

A fact Luke prayed would be borne out again when he loaded Nate and Damaris onto the train that afternoon in Huntsville.

When the moment came and they left his side to board the passenger car bound for San Antonio, Luke's heart throbbed painfully in his chest. He kept telling himself the separation was necessary, but that didn't make it any easier. It just meant he'd have to find Harbinger's henchman fast. Get him in custody and the land development company under government scrutiny so his family could come home.

Luke waved to Nate through the window, then turned his gaze to Damaris. When she put her hand to the glass, he swore he could feel her palm press against his chest like it had back in the kitchen.

A whistle pierced the air, and the train lurched forward. A sudden panic speared through him, but Luke tamped down the irrational fear as he walked the length of the platform, keeping their window in sight as long as possible. They'd be fine. Matt would be waiting for them at the depot. Luke reached the end of the platform and lifted a hand in farewell. Really, he had nothing to worry about. They were surrounded by dozens of passengers—

A pair of faces in the last car snagged his attention as the train rumbled out of the station. One refined, blond, and arrogant. The other dark, dangerous, and smirking as he raised a hand in silent, sarcastic salute. The lawyer and the rustler.

No!

Luke bounded off the platform and chased after the train, yelling for it to stop. But it chugged on, spitting steam and gaining speed, taking his family out of reach.

God help him. He'd just put Damaris and Nate on a train with the very people who were trying to kill them.

Ignoring the stares of the people milling about the plat-form, Luke raced back to the depot. For a heartbeat he considered veering to the street, leaping on Titan, and giving chase to the train. But by the time he untied the horse and wove through the buildings, the train would have gathered too much steam and be too far away to reach. Even now it was fading into the distance. Better to save Titan's strength for a strategy that had a better chance of success.

So instead of attempting dime-novel heroics, he dodged luggage carts and family reunions to get to the telegraph office. Pulse pounding and lungs heaving, he scribbled a message on a telegram blank and shoved it through the barred window.

Thugs on train. Might take Baxters to
Austin. Heading there. Send the troops.

"I need this wired immediately." Luke slapped a silver dollar on the counter, almost double the fee required. "Do it while I watch, and you can keep the change."

The clerk's eyes widened at the brusque demand. His gaze moved to the gun strapped to Luke's thigh, then crawled up the length of him. His Adam's apple bobbed in his throat as he tentatively reached for the form. Slugs moved faster than this fellow.

"Hop to it, man." Luke thumped his hand on the counter, the clap making the clerk jump. "It's an emergency."

"Y-Yes, sir."

The fellow scurried away from the counter and nearly knocked his chair over in his haste to take his seat at the telegraph table.

How had Mullins known about the train? Luke had told no one in Madisonville of their plans. Except . . . The clicking of the telegraph key pecked at Luke's skull like a woodpecker on a pine tree. His hand balled into a fist. Except the telegraph operator when he'd wired Matt this morning.

The telegrapher must have tipped off Mullins. Probably unintentionally. The postmaster who doubled as telegraph operator back in Madisonville was a bit of a gossip, and a lawyer could easily mine him for information, especially if he professed to be helping Nate and Damaris. With the slower travel speed of the Baxter wagon, Mullins could have easily beaten them to Huntsville on horseback. And if he'd avoided the roads, Luke never would have seen him.

He'd missed it. Luke bumped the pad of his fisted hand against the wall, wishing he could clobber the thin wood. After Nate's arrest, Luke had been suspicious of Mullins, and he'd known the lawyer profited from the sales he brokered for Harbinger, but he hadn't actually thought the lawyer capable of consorting with a murderer. He'd been fooled by the suit and fancy education. Mullins didn't fit the mold of the coarse outlaws the Horsemen usually pitted themselves against, yet it seemed he was equally corrupt. Maybe more so. Outlaws didn't pretend to be something they weren't. They waved their guns right in a man's face. Mullins hid his treachery behind a smile and his crimes behind conveniently orchestrated *accidents*.

The truth Luke had failed to see glared at him like a blinding shaft of sunlight.

Mullins wasn't just consorting with a killer. He was giving the orders.

Damaris and Nate would flee from the man who attacked them, but if Mullins approached them alone, they wouldn't recognize the threat. Which gave the lawyer a tactical advantage.

One Luke had to find a way to neutralize.

The telegrapher ceased clicking the key and turned his face in Luke's direction. "It's sent, sir. Do you want to wait for a reply?"

"No." He pushed away from the counter, ready to stalk out, but a railroad map tacked to the wall at his left snagged his attention. He strode over to it and traced the various rail lines leading to Austin.

As Harbinger's base of operations, Austin would provide resources to Mullins that other cities wouldn't. He'd have the advantage of familiarity and allies at his disposal. But he'd have to get there. The tickets Luke purchased for the Baxters would take them through Houston and then on to San Antonio. For Mullins to divert to Austin, he'd have to switch trains at either the main hub in Houston or later down the line in San Marcos. Waiting until the last minute would give Damaris and Nate fewer chances to escape or flag down help, so San Marcos was probably Mullins's target. Which meant Luke might be able to make up time on them if he took the line running directly from Houston to Austin.

He slid back over to the window. "When's the next train?"

"Not 'til tomorrow. We only get the two spurs a day."

"Could I catch something if I rode into Phelps?" That was where the Huntsville spur met the main line.

The telegraph operator frowned. "Only if you have a fast horse. That's a good seven miles from here."

Luke nodded to the operator and rushed out of the depot, thanking God for the impulse that had led him to tie Titan to the back of the Baxter wagon this morning, as well as the check that had kept him from running the horse ragged chasing an uncatchable train.

Your Father knoweth what things ye have need of, before ye ask him.

He tried to take comfort in the Lord's provision as he leapt onto the wagon seat and drove the Baxters' team to the nearest livery, but his concern for Damaris and Nate eroded his peace. He could feel precious minutes tick by as he arranged to board and store the wagon. As soon as the money changed hands, Luke hurried to Titan's side, tightened the cinch, and climbed into the saddle.

You revealed the danger to me, Lord, and you provided Titan, so I gotta believe you'll get me to the station in time to catch the next train. But I'm scared for Damaris and Nate. The thought of living the rest of his life without them slashed like a saber across his chest. *Protect them. Please.*

As Titan's powerful hooves tore up the ground, Luke scoured his memory for a verse to cling to, one to keep him sane during the next half hour of hard riding.

The last two verses of Psalm 37 rose to his consciousness, and he latched on to them like a drowning man to driftwood. He repeated them over and over in his mind, the words eventually matching the rhythm of Titan's stride.

But the salvation of the righteous is of the Lord: he is their strength in the time of trouble. And the Lord shall help them, and deliver them: he shall deliver them from the wicked, and save them, because they trust in him.

Help them. Deliver them. Save them.

Please.

"All aboard!"

The conductor's call jerked Damaris out of her doze and sharpened her attention. They'd been traveling for hours. The sun had set long ago, and the dim kerosene ceiling lamps illuminating the aisle did little to hold the shadows at bay. She glanced out the window and managed to make out the forms of several passengers milling about the platform. Porters with lanterns began urging people back onto the train.

Nathaniel wriggled in the seat next to her, pushing up from where he'd leaned against the side of the car. "How much longer?" he asked in a sleepy voice.

"Maybe a couple of hours?" she guessed. "We're in Lockhart now. We'll stop in San Marcos and then arrive in San Antonio." With the lateness of the hour, the train wouldn't stop at the smaller towns along the way unless they needed to take on water or coal.

The train whistle blew, and the few remaining passengers outside rushed to board. A pair of men stood beneath a lamppost, waiting for the others to board ahead of them. Something about them struck her as familiar. She leaned around Nathaniel and peered through the smoky glass, trying to make out the men's features. The one with the lighter coloring moved his hands over his mustache in a distinctive manner. The curling flourish he made with his fingers at the end was exactly like . . .

"Mr. Mullins?"

"The lawyer fella?" Nathaniel straightened and pressed his face to the window. "What's he doin' here? Is he on the same train as us?"

Damaris's stomach clenched, and a shiver snaked down her nape. She tried to tell herself it was merely coincidence, but her instincts screamed that it was more.

When the man next to Mullins stepped more fully into the light, all doubt vanished. Air whooshed from her lungs as if she'd been hit in the gut. Damaris clutched her nephew's shoulders and jerked him backward, away from the window. Her mind spun.

A plan. She needed a plan.

"Was that . . . ?" Nathaniel's trembling whisper confirmed what her eyes had told her. The man who'd attacked them in the fire was on their train.

Not only on their train, but apparently working with Ronald Mullins.

They needed to get off the train. Now. But they had to do

it in such a way that Mullins and his wicked friend wouldn't realize they were gone until it was too late to follow.

Damaris grabbed her handbag and pulled out the coin purse that carried her travel funds. She snatched the folded banknotes sitting on top of the heavier coins and shoved the money into Nathaniel's hand. "Put this in your pocket. In case we get separated."

He obeyed, then turned to look over his shoulder. "Are they coming after us?"

As much as she wanted to shield him from the truth, they didn't have time for wishful thinking. Only action. "We can't afford to find out. We're getting off this train."

She stood in the aisle, took down their two small bags from the overhead luggage rack, and handed them to Nathaniel.

"Stack them on top of each other by the window," she whispered, careful not to wake the passengers in the seat behind them, "and put your hat on top to make it look like you're sleeping."

It wouldn't fool anyone up close, but from a distance it might appear that Nathaniel was slumped in the seat and buy them a few precious seconds.

"Go to the lavatory at the front of the car, close yourself inside, and wait for me." She glanced down the aisle to where the conductor was moving through the car, checking tickets. "As soon as the conductor passes through to the next car, I'll come join you. I'll tap three times on the door so you'll know it's me. When the train starts moving, we'll sneak outside to the platform where the cars couple and hop off on the side away from the depot. The darkness should provide cover until we can find a tree or bush to hide behind. Once the train disappears, we can seek refuge in town."

"But what if they see us?"

"We'll have to pray they don't." Damaris glanced back at the conductor, now only half a car away. "If something goes wrong, buy passage to San Antonio and get to the Hangers. They'll know what to do."

Her brave, defiant boy looked more like a lost puppy as he hesitated in the aisle.

"Last call!" The shout came from the porter outside on the platform.

Damaris took Nathaniel by the shoulders and turned him to face the front of the car. "I'll be right behind you," she whispered in his ear. "Go!"

He stumbled forward. Her heart squeezed, but she pivoted away from him and sauntered down the aisle in the opposite direction, determined to hide her nephew's retreat. A few passengers looked at her strangely, but most were too concerned with their own business to pay her much mind.

Meeting the conductor in the middle of the aisle, she pasted on a bright smile and extended her tickets. "Here's ours."

He gave her a quizzical look as he handed tickets back to the man seated to his right. "I'll check yours when I get to you, ma'am. You need to take your seat."

"I'm afraid I need to run to the lavatory. I was hoping you could check my tickets now to allow me an extra minute to tend to a personal matter."

The conductor scowled. "The train's about to depart. Your personal matter will have to wait until we are under way. Please take your seat."

"I'll just be a trice, I promise."

Unfortunately, the conductor took his job too seriously to be swayed by a breezy reply. His mulish expression only tightened. "I must insist, ma'am. Whatever it is will have to wait."

"You don't understand." She leaned close. "It's a matter of a . . . delicate nature. And terribly urgent."

His face reddened, and he dropped his gaze, but he still made no move to take her tickets.

"Please, sir," she begged. "I'll take every precaution."

He straightened his shoulders. "It's for your own protection, ma'am. I'm sorry."

His protection was going to get her killed.

"Miss Baxter? May I be of assistance?"

No, no, no.

Damaris leaned to the side to see around the overzealous conductor and confirmed the dreadful truth. Ronald Mullins stood two steps from her.

Instinct insisted she turn and flee, and her pulse prepared accordingly, but her head demanded a wiser course. She would not endanger Nathaniel's escape. Even if it meant surrendering her own.

"Mr. Mullins! Good heavens. I didn't expect to see you on this train."

The conductor turned. "You know this lady, sir?"

"I do." The lawyer's gaze flicked past the trainman to the seat at the front of the car. "I'll see to her safety."

The conductor nodded, then finally accepted her tickets and punched them, apparently glad to relinquish his responsibility for her well-being into the hands of another man. Why he couldn't simply let her be responsible for herself was an annoyance of the highest order, but not her top concern at the moment. Protecting Nathaniel took precedence. Which meant she had to get Mr. Mullins and his prying gaze as far away from the front of the car as possible.

When the conductor shifted sideways in the aisle to squeeze past Damaris, she did the same to slip past Mr. Mullins, heading to the rear.

He clasped her arm as she attempted to sail past. "Where are you going? Isn't your seat up front?"

Hoping he'd overheard enough of her embarrassing conversation with the conductor to believe her frantic reaction was due more to her desire to get to the lavatory than to get away from him, she turned her face close enough to him to explain in a breathy whisper. "I need to get to the lavatory." She gave a tug of her arm, intending to proceed to the back of the car and lead him away from Nathaniel so he couldn't examine her slapdash efforts to recreate a sleeping boy out of a pair of satchels and a cap.

With an audience looking on, the lawyer had no choice but to act the gentleman, but instead of releasing her, his grip on her arm tightened. "I'll escort you."

Fear squeezed her chest. He wasn't going to let her go. In fact, after they passed between the cars, he practically pushed her down the aisle, making no effort to stop at the lavatory.

"Mr. Mullins, the lavatory." She tried to wrench her arm free, but he held firm.

"Easy, my dear. You don't want to do yourself an injury."

No, she wanted to do *him* an injury for likely hiring the man who tried to kill her nephew. But she couldn't give away her suspicions. She had to act the ignorant damsel and pretend that his hand on her arm didn't make her stomach churn.

"Here. Have a seat." He guided her to an empty bench at the front of the car. "It isn't safe to use the facilities right now, but you'll be close here and can use them as soon as we are under way. Is Nathaniel with you? I can fetch him."

"No!" She forced her voice to calm as she perched on the edge of the bench. "Please. He's resting." Hopefully in the front car's lavatory. "As soon as I visit the ladies' room, I'll return to him."

Mr. Mullins stared at the newly closed door behind him, then took a step in that direction. Damaris rose and made a grab for his arm. The train lurched forward. Damaris squealed and tumbled awkwardly against the seat across the aisle.

"For heaven's sake," the man accosted by her bruised hip muttered in disgust. "Collect your woman, sir, and sit down!"

Red-faced, Mr. Mullins righted her and steered her back to the bench. He pressed her into the seat, then sat beside her, pinning her skirt beneath his legs.

Grabbing the fabric of her skirt, she tugged it free and scooted as far away from him as possible. A movement in the darkness outside the window caught her eye and set her pulse speeding into a frenzy. Nathaniel. Sprinting away from the train and darting between a pair of stationary cars on a standby track. *Thank you, God!*

She longed to watch him, to ensure he found safety, but she couldn't afford for Mullins to notice her taking a particular interest in anything outside. She turned sideways in the seat, pressing her back against the window to block the view.

"I really must insist that you let me visit the lavatory, sir.

The train is under way now, and I can manage the gradual acceleration without a repeat of that unfortunate tumble."

"You will sit still and remain precisely where you are, Miss Baxter." Mullins's voice was low and decidedly menacing. Apparently, their game of polite pretense had come to an end.

The train rocked, and she silently urged it to pick up speed and leave Lockhart behind. Mullins took hold of her elbow and dragged her against his side. Praying that Nathaniel had already concealed himself, she did her best to give her adversary something else to worry about.

"Remove your hand from my arm." She raised her voice enough to capture the attention of the man across the aisle.

"Not until we're up to speed, my dear," Mullins responded in a falsely solicitous tone. "You know how unsteady you can be." His grip tightened painfully on her forearm at the same time that a hard, cylindrical object pressed against her rib cage. His waxed mustache brushed against her ear. "I would advise against drawing attention to yourself, Miss Baxter. It could prove detrimental to your health and the health of your nephew."

Damaris's mouth went dry.

A heartbeat later, boots clomped in the aisle, and the man who'd tried to strangle her nephew stood in front of their seat, his hand braced against the overhead luggage rack. "Need anything?"

Mullins nodded. "Kind of you to offer, Colburn. I think Miss Baxter would be much more at her ease if you would fetch her nephew to her. Would you mind?"

"Not at all."

Damaris started to protest, but Mullins jabbed his pistol harder into her side.

Colburn tipped his hat, his dark eyes laughing at her. No amusement softened his gaze, however, when he returned with Nathaniel's cap crushed in his fist.

"Kid's gone."

"How unfortunate," Mullins ground out. He pivoted toward her. "You don't seem too alarmed by your nephew's disappearance."

Damaris lifted her chin and said nothing. The train barreled down the tracks, finally at full speed. She might not live past this night, but Nathaniel would.

THIRTY-SIX

The first light of dawn streamed across Luke's face and woke him from a restless sleep. Like all good soldiers, his senses sharpened to keen points the moment his eyes cracked open. He climbed off the too-short hotel bed and padded on bare feet to the window, a prayer on his heart. Had Damaris and Nate made it to San Antonio? He wanted to believe they had, yet the unease stirring in his gut told him they remained in danger.

He'd only made it as far as Houston last night. No outbound passage had been available until morning. He'd wired Gringolet to let them know his location, bought a ticket on the first train to Austin, then stalked across the street to the Grand Central Hotel and secured an overpriced room so he could get a few hours of shut-eye before resuming his mission.

He'd slept in his clothes, so it took less than five minutes to strap on his gun belt, slide his feet into his boots, and grab his hat. After a quick visit to the community washroom down the hall, he headed downstairs to the dining room and ordered coffee and a plate of eggs, sausage, and biscuits with gravy. Not knowing if he'd have the chance to eat again, he steeled himself against the worry churning in his gut and forced down every last bite. He couldn't afford sapping strength or flagging energy. Nothing would slow his search today. He'd go until he found his family.

After swallowing the last of his coffee, he left payment on the table and strode across the street to Houston's Grand Central Station. His train didn't leave for another hour, but he wanted to check in with the telegraph clerk on duty.

Luke's bootheels echoed loudly in the near-empty station as he strode through the passenger waiting area to get to the ticket window.

A man in a green eyeshade visor looked up at his approach. "Can I help you, sir?"

"Name's Luke Davenport. Any messages waiting for me?"

The clerk twisted to survey a shelf of wooden pigeon holes to his right. He pulled out a handful of small envelopes before finding one with his name on it. "Ah. Yes. Here you are." He slid it through an opening at the bottom of the barred window.

"Thanks."

Luke tore open the envelope and read the short message.

> ## Horsemen in Austin. No sign of Baxters. Will wait at station until location is determined. Burkett

Thank God for Matt's father-in-law. Thaddeus Burkett was a former army man and would guard his post well. Damaris and Nate wouldn't know him, but Matt would have given his business partner a detailed description of them. If they arrived, he'd find them.

The thought brought Luke little peace, though. The fact that they hadn't arrived last night meant something had happened on the train. Helplessness jabbed him in the gut, followed by an uppercut of self-recrimination. He'd fed his family to the wolves and left them to fend for themselves. He wadded the telegram into a ball inside his fist—a fist so tight his knuckles whitened.

Mullins could have taken them anywhere. He could be doing anything to them while Luke paced an empty corridor miles away, unable to track them. Unable to save those he loved. A quiver vibrated through his jaw as his throat thickened. He clenched his teeth together and forced his mind away from the impotence that threatened to incapacitate him.

He glanced up at the vaulted ceiling. *Got a verse for me?*

The words his captain always asked him before a mission resonated in Luke's heart as he took them and laid them before the Almighty.

I need one awful bad, and I seem to be plumb out.

No word of the Lord descended from the ceiling tiles to soothe his ragged heart, however, so Luke returned to his pacing. If only he knew where Mullins had taken them. Austin made sense, but there was no guarantee they hadn't gone elsewhere. And even if Austin was correct, the state capital was huge. Mullins and his killer-for-hire could be hiding Damaris and Nate anywhere.

Can any hide himself in secret places that I shall not see him? saith the Lord.

The scripture filled his mind with such fullness, Luke snatched his hat from his head to make more room.

The eyes of the Lord are in every place, beholding the evil and the good.

A tear slid down Luke's face.

For his eyes are upon the ways of man, and he seeth all his goings. There is no darkness, nor shadow of death, where the workers of iniquity may hide themselves.

Luke fell to his knees. His eyes closed as the Lord's generosity overwhelmed him.

God saw. He saw Damaris. And Nate. Right this very moment. Mullins too. No one could hide from the Almighty. No one could flee his presence.

Guide me to them, Lord. Make my path straight. Lead me in the way that I should go.

He knelt in that empty corridor for several minutes. Praying. Humbling himself before his God. Opening his fist to take the Father's hand. When the mingled sounds of footsteps and voices increased and told him that his solitary place would soon be public, Luke braced a flat palm against the wall and levered himself to his feet.

His mind oddly clear, he scrubbed a hand over his face and marched back to the ticket counter. This time he had to wait in line behind a drummer and his oversized sample case, but once the peddler concluded his business, Luke stepped up to the window and asked for two telegraph blanks.

"Send this first one to the depot in San Antone, addressed to Mr. Thaddeus Burkett."

The clerk accepted the message, making a quick count of the words before looking up again. "And the second?"

"Matthew Hanger, Austin depot."

The clerk's eyes widened. "*The* Matthew Hanger?"

Somehow Luke managed not to roll his eyes. "Yep." He pushed the second blank through the window opening. "I need these sent right away." He met the clerk's eye with a knowing look. "Official Horsemen business." He'd make use of whatever advantage the Lord sent his way.

"I'll do it now, Mr. Davenport."

Luke tipped his hat. "Mighty obliged to ya."

The operator scurried over to his machine and began tapping out the code that would inform the captain of their target.

Ronald Mullins—lawyer. Harbinger Land Development Company.

After dropping the necessary coins on the counter, Luke excused himself to wander over to the platform and wait for the boarding call. As he stepped out of line, however, he felt eyes upon his back. Murmurs followed.

"Did you hear? Hanger's Horsemen are back in action."

That they were. For the most important mission of Luke's life.

Damaris blinked and tried to focus, but the room kept swimming. A room she didn't recognize. A wave of nausea roiled through her stomach. She squeezed her eyes shut and drew in a slow, deep breath. A cloying scent tinged the air, making her nose scrunch up and her mind awaken to snippets of memories.

On the train. Mr. Mullins holding her at gunpoint. His handkerchief over her mouth and nose after the rocking of the train had lulled most passengers to sleep. The sticky-sweet smell of ether. The resulting dizziness. Him claiming she was ill as he clutched her close and ushered her away from the San Marcos depot. When her legs eventually collapsed, he'd swept her into his arms and climbed into a waiting buggy. She'd had no strength to fight. Consciousness gave way to darkness.

Hazy impressions fluttered through her mind. A scantily clad woman in a room that reeked of cheap perfume. Colburn tossing Damaris on the borrowed bed, tying her wrists to the iron frame, and leering at her with cold, wicked eyes. The panic that had pulsed through her. The inability to scream when she thought he would attack. The relief she felt when the woman teased him away with a bottle of whiskey and the promise of her charms.

A private railcar had carried her to Austin. At least she thought it was Austin. Hadn't that been the name on the sign at the station? The memory was too fuzzy to pin down with complete certainty.

Collecting herself, Damaris opened her eyes again, better prepared to battle the dizziness. Sunlight outlined a pair of closed shutters on the wall in front of her. A pillow lay beneath her cheek, and her left hip sank rather comfortably into a mattress that must be filled with feathers. Logs made up the walls, but they were well-chinked. No drafts slipped through. She was in a cabin somewhere. A well-made cabin with an expensive bed. Unfortunately, that was all she could deduce from her curled position facing the wall.

She listened for additional clues, but no voices murmured behind her. No feet tapped against floorboards. Had they left her alone? How late in the day was it? Still morning? Or had the ether kept her sleeping into the afternoon?

With tiny, controlled movements, she tested her mobility. Her arms stretched in front of her unhindered. Ankles too. So no bindings.

Dare she roll over? Let her captors know she was awake? But what if she was alone and this was her one chance to escape?

Hearing nothing that warned her to lie still, she braced her hand on the bed and slowly rolled over. She *was* alone. But in a small room with a closed door and a few pieces of bedroom furniture. Not in the main cabin as she'd imagined.

Still, she was free of prying eyes. She had to make the most of it.

Careful to move as smoothly as possible to avoid a dizzy spell, she climbed from the bed and made her way to the window. The shutters were barred from the outside and refused to budge. She turned to the bureau and wardrobe next, searching for something that could be used as a weapon, but all the drawers were empty. No chamber pot beneath the bed or porcelain ewer on the washstand with which to knock someone over the head. Sudden inspiration had her grabbing for her hair, but the straw hat she'd worn for the trip—along with the pointed hatpin she'd used to secure it—was gone.

She had nothing.

No, that wasn't true. She had her wits and a reason to hope. Nathaniel would fetch the Hangers. Luke would come.

She just had to hold out long enough for her Horseman to find her.

Courage and cunning. Those would be her weapons.

Yet even as a prayer for such blessings took shape in her heart, a key rattled in the door lock, scattering her composure and setting her hands to trembling. Grabbing hold of the bed frame for support, Damaris backed away from the opening door.

Ronald Mullins stepped through, a smile stretching across his face.

A queasiness that had nothing to do with having been dosed with ether earlier agitated her stomach. How had she ever trusted this man?

"Ah," he said. "You're awake. Excellent. Time for us to get down to business."

THIRTY-SEVEN

The instant Luke's boots hit the platform at the Austin station, he used the full length of his legs to stride through the milling passengers toward the telegraph office. Hopefully, Matt had communicated with his father-in-law and left word for Luke about where to meet up with the rest of the Horsemen.

"Preach!" The captain's shout carried above the hissing steam of the locomotive and the hustle of the trainmen and porters.

Luke's head snapped to the left, his pulse leaping as he searched the platform for Matt's familiar handlebar mustache. A waving arm drew his attention, and he jogged over to the man he loved like a brother.

As they gripped forearms and pounded each other on the back, a weight lifted from Luke's shoulders. The cavalry had arrived.

"I heard from Thaddeus," Matt said. "Nate made it to San Antonio about an hour ago."

Luke gripped his captain's shoulder and leaned on him for support as his knees wobbled. "Thank God." He recognized at once what Matt hadn't said, but he needed confirmation. "Damaris?"

The small shake of Matt's head made the situation clear.

"As soon as we got your wire about Mullins and Harbinger, we put Francis Kendall to work investigating all company holdings in town. Wallace and Brooks are checking out a pair of warehouses, but I think it more likely he'll take her someplace remote."

Luke didn't know the newspaperman well, since Kendall had always communicated directly with Matt about their jobs, but having a local man familiar with the area could even the odds against Mullins. Damaris needed every advantage they could wrangle.

"Kendall was surprised to see Harbinger's name attached to the investigation," Matt said as he steered Luke toward the road where his horse, Percival, and a second Gringolet mount waited.

Leave it to the captain to think of everything. Luke had left Titan at a livery in Phelps, not wanting anything to slow him down or complicate his ability to get to Austin as quickly as possible.

"The company has a reputation for being aggressive but fair in their dealings. Are you sure they're behind the Baxters' troubles?"

Luke slowed as they reached the horses. He rested an arm on the saddle and looked over the back of his horse to where Matt collected Percival's reins. "They're the ones who benefit from the railroad building a spur into Madisonville, but I suppose it's possible that Mullins has been operating without their knowledge. It doesn't really matter to me at the moment, though. Mullins is the one who has Damaris. He's got a killer with him and access to Harbinger resources. We can sort out where the blame goes after we get Damaris back."

Matt held his gaze for a long moment, then dipped his chin. He understood. Damaris was more than just a kind woman who had nursed Luke back to health. She was his heart. His life. Justice was not the mission today. Damaris was the mission.

"Kendall has a command center set up at his home. Mount up, and I'll take you there. You can fill us in on what you know about Harbinger and Mullins, and we'll see what information Kendall has gleaned from his local sources. Lord willing, that will give us a direction to start the hunt."

The last thing Luke wanted to do was sit around in a room talking. The bloodhound inside him already strained at the leash to be turned loose. But determination alone wouldn't lead him to his target. A hound needed a scent to identify the trail. And no one was better at finding a viable scent in a pile of random information than Matthew Hanger.

So Luke mounted up without argument and followed his captain to a tidy little house near Shoal Creek. Seeing a pair of familiar horses tied up outside got Luke's blood pumping. He hurried inside to see if by some miracle Wallace and Brooks had found Damaris.

But the only woman inside the house was a middle-aged lady fluttering about a small parlor.

"This is Eloise Kendall," Matt said by way of introduction as she entered the room. "Ellie, this is Luke Davenport."

"Ah. The one they call Preach." She smiled, and the sparkle in her eyes gave her a youthful glow at odds with the smattering of gray streaking through her dark hair. "Please, come in." She called out to the group of men huddled around a table. "Francis will want to talk to you."

Luke had never considered that Francis Kendall might have a wife. But why shouldn't he? Most men their age did. Still, it was odd to think of him as anything other than the reporter who'd chronicled the Horsemen's exploits. Not a real person with a full life of his own.

"Sorry to cause such a stir," Luke said as he removed his hat and ducked around a light fixture hanging from the hall ceiling.

"Don't be silly." Mrs. Kendall winked as she shepherded them toward the parlor. "I haven't seen Francis this excited in years. He's always wanted to meet the four of you in person, but to actually help you on a case? Why, he's beside himself."

When she caught Luke's eye, her smile flattened, and compassion sparked in her gaze. She touched his arm. "No one knows Austin better than my Francis. With all the stories he's written and the good he's done in this city, people are eager to help whenever he asks, and he's been asking all morning. He'll find Miss Baxter for you. I have no doubt."

But would he find her in time?

"Preach!" Wallace strode away from the card table where a short man with a fluffy mustache bent over a crazy assortment of books, maps, and seemingly random scraps of paper.

Jonah stepped out of the shadows in the corner and strode forward as well.

KAREN WITEMEYER

Luke embraced his comrades but only found the words for one question. "Any sign of Damaris?"

Jonah shook his head. "Nothing at the warehouses but cargo. I checked all the back rooms and storage closets while Wallace kept the managers busy with his usual song-and-dance routine, but we found no evidence of anything unusual."

"Those were shots in the dark, though, made when the only clue we had to go on was the Harbinger name." Wallace slapped Luke on the back and offered a crooked smile that somehow managed to be reassuring without diminishing the seriousness of the situation. "Other intelligence has been arriving all morning. We've got much more to go on now. With you here to fill in the missing pieces, Matt and Kendall will have things narrowed down in no time."

Kendall looked up from his paper-strewn table and dipped his head in Luke's direction. "Mr. Davenport."

Luke stepped past the other Horsemen and extended his hand to the man best situated to find Damaris. "Call me Preach."

Kendall straightened. His stature barely brought his head in line with Luke's shoulder, but he exuded confidence and intelligence, two things Luke craved at the moment.

Kendall clasped his hand. "Preach." He had a firm grip. "The first thing I need is a physical description of Mr. Mullins and the man traveling with him. Matt already provided a description of Miss Baxter, but I'm afraid brown hair and eyes along with average build didn't help much in narrowing down the field. Dozens of women fit that description."

But Damaris was so much more than that. How had Matt, with his keen observation skills, failed to notice?

"She's wearing a dark blue traveling dress with one of them lacy shirts that buttons to the neck." Luke wiggled his fingers in front of his throat in case that helped draw a better picture than his inelegant words. Heaven knew his pitiful vocabulary failed to do her justice. "She wears a black mourning brooch in honor of her brother, and her hair is always braided and wrapped around her head like a crown." He looked at Matt. "Her hair's about the same color as Percival's coat."

"Good grief," Mrs. Kendall muttered somewhere behind the gathered men. "You can't compare a woman to a horse."

Maybe not in normal circumstances, but if there was one thing cavalrymen understood, it was horses. Matt was already nodding his agreement of Luke's assessment, and the other Horsemen were no doubt firming up a mental image of Damaris that was more accurate than the nondescript *brown hair and brown eyes* they'd been working from previously.

Luke went on to describe Ronald Mullins with his fair hair, fancy suit, and ridiculous waxed mustache. When it came to the lawyer's companion, Luke focused as much on the weaponry the rustler carried as his features.

"This the same fellow who carved you up and left you for dead?" Jonah asked.

Luke nodded. "Yep. But two days ago he tried to strangle a kid in the middle of a prairie fire he set." He gave Kendall and the others a quick rundown on the fire, Nate's attempted arrest before that, and the suspicious nature of Douglas Baxter's death prior to Damaris's arrival in Madisonville. "Harbinger's been buying up land between Navasota and Madisonville, using whatever means necessary. When rustling Oliver Grimes's cattle didn't convince him to sell, they moved on to bribery. Damaris and Nate are the last holdouts, and things have gone from bad to worse for them. Best we can guess, the railroad plans to build a spur and Harbinger intends to profit on the land deal."

Luke turned to Matt and held his captain's gaze. "Mullins is gonna try to force Damaris to sign away Nate's land. And the man he's got with him has no qualms about using a knife to get what he wants." Bile rose in the back of Luke's throat. He forced himself to continue. They needed to understand what was at stake and how little time they had to act. "Whether she signs or not, they can't let her leave Austin alive. Not when she can testify against them. As soon as they get what they want from her, she's as good as dead."

Matt scowled. "And if they can't get it from her, they'll go after the boy."

Grunts of disgust echoed around the room.

"I think I might know where to look."

All four Horsemen turned to Francis Kendall. The bespectacled newspaperman tapped a spot on the map spread across the table.

"A contact at the depot reported that a private car owned by the Harbinger Land Development Company arrived on the northbound train out of San Marcos late this morning. He didn't see a woman, but he mentioned a fair-haired man with a distinctive mustache who oversaw the decoupling of the car and gave instructions for its storage in the train yard. The man seems to match the description of Mr. Mullins." Kendall looked at each Horseman in turn, then focused on Luke. "The blond man left word that he expected to need the railcar again first thing in the morning."

Luke had known the timeline was short, but hearing it confirmed tightened a screw into the wall of his chest.

"One of the stable boys at Owen's Livery came 'round when he learned I was looking for a woman who might be in trouble. He reported seeing a man and a woman at the livery midmorning. The man had dark coloring and hard eyes with a manner that made the boy nervous. The woman seemed . . . limp. As if she'd crumple to the ground if her escort removed his arm from around her middle. The man claimed she'd drunk herself into a stupor after learning of her brother's sudden death, but my young friend smelled no alcohol on her when he helped get her into the closed buggy they rented. He didn't remember much about her except that she wore a blue dress."

"That's her!" Luke grabbed the edge of the table. "It's got to be her." But what had they done to incapacitate her to such a degree? He pinned Kendall with a stare. "Did the kid know where they were headed?"

Kendall shook his head. "All he could tell me was that they headed west on Fifth Street."

"But you said you knew where we should look." Luke's voice rose in volume. Matt placed a hand on his shoulder, but Luke shrugged it off. He didn't want to be calm. He wanted to find Damaris!

Unperturbed by the demanding giant hulking over him, Kendall pulled a sheet of paper from a messy pile on the far side of the table. "I made a list of all properties in the area owned by Harbinger or one of their executives. Most are warehouses or vacant lots purchased for some form of speculation or another. But there are two private residences.

One is in town and therefore ill-equipped for hiding criminal activity. The other, however, is a hunting cabin owned by one of the New York investors. It's secluded. Nestled in the hills northwest of town. I initially thought it too far away to be of much use, but that was before I understood the intentions of the parties involved." He glanced up at Luke. Compassion softened the confidence radiating from his gaze. "If one was looking for a place to dispose of . . . evidence . . . this cabin would be the place to go."

Matt squeezed Luke's shoulder, then slapped him on the back hard enough to dislodge the mental image of Damaris's body being thrown into a shallow, unmarked grave.

"Saddle up, men." The captain's voice echoed with the clang of steel. "We've got a woman to save."

⟢ CHAPTER ⟢
THIRTY-EIGHT

M r. Mullins offered Damaris his arm as if he were a gentleman asking her to dance rather than a villainous reprobate demanding to steal land from an orphan. She ignored the offer and stepped past her captor, holding her head high even as she wove unsteadily thanks to the lingering effects of the ether. She clung to the back of the brocade sofa for balance as she made her way around the sitting area positioned near the hearth. Then, on her own, she crossed to the small table and chairs at the back of the room near the cookstove.

A dark figure standing at the window by the front door separated himself from the hunter-green curtain, drawing Damaris's attention. Colburn.

"'Bout time you woke up." The sneer in his voice and the hardness in his eyes sent a chill down her nape.

It didn't help that he stood near a gun case filled to capacity with hunting rifles and no doubt enough ammunition to hold off an army.

Damaris turned her face away from the vile man and continued to the table, where a few sheets of paper sat in front of a vacant chair. She settled into the seat and reached for the papers, hating that her fingers trembled, revealing her nervousness.

She held the papers before her, but her eyes absorbed nothing of the content. Lacking the speed or strength to escape, her only option was to delay Mullins as long as possible. Give the Horsemen time to find her.

And if they didn't?

Take care of Nathaniel, Lord.

"I do apologize for all the dramatics." Mullins sat in the chair across from her, reached inside his coat, and pulled out a fountain pen. "It could all have been avoided if you had just taken my advice from the beginning and accepted the price Harbinger offered."

Damaris couldn't bring herself to meet his eyes. "You could have simply accepted no for an answer."

"Afraid not, my dear." He extracted a vial of ink from his vest pocket and unhooked it from a gold fob chain. "You see, I owe a very dangerous man a significant amount of money, and the only way to acquire that money is to gain the bonus Harbinger promised for securing all the acreage needed for the railroad spur they have planned for Madisonville. Since Oliver Grimes finally agreed to sell a portion of his land, the property in your trust is the last piece I need to complete the set."

He unscrewed the vial's lid, then withdrew an eyedropper and began methodically filling the reservoir in his Waterman pen. "Grimes proved nearly as stubborn as you Baxters. His hiring of Mr. Davenport nearly undid all my hard work. He scared off the rustlers we hired as soon as they realized he didn't have the decency to die following their altercation. Afraid of being identified or some such nonsense. I would have protected them, of course, but no matter. I found a way to get what I wanted from Grimes, and I'll get what I want from you, too."

"All this—the rustling, the attack on Luke, what happened to my brother—it was all because you owed someone money?" Even knowing how precarious her situation was, Damaris couldn't keep the scorn from her voice. "You're a murderer."

Mr. Mullins halted his deliberate ink dropping. "What happened to your brother was an unfortunate accident. My associate got a little carried away in his efforts to convince Douglas to sell." He shot a scowl toward Colburn.

"Weren't my fault the fool was so muleheaded." Colburn turned from keeping watch out the window to glare at Mullins. "I woulda stopped dunkin' his head in that rain barrel if he'd just signed the paper. Ornery cuss kept fightin'. I had to hold him under longer and longer. I didn't realize I'd drowned him 'til it was too late. Caused me no end of trouble. Loadin' his carcass in a wagon bed and coverin' him with straw so I could get him out to the lake unseen. Then waitin' 'til no one was around and rowin' him out past the shoreline. At least with the kid, I coulda just left his body to rot in the fire." His glare shifted to Damaris. "You're turning out to be as much trouble as your brother."

"But if you cooperate," Mr. Mullins said with a pointed glance at Colburn, "we'll let you go." He smiled and patted her hand. "You can be on a train home tonight."

Damaris released the papers and pulled her hand away from his touch. "Even *I* am not that naïve, sir. I can link you to a known arsonist, cattle rustler, and confessed murderer."

"You forget that I have connections in high circles. People who owe me favors. Powerful people. Colburn is an outlaw who can disappear on a whim, and without him in custody, there is only your word against mine. With my long-standing relationship with the judges in the area, I'm not worried about winning that battle. I've committed no actual crimes, after all."

He was skilled in presenting a swaying argument. She almost believed him. But not quite. He had too much on the line. He wouldn't risk his future on a chance, even a good chance, when he could assure it. Still, it might be best to let him think she believed his lies.

"You'll really let me go?"

The obsequious grin returned. "I'm a man of my word, Miss Baxter."

Yet he had not actually given his word on anything.

"And if I choose not to sign?"

His smile flattened as he shook his head. "That, I'm afraid, I cannot allow." He capped his vial of ink and tested the fountain pen on a blank sheet of paper. An elegant black slash streaked across the page. "If you choose to be difficult, my associate will offer you . . . encouragement until you decide to comply." He tipped his head toward Colburn, who unsheathed a large hunting knife and tested the sharpness with the pad of his thumb. "It will be most unpleasant, I fear."

Colburn grinned with far too much relish as he pointed the tip of the knife in her direction. The same knife, no doubt, that had caused Luke such pain. The one that nearly ended his life.

With a thick swallow, Damaris picked up the documents Mr. Mullins had prepared, placed them in front of her, and slowly began to read.

With a huff of impatience, the lawyer slid the bottom sheet out from beneath the page she was reading and slapped it onto the table near her right elbow. "All we need is a signature, Miss Baxter. No need to read the fine print." He held out the pen.

"I disagree. I must ensure this document only pertains to the sale of my brother's property. Once I have ascertained the details of the agreement, I will be ready to proceed."

He groaned but set down the pen and nodded.

It might only buy her ten to fifteen minutes, but it was ten or fifteen minutes in which God could work to bring the Horsemen.

She prayed it would be enough.

"What do you see, Brooks?" Lying flat on his belly at the top of a small rise a good hundred yards from the Harbinger hunting cabin, Matt handed the field glasses past Luke to the Horseman with the keenest vision.

It was all Luke could do not to snatch the binoculars as they passed over his head and have a look for himself, but he trusted Jonah's eyesight more than his own. And they had no time to waste. The only thing keeping him sane at the moment was the wagon and team in the grassy field to the left of the cabin. The men were still here. And if the men were still here, that meant they hadn't concluded their business yet.

"There's a guard by the front window," Jonah reported, his tone cool and matter-of-fact as he braced on his elbows to peer through the field glasses. "Dark hair, tanned skin, bushy mustache. Matches the description of the rustler who attacked Preach."

"Any sign of Damaris?" *Please let her be alive.*

"I don't have a clear line of sight. I caught some movement in the background, but nothing to distinguish man from woman." Jonah passed the glasses back to the captain.

Matt met Luke's gaze. "She's in there, Preach. There'd be no reason for him to stand guard, otherwise."

Luke nodded, but his heart pounded painfully in his chest, desperate to find evidence to support the captain's conclusion. Desperate to see Damaris with his own eyes. To hold her. Protect her. Shield her from the cruelty of wicked men.

A rustling to the rear made Luke reach for his holster, but Wallace's quiet whistle stilled his hand.

As one, Luke, Matt, and Jonah belly-crawled backward until they were away from the crest of the small rise. Staying crouched close to the ground, they made their way to a pair of live oaks where Wallace waited.

"No exit from the rear of the cabin. There's one small window, but it's boarded up."

"Could Preach fit through if we unboarded it?" Matt asked.

Wallace shook his head, and Luke bit back a growl of frustration.

"I gotta get in there, Cap. They've got the covered position.

And Damaris. As soon as we make our presence known, she's as good as dead."

A thoughtful look wrinkled Matt's face. "We need a surprise attack. Get you inside before anyone fires a shot."

"How?"

A feral light gleamed in the captain's eyes. "I have a plan."

"No more stalling, Miss Baxter." Ronald Mullins picked up his fancy fountain pen and thrust it toward her like a dagger. "Time to sign."

Damaris set the papers down in front of her but made no move to collect the pen. *Lord, make me bold.* Her time was up, and she knew it. But she wouldn't go down without a fight.

"This document indicates that I am selling the land to Harbinger for one dollar. Surely you don't expect me to agree to such terms." She pushed the paper back toward the lawyer with shaking hands. "Amend the deal to include a fair selling price."

Before she could blink, Ronald Mullins grasped her wrist and forced the pen between her fingers.

"Sign it," he gritted out between clenched teeth. "Now!"

She lurched to her feet, tipping her chair over as the instinct to flee took control of her body. But his grip was too strong. He yanked her forward and sprawled her upper body across the table. Then he lowered his face next to hers.

"I've taken great pains not to hurt you up to this point, Miss Baxter. But my patience is at an end. Sign now, and I'll ensure my associate kills you quickly and painlessly. Otherwise he'll torture you until you become compliant. You're going to die either way, but how much you suffer is up to you." Apparently, he'd decided his fiction regarding letting her go no longer had merit.

He grabbed her plaited coronet and yanked her backward. Hair tore from her scalp, and Damaris cried out. Mullins righted her chair and shoved her into it.

"Sign the paper." The words growled in his throat.

"No!"

He released her hair and slapped her hard across the face. Her head spun sideways. Tears sprang to her eyes.

"Sign it!"

"No," she whimpered.

Heaven help her. She wasn't brave. Or strong. Or heroic. One slap and she was falling apart.

"Colburn," Mullins snapped. "Get over here."

"About time." The man with the cold eyes stepped away from the window and strolled toward the table, unsheathing his knife as he came. "For a minute there, I thought you was gonna steal my fun."

Mullins circled behind Damaris. His fingers bit painfully into her collarbone as he pinned her in place. "Don't touch her writing arm."

Colburn slashed his blade through the air, then tossed it from hand to hand.

Damaris's feet scraped against the floor, trying in vain to back away. "Please." Tears rolled down her cheeks as she wagged her head from side to side. "Don't hurt me."

"Oh, it's gonna hurt, darlin'." In a flash, he lunged forward, blade swiping.

Damaris gasped.

Pain erupted across the fleshy part of her left arm. She grabbed the wound with her right hand, the sharp sting pulling a sob from her throat.

"That one's just a scratch. The next one will really hurt." Colburn grinned. "Unless you're ready to sign the paper." He waved the blade slowly in front of her, then wiped it on his sleeve. A thin red line smeared across the white fabric. Blood. Her blood.

Her eyes darted to the table. The paper. The pen.

"Ready, Miss Baxter?" Mullins loosened his grip on her shoulders just a little.

If she signed, she died. If she didn't, she suffered, but she bought time for Luke to find her. Time for the Horsemen to stop Mullins before he could threaten Nathaniel.

Lord, make me brave.

Damaris closed her eyes and shook her head.

Mullins tightened his grip. "So be it."

Colburn slashed a second time.

Damaris screamed.

THIRTY-NINE

Damaris's scream carried upward through the chimney and cracked Luke's chest open more effectively than any cavalry saber. If Wallace hadn't been gripping his arm to keep him balanced on the cabin roof, Luke would have forfeited all stealth and launched himself over the side.

"Don't give up our position," Wallace whispered, tightening his hold. "We'll have a better chance of breaching the cabin cleanly if we work together." His jaw was set in a firm line, but his eyes radiated compassion. "She's alive, Preach. Focus on that."

The fact that his friend was right didn't make it any easier to wait. Luke nodded, though, and after Wallace released his hold, he took a silent step down the sloping roof toward the front eave.

They'd taken advantage of the cabin's blind side to approach from the rear. Using a nearby tree as a ladder, he and Wallace had lowered themselves to the rooftop on the side farthest from the front room, then tiptoed over to the chimney to await the captain's signal.

"Your grip secure?" Wallace asked as he checked the rope harness crisscrossed over his chest and shoulders.

Luke wrapped another loop of rope around his gloved wrist and flexed his fingers. "Yep."

"Good. Do you see Matt?"

Luke scanned the trees again before catching a beam of light reflecting off a mirror. "There." He took two steps to his left. "All right. I'm lined up."

"Stay there so I can use you as a point of reference." Wallace picked up the slack in the rope and handed the tether to Luke. "I'll give it a tug when I'm in position."

Luke nodded and braced his feet apart, keeping his eyes glued on the flash of light directly ahead. A foot to the right or left, and he'd miss his target. He had one chance to make this work, and he needed each of the Horsemen to play a role. Matt to direct him. Wallace to serve as anchor. And Jonah to ensure no one got away.

Luke glanced over his shoulder. No sign of Wallace, which meant he was on his belly, stretched out like a human grappling hook, clamping on to the eave opposite their point of entry so Luke would have a straight shot.

Had it been two minutes since Damaris had cried out? Three? They needed to hurry. The thought of that devil in there with her—

The rope tugged. Finally. Luke raised his arm above his head to signal Matt that he was ready, then dropped the coiled slack and fit his second hand to the end of the rope. Trusting Matt to be watching through the field glasses, he nodded his head once, twice, and on the third time, he took off running. The captain would do the same—charge the house from the front.

Luke leapt off the roof, twisting his body in the air to aim himself feet-first at his target—the large plate-glass window at the front of the cabin. His arms snapped in their sockets as the rope tautened. A heartbeat later, his boots slammed into the window.

Glass shattered. A curtain covered his face as his momentum carried him into the front room. Releasing the rope, Luke fell to the floor. Throwing the curtain fabric aside, he sprang to his feet, spotted his prey, and charged.

With a roar, he launched himself at the rustler who'd left him for dead, the devil who dared touch Damaris. His enemy spun to face him, bringing up a knife, but Luke was ready. He blocked the blow with his left forearm and slammed an uppercut into his opponent's jaw. When the man staggered backward, Luke charged again, flattening him to the ground. He grabbed the knife arm and banged wrist against floor until the blade fell away. The rustler kicked and punched, but without his three compadres to even the odds, he was no match for Luke's greater size and strength. Ignoring the pelting jabs to his body, Luke fisted the rustler's shirt and yanked his head and shoulders off the ground. Then, with a mighty swing, he smashed his enemy's jaw. The rustler went limp.

"Gun!"

The captain's call had Luke spinning around and reaching for his weapon, but his revolver never cleared leather. Because the gun the captain had spotted wasn't pointed at Luke. It was pointed at Damaris.

His beautiful, brave Damaris. Her hair hung down around her ears in lopsided hanks. Tears streaked her cheeks. Blood stained her sleeve and her skirt.

Mullins stood with his arm wrapped around Damaris's middle. Gun pointed at her head as he used her as a shield. Luke's jaw tightened. As did his fists.

"Back away," Mullins demanded. "Or she dies!"

Luke unclenched his fists and held his hands harmlessly away from his body.

The lawyer's gaze darted over to Matt, who stood, gun drawn, directly outside the shattered window. "Throw your pistol into the broken glass. Now!"

Matt uncocked the revolver and loosened his grip, letting it spin around his finger so that it dangled upside down like a fish on a line. "Easy, there," he coaxed as he leaned down to drop his gun into the glass shards on the floor inside the window. "All we want is Miss Baxter. Let her go, and we'll let you walk right out that door."

"Not a chance," Mullins said, inching his way toward the door. "I know who you are, Horseman. You and Davenport are going to stay right where you are while Miss Baxter and I take a ride into town." Another step toward the door. "You follow me, she dies. You race ahead and try to stop me at the depot, she dies. But if you're smart and do as you're told, I'll leave her unharmed at the first station we reach."

Luke itched to get his hands around Mullins's throat, but he'd do nothing to endanger Damaris. A fact the lawyer knew all too well. Mullins actually smirked as he sidled past his fallen comrade to get to the door. Luke didn't pay him more than half a glance, though. He focused on Damaris. On those glistening brown eyes that looked far too defeated.

"Take care of Nathaniel for me," she said softly as Mullins dragged her past.

A muscle ticked in Luke's jaw as he pinned her with his stare. "I'll take care of him *with* you."

Her eyes widened slightly, and her step slowed until a shove from Mullins broke their eye contact and forced her to stumble toward the door.

"Open it," the lawyer snapped as he twisted her sideways so he could keep an eye on both Luke and the captain.

Not that his vigilance mattered. Luke and Matt weren't the Horsemen to be worried about.

After struggling with the heavy latch barring the door, Damaris pulled the portal open and stepped out into the sunshine. The moment she cleared the eaves, the getaway wagon raced by with Wallace in the driver's seat.

"Stop!" Mullins moved his gun arm to take a shot at the man stealing his team.

As soon as he moved, a rifle fired. Mullins yelped. His pistol fell to the ground, and blood seeped through his cuff. He bent sideways to cradle his injured wrist, but with the gun no longer pressed to her temple, Damaris discovered new energy to resist, kicking the gun out of his reach and straining against his hold.

She didn't struggle long, for the moment Luke heard Jonah's sniper shot, he ran for the door. He pulled Damaris to his chest, creating enough separation between her and her captor to chop an elbow across Mullins's bicep, breaking his hold.

Without his shield, Mullins had no choice but to run. Luke let him go a few yards while he steadied Damaris on her feet, then chased the cur down and tackled him to the ground. Luke's knuckles crashed into Mullins's jaw on the same side where Damaris's face had been reddened by a man's palm. Then he laid into his body, jabbing stomach, kidneys, and ribs until Mullins curled into a ball, covered his head, and begged Luke to stop.

Grabbing Mullins by the coat lapels, Luke dragged him to his feet. Matt stood nearby, ready to take the villain off his hands, and Luke didn't hesitate. Mullins might deserve to be covered in honey and staked out on a bed of ants for a week, but seeing to Damaris took precedence over vengeance. That was God's jurisdiction anyhow.

Luke shoved Mullins toward the captain, then jogged over to the cabin, where Damaris stood with an arm braced against the wall. A quick peek inside the door as he passed confirmed there'd be no trouble from that quarter. The rustler still lay in an unconscious heap.

"I got him." Wallace waved from the wagon he'd just drawn to a stop in front of the cabin. "Come on, slowpoke," he called over his shoulder to the black man striding across the yard from the tree that had served as his sniper's perch. "Give me a hand."

Jonah scowled as he slung his rifle over his shoulder, which of course made Mark chuckle.

"Those two are about as similar as rocks and water," Luke said with a grin when he saw Damaris watching them with a dazed expression, "but their friendship is as solid as they come." He came alongside her, his smile fading into a frown of concern. "Damaris? Are you all right?"

It took her a moment to meet his gaze, and when she did, his stomach dropped to his boots. Dullness clouded her eyes.

"Luke?" She reached for him. "I think I'm going to . . . fain . . ."

He caught her right as her knees buckled.

"Matt!" he roared as he swept her into his arms and carried her to the wagon bed.

He laid her across the tailgate, smoothed her hair out of her face, and quickly took stock of her injuries. The slash across her forearm was shallow and no cause for immediate concern. But there'd been another bloodstain on her skirt. He flipped through the fabric until he found it. A dark brown stain glaring up at him from the folds beneath her left hip.

"Here." A knife appeared in Luke's field of vision. Matt's knife. "Cut a slit so we can see what we're dealing with."

Luke grabbed the blade and carefully fit the tip through the hole in the middle of the stained fabric. In one long slice, he cut a slit from hip to ankle. Then he repeated the action with her petticoat and spread the fabric wide. Bright red blood seeped through her cotton drawers on her left thigh.

A moan tore from Luke's throat.

"Steady, Corporal. Let's get a field dressing on that wound and get her back to town. It's not too deep. We should be able to get the bleeding stopped."

Not too deep? It looked like a mini Palo Duro Canyon carved into her tender flesh.

Aching for the pain she'd endured, Luke bent close and rested his face against hers. "I'm sorry I didn't get here sooner, love. But I'll take care of you now. I swear it."

He placed a kiss on her forehead, then set his jaw and got to work.

FORTY

Damaris slowly became aware of her surroundings, tugged into consciousness by a familiar, beloved growl.

"I ain't leavin'."

Luke. A smile stretched across her heart.

"But you've done all you can for her, Mr. Davenport," a woman's voice interjected. "The doctor said she'll be fine. She just needs to rest."

"I told you, I ain't leavin'." The growl grew louder. More adamant.

"I'd be glad to sit with her for the few minutes it takes you to clean up and grab a bite to eat. The others—"

"The others have their own womenfolk to worry about. This one's mine. And I ain't leavin' until she wakes up and tells me herself that she's all right."

This one's mine.

Never had she thought to hear such words from a rugged mountain of a man who made all the heroes from her novels seem pale and anemic in comparison. A man who could take down a rustler with a single punch yet hold her with a tenderness that weakened her knees.

A man who was going to badger some kind woman to pieces if Damaris didn't pry her eyelashes apart.

"Luke?"

The growling stopped mid-sentence, and a heartbeat later her Horseman's hand engulfed hers and his unshaven, trail-dusty, incredibly handsome face bent close.

"I'm here, Damaris." His other hand traced her hairline from her forehead, around her ear, and down the braid on her shoulder that someone had brushed out and replaited. "You're safe. Mullins and Colburn are in custody. They can't hurt you anymore."

She turned her face into his touch, needing the comfort he offered, the security. "Nathaniel?"

Luke's eyes softened, and a small smile curved his lips. "He made it to San Antone this morning. He's with Dr. Jo and her father at Gringolet."

Thank you, God. Damaris's eyes slid closed for a moment as relief swelled through her soul. *He's safe, Douglas. Your son is safe.*

When she opened them, a round-faced woman with a cheerful grin came into view from the other side of the bed. "I'm Mrs. Kendall, dear. Can I bring you anything? Water?" She hesitated, then barreled ahead, answering her own question. "I know. I'll fix you a hearty beef broth. The doctor said you'll need red meat, eggs, and greens to build the iron back up in your blood after losing so much. I'll start with a broth, and we can work you up to more substantial foods later. How does that sound?"

Damaris smiled. "Lovely." Especially since the chore would take the hospitable woman out of the room and provide a few private minutes with Luke. "Thank you for your kindness."

"My pleasure." Mrs. Kendall glanced across the bed at Luke and gave him one of those looks mothers give their boys when they fail to march to matriarchal orders. "I'll expect *you* to find your way to soap and water before I return."

"Yes, ma'am." Luke chanced a wink on the sly to Damaris as the older woman bustled toward the door.

"I saw that, young man."

Damaris did her best to stifle her laugh, but when Luke grinned with all the mischief of a boy with frogs in his pockets, she couldn't hold it back.

His smile softened, and his eyes warmed. "It's good to hear you laugh."

"It feels good. Like letting go of all the bad and making room for happy memories to take up residence."

The mattress dipped as he sat on the edge next to her right hip. "How do you feel?"

She moved her left arm, feeling the bandage under the sleeve of the borrowed cotton nightgown Mrs. Kendall must have wrestled her into. Next, she tried to move her leg. Pain throbbed at the motion, but it wasn't unbearable.

"Not too bad." She tried to sit up.

Luke jumped to his feet, lifted her beneath her armpits like a toddler, then arranged an enormous stack of pillows behind her back. The pain in her thigh during the jostling made it easy to hide her grin, but her heart melted at his unpracticed yet sweetly sincere attempts to take care of her.

"I love you, Luke." The words slipped out without warning,

but she did not wish them back. Not even when he turned to stone, his hands locked on the blanket he'd been in the process of tucking.

He didn't seem any more comfortable with her declaration now than he had the first time she'd made it, but he'd grow used to it eventually. He didn't have a choice. Not when she'd be repeating it every day for the rest of their lives.

If he let her.

Slowly, he broke from his paralysis and lifted his eyes to meet hers. He opened his mouth, then closed it. Dipped his head and removed his hands from the covers. As if the bed were suddenly infested with rattlesnakes, he lowered himself to the mattress with extreme caution. Then he squared his shoulders and twisted to face the firing squad.

"As a kid, I never understood what love was," he said, his voice a low rasp. "My ma left, and my old man took his anger at life out on me. I saw other families who were happy, but I figured that wasn't meant for me. And when Matt and the others started settling down, the old wildness crept through me again. Driving me to run away from what I could never have before bitterness built a wall between me and my brothers."

Heart aching at his words, Damaris laid a hand over his and squeezed tight.

"Then I met you. And Nate. I saw myself in the kid. And you? You were everything I thought a home should be. Kindness. Nurture. Sacrifice. Even all those doilies and embroidered samplers fit my mental picture of what an ideal home would look like."

He shook his head at himself, the act so endearing that

she wanted to kiss his cheek. Then maybe go stitch him a sampler.

"My vague notions of family took on specific form and shape, patterned after you and Nate. I wanted to be a part of you. To . . . belong to the two of you." His gaze heated. "I wanted soul-deep love between a man and a woman. A woman with soft brown eyes and a smile that turns my insides to mush every time she aims it my way."

Warmth infused her cheeks, and a smile blossomed at his words.

"Just like that," he whispered, the gravel in his voice making her light-headed. He rotated the hand she held until he was the one holding her. "The Bible says a man is supposed to love his wife the way Christ loved the church, giving himself up for her. If you'll have me, Damaris, I promise to give myself up for you every day. Put your needs ahead of mine. Value you above all others. And lay down my life to keep you safe. I don't know much about lovin', but I know I don't want to live my life without you in it. I'm hoping you can teach me the rest."

Love squeezed her chest so hard, she nearly lost her breath. "Seems to me you have a pretty good handle on the concept already." Ignoring the pain in her leg, she leaned forward and cupped a hand around his jaw. She rubbed her thumb over the stubble on his chin, adoring every inch of this rough, imperfect man. "And if that was a proposal of marriage, I accept."

Joy lit his eyes a second before he took her face in his hands and kissed her with a thoroughness that curled her toes. Having a little wild in her man definitely had its advantages.

EPILOGUE

Two days later, three of the four Horsemen rode into Gringolet to be met by a parade of family. The fourth rolled in on a wagon, but he didn't mind his lack of mount, not when the woman he loved sat beside him.

"Aunt Maris!" Nate separated himself from the younger kids and ran up to the wagon. "You're all right."

"Thanks to the Good Lord and four good men." She tossed a quick glance at Luke, one he wished he had time to explore more in depth, with all the love and appreciation sparkling there. But now was not the time, for after bestowing an apologetic pat to his leg, she scooted away from him and waved to her nephew. "Help me down."

Nate didn't hesitate. He stepped close and held up his hands.

"Watch her left leg," Luke cautioned. "It's bound to be sore after two days on the road."

He had tried to convince Damaris to rest for at least a day at the Kendalls' home before setting out for Gringolet, but she had insisted on seeing her nephew as soon as possible. Apparently, Nate had needed to see her as well, for as soon as he helped her alight, the two embraced and wept.

Luke hopped down, turned the wagon and team over to one of the Gringolet hands, then circled behind the wagon to join Damaris. As happy as she was to see Nate, Luke knew the journey had taken a toll on her, and he aimed to get her to a chair on the veranda as soon as possible.

"Hi, Mr. Luke." Abner, one of the kids from Harmony House, waved as he and his pal Rawley trotted up to Nate's side.

Luke glanced over the yard, where close to a dozen other children scampered all over creation. Apparently, Wallace and Brooks had packed up their entire passel of foundling home kids and brought them for a visit. No wonder the other Horsemen had been ready at a moment's notice when Luke wired the captain for help.

Luke tipped his hat to the boys. "You scamps stayin' outta trouble?"

"Yes, sir." Abner nodded.

Rawley, on the other hand, shrugged, his face stoic except for the mischief dancing in his dark eyes. "Mostly."

Luke chuckled. Then he looked at the scene again. Wallace swung Kate around in a circle before doing the same for each of the girls in their care. Jonah pulled off his hat, dragged Eliza to him, then used his brim as a shield to hide his welcome-home kiss from the rest of the kids. As if they didn't know perfectly well what was happening behind that

hat. The hoots and hollers told the truth and earned Jonah a slap on the arm when he finally released his wife. But the way Eliza slid her arm through his and leaned against his side made it clear she bore him no ill will.

Matt had already made his way to the veranda, where Thaddeus gladly commandeered his sleeping granddaughter from the arms of her mother so Josephine could wrap those arms around her husband's neck instead.

A couple of months ago, Luke would've been battling jealousy and discomfort about now, hurrying away with the hands so he could put himself to use in the barn. But not today. He settled his palm at Damaris's back and smiled when she glanced at him over her shoulder. Today he had his own family. A family he'd honor and defend and love until the day he died.

"C'mon, Nate," Abner said, tugging on the older boy's arm. "Wart wants you to teach him how to sword fight, too."

Nate had managed to untangle himself from his aunt's embrace and rub away any emotional leaks with his sleeve before the younger boys arrived. He gave a quick sniff, and then, instead of running off, he paused and looked to Damaris for permission.

"Can I, Aunt Maris?"

A slight tremor ran through Damaris at the question, and Luke recognized the significance of the moment. Whatever barriers Nate had built up between him and his aunt had crumbled to silt in the last few days.

She smiled, and the beauty in the expression stole Luke's breath. "I don't see why not."

The boys whooped, but Luke didn't let them run off just yet.

"He'll be there in a minute," he said. "I need to have a word with him first. Man to man."

Rawley and Abner exchanged looks, then grins, then gave a salute and ran off to join the others. Nate's brow crinkled, but he dutifully remained behind.

Suddenly nervous, Luke cleared his throat. "I, ah, need to ask you a question."

"All right."

"I'll be writing a letter to your grandpa too, but since you'll be affected most, I wanted to ask your permission first." Good grief. He was stumbling around worse than a blind buffalo. *Just spit it out, for Pete's sake.* "I want to marry your aunt."

Nate's lips twitched, but he crossed his arms and forced his mouth into a straight line. "Does she want to marry *you*?"

"*She* happens to be right here, gentlemen, and can speak for herself."

Both male heads swiveled in her direction. Thankfully, she was smiling, so she wasn't too perturbed.

She dipped her chin toward Nate. "Yes. I want to marry him very much."

Nate raised a brow as he turned back to Luke. "You know you're gonna have to put up with her terrible cooking, right?"

"Hey!"

Luke chuckled. "She's worth it."

Nate finally let his grin loose. "Yep. I suppose she is." A new light came into his eyes. "Does this mean I can call you Uncle Luke?"

His heart squeezed. "I'd like that."

"Wait 'til all the kids at school find out my uncle's a

Horseman! I'm gonna be the most popular kid in town."
He sprinted off to join his new friends. "Hey, Rawley! I'm
gettin' an uncle!"

"You better come up here and tell me all about that little
announcement, Luke Davenport," Dr. Jo hollered from the
veranda railing. "Don't make me send Matt to fetch you."

Luke held up a hand in surrender. "I'm coming."

For the next hour, the women told tales of how each of
them came to be married to a Horseman while the menfolk
nodded and grunted agreement at the appropriate times.
Eventually, though, talk turned to Harbinger and what would
become of the railroad spur planned for Madisonville.

"Kendall said the US Marshals would be launching an
investigation into the Harbinger Land Development Company to see if there is any evidence of wrongdoing on their
end," Luke explained. "In the meantime, the land Mullins
purchased on their behalf will be considered evidence and
therefore unavailable for sale. If the railroad wants to build
a spur to Madisonville, they'll have to do it over more rugged terrain. The land won't fetch the lucrative price that the
Harbinger deal would have produced, but it will circumvent
Nate's land."

"You know," Wallace said, leaning a forearm across his
knee, "Kendall and I were talking about this. If the five of us
pooled our money, we could buy up that land before anyone
else gets word of the spur. Might turn a tidy profit."

Kate gave her husband a thoughtful look. "Harmony House
could use a new revenue source."

"Jonah could expand his herd," Eliza added.

Dr. Jo slowed her rocking and looked up from baby Ellie

Lou to meet the captain's eye. "You've been talking about bringing in a new mare."

"So I have." Matt turned to the rest of the Horsemen. "Well, boys, what do you say? Colburn's got a nice-sized bounty on his head. If we track down the rest of his gang, we could put the funds toward some land speculation."

Wallace slapped his knee. "I'm game."

Jonah nodded.

Matt turned to Luke. "Preach? What say you?"

Taking Damaris's hand, he pressed a kiss to her knuckles. "I've been thinking about opening a livery in Madisonville. Working with horses. Providing for my family while staying close to home."

They hadn't talked about it yet, but the warmth in her eyes seemed to indicate that she didn't hate the idea.

He turned back to Matt. "A little extra seed money could help that along."

"Sounds like Hanger's Horsemen are getting into the land development business."

Putting down roots. Ones that would run deep and weather any storm. Something Luke never thought he would do. Yet as Damaris rested her head on his shoulder and nestled within the curve of his arm, he could think of nothing he wanted more.

Christy Award finalist and winner of the ACFW Carol Award, HOLT Medallion, and Inspirational Reader's Choice Award, bestselling author **Karen Witemeyer** writes historical romances because she believes the world needs more happily-ever-afters. She is an avid cross-stitcher, tea drinker, and gospel hymn singer who makes her home in Abilene, Texas with her heroic husband who vanquishes laundry dragons and dirty dish villains whenever she's on deadline.

To learn more about Karen and her books and to sign up for her free newsletter featuring special giveaways and behind-the-scenes information, please visit karenwitemeyer.com.

Sign Up for Karen's Newsletter

Keep up to date with news on Karen's upcoming book releases and events by signing up for her email list at karenwitemeyer.com.

More from Karen Witemeyer

On a mission to deliver a baby to a nearby foundling home, Mark Wallace and Jonah Brooks encounter two women who capture their attention. When a handful of children from the area go missing, a pair of Horsemen are exactly what the women need. As they work together to find the children, will these two couples find love as well?

The Heart's Charge
HANGER'S HORSEMEN #2

You May Also Like . . .

Ex-cavalry officer Matthew Hanger leads a band of mercenaries who defend the innocent, but when a rustler's bullet leaves one of them at death's door, they seek out help from Dr. Josephine Burkett. When Josephine's brother is abducted and she is caught in the crossfire, Matthew may have to sacrifice everything— even his team—to save her.

At Love's Command by Karen Witemeyer
HANGER'S HORSEMEN #2
karenwitemeyer.com

Spiced with Witemeyer's signature blend of humor, thrilling frontier action, and sweet romance, this charming holiday novella collection includes three novellas, "An Archer Family Christmas," "Gift of the Heart," and a brand-new story, "A Texas Christmas Carol," along with a Christmas devotion, holiday recipes, and fun facts about 1890s Christmas celebrations.

Under the Texas Mistletoe by Karen Witemeyer
karenwitemeyer.com

After being railroaded by the city council, Abby needs a man's name on her bakery's deed, and a man she can control—not the stoic lumberman Zacharias, who always seems to exude silent confidence. She can't even control her pulse when she's around him. But as trust grows between them, she finds she wants more than his rescue. She wants his heart.

More Than Words Can Say by Karen Witemeyer
karenwitemeyer.com

BETHANYHOUSE

More from Bethany House

British spy Levi Masters is captured while investigating a discovery that could give America an upper hand in future conflicts. Village healer Audrey Moreau is drawn to the captive's commitment to honesty and is compelled to help him escape. But when he faces a severe injury, they are forced to decide how far they'll go to ensure the other's safety.

A Healer's Promise by Misty M. Beller
BRIDES OF LAURENT #2
mistymbeller.com

While Brody McQuaid's body survived the war, his soul did not. He finds his purpose saving wild horses from ranchers intent on killing them. Veterinarian Savannah Marshall joins Brody in rescuing the wild creatures, but when her family and the ranchers catch up with them both, they will have to tame their fears if they've any hope to let love run free.

To Tame a Cowboy by Jody Hedlund
COLORADO COWBOYS #3
jodyhedlund.com

Michelle Stiles has stayed one step ahead of her stepfather and his devious plans by hiding out at Zane Hart's ranch. Zane has his own problems, having discovered a gold mine on his property that would risk a gold rush if he were to harvest it. But soon danger finds both of them, and they discover their troubles have only just begun.

Inventions of the Heart by Mary Connealy
THE LUMBER BARON'S DAUGHTERS #2
maryconnealy.com

BETHANYHOUSE